CONQUEST

Also by Julian Stockwin

Kydd
Artemis
Seaflower
Mutiny
Quarterdeck
Tenacious
Command
The Admiral's Daughter
Treachery (US title: The Privateer's Revenge)
Invasion
Victory

JULIAN STOCKWIN

CONQUEST

HODDER &
STOUGHTON

First published in Great Britain in 2011 by Hodder & Stoughton
An Hachette UK company

1

Copyright © Julian Stockwin 2011

A CIP catalogue record for this title is available from the British Library.

Hardback ISBN 978 1 444 71196 7
Trade Paperback ISBN 978 1 444 71197 4

Maps drawn by Sandra Oakins

Typeset in Garamond MT by Palimpsest Book Production Limited,
Falkirk, Stirlingshire

Printed and bound in the UK by Clays Ltd, St Ives plc

Hodder & Stoughton policy is to use papers that are natural, renewable and recyclable products
and made from wood grown in sustainable forests. The logging and manufacturing processes are
expected to conform to the environmental regulations of the country of origin.

Hodder & Stoughton Ltd
338 Euston Road
London NW1 3BH

www.hodder.co.uk

To the Lady Anne Barnard, Capetonian diarist and chronicler

1750–1825

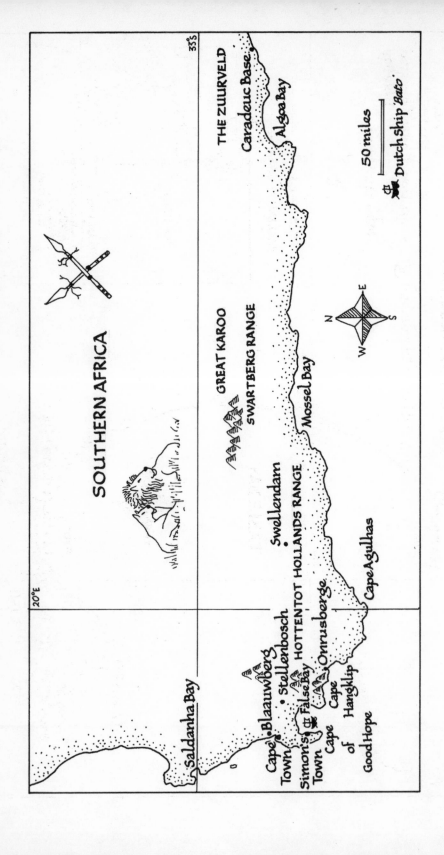

SOUTHERN AFRICA

THE ZUURVELD

Caradeuc Base

Algoa Bay

GREAT KAROO

SWARTBERG RANGE

Mossel Bay

Swellendam

HOTTENTOT HOLLANDS RANGE

Cape Agulhas

Saldanha Bay

Cape Town • Blaauwberg

Stellenbosch

Simon's Town • False Bay

Onrusberge

Cape Hangklip

Cape of Good Hope

20°E

33S

50 miles

Dutch Ship Bato

N   E   W   S

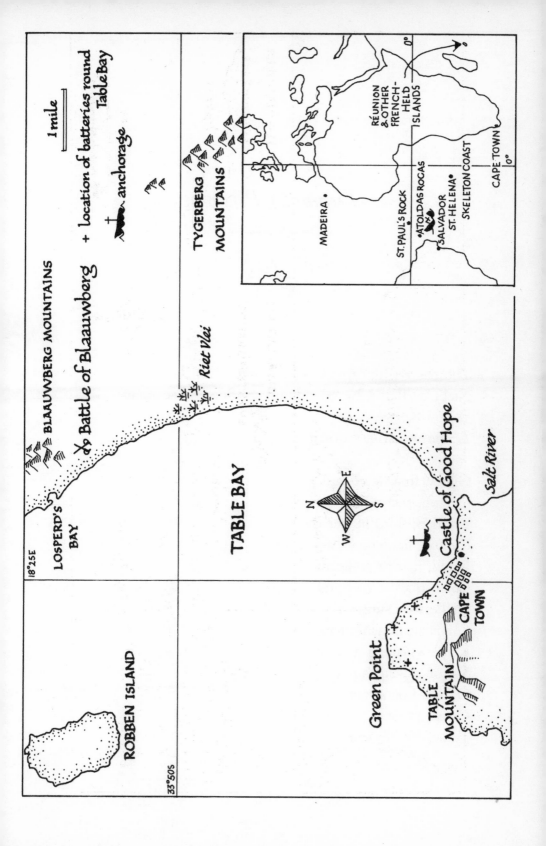

ROBBEN ISLAND

33°50'S

18°25'E

LOSPERD'S
BAY

BLAAUWBERG MOUNTAINS

Battle of Blaauwberg

Riet Vlei

TYGERBERG
MOUNTAINS

1 mile

+ location of batteries round
Table Bay

anchorage

TABLE BAY

N
E
W
S

Green Point

TABLE
MOUNTAIN

CAPE
TOWN

Castle of Good Hope

Salt River

MADEIRA

ST. PAUL'S ROCK

RÉUNION
& OTHER FRENCH-
HELD ISLANDS

ATOL DAS ROCAS

SALVADOR

ST. HELENA

SKELETON COAST

CAPE TOWN

0°

0°

Dramatis Personae

Thomas Kydd, captain of *L'Aurore*
Nicholas Renzi, his friend and confidential secretary

L'Aurore, ship's company

Gilbey, first lieutenant
Curzon, second lieutenant
Bowden, third lieutenant
Clinton, lieutenant of marines
Dodd, marine sergeant
Cullis, marine corporal
Dr Peyton, surgeon
Calloway, midshipman
Kendall, sailing master
Saxton, master's mate
Oakley, boatswain
Owen, purser
Tysoe, Kydd's valet

Stirk, boatswain's mate
Poulden, coxswain
Greer, sailmaker
Olafsen, sailmaker's mate
Pinto, seaman
Ah Wong, seaman
Harmer, 'Buttons', seaman

Officers, other ships

Commodore Home Popham
Captain Honyman, *Leda*

Army officers

Major General Sir David Baird
Lieutenant Colonel the Lord Geoffrey MacDonald
General Lord Beresford
Brigadier General Ferguson
General Yorke
Colonel Pack
Lieutenant Grant
Dr Munro
Tupley, quartermaster general

Cape Town

General Janssens, former governor of Cape Colony
Willem van Ryneveld, fiscal
Barbetjie van Ryneveld, his wife
Oudsthoorn, chief clerk

Höhne, Renzi's sworn translator
Stoll, personal aide to Renzi
Knudsen, Danish shipwreck survivor
Ritmeester Francken, captain of Fort Onrusberge
Van der Riet, *landdrost* of Stellenbosch

Others

Frederick Stanhope, Marquess of Bloomsbury
Marchioness of Bloomsbury
Cecilia Kydd
Lord Grenville
Marie Thérèse Adèle de Poitou
Baron de Caradeuc
Poncelot, Chef de Bataillon des Chasseurs de la Réunion
Robert Patton, governor of St Helena

Chapter 1

Captain Thomas Kydd held his impatience in check. Still in thrall to the all-so-recent cataclysm of Trafalgar, he and his ship had played escort to the body of Admiral Nelson in their grief-stricken return to England. Then, immediately, he had been given orders for sea, falling back on the Nore to victual and store with the utmost dispatch before setting forth to attempt urgent rendezvous with Commodore Home Popham in Madeira.

Much affected by the loss of the great commander, Kydd had at first resented not being able to attend what would no doubt be the greatest funeral of the age, but as all of Nelson's victorious battle-fleet, save the legendary *Victory*, were still faithfully on station, who were he or his men to complain?

Under a press of sail, *L'Aurore* had braved the hard south-westerlies and was now rounding the last point before the deep anchorage of Funchal Roads opened up.

Madeira was peculiarly well located at the crossroads of the pattern of trade routes that led to Europe; merchant shipping and naval vessels alike gratefully raised landfall before the last few weeks of far voyaging – or girded for long months outward bound. Now, in winter, the little island was at its best: an emerald jewel in the warmer reaches of the Atlantic, with crystal water, succulent fruits and blessed rest for mariners who had won clear of the Channel's bluster on their way to exotic destinations.

Kydd peered through the throng of shipping to a denser group, and caught sight of the swallowtail of a commodore's pennant high aloft in an elderly 64-gun ship. They were in time!

He assumed a strong quarterdeck brace. Kydd knew that his ship – a thoroughbred light frigate captured from the French a bare year ago – was at her best, even with all the haste in getting back to sea. His head lifted in pride at the impression she must be making on the eyes now upon her – and he remembered how, in a similar frigate, he had passed this way all those years ago, a young sailor before the mast, making skilled seaman from humble press-ganged beginnings. And now he was captain of his own frigate . . .

This was no time for reminiscing: he had served with Popham before and was eager to make his acquaintance again – and find out what was in store for *L'Aurore*.

Shortening sail, they threaded their way through the packed shipping, no difficulty for the nimble frigate on a favourable wind, and in short order their anchor plunged down and their thirteen-gun salute cracked out.

He was met on *Diadem*'s quarterdeck with all the ceremonial of a post-captain coming aboard a flagship. 'A swift passage, Mr Kydd,' Popham said, the intelligent eyes appraising. 'I count myself fortunate that you shall now be able to join our little enterprise.'

There had been just the barest details about it in his orders, Kydd reflected, but he replied respectfully, 'I'm honoured to be here.' Then he ventured, 'Er, you did say "enterprise", sir? I'm as yet mystified as to its purpose.'

Popham gave him a quizzical look, then dealt with a hovering first lieutenant before inviting Kydd to a sherry below. He wasted no time on pleasantries. 'The French fleet has been destroyed and the way is made clear for us to take the offensive. This is nothing less than the first move in a race to empire!'

'Sir, I don't—'

'Are you in doubt of empire, Mr Kydd? The world is populated by quantities of benighted heathens who, in the nature of things, will be ruled by one or other of the Great Powers until they be of stature to stand alone. It were better for them that it be us, with our enlightened ways, than the selfish and rapacious Mr Bonaparte, do you not think, sir?'

There could be little arguing at that level, or with the notion that this war of Napoleon would not continue indefinitely. Whoever had the greatest empire at its end would dominate the world and its trade. Kydd finished his sherry. 'Sir, may I know where we shall, er, strike?'

Popham frowned. 'You haven't been informed?' He leaned forward in his chair. 'Then tonight will be a capital occasion for you to learn at first hand. We sail in thirty-six hours and this evening will be the last chance for some time for the principals of the campaign to dine together in anything approaching civilised comfort. I hope I may see you there.'

At Kydd's look, he added, 'And never fear, sir, tomorrow you'll have the requisite orders and details that shall see you satisfied in the particulars.'

Funchal, the capital of Madeira, was set in a natural amphitheatre among stern mountains, its neat white houses nestling in ascending rows. Surrounded by vineyards and plantations and well supplied by streams from the craggy uplands, it had an unusually attractive scenting from the many groves of figs, mangoes and red-fleshed oranges.

Admiring the pleasant vista from the quarterdeck, Kydd said, to his friend and confidential secretary Nicholas Renzi, 'I suspect this dinner will be long. If you—'

'Do not concern yourself on my account, dear chap,' Renzi murmured. 'I believe we shall have a tolerable enough time of it ashore.' The port was well regarded by a number of the ship's officers, who'd confided they were familiar with where the most agreeable entertainments could be found.

After Trafalgar, Kydd knew *L'Aurore*'s ship's company was hard, experienced and reliable – men like Poulden, his coxswain, in the past a stout-hearted seaman who had stood by him when he was a newly promoted lieutenant in those days of endurance in the old *Tenacious*. Stirk, at a forward six-pounder, hard as nails and from whom, as a raw landman, Kydd had learned lessons of fearlessness and the rough moral code of the lower deck; and Doud, spinning a yarn with the boatswain's mate, another long-ago messmate who had come to join others from his past, wanting to share fortune with Tom Kydd, their old shipmate.

L'Aurore's officers had seen three changes. Kydd's former first lieutenant, Howlett, had been promoted out of the ship, and his second, the tarpaulin Gilbey, had taken his place, with the well-born Curzon moved up to second lieutenant.

The last-minute replacement for third now stood stoically on the quarterdeck, as most junior, to remain on watch aboard while his seniors disported ashore. Before Kydd went below to change, he crossed to the young man. 'So, do I see you contented with your lot, Mr Bowden?'

4

He beamed. 'That I am, Mr Kydd,' he said proudly. 'You may depend upon it.'

Hiding a smile, Kydd tested the tautness of a line from aloft. 'Do you take care of my ship while I'm away, sir. I'll not have it all ahoo when I return.'

'I will, sir,' Bowden replied, and turned to glare at the inoffensive mate-of-the-watch.

The young man had started his naval career as a midshipman under Kydd in the Mediterranean some years before, and then had gone on to be signal midshipman in *Victory*. In the wave of promotions following the famous battle, he had achieved his lieutenancy – able to claim a reduction in the strict requirement for six years at sea before his lieutenant's exam – as a passed student of the Naval Academy.

Kydd had initially been puzzled as to how Bowden had managed appointment into a prime 32-gun frigate. Then he'd remembered that, in the young man's ancient naval family, his uncle was a very senior captain at the Admiralty. It was, however, a most sincere compliment.

At four precisely Kydd stepped out of his carriage into the dignified but antiquated St Jolin's Castle, nobly perched above the town. An army subaltern in kilt and full Highland regalia came forward to receive him. 'Captain Kydd? We are expecting you, sir. Come this way, if you will.'

The castle had been borrowed for the occasion and Portuguese soldiery in colourful finery faced stolidly outward from the wall, their eyes ceremoniously following the visitors' movements in the Continental style.

Met by a rising hubbub of noise, Kydd emerged into a medieval banqueting hall filled with army officers in scarlet and gold, and here and there the dark blue of a naval officer.

With the barbaric splendour of massed candles and the glitter of ancient armour and hangings on the lofty walls, it seemed to him a fitting place for the meeting of lords of war on the eve of battle.

He paid careful respect to the aged and pompous castellan wearing dress of another age, and then Popham found him. 'Kydd, old chap, do come and meet the others.'

There were fellow naval captains: Downman of *Diadem*, Byng of *Belliqueux*, Honyman of *Leda*. And then the army: brigadier generals and colonels, fierce-gazed and each in the warlike colour of Highland regiments.

Finally it was a formal introduction to the principal himself. 'Sir, may I present Captain Thomas Kydd of *L'Aurore* frigate of thirty-two guns, new joined. Mr Kydd, Major General Sir David Baird, commander of this expedition.'

Kydd bowed politely, frustrated that he still knew so little of what was afoot.

'Well, now, sir, and it's been a long time!'

Taken aback, Kydd noted calculating eyes and a tall, handsome frame. 'Er, you have the advantage of me, Sir David,' he said carefully.

Baird's eyebrows drew together. 'Come, come, sir! You'll be telling me next you've altogether forgotten our little *contretemps* in the sands o' the Nile.' He threw a look of mock exasperation at Popham. 'The plicatile boats, was it not? Quite took Kleber's veterans in the rear – heh, heh! Why, sir, do you think I've asked for you specifically in an expedition of a sea-borne nature?'

Kydd realised his summons to Madeira must have been in consultation with Popham, who had been naval commander in the Red Sea at that time, the occasion when a successful landing from the sea had put paid to Napoleon's stranded

6

Army of Egypt. Baird had been at Alexandria with them for the final scenes. It had been one of the few victories the army could boast of in the last war.

He inclined his head. 'Ah, on the contrary, sir, that is a success-at-arms that will remain with me for ever.'

'As it should.'

'General Baird has a high regard for the Navy, Mr Kydd,' Popham interposed smoothly.

'As will be tested to the full at the Cape!' Baird snapped.

'The Cape, sir?'

As if to an imbecile, Baird spluttered, 'The Cape of Good Hope, of course, man!'

The next day Popham duly sent for Kydd. 'Some refreshment?' he asked solicitously, beckoning to his steward in the great cabin of *Diadem*.

Kydd was well aware of the capricious humour of his superior from their shared experience of the American inventor Robert Fulton and his submarines, but he was tired of being left so long in the dark.

However, as Popham began providing details of the enterprise he could see it was a bold, imaginative and daring stroke. In this first thrust of empire the British would move not against the French but the Dutch – to take the strategically vital colony at the very furthest tip of Africa that the Hollanders had settled as far back as 1652.

To date they had done little to antagonise the British, their interests lying more in safeguarding their Spice Islands trade to the east, but as the vessels of every nation heading for India, China and even the new land of Australia must necessarily pass close by, any stiffening of attitude would cause catastrophic harm.

It had been resolved that the situation could not be suffered to continue. The British would seize the Cape so that in any further thrust for empire they would be sitting squarely astride the trade routes of the world.

It was easier said than done. The Dutch were a proud people and could be counted on to resist. An opposed landing on a hostile shore all of seven thousand miles from home would be the most ambitious warlike endeavour Britain had yet contemplated.

The enterprise had been planned and launched in great secrecy; the military transports had sailed from Cork and the naval support from other ports – it was here at Madeira that the final assembly of the fleet had been concluded. It was to be a joint army and navy operation, which was not uncommon, but with the different perspectives of these two arms of the military there was always potential for unforeseen problems.

'What is our force, sir?' Kydd asked.

Popham frowned. 'Not as it will terrify the enemy,' he muttered. 'In a descent of this importance we are granted no ships-o'-the-line save three old sixty-fours and a contemptible fifty. For the rest we have but two frigates, a brig-sloop and a gun-brig.'

Kydd blinked, astonished. This was fewer than there had been in many minor operations he had witnessed and he felt a stir of misgiving. Was this a measure of the importance Whitehall was giving the enterprise?

With a sudden cynical insight he saw the reason: if the venture failed, as well it might, the costs would be minimal and easily explained away.

'And for the landing?' After his experiences in Egypt and Acre he was well aware of the difficulties facing troops attempting to establish a foothold on a fiercely defended shore.

'Beyond our preceding gunfire support, nothing. Once landed, the army is on its own.'

'With—'

'Soldiers of the Seventy-first and Seventy-second Highland Regiment of Foot, the Seaforths; the Sutherlanders – that's the Ninety-third – and the South Wales Borderers out from Egypt. For cavalry they rejoice in the Jamaica Light Dragoons. Light artillery: some, the Royal Artillery with six-pounders, providing we can get them landed. And . . . well, shall we say but two brigades in all, of some two to three thousand effectives?'

Against who knew how many troops on their home ground, easy supply lines inland and the ever-present threat of French reinforcements, it was a breathtaking assumption that at the end of a lengthy and wearying voyage they would be fit enough to stand and fight, equipped only with what they could carry with them.

'If you'll be frank with me, sir, can you tell me a little of the army commanders?' It was perhaps presumptuous but Kydd knew that Popham would be open in his opinions: it was his way to allow his subordinates to know his thinking.

'The Highlanders, a hot-blooded enough lot. Colonel Pack, a firebrand, Lieutenant Colonel the Lord Geoffrey MacDonald, Lord of the Isles – like 'em all, hungry for glory. Well led, they'll give a good account of themselves, I believe.

'The generals: there's Lord Beresford, a prickly chap, second to Baird but competent enough. Yorke, with the artillery – an old-fashioned sort, stickler for the forms but brave to a fault.'

He paused. 'Major General Baird is likeable enough – we

9

get along. He's shrewd, a calm thinker and sees things through. I have no doubt but if he sees a chance he'll not hesitate to take it.'

'And if not . . . ?'

'He'll not sacrifice his men, not after what he's been through.'

'Oh?'

'You saw the sword he wears?'

Kydd remembered a rather outlandish and extravagantly ornamented curved Oriental weapon.

'He seized that from the still warm body of Tippoo Sahib after Seringapatam and has worn it since. Can't find it in me to blame him – Baird was once incarcerated by him in chains for three years, with his men of the Seventy-first, in atrocious circumstances, after being overwhelmed in battle by the man's father. It must have been a sweet revenge indeed.'

'Just so,' Kydd said uneasily. 'Not as if he has a thirst for blood still?'

'Hmm. Can't really say. Now to details, sir. I'm to be flag officer afloat for this expedition and you'll have my orders and form of signals. These will be straightforward enough, your role in this as escorting frigate to the transport convoy, and at the landing, close gunfire support. After that, well, we'll see how it all goes.'

Drawing his chair closer, Kydd followed where Popham was indicating in a list.

'This is the composition of our convoy. Thirteen Indiamen for the regiments and artillery, and thirty-seven of all sorts for their impedimenta and stores.'

Kydd gave a tight smile. With their derisory force, it was a frightful risk: if even a single modern French sail-of-the-line came upon their expedition it would result in a massacre.

The longer they were at sea the more exposed to this risk they were, and it would prove a nightmare to provide water and victuals to the thousands of soldiers as they sailed through the fearsome equatorial heat down the length of Africa. And their horses would suffer horrifically, clapped under hatches as they passed through the burning desert of the doldrums.

As if reading Kydd's thoughts, Popham nodded. 'Long weeks at sea, yes. However, we shall be touching at the Brazils to water and recuperate before the final leg.'

The anti-clockwise wind-circulation pattern in the South Atlantic made the longer semi-circular passage away from Africa across the ocean to South America the more efficient. But that last leg remained more than four thousand miles and Kydd's heart went out to the soldiers who must endure for so long, then be called upon to give their all in a convulsive life-and-death struggle.

'In course,' Popham added lightly, 'before we get under way we will purchase replacements for any horses that may die on passage.'

Popham's responsibility was to ensure the safe arrival of the whole complex structure to its climax at the landing: the jocular tone hid deep worry. Despite his reservations, Kydd asked, with brisk enthusiasm, 'Then, sir, what is our plan for the final assault?'

'Why, Captain, that rather depends on the report of the frigate sent to reconnoitre before our arrival, don't you think?' he said, with an innocent smile.

In the cold light of morning, the invading fleet made ready to sail. To a casual onlooker it was impressive: fifty or more sail crowding Funchal Roads, a mighty armada about to descend on a luckless enemy.

But to any knowledgeable observer the truth was very different. A dozen of the very largest were nothing more than Indiamen, some with troops – but, as well, laden with luxury cargo and passengers, intended in the event of a dismal failure to continue on to Calcutta and the Raj. Other ships, crammed with artillery and stores, were slow and vulnerable. Still more were anonymous utilitarian hulls, of varying size down to the pipsqueak *Jack*, a Botany Bay ship hired for the task by a harried Transport Board and of questionable fitness for the long voyage.

And all that had been spared to escort them could virtually be counted on the fingers of one hand.

It was madness. Compelling evidence lay at anchor away to one side: a survivor of an Indies convoy found by Admiral Allemand and his squadron, which had sortied from Rochefort, the so-called 'invisible squadron' sent to play havoc off the coasts of Africa.

This convoy, escorted by a single ship, the 50-gun *Calcutta*, had been set upon by five ships-of-the-line, frigates and corvettes, but in a magnificent yet doomed show of defiance and resolution she had fought the odds, leading the enemy away from her convoy. She had finally struck her colours to prevent further loss of life but all except one of her charges had been able to escape.

Allemand was still at sea, whereabouts unknown. So, too, was the breakout fleet of Admiral Jean-Baptiste Willaumez, even larger and reputedly including Napoleon's brother – both somewhere in the wastes of ocean, looking for prey and revenge for Trafalgar. If either came up with Popham's fleet, there would be a massacre.

'This will do, Mr Kendall,' Kydd told the sailing master, satisfied with their offshore position, which was well placed to receive the ships now awkwardly getting under way and endeavouring to assemble in some sort of order. The seaward approaches were secured by the other frigate, *Leda*, and the two sloops, and the convoy, in two loose columns, began falling in behind *Raisonnable* and *Diadem*.

As if in concord with their mood, the sky was leaden and louring, the seas with an irritated slop and hurry, while Kydd manoeuvred *L'Aurore* back and forth in the inevitable never-ceasing efforts to encourage stragglers. Eventually the lines of ships, backing and filling with impatience, were rewarded by the Blue Peter in *Diadem* whipping down. They were on their way.

At first it was fresh going, running the north-east trade-winds down, the airs warming by the day until in flying-fish weather the convoy laid the Cape Verde islands to larboard to enter the deep Atlantic.

They were lucky: it was at all of three degrees north latitude before the winds eased to a pleasant zephyr and settled to a wispy breeze, fluky and baffling. The doldrums.

Sails hung in their gear, slatting lazily, while the heat descended in a thick, inescapable blanket, melting the tar in deck seams, turning the enclosed mess-deck into a torment to be endured. For three days it continued, ships scattered in random stillness over the glittering furnace, each with its burden of suffering.

On the fourth the first blessed whispers of air from the south-east arrived, playful cats-paws on the sea surface that lifted canvas and set lines from aloft to a cheerful rattle. Sweating sailors braced around and *L'Aurore* glided forward, the chuckling of water at her forefoot bringing pleased smiles to every face.

However, what could set a fine frigate to motion was not enough for the cumbrous transports, which lay obstinately unmoving. Even when the wafting breeze firmed, it left some like massive drifting logs, and as the day wore on it became clear that the convoy was in danger of disintegrating because those who were able to sailed on.

Kydd was summoned to pass within hail of Popham and received orders to stay by the laggards as a separate formation. He watched the others sail off at speeds not much more than a baby's crawl; they were still distant white blobs on the horizon in the morning when he set about marshalling his brood.

They were a round dozen sail, including the important *King George*, with General Yorke and the expedition's artillery aboard, the *William Pitt* transport, others with Highland regiments in fearful conditions below decks – and *Britannia*, laden with specie for paying troops and the laying in of supplies.

The south-easterly wafted about but then held steady and the little fleet got under way, heading for their rendezvous at Salvador, the last point of land before the assault on the Cape. *L'Aurore* prudently held an upwind rearward position.

They made better time once the south-easterly trades had got into their stride, soon nearing the Brazilian coast. However, as they reached southward the same south-easterly turned first brisk, then decidedly boisterous.

It stayed that way for the best part of a day, but when it subsided, Kydd spotted a signal of distress flying from *William Pitt*. If the vessel fell behind he could not risk the others, and it was out of the question for the fine-lined frigate to take the lumbering transport in tow. He ordered the convoy to heave to: he would see for himself. With the mild and obliging Legge, *L'Aurore*'s carpenter, sitting awkwardly next to Kydd, along with his mates and half a dozen hands, the captain's barge pulled over to the big ship lying with backed topsails.

It was raining on and off, and Kydd mounted the dripping side-steps in the oppressive damp heat with care. Waiting to greet him were a pair of colonels and an apologetic ship master. 'Captain Kydd, might I present—'

'Damn it, the man wants t' know what's to do,' growled the taller of the colonels, fixing Kydd with a flinty stare. 'An' I'll tell him. Oh, Pack, o' the Seventy-first Highlanders. Think we met briefly at St Jolin's,' he added, without waiting for a reply. 'Sir, we're served ill by the parcel o' knaves who outfitted the *Pitt* for this expedition. A right gimcrack job they made of it.'

Kydd's eyes narrowed. 'Colonel, a signal of distress from this ship was observed and I'd be obliged to know—'

'Come below,' ordered Pack, without explanation, leading down the hatchway. A wafting stench thickened as Kydd followed him to the main-deck where a musty gloom enveloped them.

As his eyes became accustomed to the shadows he saw the whole deck had been partitioned into horse stalls. But many were empty, and the horses remaining were standing listlessly, swaying with the ship's movements and occasionally staggering.

'Sir,' said Pack, heavily, 'I ken this is none of y' doing, but I'll have ye know we're in a sad pass. Without horses on the field o' battle we're helpless to turn an infantry attack, repel cavalry, press home an advantage – in short, sir, I'm sore puzzled to know how we can claim to be an army without 'em.'

They reached a stall where a grey horse lay on its side,

neck extended, breathing in short, rapid gasps. A groomsman and other soldiers in soiled uniforms looked up helplessly.

'We've lost eleven b' breaking their legs, losing their footing in this damn sea. Others takin' a fever in this damp and more refusing t' drink because the water's sour – some fool thinking to put it into old beer casks – and that's o' those that made it through that hell across the equator!'

Pack knelt beside the animal. 'This is my faithful Lory.' He looked up with great sorrow. 'We charged together at Pondicherry and again in Egypt. Now, d'ye see?' he said, gently lifting the horse's eyelid. There was an acrid discharge from an eye that held the greatest depth of misery Kydd had ever seen in an animal.

The colonel glared at the groomsman, who muttered defensively, 'Aye, an' there's nowt more we can do, sir. Obedient to y'r orders, th' best oatmeal in gin an' hot water three times a day, but I'm grieved t' say he's never touchin' it now, sir.'

Pack lowered his head in dejection – then jerked to his feet and thrust his face at Kydd. 'Distress! You lecture me o' distress! I'm to land my regiment in the face o' the enemy with – with animals only fit for the knacker's yard.'

He drew in a ragged breath and fixed Kydd with a terrible glare. 'What are ye going t' do, man? I say, what's the Navy going to do about it, hey?'

Kydd returned his stare with a look of mute obstinacy for there was not a single thing he could do.

The noon sight placed them safely south of St Paul's rocks, a lethal sprawl located squarely across the path of ships crossing from one continent to another, nearly a thousand miles out in the middle of the ocean. However, their position was well known and the track of a vessel could be set ahead of time to clear them. What mariners most feared were hazards to be encountered off continental coasts, under-sea extensions of land that reached out to disembowel incautious ships venturing too close.

But with two powerful enemy squadrons on the loose, Kydd needed to quit the broad sea-lanes, where he knew they would be ranging, to reach the closest point of South America now just a few hundred miles away, and then keep well in until he made Salvador.

Before dusk, with the prospect of Brazil in a day or two, *L'Aurore* took the lead, Kydd wary of any predators that might be lurking inshore.

Eventually he turned in, his mind alert to the dread cry of 'Sail!' Would he wake to be pitched into chaos? How could he shield his flock against a line of battleships? Would it all end with *L'Aurore* being pounded to a wreck to buy time while his charges fled desperately? As his imagination brought him images of blood and ruin, Kydd turned restlessly in the hot darkness and drifted into sleep.

An urgent cry woke him in a wash of cold shock – but it was not the French. The shriek *'Breeakers! I see breakers dead ahead!'* was joined by another until all three lookouts were shouting together.

He threw himself out of bed and raced for the hatchway. As he thudded up the steps he heard Gilbey bellowing above, rousing the watch to wear ship. 'A gun!' Kydd shouted breathlessly, as he made the deck. 'Signal the convoy!'

In the inky darkness men pushed and stumbled to their stations, joined by others boiling up from below. Braces and tackles thrown off, the helm went down and the frigate began to pay off, Kydd picking up on the betraying flash of a line of white in the gloom ahead.

The fog swivel forward cracked out at last and was joined by the deeper flash and bang of one of the quarterdeck guns. The level-headed master's mate Saxton had men around the other guns, and a steady banging started into the night, *L'Aurore*'s desperate warning to the ships trustfully following her.

Suddenly another cry went up. '*Land hooo! Land all t' loo'ard!*' The lookout had made out a denser mass of blackness that lay low and ominous on the other side, betrayed only by occasional flecks of white at the shoreline.

Committed to their turn away it seemed that they had run into some kind of bay or inlet and Kydd could not see how they would beat out against the wind into the unknown rock-strewn night.

'I have the ship, Mr Gilbey,' he bawled, and wheeled on the quartermaster. 'Midships your helm.' Then, roaring down the deck at the boatswain, 'Mr Oakley, belay that wear — we anchor!'

Cancelling a manoeuvre in mid-action in the darkness and substituting another was incredibly risky. He knew his crew to be the best — but what of the convoy following? Spotting Curzon in a laced nightshirt, loyally with his men at the main-mast, he hailed, 'Take a crew. And fire any gun to larboard you find charged!'

It was usual to meet the dawn with guns ready loaded and he was in effect ordering a rolling broadside. Any ship following would have no doubt there was deadly danger ahead.

By degrees the confusion lessened. The brailed-up sails, flogging murderously in the stiff wind, were brought under control as a first anchor was readied and let go. Riding lanthorns were rigged in the tops, and soundings were taken that had Kendall pursing his lips in worry.

Answering gun-flashes came out of the night; one by one pinpricks of lights flickered into existence as other captains saw the peril and decided to ride it out at anchor until daylight revealed the situation.

Were they in time? Anything could be happening in the invisible darkness, and the hours until dawn dragged unbearably for Kydd. If any of his charges was wrecked, the consequences to the expedition would be disastrous and he would answer for it.

When a grey dawn reluctantly drew back the dim veil yard by yard the scene became clear. They had stumbled across an atoll unlike any Kydd had seen before. It was an utterly desolate low complex of sand and rocks, distorted and evil, in the rough shape of a crescent, and they lay deep within its hollow curve.

Of his dozen sail, ten were safe. Under bare masts they jibbed at anchor, some uncomfortably but, as far as it was possible to see, unharmed.

However, two were in serious trouble. *King George*, deep laden with artillery and stores and carrying not only General Yorke but reportedly regimental women and children, lay at an angle within an appalling tangle of broken rocks. The Atlantic seethed white around the ship and in the cold early light, black figures could be seen milling about her canted decks.

Britannia, the large Indiaman with near five hundred soldiers and £300,000 in chests of Spanish dollars on board, had clearly been in a collision, her bowsprit broken off short and foremast down, but she was clear of the rocks, drifting along the shore. She would have to be left while they did what they could at the doomed ship.

'Away, all boats!' Kydd rapped. Gilbey in the pinnace would

take charge at the scene. In a very short time, dozens of other small craft were stroking vigorously for the stricken *King George* from the ships at anchor.

Kydd took a telescope and trained it on the wreck. Gilbey had the boats coming alongside in an orderly manner and passengers were being made ready to be handed down into them. Over the rearing bows a spritsail yard had been lashed, a precarious bridge to a larger rock clear of the surf; the soldiers were being directed down this to wait in a huddle for the boats.

He handed back the glass. In the best traditions of the sea, lives were being saved by calm and resolute action, and there was every prospect that it would all end without grievous toll.

The boats began to return, survivors heading for the blessed security that was a King's ship. Some were hauled aboard, crowding the deck. But *L'Aurore* was a fighting frigate and Kydd waved off any boat not theirs. With these numbers most would have to be redistributed among the other merchantmen.

At last Gilbey made his way back and pulled himself aboard wearily. 'All off, sir, a good day's work.' He hesitated then went on, 'That is, all save one.'

'Oh?'

'The general, I'm grieved t' say.'

'General Yorke?' Kydd said, disbelieving what he heard.

'He's – that is to say, he was an old man an' not so sprightly, sir. When his soldiers went over the sprits'l yard and the passengers an' women lowered over the side in a bowline he was begged to go with 'em but wouldn't hear of it. Said high words about honour an' being a gentleman and insisted on going out on to the yard like his men.'

'And then?'

'Well, sir, he waits till all his men are off an' then gets out on the spar. But, sir, he . . . he took fright as some do an' froze. Wouldn't hear of we takes a bowline to him, no, sir. He stayed there till a wave took him and he slipped off below . . . into the surf aroun' the rocks, an' we . . . we never found him after.'

'I'll need your report in writing on this, Mr Gilbey,' Kydd said dully. The old soldier, with distinguished service going back to the American war, to end like this . . .

His attention returned to *Britannia*. It looked as if, with her bows in ruin from the collision, she'd had difficulty in getting an anchor away. Although still drifting, she appeared in no immediate danger.

Then she stopped abruptly. Kydd peered through the glass and saw she had driven into a crag forward. Slewing round under the impetus, she tore off and continued her down-wind drift, but within a short time her colours jerked down and were re-hoisted upside-down.

The level-headed master of *Britannia* was not given to gestures. 'Buoy 'n' slip the cable, Mr Oakley!' Kydd roared down the deck and turned to order sail set. Every minute counted. There was no time to hoist in the boats and they were towed in a gaggle astern as *L'Aurore* fell off the wind and turned to make for *Britannia*.

'Must be bad wounded, them gettin' their distress flag up s' quick an' all,' muttered someone behind Kydd.

The frigate spread her wings and was soon up with the hapless Indiaman. 'Lost our rudder,' cried a figure on her quarterdeck. 'Our bows stove – no hope for it.'

'You'll abandon?' Kydd hailed back.

'This moment!'

The upper-deck of this prime vessel of the East India Company was crowded; she was much sought after for comfortable berths and gentle living and had been first choice to freight the expedition's treasure.

Kydd saw boats by the dozen putting out again from the rest of the ships. His duty now was to secure the bullion. 'Poulden,' Kydd addressed his coxswain standing quietly by the wheel, 'take away my barge with your trusties and do what you can to lay hold of the pay chests.'

Confused shouting, muffled screams and female shrieks rising above an excited hubbub drifted across the water.

'Mr Kendall,' Kydd called to the sailing master, 'I want to see us lying off no more than a half-pistol-shot, as will give the boats less distance to pull.'

Poulden returned with twelve heavy chests in the bottom boards. A yardarm whip was quickly rove to sway them out and then he hastily set out again.

Not long after they had left, it became clear that *Britannia*'s time was upon her. Down by the head, she had taken a pronounced list towards them and those remaining aboard hastened to find a place in the boats. A dull rumble and agonised cracking came from deep within and the heel increased visibly.

Where was Poulden? Kydd saw the last few aboard the Indiaman tumble into the boats but there was no sign of the barge.

Britannia lurched spasmodically, and slowly, grandly, her masts arced down as she lay over for her final moments. Was Poulden below, heroically bringing up the last of the chests? There was no time for delay: *L'Aurore* had to be manoeuvred clear of the sinking ship.

The end was abrupt: in a corkscrew motion she plunged

and capsized, her huge bare hull glistening obscenely before she vanished in a final paroxysm of vast bubbles and plumes of spray.

Beyond, where they had been out of sight behind the big ship, *L'Aurore*'s barge bobbed disconsolately, waiting while the sea disgorged its wrecked spars and floating debris from the depths before it began pulling back.

Poulden was at the tiller, but when it hooked on at the chains it was plain there were no more chests. 'Tried, sir, but . . . but there was this – this madman!' He trailed off, lost for speech.

Stirk, one of the boat party, took up the tale with relish: 'Aye, a right reg'lar-built loon! Stands athwart th' chests wavin' a cutlass, his pockets stuffed wi' Spanish cobbs, swearin' as how he'd been a poor man all his days but bigod he was going t' leave this world stinkin' rich!'

Salvador was raised within the week without further incident, and *L'Aurore* thankfully rejoined the expedition fleet at anchor in the majestic sweep of the Bay of All Saints. Popham heard Kydd out courteously, visibly saddened at the news of General Yorke.

But other matters were pressing. Surprised and gratified by the arrival of so many ships in want of repairs, with thousands of mouths to feed and provision for, the merchants and speculators of the tawdry little town immediately trebled their prices, the goods of contemptible quality. And to a man the merchant community refused to accept paper credit on the British Treasury, the news of Trafalgar not yet current.

Many of the horses had died at sea and those left were in a sickly condition. Prices for replacements and additions were ridiculous and subalterns were sent up-country with what little cash remained after the loss of *Britannia*, but this resulted only in a string of a dozen rangy ponies, beasts untrained for war.

It was not possible to delay further: it was essential to be under way on the last stage before word about their destination slipped out. With as little fuss as possible the fleet put to sea, their destination – the shores of Africa.

Leda was far out on *L'Aurore*'s beam, a tiny smudge of white on the deep blue horizon. The two frigates racing across the South Atlantic were on a mission of reconnaissance and their orders were clear: if at any time a French battle squadron was sighted, the fastest – *L'Aurore* – would return down the expedition's designated track to warn, while the other stayed to track the French.

Otherwise it was a matter then of *Leda* ranging north up the African coast, *L'Aurore* south around the Cape with the aim of ensuring there were no lurking enemy waiting to fall upon the rear of the assault. On their return they were to seek what intelligence they could concerning defences and military capability before making rendezvous at the landing.

It was direct evidence of Popham's anxiety that he had detached his only two frigates for the task, leaving his fleet to sail on blind.

The stakes could not have been higher.

Chapter 2

They made landfall on Africa together, just south of the thirty-fourth parallel. This was close to the southern tip of the continent, and after a mutual wishing of good fortune, the two frigates parted as planned.

'A penny for 'em, Nicholas,' Kydd said, coming up behind his friend, who was gazing dreamily at the placid, slumbering coast ahead – that should, nevertheless, be accounted an outpost of the most stirring and wondrous place on earth.

'I would they were a guinea in the asking, dear fellow,' Renzi answered absently.

Kydd was long used to his friend's occasional scholarly detachment from the world; he had been able to provide Renzi with the time and space aboard to devote to his *magnum opus* on societal imperatives as informed by his far voyaging. That the London publishers were far from receptive to the work must be so discouraging for him.

Renzi turned, his wistful expression almost comical. 'Should ever I desire a perfect zoo of ethnical curiosities then Africa . . . The humble savage, he must learn not only how to secure his daily bread – or should it be taro or similar? – but to lie down in amity with the lion and crocodile that may be contemplating his devouring.'

They began pacing together companionably. 'And these savages from the dark interior, what of their pride, their hopes, when encountering strangers from another world? What can they—'

'Easily enough answered by those who know the Caribbean, my friend,' Kydd interrupted cynically. 'They're taken up as slaves and need not fear for their prospects.'

'None the less, I should take joy to see them at their native pleasures,' Renzi said huffily.

'Excepting for this you must step ashore, old fellow, and that will not be possible unless we first persuade the Dutch to part with their possession, which I'm tolerably certain they'll resent.'

Renzi gave a half-smile.

Eight bells dinged from the belfry forward signifying the relief of the watch-on-deck. The men of the first dog-watch waited while Curzon went through hand-over with the off-going Bowden. The quartermaster then took his slate and the mate-of-the-watch went with his men to the bitts, ready for the inevitable sail-trimming.

After things had settled down, Kydd and Renzi resumed their pacing, a broad sunset developing astern while the line of land ahead turned dusky and mysterious.

'Touching on the Dutch, Nicholas, don't you think it perverse o' them to fall in with the French? I'd not think Bonaparte a fit bedfellow for any.'

'*Faute de mieux*, old trout. They are situated much too close to the revolutionary storm to think to remain neutral, while if they ally with Napoleon he will desist from seizing the country.

That's not to say they're independent – not at all. They must suffer a foreign army of protection and immense interference in their affairs. But this they deem preferable.'

'So as allies o' the French it puts 'em as enemies to us. They fight like tigers let loose, and I'll confide to you, Nicholas, I have my qualms about our enterprise.' To Kydd, the fraught battle with the Dutch at Camperdown in 1797 had been on a par for bloody brutality with Trafalgar.

'Just so. And considering the strategics I'll not be surprised to hear they've reinforced their vital waypoint to the east at the Cape – or the French, distrusting them, have sent their own forces.'

They paced along, silent for a space. Then Kydd said quietly, 'They've much to be proud on, Nicholas – a century or so ago they had a navy and trade to conjure with before we rudely gathered it all in from them. And now t' be brought so low . . .'

'It's not the Dutch people we oppose, only their present government – the Batavian Republic as is controlled by Napoleon. I suspect the ordinary people have their views. Or not – recollect that the country is riven between the republicans, who applauded the French Revolution, and the Orangists, who want nothing more than a restoration of the monarchy. How deep does this go?'

Any further musing was cut short by the appearance of Midshipman Calloway, who had been dispatched by Lieutenant Gilbey to inform the captain that gun crews were closed up for drill and inspection.

This was Kydd's invariable practice: the guns in the forward half of the gun-deck were manned on both sides and practice would then take place, starboard against larboard. The winners would have the satisfaction of looking on lazily while

27

the losers were obliged to go through their motions once more, this time to ribald encouragement.

Later in the evening Kydd and Renzi relaxed in his cabin, admiring the last of the sunset. 'A singular continent, Africa,' Renzi said expansively. 'Egypt and an ocean of desert in the north, the prehistoric darkness of equatorial forests in the centre and – and whatever we will find in the south. Elephants, giraffes and quantities of snakes, I've heard.'

Kydd grimaced. 'Did you hear of Mungo Park's explorations to Timbuktu at all? Sent by Sir Joseph Banks to go up some river and after two years came back with aught but his horse, a compass and a tale as would put any fo'c'sleman t' the blush.'

'Yes, I did read something of it,' Renzi murmured, aware that the account of the adventure had been put out by John Murray, the publisher who had turned down his own tome. 'And he was given another perilous exploration and is now vanished from the ken of civilisation.'

He put down his glass. 'But what sights he must have seen! Giant waterfalls, grand mountains – wild beasts unknown to civilised man, tribes of pygmy savages—'

Kydd chuckled. 'As if you would wish to get lost with the poor wight among all those cannibals and such.' The look he received in response made the smile fade from his face.

As they closed with the coast, tensions increased. These were unknown waters to all aboard – Kydd had rounded the Cape several times but always at a respectful distance; the grand sea route to the Indies was a relatively narrow band of waters some dozen miles offshore to the south. If the French were at large they'd be there. With their numbers and force, they had nothing to fear from the British and everything to gain by straddling the shipping lanes.

This was where *L'Aurore* would venture in her sweep eastward, a week's sail around against the wind and current, then a fast week or less back. They had the advantage that a large squadron would be easier to spot and their own rapid retreat would be put down to reasons other than scouting for an invading force.

The sailing master knocked softly at the great cabin and entered.

'Ah, Mr Kendall – you're not so familiar with African waters, I hear,' Kydd said.

'No, sir,' he replied levelly, 'but I've good enough charts 'n' rutters. They did a fine piece o' work afore in the surveying hereabouts.'

'Good. Shall you now tell me your understanding of these parts?'

Kendall said gravely, 'Why, sir, I c'n do that in one. This is not y'r northern seas, English Channel an' similar. This here is all ruled b' the oceans.'

He went on to explain. Much simpler than the complex weather patterns of the north, here the continent ended, extending into the Southern Ocean, a globe-encircling mass of water that endlessly marched on eastwards with mighty seas driven up by the virtually constant westerlies.

Where Europe was dominated by the vast land mass of Asia to the east, here there was only the empty expanse of the Indian Ocean stretching all the way to Australia, but subject to a seasonal wind reversal as regular as clockwork – the monsoons.

Therefore the Cape could rely on predictable wind patterns – a strong north-westerly with heavy rain in winter, and brisk, dry south-easterlies in summer. And now, of course, here in the southern hemisphere it was high summer. There was notorious variability at times, but the ruling pattern was there.

For the sailor there were further points of interest. To the east of the Cape a warm current swept down from the tropical north, the Agulhas, narrow and strong, which, with the powerful north-east monsoon, sped rich Indiamen rapidly homeward. Down the east coast it also kept the luxuriant rain-forests suitably wet and humid.

To the west of the Cape it was the opposite: from the south polar regions the cold Benguela current pressed northward along the coast. And once the Mediterranean pleasantness of the Cape had been passed, some of the most arid and desolate desert regions on earth resulted.

'What of the ports – harbours o' refuge and such?' Kydd wanted to know.

'Aye, well, it's a God-forsaken place, no need for 'em, just a few settlements as can trade wi' the natives.'

'So there's nowhere our French battle squadrons may lie to refit and store?'

'No, sir,' Kendall said positively. 'We meet 'em at sea or not at all.'

They made rapid progress along southern Africa as it trended around and up the east coast. The days were balmy, a long, languorous swell doing nothing to slow them, the distant land always to larboard, blue-grey and mysterious.

Then their course began shaping north as they rounded Cape Agulhas. Kydd was now satisfied that there was no enemy fleet abroad and the two innocent neutrals he had stopped had confirmed this. It was time to return.

On this leg they would keep with the land, lookouts alert for betraying clusters of masts inshore.

Kydd consulted the charts once more. The notes in the pilot were insistent that mariners be not trapped into error: vessels from Europe sailing from the other direction should never feel tempted to put over the helm after rounding the Cape of Good Hope for the run up the east of Africa; if they did, they would find themselves in a vast cul-de-sac, False Bay, which, if the wind was in the south, they would never get out of.

Yet it seemed this directly south-facing bay had its uses as a welcome haven during the winter months when the north-westerlies hammered in on the open roadstead of Cape Town. The Dutch apparently maintained a small maritime establishment in the most sheltered part, Simon's Town, to supply the ships waiting out the gales there. Kydd could see that such facilities would be attractive indeed to any commander with large ships and far from home. He decided to look in on it.

The chart showed False Bay as being in the shape of a lobster claw, the unattractively named Cape Hangklip on the east tip and the Cape of Good Hope to the west. On the open sea the wind was steadily in the south-south-east but he was too much the seaman to think that it would necessarily prevail within the bay.

They were coming up with Cape Hangklip: it was sometimes confused with the real Cape, out of sight on the other side, and unwary westbound ships thinking to turn up for the final run north would similarly find themselves embayed, hence the name – False Bay. Kydd, though, was noticing its steep, rearing form: there would be useful winds curling around in its lee, and prudence suggested they made use

31

of this feature for a rapid exit should there be an enemy within.

The broad bay, enticing in the sunshine with its emerald-green sea, was near twenty miles deep and fifteen across. So close at last to the shores of Africa, *L'Aurore*'s decks were filled with interested spectators, but the brown and hard-green mountainous landscape kept its secrets.

Judging the wind, the frigate wore about and angled across towards the fabled Cape just as a hail came from the fore-top lookout: '*Sail* – I see eight or more, er – an' one a ship-o'-the-line!'

Kydd leaped into the shrouds and mounted rapidly to the tops. This had to be a French squadron member undergoing repair or a Dutch sail-of-the-line. Either way the threat to the landing was grave – and if it had friends . . .

Aware of every eye on him he steadied his pocket tele-scope against a shroud until he had a good image. It was indeed a ship-of-the-line, perhaps a 74, more powerful by far than anything the English expedition possessed.

He looked again. It was of an older, more elaborate age; the ships at Camperdown had not been as elderly. Puzzlingly, it had its topmasts down and was moored bow and stern. Then he had it: this was a ship not intended for the sea; it was merely a floating battery guarding whatever amounted to the Dutch marine settlement at Simon's Town. The others were harmless merchant ships, small fry, coastal vessels. He snapped the glass shut and descended. 'A liner, it's true, but a guardship only,' he announced. At the relieved murmuring, he added sternly, 'But who's to say he hasn't friends?'

Before them, the Cape of Good Hope was approaching, a legendary place of romance and antiquity that they would pass closely.

Renzi appeared next to Kydd, engrossed in the spectacle, gazing intensely at the narrow, precipitous finger of rock projecting into the deep green seas. 'Conceive of it, my friend. The uttermost south of Africa! Should you lay foot on that pinnacle you may walk on due north for miles without count, never getting your feet wet until you arrive at the shores of the Mediterranean Sea. Or detour through the Holy Land and eventually you will stand at Calais observing the white cliffs of England itself, still dry-shod . . .'

'I'm devastated to contradict you, old fellow, but this is far from the most southerly point, which being Cape Agulhas we recently passed, some thirty miles of latitude south. And the fine foreland you're admiring is never our fabled Cape – you'll find it the more humble point a mile on your left, past the beach.'

'I see,' said Renzi, with a sniff. 'I haven't had the sight of a chart this forenoon. However, I do note that our doughty forebears are right in one particular – the rounding of the Cape of Good Hope involves a decisive change of course from south to east, and thus, whatever its deficiencies of grandeur, it must truly be considered the hinge-point on the road to India.'

Honour thus satisfied, they stood together as *L'Aurore* duly turned her prow northward for the last two score miles up the peninsula.

So far they had done little to alarm the Dutch. English cruisers were no rare sight as they passed on their way to the Indian Ocean or homeward bound, and Kydd intended to keep it that way. His plan was to enter Table Bay, the expansive roadstead before Cape Town, as if on the prowl for prizes but in reality observing as much as he could of the shore defences.

It was out of the question to land scouts on the hostile shore – they would be instantly taken as strangers – but there was always the possibility of intercepting and questioning a fisherman or coastal trader. Time was pressing, however, and—

'Good God!' Curzon spluttered, pointing ahead. From around the next headland had suddenly appeared a ship, close-hauled under full sail, standing south, heading directly towards them.

Kydd hesitated in shocked surprise. *L'Aurore* was not at quarters but probably neither was the other – but then it shied away, falling off the wind to race back whence it had come.

This gave them a chance to see that it was of substantial size, well armed but somewhat smaller than they. Kydd's mind raced. Their mission was reconnaissance, not to engage in battle; any damage to mast or spars could jeopardise their vital task to return and report. They would let it go.

'Hold your course!' he threw at the conn. This would give the other ship the opportunity to make the open sea and escape, but incomprehensibly it did not. The turn-away slowed and it came back to its original course, directly for them. It was going to fight.

Only a few hundred yards now separated them and *L'Aurore*'s guns were not yet cleared for action. And they could not buy time by seeking room to manoeuvre because the hard coastline was to one side and the stranger to seaward. 'Get those men to the guns!' he roared, in a fever of frustration.

Then the vessel was up with them – a cheerful hail in French and a wave came from its fo'c'sle. Kydd stared for a moment, then gave a grim smile. 'He asks for news, believing we're a Frenchman homeward bound from the Indies, our build so clearly theirs, and disbelieving an English warship this close in to the Cape.'

It put over its helm to wear about and run companionably along with them; at sea, to save wear and tear, a ship normally wore no colours and so far neither had hoisted them.

Suddenly a sharp cry rang out from among the sailors on its deck, then a hoarse bellow and the ship hastily sheered away. Something had spooked them to the true situation and now they were making off as fast as they could.

'Well, I'll be . . .' Kydd murmured. It was precisely what was wanted – but then a thought struck. If he held back from engaging, it would signal that he was here for another purpose and the Dutch would immediately be on the alert.

He had no alternative. 'We go after him,' he growled.

It had to look convincing. The other vessel was most likely one of the corvette-sized privateers that were preying on the India trade and therefore heavily manned. Boarding was out of the question but a running gun duel was the last thing he wanted.

'Brace up sharp, there!' he roared down the deck. The privateer was angling out to sea as close to the wind as it could lie, but it would take a much finer-lined craft to outdo *L'Aurore* on a wind.

'Gun crews closed up, sir,' Gilbey reported, eyeing their chase with smug satisfaction.

'Thank you,' Kydd said coldly. If the man thought they were taking prizes he would disabuse him, but not just yet.

It would solve all problems if the privateer got clean away. But the distant captain had seen *L'Aurore*'s effortless forereaching and threw over his helm to go directly down-wind

– back into the embrace of the craggy coastline. Kydd followed suit; in a twist of irony he was trying to lose the race but the other man was playing into his hands.

Short of deliberately slowing, which would be noticed, there was little he could do, for the privateer had allowed himself to be boxed in against the land, and with the down-slope afternoon winds coming in from near abeam, *L'Aurore* was at her best, at less than half a mile astern and closing.

Should he reluctantly board or stand off and cannonade it to a ruin? A prolonged roll of heavy gunfire would wake up everything for miles and Cape Town itself was only some twenty or so miles ahead. Damn and blast the useless swabs!

A quick check of the chart revealed a forbidding steep-to coast stretching into the distance. There was a good chance they would have to take the privateer on when it was forced seaward by the blunt promontory ahead, marked 'Olifants Bos Point'. Some unknown hand had ominously inked in a graveyard cross and a date pointing to its offshore reef, Albatross Rocks.

It would soon be over: they were overhauling to seaward, and when the hapless vessel came out to round the breaking seas that marked the reef, they would be waiting with a broadside.

L'Aurore edged further seaward; without local knowledge, it would not do to come too near those wicked sub-sea fangs – but the privateer seemed not to care. Or was it that he intended to go between the reef and the point? It was odd: he would gain little by it for *L'Aurore* would simply take him on the other side and, unless he had faultless local know-ledge, with the state of tide, inshore currents and the like, he was taking a terrible risk.

The gap closed – but as *L'Aurore* sheered clear of the

reef the privateer insanely careered on under a full press of sail.

'He's mad, the bugger!' shouted Gilbey, outraged at the foolishness of their rightful prize.

At full tilt the privateer drove on to the rocky plateau at the base of the cliff, rearing up and crashing down, the masts teetering before tumbling in a tangle of rigging until all motion ceased and it lay there, an utter wreck. He had destroyed his ship rather than let it fall into their hands.

Gilbey raved at the madness until Kydd silenced him curtly. This could not have acted out better: not a shot fired, the privateer destroyed, all in a desolate region where the survivors could be expected to take a long time to straggle out and raise the alarm.

Even as he watched, figures were tumbling out of the wreck and crowding on the stone-strewn shore. 'Ease around, Mr Kendall, and we resume our course,' he said, in grim satisfaction.

The next and last stage of the reconnaissance was going to be the hardest. An incursion into the very heart of the enemy's territory: Table Bay itself.

Kydd's charts were good: they showed how the settlement of Kaapstad – Cape Town – was on the lower slopes of a spectacular mountain within the sweep of a broad bay open to the north-west. Unusually, there was no harbour marked, simply a single jetty out from the long, sandy foreshore.

When he rounded Green Point to open into Table Bay, half of his anxieties would be settled. If there was an enemy battle squadron he would find them at anchor opposite the town, and in this near southerly he was confident *L'Aurore* would be able to make her escape seaward and sail to the rendezvous to bring the expedition word in time.

However, if there were no waiting battleships this was only the first act. Establishing how the Dutch would defend their possession was crucial. Kydd could think of no easy way to discover the defences to a landing other than to show his colours and flaunt them along the foreshore, provoking the batteries and gun positions to unmask. It would be dangerous but he was relying on the military's unfamiliarity with gunnery ranges over sea and their probable lack of live practice.

He studied the chart again. There were batteries marked Chavonne, Amsterdam, Fort Knokke and others. And ominously, just below the town at the shoreline, a major fortification in the shape of the Castle of Good Hope. There was nothing for it but to go in.

'All plain sail, Mr Kendall,' he said evenly, to the master. 'After we've cleared Green Point, if there's no French at anchor we'll follow along the six-fathom line as near as we dare.' This would place them at a tempting half-mile range but with sufficient water under the keel.

'Colours at main and mizzen, Mr Gilbey, and I'll thank you to beat to quarters.' The die was cast.

As they made the run, to their starboard the grey-brown slopes of the peninsula spine began to rear up massively, near vertical as a great mountain mass loomed, the rearward ramparts of Table Mountain. And the last feature before they turned the corner into Table Bay was the large cone-like peak called the Lion's Head, the Lion's Rump its smaller continuation. White-fringed rocks below were marked as North and South Lion's Paw.

Atop the Rump there was a signal station, and the thin crack of a gun and wisp of smoke drew attention to the rapid flag hoist on the mast. They had been seen and reported. No doubt there was now the furious drumming and *tan-tara* of trumpets at the batteries and castle, which was what Kydd wanted – but would there also be the sudden appearance of Willaumez's frigates?

Keyed up to expect anything, *L'Aurore* rounded the low flat of Green Point until the whole bay opened before them – with no dread sight of a massed squadron.

There were vessels at anchor: a large one close in, several of medium size and a huddle of smaller, all as near as they could get to the shore and its protection. As *L'Aurore* paused to take in the situation, a series of low thuds sounded from the shoreline, then smoke rose from a small fortified battery at the end of the point and was snatched away by a businesslike breeze.

Standing next to Kydd, Renzi dutifully noted its existence. 'Twelves, do you think?' he said matter-of-factly, as the balls slammed past and sent up vicious plumes nearby.

Close-hauled to the southerly as she was, Kydd knew *L'Aurore* must look a picture from the shore: a beautiful, lethal and utterly graceful man-o'-war arrogantly entering the bay. But he had to show purpose or their real mission would be betrayed. 'Around and through the anchorage as if we mean to take our pick, Mr Kendall,' Kydd said, as though it were an everyday affair to penetrate casually into the heart of an enemy port and out again.

Another battery took over, the concussions heavier and with more venom. 'The Chavonne, I'd believe,' Renzi said, with interest, counting the embrasures with gunsmoke issuing from them. Kydd spared a glance at the panorama of Cape Town opening up: a curiously neat town on the slopes, regularly spaced streets amid mainly whitewashed houses, dominated by the colossus that was Table Mountain.

He had seen illustrations but the reality was dramatic. Its perfectly flat summit stretched along for several miles. At three thousand feet high, with a near-vertical face, it gave an impression of grandeur only approached by what he'd seen at Gibraltar.

Tearing his gaze away, he took stock. There was the castle at the foreshore. It was unmistakable, with its curious low-built bastions and star-shaped design. It was joined by a wall to a fort further along, both completely dominating the only landing place, the jetty.

Another battery opened up as they approached the inner anchorage; by now there was continuous fire on the presumptuous intruder but so far with little effect. They were going to get away with it.

The wind's direction meant that the anchored ships streamed to their cables, presenting a bows-on appearance and therefore unable to fire back. It was nonsense to think that it was possible to board and take one – so near to each other there would be reinforcements by boat on the way before they could bend on sail and put to sea.

He had to make an aggressive gesture – but there was a catch. He called over a master's mate. 'Mr Saxton, go down and tell Mr Bowden it's my desire to fire on the largest, ahead there. Now – mark me well. He's not to hit his target, do you hear? Not one shot to strike him.'

'Sir?' spluttered Saxton, in perplexity.

'Do you not understand plain English, sir? I will give orders to fire and he is to miss. Or shall I have to instruct Lieutenant Bowden myself?'

He hid a smile at the wry thought that on a day of ironies

this was possibly the biggest. He could not fire into the enemy because, if Baird's enterprise was triumphant in the field, all of these would be British.

Plunging through the middle of the anchored vessels, Kydd gave the order. As if in too much of a hurry, *L'Aurore* fired off her broadside early, the savage gouts of shot-strike rising all about the large three-master. They seethed past the untouched ship and Kydd saw the ensign of the French Republic at the staff. It must be a transport, the French reinforcing the Dutch garrison.

Still more batteries were waiting for *L'Aurore* beyond, but had as little success. *L'Aurore* followed the line of the shore. All who could aboard had a telescope up, squinting through the hard midday glare at the alarm ashore.

There appeared to be a coast road following the long curve of the bay, and after the buildings petered out, the land grew flat and uninteresting, a uniform light ochre and dusty green. As far as Kydd could see in either direction, apart from the single jetty under eye from the castle, there were no port facilities to disembark soldiers and equipment, a grave drawback.

Robben Island, flat and barren on the charts, gave a natural conclusion to the bay and made a perfect blind for their rapid exit out to sea and the rendezvous.

What could he report? The most significant fact was that the fearsome battle groups of the French had not been sighted close by. Therefore they had a bracket of time of perhaps one or two days. The presence of the transport was a troubling unknown – how many troops had it brought? As for the defences, it was out of the question to repeat their surprise penetration. They had good information on the siting and calibre of defensive batteries but, on the other hand, clear evidence that without a port only a beach landing was open to them – and that in the face of hostile fire.

But those were considerations for others. 'Course nor'-west after we round the island, Mr Kendall,' Kydd said. Time was short.

General Baird rose to his feet. The muted conversations around the table in *Diadem*'s great cabin died away until there was perfect quiet. He did not speak at first, looking about gravely at the senior officers, an imposing group in their regimental and naval dress.

Kydd sat respectfully alert; he was not at the table with the commodore and brigadiers but with others in the outer ring.

'Today I received my latest intelligence concerning the situation obtaining in the Cape,' the general said quietly. 'And it is that there are no signs of superior French forces in the vicinity. Had there been, be assured, I would have summarily cancelled the expedition and fallen back on St Helena.'

'We go in,' said Colonel Pack, with a savage smile, but he was pointedly ignored by Baird, his face lined with worry.

'I shall not hide it from you – the decision is hard. Our forces are reduced. We have lost men at sea and the remainder must be accounted in weak condition from so long on ship-board. Moreover, we've now few horses left to us available to turn an attack by column.'

He drew in a deep breath. 'Not only that, but most of our artillery is lost to shipwreck. If we make an assault – if we land successfully – then it will be but infantry on the field of battle against cavalry and guns. These are not odds most favouring those attempting a descent on a hostile shore.'

He paused, letting it sink in. Sea-glitter played prettily on the deckhead through the expanse of ornamented stern windows, moving slowly from side to side with the long sway of a South Atlantic swell.

'But, yes, I have decided we will go forward with the landing, and with no further delay.' A ripple of satisfaction went around the cabin.

'From intelligence I have received so far we have a fair idea of what opposes us. First, there are the Dutch regulars. They garrison the castle and man the many batteries around the Cape. In addition to grenadiers and fusiliers, they maintain six companies of horse artillery deploying six-pounders together with foot artillery and dragoons.

'As well as regulars, the Dutch command a battalion of Waldeckers, well-paid Westphalian and Hesse German mercenaries. Then there is the Java Foot Artillery, Malay slaves who have bought their freedom by enlisting. And also the Kaapsche Jägers – a line regiment of sharpshooters equipped with accurate rifles who will no doubt harry us as skirmishers on the flanks.

'For cavalry they have what they term a "mounted commando" of light dragoons. These are irregulars but a formidable foe. Raised locally from the Boer country-folk, they fight for their land and their homes, and although individualists come on like tigers, it's said their favoured method of charge is firing their carbines from horseback and other tricks.'

There were comradely chuckles of amusement at this evidence of rank indiscipline but Baird cut through it: 'Be sure of it, the moment our force is sighted, a chain of signal cannon will send an alarm to the interior and this "burgher cavalry" will come swarming upon us.'

Kydd hadn't any idea what a Boer was but there was no

doubting Baird's deadly seriousness. The general continued, 'And, of course, there are the Pandours – and not to be despised, I'm persuaded. They are fine marksmen, locally raised men of colour. The Dutch call 'em the Hottentot Light Infantry and we shall meet at least a regiment of them in the field.'

An older colonel shifted in his seat. 'Sir, we have heard nothing of French reinforcement. Captain Kydd reported a large transport at anchor and we can only infer that there's—'

'I know nothing of recent accessions to strength. At the least there are some hundreds, possibly a thousand of Bonaparte's troops or marines. But we should not overlook the fact that they are not an organic part of the Dutch Army and, new arrived, may not fit well into their command structure. Nevertheless, we shall face them as we do the rest – as British soldiers!'

As stout murmurs of agreement went around the table, Honyman, captain of *Leda*, leaned across to Kydd and whispered, 'Be damned to all this battlefield gabble – it's getting 'em ashore I'm concerned with. Boats? Under fire? A night landing?'

Baird's expression did not ease as he picked up his thread. 'So, on to my plan. I've considered it well. With our forces as they are, we cannot contemplate a frontal assault on the town for I've no siege engines of any kind.

'An attack overland from False Bay? I've been advised by the Navy' – Popham nodded gravely – 'that in view of the reigning winds in summer being in the south-east this also cannot be in contemplation.

'Then a surprise landing behind the town, say at Camps Bay? There's a pass just above at Kloofnek leading between

44

the Lion's Head and Table Mountain that could see us massing above for a descent on their unprotected rear. But again I'm cautioned by the Navy that, given the tight constraints of the landing place, insufficient men might disembark before the enemy retaliates.'

He paused for effect. 'So! What is left to me is a massed landing by boat. At a place far enough from the fixed defences to allow us a chance to establish a foothold but not too far away that the enemy has time to prepare in depth.

'Gentlemen, there is such a place, no more than fifteen, eighteen miles from the centre of Cape Town. Er, if you'd kindly assist me . . .' Two officers took a corner each of the map and held it up for all to see.

'Now, as you may observe, Table Mountain is at their backs. Where the ground levels to the north we have the castle. Beyond the castle is a fort, and past that – nothing. A ten-mile length of beach up to and past Robben Island here. Now, there is a coast road, a contemptible thing that will take an ox-wagon or four men abreast, not enough to send troops in haste.

'Losperd's Bay is here, at the end of the beach, past the island. And, gentlemen, this is where we go in.'

Military and naval heads craned forward together to peer at the map. 'I'm supposing we can get our troops landed before the Dutch can reach us. We form up and accept battle, driving them back on the town.'

He looked back sharply at a muffled 'Without guns, without cavalry . . .' but continued grimly, 'I'm only too well aware that an opposed landing may be bloody but I'm sending in the smaller navy ships to cannonade the landing place as the boats approach.'

Kydd knew full well who this would be, and the problems

he and *Leda* must face. Were they to present their broadsides to the enemy, cutting across the path of the boats, or fire over their heads at fearful risk to them with rolling seas on the beam? And who would be there to help the soldiers and their kit disembark on an open beach? And what of the risk to the ship? Enemy guns lined up on solid ground could hardly miss, and a damaged ship out of control would be a wreck in a short time, wreaking chaos.

Baird's iron gaze moved slowly around the table. Then he said, 'I will not accept anything except that we are ready to invest the castle within a very short number of days. Else we stand exposed to any forces the enemy summons. I shall make my meaning clearer, gentlemen. We move on the Dutch tomorrow.'

Chapter 3

It was as if a sign had been given: no sooner had they returned to their ships than the wind veered from the usual south-easterly directly for their objective. It settled to a broad westerly during the night and increased to a respectable briskness.

In the dawn's light the little armada saw the mountains of the Cape ahead and set their course for the climactic act of the drama. Within hours they had cast anchor in fifteen fathoms just to the north of the grey-green anonymity of Robben Island, two miles offshore from the landing place.

Kydd glanced over to the mainland and took in a low, flat coastline, a long beach ending in a twist of shoreline and a knot of dark rocks. Away in the distance was the grand sight of Table Mountain, at this angle picturesque and magnificent. A mile or so inland a blue-grey pair of hills rose abruptly from the flat plains, and in the far distance a light-grey craggy mountain range limned the horizon.

And not a sign of the enemy! Had they achieved the surprise they so much needed? The looming of an invasion fleet at their very doorstep must surely be causing dismay and alarm among the Dutch.

There was little time to ponder, however, for the flagship immediately summoned all commanders for a last conference before the assault was unleashed.

Kydd boarded *Diadem*, feeling the excitement and tension. On her quarterdeck a piper in kilt and bonnet stood at the ready.

In the great cabin Baird waited calmly for the meeting to come to order. Then he said briskly, 'It seems we have our wish, gentlemen. I propose to dispense with preliminaries and proceed without delay.'

Fierce grins showed among the army officers: the endless weeks at sea had been a sore trial for them but now there would be action at last.

'We begin embarking in the boats immediately. These will depart on my command for Losperd's Bay. This is a clearly defined stretch of sand between two points of rock. To occupy the dunes immediately inland is our first objective. Commodore?'

Popham's glance took in all the naval captains. 'Offshore bombardment will be by *Diadem*'s thirty-two-pounders, firing over the heads of the boats going in. *Leda* and *L'Aurore* will go to two anchors as close to the shore as practical and pass springs for adjustment of aim. Their positioning will be to either side of Losperd's Bay. A continuous fire will be maintained before and, as signalled, after the landing.'

'Thank you,' Baird said. 'It will keep the enemy tolerably entertained, I believe. I shall remind you again – the rapid establishing of a foothold is critical to our success. We must move before the foe wakes to his situation.'

Kydd felt muffled thumps and scrapes through the deck,

which he recognised as boats coming alongside in the brisk seas. The embarkation was beginning even as they sat.

'Nevertheless, as a prudent commander I will make a last reconnaissance. Brigadier General Ferguson has claimed that honour for himself but begs he might be accompanied by a senior naval officer.'

Ferguson, a bewhiskered Highlander, red of face but with piercing and intelligent eyes, acknowledged the table and Popham nodded pleasantly. 'It can be arranged. A ship's pinnace under sail will be adequate to your purpose, which Captain Kydd, I'm sure, will be delighted to command.'

While *L'Aurore*'s pinnace was readied Kydd and Ferguson watched the embarkation. The same brisk westerly that had sped them to *Diadem* had produced a sizeable swell and white wave-crests, and the soldiers with their equipment were finding it difficult to get aboard.

Every boat was being pressed into service: big launches seating sixty soldiers, with twenty oarsmen, through to barges and cutters crowded up to the larger ships. The troops were assembled on deck by file, their kit beside them. As well as their muskets and bayonets, each man had to carry sixty rounds of ball cartridge, spare flints and haversack rations for three days.

They climbed into the bucking craft awkwardly, trying to keep in the centreline away from the seamen at the oars and looking at the hissing seas nervously. The boats backed off and joined the assembling armada.

L'Aurore's pinnace came alongside, cutter-rigged with a mainsail boom and long bowsprit. Kydd took the tiller, with Stirk at the main-sheets and Poulden with Doud forward. Ferguson boarded, sensibly clad in a plain uniform and accompanied by two blank-faced soldiers.

49

'Shove off,' Kydd ordered, and the boat swung out of the lee of the 64, catching the westerly squarely. Under a single-reefed main they surged towards the shore on the backs of the combers.

'A mite lively,' the major general said peevishly, as the pinnace took a foaming crest over the gunwale, soaking his breeches. The boisterous seas grew steeper as they felt the shallowing seabed rise under them.

Kydd held his tongue. This was a lightly manned boat under fast sail – he feared how it would be for deeply laden craft under oars.

They approached the beach, Ferguson leaning forward in his eagerness to sight ashore. 'Up 'n' down, if you please,' he rapped. Kydd chose his moment, then put down the tiller.

Broadside to the waves, the boat rolled wickedly, bringing cries of alarm from the soldiers, but Ferguson held on grimly as they wallowed and bucketed along. With the wind abeam, the boat was canted higher on the weather side, which served to keep the worst seas at bay, bobbing skyward as a massive swell drove beneath and then, with a precipitous lurch, dropping dizzily as the wave charged inshore.

They went about after half a mile and did a pass further up the coast. There was no gunfire or sudden movement, and Ferguson abruptly turned to Kydd. 'Put these men on the land, sir.'

The two soldiers, hanging on for their lives, looked back in dismay and Kydd tried to smile encouragingly, despite his misgivings. 'Poulden, ready the oars. I'll bear up into the wind and at that instant brail the main, let fly fore-sheets and then out oars.'

Sail doused, it was nearly impossible to keep head to sea. The seething combers met the bow, flinging it skyward to crunch back at an awkward angle, which frantic work at the oars could only just meet. Kydd could see that even if he brought the boat to land through the surf they would never get off again, given this force of wind and sea.

'Set the fores'l 'n' jib!' he roared, above the thunder of the waves. They clawed off, every man soaked and Doud frantically bailing over the side. 'We can't make it, sir!' Kydd bawled, at the hunched-over figure of the general.

Ferguson looked up and met his eyes. If a well-found ship's pinnace could not get through to the shore, then sending in heavily laden, crowded assault boats would risk catastrophe. 'No. I've seen enough. We return.'

At the flagship further out, the seas gave little hint of their bull-rampaging power at the shoreline. 'Sir, it's my firm opinion they'll never get on shore in this,' Ferguson told Baird urgently, as the general came up to meet the returning party. 'We must not attempt it.'

Baird looked at him as if he were demented. 'Not proceed? Sir, by your own report the enemy has not reached the landing place. You're proposing I suspend operations, recall the boats and lie in idleness while the enemy finds time to complete his deployment?'

To shoreward of *Diadem* the boats were assembling in concourse for the line of assault, bobbing and sliding on the swell and perilously full of soldiery; the embarking was near complete.

The tension on the quarterdeck was electric.

'Sir! Might I . . . ?' Kydd interposed, unsure of the proper form for contradicting a commander-in-chief.

'Captain?'

'I fear General Ferguson is right. These beaches are open

to the full force of the Atlantic. Our seamen will try their best but with all those soldiers on board . . . That is to say, with their oars they'll need . . .' He trailed off at Baird's thunderous expression.

'You're trying to say the Navy can't find a way to land my men on an unopposed shore?' Baird said, with biting savagery. 'That a vital strategic move against the enemy, devised and planned by His Majesty's War Council in Whitehall, is to be overborne by – by you, sir?'

Despite his vitriol, Kydd felt for the man – with all his detailed plans and hopes, he now had an impossible choice: to go ahead and risk disaster before his very eyes or wait for someone to tell him that he could go – and take responsibility when he was bloodily and decisively beaten on the beaches by a prepared enemy.

'Er, may the commodore and I consult, sir?' Kydd said evenly, seeing Popham arriving on the quarterdeck.

At Baird's grunt, he motioned Popham aside. 'Sir, the conditions are insupportable. This westerly has kicked up a long swell that's pounding the sand. No boat can live in that surf. You must . . .'

The commodore's brow creased and he paused before he replied. 'I see, Mr Kydd. You will appreciate, however, that this cannot be received by the commander-in-chief with anything but resentment and more than a trifle of anxiety but I will speak with him.'

He approached the fuming general and took him by the arm. 'David, I really do feel we must discuss this further. Shall we go below?'

A little later Popham returned alone. 'Well, now. The general has a pretty dilemma but I flatter myself we have a naval plan that shall see him mollified.'

Kydd's spirits rose. 'Then how shall we get them ashore, sir?' That was the nub, but the commodore probably had ideas such as pontoons on a line through the breakers or—

'We don't.'

'Sir?'

'Consider. We had notions of landing here because we had a chance of getting 'em ashore and established before the enemy had time to advance up the coast to contest the landing. Now he has the time. Therefore do you not think that our primary purpose is to dissuade him from such a course? To remain where he is and allow us to land here when the weather improves?'

Popham's look of smug superiority irked Kydd, but he would play the game. This was the man who'd devised a radically new system of signals that had been adopted by the whole Navy and whom he'd witnessed devise an ingenious solution for delivering Fulton's torpedoes when his submarine was seen as not practical.

'Er, a feint as will draw his attention away?'

'Umm?'

It was beginning to come. He remembered Baird's reasoning behind his decision to land in this particular location. 'Make a motion in his rear, say Camps Bay, as will persuade him we intend to cross, um, Kluffnick Pass—'

'Kloofnek.'

'– to fall on him from behind. In this way he'll not want to be caught with his army straggling out in the open if there's a chance we'll strike at his centre.'

'Very good. Pray continue.'

Of course! That was the solution. 'So we are giving out that the Losperd's Bay show with boats is merely by way of enticing him out – and the real landing is at Camps Bay.'

'Bravo!' Popham said. 'Their field commander and governor, General Janssens, is a wily bird. He may or may not fall for it, but at the very least he'll hesitate before committing his troops this far out from the town and castle.'

At a hurriedly reconvened council-of-war Baird wasted no time. 'Gentlemen, I've given orders that the landing is *not* to proceed.'

A dismayed hubbub died away at his calm smile. 'Instead we turn the delay to our advantage. I'm asking Commodore Popham to make a flourish at Camps Bay for the purpose of getting General Janssens to think again of where the landing will be taking place. No army commander would dare to be caught with his column of advance strung out and a landing in his rear.'

There were murmurs of appreciation and Popham avoided Kydd's eye. 'Nevertheless, I'm to take precautions, I believe. It's my desire to set troops on the shores of Africa and to this end I'm dispatching General Beresford with the Twentieth Regiment of Dragoons to the closest sheltered harbour, which is Saldanha Bay in the north. Having established a presence there, he will march down to meet us at the landing or alternatively hold a position. Any questions?'

Kydd had none, but Saldanha Bay, while less than a day's sail away for a ship, was a march of seventy miles across African wilderness for soldiers weakened by the voyage. If the weather stayed from the west and the main landing was impossible, on arrival they would be cut to pieces while he and the others looked on helplessly.

Any watcher from the dunes would have seen, in the last of the daylight, first a frigate and then other ships detach from the invasion fleet one by one and slip south, in full view, past the castle with the colours of the Batavian Republic and continuing by Cape Town itself, before rounding the point out of sight as a sunset blazed in from the sea. The conclusion would hopefully have been that the British were readying for a dawn assault – and the Dutch commander could congratulate himself for not falling for the gesture at Losperd's Bay: his forces were still in place and fully capable of defending the town.

Kydd's little fleet of a single frigate and harmless transports, however, were waiting for a sign. It came in the darkness at a little after two in the morning. Under easy sail well offshore, they felt the wind die to a whisper and then, an hour before dawn, it strengthened – from the south-west.

Signal lanthorns were hung in *L'Aurore*'s rigging and sail was set for the north. When day broke, they were back in the lee of Robben Island with the invading force and a very different prospect.

The seas were now subdued and the wind, backing yet further into its accustomed summer direction, was no longer a threat. The landing was on.

Brigadier General Ferguson returned from the beaches in fine spirits: he had landed his scouts, who had sighted lookouts but quickly determined that there were no enemy troops in strength lurking under cover behind the sand dunes.

Baird gave his orders for an embarkation. It was going to be a race against time: there could be no doubt now that the landing was taking place and the Dutch must be rushing troops to meet the threat. Only if they could get his own men ashore in time would they have a chance.

While soldiers boarded their boats once again, *L'Aurore* and *Leda* manoeuvred to take their bombardment positions each side of the sea-lane the boats would use, anchored both fore and aft and with the springs attached to the cables that would allow the whole ship to be oriented to lay down fire as requested.

At the head of the sea-lane, *Diadem* was ready with her big guns while the other two 64s lay defensively to seaward and the remainder ranged up and down the shoreline.

Before noon the stage was set and the signal was given. Galvanised into motion, the boats began the fearful passage to the beaches under a hot sun. But from their lofty height lookouts had spied a disturbing turn of events. There had been no time for the Dutch to march up to confront the landing but a commando of the burgher cavalry had been spotted: their horses had enabled them to be quickly on the scene and now they would be taking position in unknown numbers up and down the dunes to blaze fire into the helpless boats.

High in the tops of *L'Aurore*, sharp-eyed midshipmen relayed bearings to the gun-deck and her guns opened up in a slam of sound. A storm of iron tore into the dunes, sending up high gouts of sand and scattered clods all along the dune crests. When *Leda* joined in, the fire intensified into a continual bombardment that numbed the senses.

It was a hideous experience for the Dutch, but it gave heart to the seamen, straining in their heroic dash at the oars, and the soldiers sitting helplessly. War pennons fluttered bravely from some, the legendary colours to plant on the beach as their rallying point. From others, kilted pipers nobly played their defiance, and in all, the feathered bonnets and splash of scarlet of the famed regiments of Scotland.

When the boats reached the beach it would be another matter. The cannonade must lift and then they would be on their own. All would then turn on whether the enemy had fled or merely taken cover to rise again.

As they neared the shore Kydd ordered his guns silent. At first nothing stirred among the dunes. Then a tell-tale puff of white smoke rose, and another, until a regular fire was coming from up and down the beach. These were the heroes among the enemy who had not abandoned their post and were going to dispute the landing – but thankfully the ominous concussion of a field gun charged with grapeshot, which could quickly turn the landing into a bloodbath, was absent.

He watched as the many boats began to converge on the assault beach between the two rock ledges in a congested surge; if they could land together they stood a better chance but this was at the cost of fatal crowding – over to the left a boat slewed sideways as it took a rock. Under the impetus of the surf it rose and fell, capsizing instantly and throwing the heavily encumbered soldiers of the 93rd into the depths. Kydd craned to look, but of the forty-odd in the boat there were only three or four heads in the water, the rest choking out their last moments of life beneath the sparkling green sea.

The first boat grounded, soldiers clambering out awkwardly in their haste. Making the beach, an officer turned to gesture imperiously for his standard. Not far behind the green-feathered light infantry, stumbling at first in the soft sand, began moving out, some firing from the kneel and others pressing on up the beach.

They were taking casualties; men were dropping. An officer spun and fell – Kydd thought he recognised the fiery Pack – but troops were spilling ashore fast and the musket fire from the dunes began to slacken.

The experienced Highlanders of the 71st knew their business. Picked squads of agile light companies trotted up and down the beach and disappeared into the sand-hills. A sizeable company assembled in extended order and, muskets at the port, stormed inland.

More boats crowded ashore; now field equipment was being landed, portable howitzers, light field-pieces, even horses, as all hostile fire was silenced. Knots of men gathered at the standards waiting for orders, while an improvised signal mast let fly the hoist that declared the beachhead secure. Against all probability, the expedition had seized a foothold on the shores of Africa.

Somewhere out of sight beyond the fringing dunes, defensive lines were being set up, pickets told off and troops placed in readiness for the expected counter-attack. A determined strike could see them in serious trouble for their tenuous hold must urgently be translated to real strength — stores of all kinds, rations, ammunition, water in the keg: all had to be landed to make this possible.

Word came that a strong body of troops had been seen issuing from the castle, joined by others further along in what could only be the deploying of an army, but it was too late in the afternoon to fear action that day and the vital stores continued to flood ashore.

Aboard *L'Aurore* there was great satisfaction. They had done their part and the Army had done theirs. The British flag was well and truly planted ashore, and in the near future there would be a bloody battlefield where the Dutch would have to make their stand against the invaders.

The ship had performed creditably and would still have a part to play in support, but for now Kydd contented himself with reverting to single anchor, the cable buoyed for quick release. They were ready for any orders – but when they came they were completely unexpected: Kydd was to attach himself to the general's staff as naval liaison.

He was to land with a lieutenant of signals set up to communicate with his ship, which, with the shallowest draught, had been chosen to act as close-in gunfire support, a fearsome mobile battery. The main coastal road ran close to the foreshore and it took little imagination to conceive of the havoc that would be inflicted by a broadside against columns of troops marching up in reinforcement. Although he would do his duty ashore, Kydd did not relish being out of his ship – the French squadrons could still make an appearance – but at least with *L'Aurore* so close he could be back aboard quickly.

'Mr Bowden!' he called.

'Sir?'

'Find yourself a likely midshipman and two hands – you're going a-signalling in Africa!' The details of how communications would be maintained he would leave as an exercise for the young man to present later.

What should a naval captain wear at a campaign headquarters on the field of battle? If the ancestral portraits he had seen were anything to go by, then only the most ornate full dress would do. Uneasily he remembered his experiences with the Army ashore. As a young lieutenant in Menorca, seconded to the land forces, he had returned on board his ship, victorious but hopelessly tattered and dusty, in stark contrast to the imposing Major General Paget, whose turnout had always been impeccable.

'Tysoe!' He summoned his valet. 'I'm to join the Army for a spell. Pray lay out some kit.'

The sun was sinking out to sea in glorious golds and reds

when he boarded his barge and was taken ashore with a single sea-chest. The summer evening wafted alien scents to him as he stood on the beach waiting for his escort. Harsh chittering and hidden rustling among the dune grasses spoke of the mystery and danger of the great continent, but in a way he felt disappointed: this was nothing like the steaming jungle of his imagination.

'Sah!' A splendid-looking sergeant major saluted and a pair of orderlies hefted the chest. They climbed into the dunes and found the path. Off the beach the roar of the surf turned to a muffled boom, and away from the sea breeze, the air became close and hot. They passed chains of soldiers handing along stores, and burial parties, stripped to the waist, inter-ring the dead where they had fallen.

Away in the distance a trumpet brayed, shouted orders faintly on the air. Kydd was conscious of the soldiers panting behind with his chest for it was heavy going in the soft sand. They left the dunes and were crossing a field of greens, sadly trampled and obviously belonging to the whitewashed farm with thatched roof ahead.

Kydd felt resentment that Tysoe had insisted on full undress uniform and sword. In his formal coat and large bicorne fashionably over his nose he was beginning to itch and sweat; on the open battlefield in the full heat of day it would be unendurable.

With much stamping of feet and crashing of muskets his presence at the farm was recognised and he was greeted by an affable major. It seemed he was now at Baird's head-quarters and was most welcome.

Inside, the comfortably worn flagstones and thick walls held a surprising cool and Baird came to greet him. 'A fine show by the Navy!' he grunted. 'Their lordships shall certainly hear of my approbation of their conduct this day, Captain!'

Seeing the major and general-officer-commanding faultlessly attired in the ceremonials of a Highland regiment, Kydd had now to be grateful for Tysoe's insistence in the matter of dress.

'You'll join us at supper?'

Kydd bowed politely and was shown into a cosy room, obviously the farmer's pride, with its quaint Dutch furniture and tableware on display in the dresser racks. Now it was a senior officers' mess, and round the table, jovial colonels and brigadiers sat and chatted expansively about the day's events.

'A dram wi' ye!' said the red-faced MacDonald, Lord of the Isles and colonel of the 24th Regiment of Foot, handing Kydd a glass. The golden sparkle was the best malt whisky and quickly set him aglow.

'A right true drop!'

'Och, as it's a Speyside out o' yon Duncan Knockdunder's casks,' MacDonald admitted smugly. There was movement in the dark outside – a massive bulk loomed against the window. MacDonald beckoned and the door opened.

An enormous figure in kilt and feathered bonnet stepped into the bright candlelight holding himself with intense pride. It was the pipe major of the 71st, his bagpipes at the ready, the light glittering on his elaborate accoutrements.

The conversation died and the piper looked at Baird, who glanced about him. 'A Pibroch!' came a cry. It met with instant acclamation and a grey-haired colonel called across, '"The Rout o' Glenfruin"!'

Baird nodded his approval. In the confined space the squeal and drone of the pipes overwhelmed the senses but their barbaric splendour was deeply stirring. The martial wail set

61

Kydd's blood racing. Would the man be leading his clan into battle on the morrow? How could any not be moved to deeds of valour by such a sound?

Supper was plain. While common soldiers were out gathering wood for cooking fires to boil their salt beef to gnaw with their biscuits, their general was not about to insist on the formalities. Wine was conspicuous by its absence and there was no napery – but the talk was all of the coming day.

Three terrified Hottentot soldiers had been captured. They had readily shared all they knew: that they came from a large hidden encampment before the Riet Vlei, a marshy area to the south, and that General Janssens was at this moment with his army marching north at speed in the darkness to confront them the next day.

At one point a diffident lieutenant reported: a determined sweep by scouts had secured eight more horses and a picture of the enemy's forward positions. It could only have been acquired the hard way – in the blackness of the night, stealthily creeping about in the African bush with all its terrors, keyed up for a sudden challenge from an outpost, then a stumbling flight back into the anonymous dark.

They had established that there was a light cavalry position at another farmhouse not far away beyond the ridge and other mounted vedettes in a line to the south. Further, fires had been observed on Blaauwberg, the massive bulk of blue-grey bluffs Kydd had seen from the sea. These would be lookouts in an impregnable situation that would report their every movement when battle was joined.

The foe was closing in, but there was no nervousness that Kydd could detect, just the same brotherly laughter and concern as in a naval wardroom, the precious feeling that was only to be found in a company whose lives the next day would be in each other's hands.

'Gentlemen! Be so good as to gather about me,' Baird announced unexpectedly. An aide passed him a large map, which he smoothed on the table. Two stands of candles were brought near. Their light caught the officers from beneath as they crowded around, their grave expressions a sombre acceptance of what lay ahead.

'My plans for the day.' An expectant silence descended. 'I won't pretend we're in a favourable position – far from it. No cavalry, just a few guns, and against us everything the Dutch care to bring to bear.'

He paused, then spoke in measured tones. 'However, this is no new circumstance for Highlanders and I place my trust completely in their qualities of soldierly ardour and unflinching bravery.'

Grunts of appreciation came but there was no easing in the unblinking stares.

'Tomorrow we shall be taking the initiative. I now know General Janssens – who is no dilettante – is forming up in line in the plain beyond Blaauwberg. He's discovered we have no cavalry and is extending his force to dominate the road to Cape Town.

'In his centre will be his guns – how many I know not, nor his numbers. What I do know is that the French are wholeheartedly with him, both the reinforcements we know of and apparently some hundreds from a privateer the Navy ran on the rocks.'

Kydd started guiltily, but there was no way he could have landed and pursued them in that hostile country.

'Therefore this shall be an infantry battle, save for our few guns, and all objectives must be taken by storm and main force. I shall attack in column with two brigades, the First on the left, consisting of the Seventy-first, Seventy-second and Ninety-third regiments; the Second on the right, with the Twenty-fourth, Fifty-ninth and Eighty-third. When we are before the enemy, we shall deploy in line. Questions?'

Hazily, Kydd understood that they were advancing with a minimum front while the Dutch artillery was in action and when in musket range would open up to full width opposite the enemy.

'We do have some guns, sir?' came from one officer.

'Six six-pounders and only two small howitzers. I'm at a loss to know how these can be termed a battering train if it comes to a siege. Nevertheless, I'll point out, if I may, that in this, as in so much other, the Navy is coming to our aid. In the absence of horses, and to release soldiers for duty, they are landing a Sea Battalion whose duty it will be to man-haul the pieces into action and keep up a supply of cannon-balls and powder.'

It was the first Kydd had heard of it but he recognised Popham's style, a vigorous response to a need. His own orders in respect of the roving battery that was *L'Aurore* had been properly acted upon. But would his part in the next day's events be as a spectator or would he be fighting for his life as they were overrun by those Dutch, Malays, Hottentots and Waldeckers?

He sat quietly, listening as the details were laid out. In all his experience he'd never been in a formal clash-at-arms between armies – Acre didn't count and he'd been away in a sideshow at the final defeat of Napoleon's army in Egypt. Did the opposing armies perform a courtly salute, a displaying of colours in much the same way as men-o'-war did before opening fire? If nothing else, tomorrow would be an interesting day for a sailor.

The discussion concluded tidily, formal written orders were issued and suddenly there was no more to be done. A toast to the health of Colonel Pack, who had indeed taken a bullet on the landing beach, and a final one to His Majesty, and it was time to retire.

Kydd found it hard to sleep in the hot dimness, smelling the reek of army canvas preservative. The dead feel of the earth under his campaign cot instead of the gentle heave of his ship was unnatural and the strange night sounds of the African bush – any one of which could have been the enemy closing in – were disquieting.

Well before dawn the camp was astir. After watch-keeping at sea Kydd was untroubled by the hour – it was rather what it implied: they were readying themselves for battle, and the first moves would be theirs.

He could sense the tension. The men were taking their breakfast quietly, his own brought by a stolid redcoat, who waited while he finished and then left noiselessly. He stayed where he was until first light stole in and a distant trumpeter played an elaborate air to be taken up on all sides. Shouted commands mingled. He heard the rush of feet and the occasional whinny of a horse on the cool morning air – and then massed drummers began a thunderous tattoo. It was the call to arms.

He emerged from the tent to see the battalions forming up in a complex pattern, the nearer column being dressed off by sergeant majors as if on a parade-ground, the other more distant, marching in file and then line, miraculously achieving a stronger cohesion at every manoeuvre.

A bewildering number of men were urgently about their business, quite ignoring why a naval captain should be wandering about – and then he heard a sound so out of place but so familiar he shook his head in bemusement: the clean shrill of a boatswain's pipe sounding the 'Tail on fall', the demand for seamen to take up a tackle line.

It was the Sea Battalion, hundreds of sailors standing loosely in lines ahead of the field pieces, looking about them gleefully. He walked over to talk with their lieutenant-in-charge but was quickly spotted and, to his embarrassment, a spontaneous cheer went up. He doffed his hat – all ships must have been stripped of gun crews and there they were, in all their individuality, so different from the uniformity of identical files of soldiers – and his heart warmed to them.

Many wore a leather harness, which hooked on to the dragrope shackled to the guns, six-pounders but with narrow iron-shod wheels that would dig into the sandy topsoil, turning them into a ferocious dead lump to pull. Two howitzers were also there, needing to be dragged into battle; squat army pieces that threw explosive shells and therefore had to be heavily constructed, brutes to move.

The hundreds not at the traces would either be hauling the howitzers, or carrying iron shot and powder. In addition each man was fully armed: a brace of pistols, cutlass and even a boarding pike. If the tide of battle went against them and the guns needed defending, they would do the job. Kydd tried not to think of how they could stand and fight against a sabre-wielding charge by heavy cavalry.

Baird and his staff were at the head of the army. Distinctive on a white charger, the general was in the centre of a group of splendidly attired officers, all mounted and in animated conversation.

As Kydd approached, a breathless young ensign found him. 'S-Sir! Your horse!' Despite a critical shortage of mounts on the battlefield it would be unthinkable that Kydd, a senior officer, should be seen on foot like a common soldier.

He climbed aboard awkwardly, the odd-looking brown creature clearly one of those lately gathered locally. It jibbed and snorted at Kydd's alien scent, and he strove to subdue it while setting off cautiously to join the group around Baird.

'Captain Kydd, sir,' a colonel said urbanely, gesturing impatiently for him to approach nearer.

'Sir. I've given my orders—'

'Then I'll wish you well of the day, sir,' Baird said, briefly looking up from a paper. 'For Brigadier General Ferguson this minute,' he snapped, passing the document to a waiting subaltern, who cantered off through the assembling columns.

Kydd held well back while the forming up took place; it seemed to take hours but he knew that any weakness or over-looked detail might cost lives, even the action. It must be worse for the waiting soldiers: Baird had a good reputation in India but would that translate here to reckless abandon, given the stakes?

Finally, it was time, and the order to advance in general was given. Taking the lead Baird walked his horse slowly forward, closely followed by his staff. As they passed, the head of the column's screamed commands started the tramp of feet and the monotonous *ker-thump* of a drum. Apparently the pipers were reserving their wind for the future.

It was unnerving. The scrubby landscape was flat and sandy, absorbing sound, and stretched away in a gentle rise ahead. There was no sign of the enemy, no hostile threat, but while Kydd was conscious of the army behind, he felt very exposed in the little group at the front. On the other hand he was witness to the grand spectacle of an army on the march into battle, which he knew he would never forget.

They stepped slowly on, the thousands of men marching

in patient unison, standards aloft, squadron colours with their bearers.

After an hour or so the sun was making itself felt. The pale soil reflected the brightness and was quickly absorbing heat, radiating it up uncomfortably. There was no keen horizontal sea breeze here, only a hot, breathy, vertical shimmering.

A horse and rider appeared above the skyline at the ridge ahead and stopped. Another rose some distance to the left. Baird reined in and signalled a halt. Screamed commands echoed back and the drums abruptly stopped. An eerie silence slowly spread. Then the general urged his horse forward. Was this some sort of grave martial rite that must be performed before the two armies grappled in mortal combat?

Kydd followed with the others. Baird seemed hardly to notice the two riders, acknowledging their smart salutes with a distracted wave and peering intently ahead. Then Kydd understood: these were their own scouts and consequently the general must be in sight of the enemy.

They drew up level and he found himself along the top of a gentle ridge. There, spread out over the plain below, the Dutch host waited for them. With a tightening of his stomach Kydd saw what seemed to be an uncountable number of tiny figures in their battalions, which stretched squarely across their route.

He tried to take in the wider scene. To the right was the dull-blue monolithic bulk of Blaauwberg, a smaller mountain a little further on. To his left was the same flat, sandy scrub that stretched for some miles inland before another blue mountain range, a larger formation beyond. But straight before them was the gentle slope that led across the baking plain to the Dutch Batavian lines, and in the far distance, the grand sight of Table Mountain.

Baird had a telescope up and was quartering the ground in front of him with the utmost concentration. Around him his officers waited with patience: this was nothing less than decisions for the final commitment – if anything were overlooked, it would be too late to remedy in the heat of battle.

'Um, a stern sight, sir,' Kydd said hesitantly to the officer nearest him, who had holstered his telescope after his own survey and now sat calmly.

'Possibly,' the man said, with a curious glance at Kydd.

'Sir, I'd be most obliged should you give me an account of what faces us.'

'Very well.' He deliberated for a moment, then said, 'Before you are the Batavian lines in extended order as they are not expecting our cavalry to outflank them. On each wing is an artillery detachment with more in the centre, which I'm diverted to observe seem to be served by a species of Malay.

'To the left you'll see a Waldeck Jäger battalion whose rifled barrels are much to be respected. The Dutch infantry are next towards the middle, where you'll note more Waldecker mercenaries in support behind that forward troop of guns in the centre.

'On the right is a strong showing of Hottentot infantry supported by additional Jägers and on the far right is where much of their cavalry are assembled.'

Kydd could now make out the differing uniforms and standards distinguishing parts of the array facing them but how all these could come together as a whole was beyond him. Then he saw in the exact centre a disciplined mass of blue – and the tricolour proudly aloft.

'And the French,' he said.

'Ah, yes,' the officer came back drolly.

Baird lowered his glass. 'Well, they seem to be awaiting us, so I shan't disappoint them.'

He let his glance rest on the scene for one last moment. 'I shall attack in two columns as planned,' he rapped. 'The Second Brigade will follow the base of the Blaauwberg massif to storm the lesser mount – Kleinberg. The First Brigade will march to the front. I will have the howitzers in play from the start.'

A two-pronged attack at a prepared army – but occupying the high ground to the right, above the Dutch, was a strong move.

Baird leaned over and took a wooden contraption from an aide, which turned out to be an ingenious desk that fitted over his horse's neck. He began scratching orders at great speed, handing them down impatiently. Each in turn was snatched by a dispatch rider, who put them in his sabretache and sped off in a wild thud of hoofs.

Their own cannon – such as they were – must now be brought forward. The howitzers with their explosive shells were small but could create dismay among the enemy ranks beyond their size. Kydd gave a grim smile at the irony that the first shots of the battle would be fired by sailors. The Sea Battalion had hauled their bronze beasts under the hot glare of the sun to the front of the British lines and were now deployed to either side of the centre. Knowing they were under the eye of the entire army, they were serving their guns with energy and skill.

The first shell landed not far from the front rank of the enemy, its orange flash and instant gout of white smoke followed by a distinct *crump*. The other howitzer followed suit, its shell causing a swirl in the opposing ranks.

To the right the pipers opened with a squeal and a drone, and the brigade stepped off in a compact column, as regular a march as ever to be seen on their home parade-ground. The howitzers fired again – but this time there was a reply from a troop of unseen guns located on the very high ground of Kleinberg they had intended as their own.

'First Brigade, advance!' Baird snapped. The sooner they closed with the enemy the better – if they could survive the guns. Behind, the pipers skirled into life and the column began to move up to crest the ridge. Passing on both sides of the general they marched towards the enemy.

The battle had begun.

MacDonald's brigade, to the right, had increased their pace, knowing the vital necessity of silencing the guns on Kleinberg, and Kydd needed no telling that throwing infantry against guns would be a deathly affair.

More enemy guns opened up – from the centre, the focus of the attack by the First Brigade. These Highlanders must in consequence advance through the hell of cannon fire before ever getting within range of their own muskets.

It was a trial for Kydd to act the spectator while others went into danger, but it was his duty.

Now at the base of Blaauwberg the Second Brigade, still in close order against cavalry attack, would be an easy target for enemy guns but they marched on under the blazing sun.

Kydd tore his gaze away and watched the other column stolidly moving forward. Now the guns were telling: a ball reached the Highlanders, its passage marked by wheeling bodies and gaps in the ranks. Another – it couldn't last!

A series of puffs showed on the flanks of Kleinberg. 'Jägers,' the officer watching with him said, with concern. A rifled weapon wielded with skill could always out-range a standard musket, even if the rate of fire was slower. These sharpshooters must have been set to defend the guns and were doing so: some lonely figures on the line of march lay sprawled and still.

'Damn it – where's those cannon?' Baird demanded irascibly, twisting in his saddle.

At that moment the Sea Battalion came over the rise, the sailors near prostrate in the savage heat from the muscle-burning effort of heaving the iron brutes through the soft sand. Yet they hauled on valiantly, trying to keep with the fast-marching troops. One gun, two – four six-pounders were now in the field.

Matters were now critical. The guns on Kleinberg were easily reaching the advancing brigade and gaps were being torn in the close mass of men; at some point the column must halt and form line to face the main enemy – and then the cavalry massing on Kleinberg's slopes could charge down on them.

Heroically, the exhausted seamen pressed on, and when the order was given for the column to halt and form line they man-hauled through to the front and, exposed as they were, manoeuvred their pieces around and set up to return fire.

Now the enemy would be suffering cannon fire and must make some response – but would the Dutch cavalry dare a charge across open ground?

The line was formed. Baird was going to make a frontal assault on the mass of the enemy, guns, cavalry and all, trusting in the spirit of the Highlanders to see it through to the end.

The pipers wailed into life and the line stepped forward at a measured pace, directly for the waiting Dutch. It was bravery of the highest order to keep discipline and formation while at any moment from the massed ranks opposite there would be a sudden crash of musketry, and death would sleet in to meet them.

The officers' decisions made now would have consequences over so many: to fire when in range, then helplessly endure the enemy's response while reloading, or accept the punishment of a first volley and vengefully take the time for a pitiless rejoinder?

Men were going down in numbers, the guns at the enemy centre firing grapeshot, and there on the flank, high up on Kleinberg, the cannon were taking victims. Everything now depended on the bravery of the Scots regiments up there in closing with the foe.

'I say, that's as damn well done as ever I've seen!' The officer handed Kydd his glass and gestured at Kleinberg. At first it didn't register – puffs of gunsmoke from invisible positions between the marching column and the guns. Was it yet another threat? Then he saw that the sharpshooter fire from Kleinberg was slackening, and well ahead of the advance he could just make out nearly invisible green-clad figures scrambling from one vantage-point to another.

'The "light bobs". Amazing fellows – specially trained at Shorncliffe with rifles to act as light infantry in any regiment. Work in pairs always, and can be relied on, out on their own. See now? I do believe they've got the Dutch rattled!'

The Kleinberg cannons were silent now: an attempt to slew them round to meet the marching 24th Regiment was stopped by the light bobs, who were systematically picking off the gun crews.

Trumpets sounded faintly from the 24th and the glitter of steel showed as bayonets were fixed. After a crashing volley, the redcoats broke into a mad charge directly at the cannons.

It was too much for the Dutch who hitched up their guns and fled downhill, leaving their now exposed position to join the main army.

Baird's tense expression cleared. 'Ah! Those brave fellows have done fine work this day. Now it's the turn of our other Highlanders.'

The line of kilted warriors tramped implacably straight ahead. Suddenly the entire front of the enemy erupted into musket-fire. Some of the Highlanders went down but the others marched on, the gaps filled immediately. At 250 yards a halt was called to bring their weapons to the present and open fire for the first time.

Smoke swirled over them as they reloaded, then the relentless advance continued. Kydd had seen nothing like it – the march into the very mouths of the enemy guns, the silken colours proudly floating above, the pipers in the forefront, their cold courage striking the fear of the devil into their opponents.

An officer was shot from his horse. He tumbled to the ground but gamely dragged himself to his feet and hoisted himself back into the saddle.

The lines were closing. It was now more than possible that the armies would meet in the shock of close combat.

A hundred yards – then fifty. Even to Kydd's eyes there seemed to be an edgy turbulence in the opposing ranks at the approach of the ferocious Scots. The line stopped: a final crashing volley erupted and out of the smoke with a triumphant yell came the Highlanders in a wild charge. It was a fearsome and glorious sight: in the dust and smoke the gleam of steel as bayonets and broadswords clashed, man stood against man, strove and died – and in the chaos and noise the day was decided.

The Dutch centre gave way. The vaunted Waldeckers had fallen back, then turned and fled, and kilted troops punched into the very heart of the enemy. The cannon were overrun, the Javanese artillerymen slaughtered to a man. The French heroically attempting to close the line gave ground under the terrible onslaught and more Scots demons flooded through.

Their army now broken and isolated, there was little the Dutch could do except call a general retreat. Trumpets bayed, and while gallant bands still held their ground and fought, most took flight. It turned to a rout, fleeing Batavians throwing aside their equipment in their terror as they made off south.

Baird punched the air in elation. 'That I had the cavalry to harry them now!' He swore, then recollected himself and raised his telescope to scan the scene. Abruptly he lowered it and looked about him. 'Ah, Captain Kydd,' he called pleasantly. 'If you would oblige me, sir?'

Kydd rode up to the beaming general.

'The Dutch are in headlong retreat and my brave Highlanders are too fatigued to pursue them. I fancy they are heading for their camp at Riet Vlei to regroup and I wish to dissuade them by means of your excellent frigate. Shall you . . . ?'

'Aye aye, sir,' Kydd said promptly, raising his arm expectantly. 'To be signalled,' he told the waiting galloper, and handed him an order. The officer saluted, wheeled his horse around in the direction of Bowden at the shore signal pole and thudded off.

The arrangement was simple: on their joint diagrams the length of the shore was divided into lettered units of one hundred yards. The point specified, together with a number indicating the required distance inland, would be signalled to

L'Aurore. It would be a matter of minutes only before the position would be under a cannonade far more intense than any seen on the battlefield that day. Riet Vlei, some miles to the south, would not be the refuge the Dutch expected it to be.

Baird walked his horse forwards, down the slight gradient over which the First Brigade had marched to glory. The smoke and dust had nearly dissipated and the pitiless glare picked out the trampled field, scattered pieces of kit, and hundreds of bodies lying at random over the arid land. Some still moved, giving out their life in the torture of thirst under the scorching sun; others were still and lifeless, fat black African flies gorging on their congealing blood. Scattered groups of men roamed over the battlefield – whether in plunder or mercy was not clear.

It turned Kydd's stomach: at sea there was none of the dust, stink or flies; no casual acceptance of heroism and lonely suffering. It was another, cleaner existence where men fought and died but with their shipmates. They were not left to choke out their lives under a cruel sun without a soul to know of it.

They picked their way over the desolation, the general's face now a mask. A dispatch rider cantered up with a message, which he read with evident satisfaction. 'They're on the run, gentlemen. I have it here – they're attempting to regroup at Riet Vlei.' He thought for a moment and grunted, 'I'm told there's a farm ahead. We'll set up there until things become clearer.'

It turned out to be one of the pretty whitewashed farmhouses, a little larger than the others and with the infinite blessing of a small pond and spring. Dozens of soldiers drank there thirstily while hundreds more weary infantrymen just sat on the ground, hunched and dazed.

Inside, Baird welcomed his commanders. Dust-streaked, their breeches torn by thorny scrub and hard fighting, their features were lined and marked by their experience. 'We'll press on, shall we, sir?' a grizzled colonel muttered. 'My lads need a spell only, then they'll—'

'They'll be sore tired. Issue 'em with rum and biscuit after they've had their fill of water and we'll wait to see what the Navy can do to stir up Janssens's camp with their cannon. He's yet to receive his reinforcements from inland and I've a suspicion we'll have a tight run of it when he does.'

Kydd knew Bowden would have shifted the signal post down the beach to keep with the tide of battle and would let him know anything of significance. In fact the bombardment would be well under way by now, just as the first of the fleeing army were streaming in. He fancied he could hear the faraway mutter and grumble of the guns of his ship on the still, fetid air.

There was desultory conversation. This farmhouse did not have the cool tiled floor of the other and it was hot and close. Kydd felt an urge to get outside, but not far away, near the waterhole, a field surgeon's tent had been erected and carts of wounded were arriving, their cries piercing the air. He stayed where he was.

Time dragged. Then a thud of hoofs and a breathless dispatch rider appeared at the doorway. Baird looked up in sudden interest.

'General, sir!' the officer acknowledged, extracting a message, which he carried over to Kydd.

It was in Bowden's young, bold hand. Hurried but precise, it detailed a landing – an unauthorised but successful assault by the Royal Marines under cover of *L'Aurore*'s bombardment not far from Riet Vlei. Popham must have stripped every ship in the fleet to find enough marines to send in but the bold initiative was a brilliant stroke.

It seemed they had brought a small gun with them, which they had set up atop the dunes and were firing directly into the encampment. A hurried defence had been improvised but had been beaten back by the marines. At the time of writing, his camp denied him, Janssens was attempting a rally further inland.

Baird met the news with barely concealed delight. 'He'll have to act boldly if he's to preserve his army,' he said gruffly, 'but Janssens is a wily old bird. Let's just see what happens.'

Barely an hour later another rider brought a message from scouts out to the south-east. There was no doubting it: the whole Dutch army was on the move. But not to strike back at the weary British – puzzlingly, they were marching at right angles away to the dry, wild country leading to the interior.

'That will do,' Baird said crisply. 'We advance and occupy Riet Vlei. Gentlemen, we'll sleep in beds tonight. I'm to set up headquarters where the Dutch commander did, I believe.'

The farm buildings at Riet Vlei were extensive and comfortable. In the glory of a setting sun, camp was established and foraging parties fanned out. As the evening drew in, a most extraordinary odour began to hang on the air. It was a space before Kydd could identify it: roast lamb! For the first time in many weeks they were to be granted fresh meat.

Later, replete, and grateful for the absent farmer's taste in wines, the officers pondered the enemy's next moves.

'Then he's running, sir?'

'No, Colonel,' Baird said thoughtfully. 'But I fear we'll hear more of Mr Janssens. No – he's heading for the Tygerbergs no more than five miles or so off, a thousand feet high and steep. My wager is that he's to throw up a redoubt there while he gathers strength.'

'Ah – there we have our dilemma, do we not, sir?' another interjected. 'Should we move on Cape Town, he lies in our rear and we cannot face both ways.'

'So I must go after him? There'll be no easy storming of the Tygerbergs. And I conceive it would be a fine trap for us, should he be luring us to the reserves he's concealing there.'

'Then to invest and storm the castle?'

'Without I have a siege train? Rather the opposite – recall that the majority of Dutch troops must be in the Castle of Good Hope and may sally against us at any time to reverse their fortunes.'

'The Navy to lay ruin to it?'

Kydd came back immediately. 'No! The fortifications are too strong and we'd be under fire from heavy guns the whole time. And to lie off in this westerly . . .'

After an awkward silence around the table Baird slowly and deliberately emptied his glass. 'Then, gentlemen, I'm presented with a quandary. Quite apart from the French arriving at any time to relieve, where are the provisions and water that will supply my soldiers for a lengthy siege? The nearest friendly territory is to be reckoned in thousands of miles away, I'll remind you.'

'Er, may we know what you plan now, sir?' one ventured.

At first Baird didn't answer. Then his face closed and he said abruptly, 'I see no alternative but to go against the castle – and we cannot delay.'

Chapter 4

Kydd took in the now-familiar bustle as the hoarse commands of an army on the move filled the morning air. The troops were forming up in disciplined columns to march the final five miles to the gates of the castle. It was a sombre advance: no piping, no good-natured chaffing, just subdued singing in the ranks. Ahead lay a formidable and bloody task: to reduce a powerful fortification and storm it with nothing but bayonets and heroism.

Kydd rode behind Baird at some way back. There was still awkwardness between them after he had stood firm on the impossibility of a seaward bombardment close in. Situated in the crook of Table Bay, the castle had many guns and there were batteries up and down the shoreline; it was only too apparent to Kydd how these could completely dominate the stretch of water opposite.

There was no doubting the general's imperative to do something about the odds facing his men but what could he offer? And if it came to rescuing a desperate situation Popham would never allow the larger ships in such shallow, crowded conditions. In any event, given the possibility of a sudden appearance by a French battle squadron, his first duty was to remain ready to stand to seaward.

The tramping column passed Riet Vlei lagoon, a reedy mere with clouds of birds rising to dispute their presence. The coastal road was deserted, not a sign of life on either hand, but Baird had a rearguard posted that could give warning of the sudden issuing of Janssens from his mountain retreat, and others far out on the wing to keep watch for the Dutch reinforcements.

The bay curved around, and as they neared their objective, Kydd felt Table Mountain's huge presence, frowning on their impertinence, the spacious white streets and houses of Cape Town seeming too fair and charming at this distance to contemplate inflicting military horrors upon them. What terror must be going through the minds of the inhabitants at their approach? They would be aware also that, at any moment, the long-expected Dutch reinforcements might appear over the crest of the foothills and they would be caught between two armies.

The castle came into view: low and compact, it was nevertheless large, star-shaped and with extensive outworks. Floating proudly above all was a huge Batavian standard. And well before they closed with it, they heard, from a lesser fortress at the forward corner of the outer wall, the heavy *crump* of a single round of artillery. They were being warned.

'Halt!' The order echoed down the column. Kydd moved up as Baird took out his telescope and carefully inspected the terrain – the castle, its surrounding cover, the foothills at the base of the massive Table Mountain. At length he lowered it, his face set.

'There's no getting past it. It will have to be invested.' There was a murmur of dismay at the talk of beleaguering the town. 'And there's so little damned time,' he added bitterly.

Kydd looked at him in some sympathy. This was the man who had commanded at the dreadful slaughter that had closed the siege of Seringapatam, and those dark memories must be haunting him now.

Baird snapped the glass shut and turned to his staff. 'We fall back out of range and set up camp behind that ridge,' he said, indicating the low rise they had passed. He glanced at Kydd and gave a tired smile. 'The good captain here has pointed out the difficulties attendant on a sea bombardment. Perhaps he'd be kind enough to advise on the landing of navy cannon as must be in the character of our siege train.'

Kydd nodded uncomfortably. 'I shall try, sir.' With an entire army waiting, regiments consuming rations and the Dutch, no doubt, calling in their outlying forces to counter-attack triumphantly, Baird urgently needed answers, not objections. But to land massive naval guns as he wanted would be near impossible. The heaviest, the thirty-two-pounders of *Diadem*, were monsters, three tons of cold iron. They would have to be slung beneath two launches in order to be moved, and such a contraption coming through the booming surf would result in an uncontrollable, bone-crushing rampage.

And there was the question of the gun carriage. Aboard ship these were precision devices to level the gun, absorb recoil and, in general, lay and control the gun. They were fitted with trucks, small wheels expecting a hard deck, which would be utterly useless ashore. The standard army cannon in the field was a six-pounder so there was no question of trying to fit a thirty-two-pounder to its tiny carriage.

Then Kydd tried to bring to mind what they had achieved at the defence of Acre – but conditions had been different there: a sheltered harbour, a stone wharf, and they had been the defenders, not the attackers. The effect, though, had been dramatic. At three times the size of army cannon, even the smaller naval weapons were not to be scorned. And perhaps four – six of them? Yes, this might work. 'Sir, in this surf I fear we cannot expect to bring in the biggest guns. Should we fashion a kind of raft it might be possible to get eighteen-pounders to you, the carriage in the nature of a slide as we do employ for our carronades.'

'Very well,' Baird said heavily. 'Make it thus, if you please.'

'Then I'll return to my ship if I may, sir, and—'

'I'd rather you stayed, Mr Kydd,' he said, adding quietly, 'I value your counsel. Is there not a lieutenant you might send?'

'Yes, sir, if you wish it.' He would do his duty but he had little stomach for land wars and the horrific scenes of a sacked city – he yearned for the clean salt tang of the sea and blessed naval routine.

The camp sprang up in remarkable time, rows of tents at exact spacing covering acres of ground, a flagpole at the centre at the commander-in-chief's headquarters and sentries posted on all sides.

A flurry of activity resolved to a dispatch rider arriving. 'Sir, from Lord Beresford.' The general had been posted to keep watch on Janssens's Hollanders, left in the mountains after the Blaauwberg battle.

Baird read the message with a frown and stuffed it into his waistcoat. He glanced around his officers. 'We're in it for the long haul, it seems. Janssens has crossed over the Tygerbergs and, circling around Stellenbosch, has taken residence in the Hottentot-Hollands range only some twenty or thirty miles away. Not only that but the castle has dispatched a substantial wagon train of cannon and supplies to him there.

'Gentlemen – we have decisions to make.'

The worst fear of a commander-in-chief at siege – that a powerful army threatened his rear – was a reality. Janssens had a secure mountain stronghold, which would serve as a point of concentration for the reinforcements now converging. When the time was right he would descend to crush the invaders.

The headquarters tent was unfurnished. It served to keep the fierce afternoon sun at bay, but every officer had to remain standing. Baird drank thirstily from a soldier's canteen, wiped his mouth and turned to address them.

'My fellow officers. I will not hide it from you. We are—'

'Sah – Gen'ral Baird, sah!' It was the regimental sergeant major of the 71st at the door-flap. 'L'tenant Grant's compliments an' he begs you'd come, um, now,' he finished woodenly, with an odd expression.

'Very well, Sar' Major,' Baird said, and followed him, his officers hurrying along too: nothing short of a grave threat would have impelled the young lieutenant to intrude.

Standing at the edge of the camp, Grant pointed across the flat ground before the castle to a cavalry officer on a white horse picking his way carefully towards them. He bore a large white flag. When the halfway point was reached he stopped and waited.

'Good God!' blurted one officer. 'The gall of 'em, calling for our surrender before the first shot!'

'It's a trick,' growled another.

'No, it's not,' said Baird, sternly. 'The Dutch are an odd

84

lot but they know the meaning of honour. L'tenant – do see what it is they want.'

The young man went for a horse, swung up and crossed to the waiting officer. Hats were doffed, words were briefly exchanged and a letter was handed over. With a civil bow, they wheeled their horses around and returned whence they'd come.

Grant handed the letter to Baird. 'Sir, I'm desired to give you this from the commandant of the castle.'

He took it and gravely broke the seal. As he read it his face worked with emotion. He scanned the words again, then lowered the paper and looked about him, overcome.

'Read it aloud,' he choked, handing it to his aide.

'To the officer commanding His Britannic Majesty's Army.

Sir, To prevent the consequences which must ensue from the Town and Castle being defended, I hereby propose to you a Cessation of Arms for forty-eight hours to enter negotiations.

I have &c.

Signed,

Lieutenant Colonel Hieronimus Casimirus Baron von Prophalow

Commanding the Town and Castle.'

In an instant the situation had changed beyond belief. The Dutch were asking to treat for conditions leading to a surrender. What had compelled them to do this, when so much was in their favour, was a mystery.

'If they wish to capitulate, they may do so!' rapped Baird. 'General Ferguson, do attend on me at once. *Where's my bloody writing desk?*'

Within an hour Ferguson was on his horse, wending his way to the castle under a white flag. He disappeared inside. Shortly afterwards, as the sun was prettily descending into the sea on the right, he emerged and rode back.

He dismounted and approached Baird, his face like stone, then saluted stiffly and reached into his waistcoat. 'Sir – I have it!' he growled and waved a folded and sealed document, only then allowing a triumphant smile.

It was no less than the Preliminary Articles of Capitulation, duly signed, which provided for the immediate cessation of hostilities, the surrender of the Castle of Good Hope and the settlement of Cape Town to His Britannic Majesty.

'Damn it, would you smoke it? It's ours now. The Cape is ours, b' glory!'

Baird had given his orders: in the formal matter of marching in to take possession of the Castle of Good Hope, the massed pipers and drummers of all three Highland regiments would figure, but he had insisted that the Sea Battalion, whose dauntless courage and tenacity had shone on the battlefield, would lead the parade.

Hauling a pair of guns for the last time, their task would be one of peace and triumph: the gun salutes that would proclaim to the world that the castle had now changed hands. Kydd had requested the honour to march with the men, so when the grand parade stepped out with a crash of drums and skirl of pipes, he and Bowden swung along with the seamen.

His heart swelled with pride as they marched around the bastions and casemates of the fortification to a vast parade-ground on the far side. A richly ornamented sergeant major then strode forward to take charge of proceedings; the Sea

Battalion and their guns were directed to be drawn up with gun muzzle pointing seaward while regiments of the line marched and counter-marched in a fine show until they were positioned in two blocks, an open lane between them leading to the gates of the castle.

It was not a castle an Englishman would easily recognise: low, and soft mustard yellow, it had a certain Dutch quaintness about it, with a colonnaded bell tower high above the main entrance, the double gates dark and closed.

The pipes and drums stopped, the long ranks rigid and disciplined in the blazing sunshine.

Major General Baird, in full dress uniform, walked his white charger slowly up to the gates and dismounted. They slowly opened and out stepped a single figure in a restrained dark blue uniform. Kydd watched in fascination as the two men bowed extravagantly and spoke together for what seemed an age. Then, with another bow, the officer presented Baird with the keys to the Castle of Good Hope. Both men retired.

A military band started up inside, sounding unfamiliar and outlandish to Kydd's ears. The Dutch garrison came out, individuals all, but subtly alien: long dark moustaches, swarthy, a foreign cross-swing as they marched. Unlike the striking colour of the British redcoats – in the chaos of a battle a soldier had only to look round to know that he was not on his own and be heartened – here were muted greens, browns and blues, a dark tonality that to Kydd looked anything but rousing.

The Dutch soldiers' bearing was neither sullen nor mutinous but their faces carried a studied blankness. What were they thinking? That their land, homes and future had been given up by their commandant without a shot fired? That while they languished in captivity in the town where they had taken their ease, British soldiery would now flock to taste the fruits of victory?

The marching ranks headed down the open lane, an endless tramping line of defeated men. At the point where they emerged they were directed to one side, their arms deftly collected and their officers given orders to march them to their barracks.

Eventually the long column ceased. The last of the Dutch had left, and Baird strode forward into the castle followed by his commanders, which included Kydd as the senior naval officer present. They stood for a space, relishing the moment.

The forbidding stronghold was unpretentious, but neat and attractive, the yellow and white finish on the stonework suited to its African setting.

The Batavian standard was still close up at the flagpole. At its base a last Dutch soldier stood to his post, a trumpeter at his side. He saluted Baird stiffly, and while the trumpeter played a thin-sounding call, the colours were struck. He saluted once more, then marched off.

A sergeant major stepped forward, clipped the Union Flag of Great Britain to the halyards and paused. Kydd nodded. At the gate Bowden signalled, and the first of the minute guns thudded out. It was answered joyously by every ship at anchor as the flag was slowly and ceremoniously raised for all to see. The castle and town were theirs.

Baird put down his sword and scabbard with a clatter on the beautifully polished dark table and sank into one of the chairs, staring into space. Around him, a babble ebbed and flowed as officers commented on the tasteful mix of yellow-wood beams and skilful embellishments in the long room.

88

'A damn fine day's work!' snorted Colonel Pack, and was heartily echoed by others.

Brigadier General Ferguson, standing in admiration by a dark-stained painting, guffawed. 'See here, Jeffrey – they've taken after Vermeer!'

'Kydd, old bean, clap your peepers on this – here's a rattlin' fine parcel o' ships for you!' said another, peering at another oil.

'They say for wines the Cape can't be beat!' said one, with a fruity chuckle.

'A right agreeable place t' be in winter, I'm told, what with—'

'*Be silent!*' roared Baird, galvanised out of his chair.

The room fell into a hush. 'Sit, if you please,' he growled, remaining standing. He went to the small, mullioned windows, looked out moodily, then swung round on them. 'For reasons that escape me, in taking this castle we've had an easy time of it. It makes me uneasy – it makes me suspicious! In the next few hours we're to move on Cape Town to take peaceful possession. What will we find? That we're outnumbered by a hostile population intent on selling out to the French? A Hollander army coming over the hill? A trap, well sprung?'

No one stirred. 'And do I have to remind you that we've only this castle and the one town? The governor of Cape Colony has by no means surrendered to us and is still at large – and at the head of a powerful army, which, no doubt, is increasing in size daily. Unless he decides tamely to lay down his arms and capitulate, the rest of the colony is duty bound to rise against us. An area half the size of Europe!'

He sat down, suddenly looking very tired. 'Gentlemen. We have a task worthy of Hercules himself ahead of us, for while we've secured a military victory, if we're to cling to our toehold on this continent then we must turn a defeated people to accepting our rule, preferring such to any other.

'Dutch ruled by English – the fruits of this colony instead to flow to London, an alien flag, customs, language. Will they accept it? Do we force them to bend to our laws, pay taxes in the name of King George, speak English to each other? And what of the common currency? Is now the guinea to supplant the Netherlands dollar? Do debts to the Batavian Republic now accrue to the English Crown?'

In the details it was almost beyond comprehension: an entire government and civil service to be brought into being, administration with the devising of rules and ordinances suited to the regulation of a people in the exotic territory of Africa.

'Yes, gentlemen. Tomorrow we step out and show ourselves to the worthy inhabitants of Cape Town. I will have no indiscipline, still less plundering. This is the newest jewel of empire in the Crown of Great Britain!'

There was a cautious murmur of appreciation, but Baird did not respond, letting it die. He continued in a quite different, muted tone: 'Gentlemen, we are so few. And at so many thousand miles from England, I pray you will not forget, for I never will do so, we are entirely – and completely – on our own.'

A bitter south-westerly flurried and bullied the immense crowds that pressed up to the bank of the River Thames. They had been there since before the pallid dawn. High-born and low, none was about to miss the greatest occasion that London had ever seen, one that could be talked about for a lifetime – one that they themselves had witnessed.

Frederick Stanhope, Marquess of Bloomsbury, and his wife

were spared the crush, guests of the Lord Chancellor at the Inner Temple Gardens of the Inns of Court, and with a splendid view of the river. They, too, had braved the raw weather, determined not to miss the extraordinary spectacle.

For the lady companion to the marchioness, snuggling into her fur-lined pelisse, the day was one of special meaning, touching on the two men closest to her. England was preparing her greatest honours for the hero saviour Lord Horatio Nelson, their late commander-in-chief, whose body at that moment was approaching in the mourning barge of King Charles II, at the head of a river procession that stretched for miles.

From Greenwich, where it had lain in state for three days, the body was to be transported to Whitehall Stairs, to lie overnight in the Captain's Room of the Admiralty before the pageant of a state funeral at St Paul's Cathedral the next day.

'You're not too chilled, Cecilia?' the marchioness asked, glancing askance at her cold-numbed face.

'Not as would stand next to what our brave sailors endure out at sea, m' lady,' she replied, with spirit. Who knew where her brother and the man she loved were at that very moment?

Having just missed them at Portsmouth when they had sailed with Nelson, she had sent a heartfelt letter telling Renzi of her deep feelings for him, promising she would wait for ever. Even though he had confessed he loved her, he had absolved her of any implicit obligation, believing it unprincipled even to imply matrimony while he was impecunious. Her letter might or might not have found him, and then the news of the great battle had reached England and, like so many others, she had waited with fear in her heart as detailed casualty lists had been made known.

When the body of Nelson had arrived in his battered

flagship she had discovered too late that Kydd and Renzi's ship *L'Aurore* had been the one with the honour of bringing it upriver to Greenwich and then was immediately dispatched to sea again.

It was odd that the particular fleet they were attached to was not specified – word was that they were to join some mysterious expedition but, cloaked in secrecy, details had been impossible to come by. She had, however, the infinite boon of knowing they were safe and well – a hurried letter from Kydd at Greenwich before they left had asked her to let their parents know this.

No reply had come from Nicholas . . . but then, almost certainly, he had not received her letter and when he did . . .

But nothing could be certain as far as he was concerned. How would he take her outpouring of passion, her indelicate revealing of ardour and need? As a man of scrupulous sensitivities, how must he regard—

'Oh, do look, Frederick!' exclaimed the marchioness, gripping her husband's arm. 'I do believe they're coming!' From between the piers of Blackfriars Bridge the first of the ceremonial barges was emerging.

The river was alive with craft, some keeping pace, others moored at the embankment, figures clinging to the masts and rigging, naval boats on flank escort. But all eyes were on the four mourning barges in the lead: draped in black with a dash of vivid colour, one after another they issued out in solemn procession, the regular muffled thud of three-minute guns from the Tower of London a fitting dirge.

The marquess consulted a paper. 'Ah, the first does carry at its head Lord Nelson's personal standard, his guidon and banners each to be borne by a Trafalgar captain.' It drew nearer, its sweeps drawn by liveried oarsmen in a rhythmic rise and fall. Under the canopy aft stood a number of richly caparisoned individuals. 'And aboard from the College of Arms are Rouge Croix and Blue Mantle senior heralds, with their pursuivants.'

Closely following, the next held Nelson's gauntlet and spurs, helm and crest, four heralds bearing his banner as Knight of the Order of the Bath, another Trafalgar captain with surcoat, target and sword.

And the third – noble, dignified, with no standards, banners or pennons aloft except one: the Union Flag of Great Britain at half-mast.

With a thrill of unreality, Cecilia realised that the mortal remains of Lord Horatio Nelson himself lay under the black-plumed canopy, the four shields of his armorial bearings bright against the black velvet enshrouding all. Three bannerolls of the Nelson lineage were borne by officers of *Victory* known to him – Signal Lieutenant Pasco, Mr Atkinson the sailing master, and others who had done their duty at Nelson's side on that fateful day. Norroy King of Arms himself bore the viscount's coronet on a sable cushion.

Following in the fourth barge was the chief mourner – known in the processional as Admiral of the Fleet Sir Peter Parker, senior officer of the Royal Navy, but within the service as the captain of *Bristol* who, in 1778, had taken into his ship a raw Lieutenant Nelson. Now in his eighties, he shared cere-monials with sixteen admirals and two captains – Hardy of *Victory* and Blackwood of *Euryalus*.

Beyond the sombre blackness of the mourning craft came the splendour of His Majesty's barge, with dignitaries repre-senting the Crown of Great Britain, followed by the Admiralty barge immediately astern, with all the pomp of the Lords

Commissioners for executing the office of Lord High Admiral.

Then it was the flamboyantly ornate trappings of the City State Barge, with the Lord Mayor of London and other officials, all in elaborate mourning dress.

Seven seamen from *Victory* were deployed in the next, two openly weeping: from time to time they held aloft the shot-torn colours worn by their ship to heartfelt huzzahs echoing out from the riverbank.

Then stretching away behind was the rest of the processional: the great livery companies of London in their ceremonials – the Merchant Taylors' Company, the Goldsmiths, the Apothecaries, the Drapers and more.

It was pageantry on a national scale. And nothing less could do justice to the stupefying feeling that the nation shared of the world shaking on its foundations at the passing of both a hero and an age.

Cecilia stood numbly as the procession passed, barely able to take in that this day she was to be the one honouring the great admiral while those who knew him and loved him were far away at sea. For them she would see it through as they would have done, and later tell them of this momentous day.

The head of the river cortège had rounded the bend on the way to Whitehall Stairs and the Admiralty, and still the immense waterborne cavalcade moved past. It was an extra-ordinary expression of popular and imperial grief, and could never be forgotten.

'Come, Frederick – we're to be early at St Paul's tomorrow, I'm told,' said the marchioness, in hushed tones, and led the way to the carriage.

The next day was as bitterly cold, with lowering grey skies, but mercifully less wind. The streets began filling before dawn, the crowds jostling for the best vantage-points. More still packed the line of procession, from the Admiralty to Charing Cross and then along the Strand and through the City, but it was not until noon that they were rewarded with the sight of the first of the great cortège: the scarlet of battalions of soldiers in drill order advancing with the slow thump of a bass drum draped in black. Then came the colour and grandeur of heralds, and the massed figures of the great in the land, princes of the Blood Royal, nobility and gentry. But none of these could command the intense respect and attention that the next carriage did.

The funeral car of Lord Nelson. Drawn by six black horses, it was made up to be a simulacrum of HMS *Victory* in black and gold, a figurehead with laurels at the stem and an ensign at half-mast above an elaborate stern. Under a sable-plumed canopy was the richly worked coffin – crafted from the main-mast of *L'Orient*, the flagship of the French admiral at the Nile and preserved for its ultimate purpose.

Around the pillars of the canopy were laurels and Nelson's motto – *Palmam Qui Meruit Ferat*: 'Let he who deserves it wear the palm.' Atop the whole was his viscount's coronet and within were heraldic devices and trophies from a life-time at sea.

A rustle, as of a long sigh, was the only sound as it passed: the simultaneous baring of heads. Many were visibly moved, silent, weeping, evidence of the depth of feeling at the loss of their paladin. At Temple Bar the procession was joined by the Lord Mayor with the City Sword, accompanied by the aldermen, sheriffs and other notables of London.

At the cathedral a strict discipline kept the crush of people from overwhelming the ushers. Only those with tickets personally issued from the College of Arms were admitted within. In respect to his diplomatic status, the Marquess of Bloomsbury's party was accorded the envied privilege of seats under the dome.

Cecilia was awestruck: the lofty sweep of the dome's catenary curves, with its noble paintings of St Paul, the richness of the pew's carving, the splendour of the arrayed nobility of England. From the galleries hung vast battle-stained ensigns of enemy ships captured at Trafalgar, so evocative of what had recently passed out at sea. And before them the empty place reserved for the body.

After hours of patient waiting, there was a flurry of movement at the grand western portico. It was the seamen, taking position for the arrival of the catafalque. Soldiers of two Highland regiments filed in on each side, gravely marching in slow time until they had lined the processional route inside the cathedral. They halted, turned about inwards and rested on their arms reversed.

And then it was time. The *Victory* seamen lifted the coffin from the funeral car with infinite care and, with pallbearers and supporters, began the journey to their admiral's final resting place. As it entered, the organ majestically filled the cathedral in homage until the coffin was reverently placed in the quire for the service of evensong.

The gathering shadows of the winter dusk added to the solemnity, and a special chandelier of 130 candles was lit and hung suspended within the dome, its light spreading grandeur for the final act of the burial service.

When the coffin with Lord Nelson's earthly remains had been carried to the centre of the dome under a funeral canopy of state, it was placed on a raised platform. His relatives and close friends gathered by it – and the seamen of *Victory*, who still carried the colours under which he had fought.

Age-burnished words rang out clear and certain in the echoing silence. "'Man that is born of a woman hath but a short time to live . . . and is cut down like a flower . . . Forasmuch as it hath pleased Almighty God of his great mercy to take unto himself the soul of our dear brother here departed . . .'"

A choir of a hundred men and boys, which included those of the Chapel Royal and Westminster Abbey, sang the concluding anthem, the pure, soaring resonance a paean of sad beauty.

And then the burial service was complete.

Stepping forward, the Garter King of Arms pealed forth words hallowed in orders of chivalry since the days of Henry V. "'That it hath pleased Almighty God to take unto his divine mercy the Most Noble Lord Horatio Nelson, Viscount and Baron Nelson of the Nile and of Burnham Thorpe in the County of Norfolk, Knight of the Most Honourable Order of the Bath, Vice Admiral of the White Squadron of the Fleet, Duke of Bronte in Sicily, Knight Grand Cross of the Sicilian Order of St Ferdinand and of Merit . . . let us humbly trust, that he is raised to bliss ineffable and to a glorious immortality.'"

While the ringing words sounded the length and breadth of the cathedral, the steward, comptroller and treasurer of Nelson's household solemnly snapped their staves of office and threw them on to the coffin, stepping back to allow the seamen with the colours to spread the flag as a pall in a last act – but, before the horrified gaze of the princes of heraldry, they did not. Instead they ripped and tore at the flag until each bore away something to retain of the commander they had adored. A rippling murmur of understanding arose from the pews.

The organ, played by a pupil of Mozart, again filled the air with a grand and melancholy piece and the coffin sank from sight to its rest.

It was over.

'The price of victory was too high, I'm to believe,' Stanhope said, his tone subdued as though still under thrall to what they had seen.

Baron Grenville raised his glass in solemn salute. 'It must be admitted, dear chap. Lost to his country at the very moment of his triumph. I do hope the people won't forget him now he's gone, poor fellow.'

In the opulent drawing room a large fire was the only cheerful presence among the murmuring, black-decked throng gathered there after the burial. 'I saw that your cousin did not attend,' Stanhope reflected. 'I know the man would have been there if it had been possible, so must only conclude that the waters in Bath have not effected a relief.'

That cousin was William Pitt, prime minister of Great Britain and known to be gravely ill. Grenville sighed. 'It grieves me to say it, but I'm sanguine he's not to be long for this world either – days at most. He's much cast down since hearing of the cost of Trafalgar – and so soon following, that damnable rout at Austerlitz.'

'If there is a tragic outcome, in these dolorous times the King will wish to form a government with all expedition. And if Hawkesbury declines – as I believe he will – then His Majesty will peradventure call upon your own good self, dear fellow.'

'I must allow it, Frederick.'

'Have you . . . ?'

Grenville gave a lopsided smile. 'An impossibility to conjure a world without a Pitt, as all must declare. I have a mind to gather in a ministry of all the talents, as it were. I shall bring back Windham as secretary of war, young Charles Grey comes to mind for the Admiralty, and Fox – well, he'll be cock o' hoop to be made foreign secretary. Oh, and that freelance intemperate Richard Brinsley Sheridan, why, I'll make sure his energies are absorbed as treasurer of the Navy – plenty of accounts to pore over, what?'

Stanhope paused at the jocular tone. 'You're not, who might say, overcome at the prospect? I rather fancy your greatest challenge will not be in domestic politics, my friend.'

'Ah, yes. Of course, the war.'

Frowning, Stanhope continued, 'The Tsar and Austrians beaten squarely in the field – it means the utter ruin of the Coalition – and with the Russians withdrawing over the border and Emperor Francis treating for a peace we're left where we started, without a single friend. I can only see as our crowning challenge the prosecuting of this war when all the chancelleries of Europe are against us.'

Grenville sobered. 'Old horse, don't take on so. You're forgetting that things have changed now. Nelson may be gone but he did his duty – the French are driven from the seas. Your Napoleon can rage up and down all he likes, but with our blockade he's securely locked up in Europe and we hold the key.'

He smiled expansively. 'And while Bonaparte's thus impotent we've got that sea as a royal road to every French colony and possession. Don't you see, Frederick? While we pluck his pieces one by one, the way lies open for us to create an empire such as the world has never seen.'

'While we rule the seas.'

'Quite. And, mark you, the process is already under way.'

'The Cape?'

'Indeed.'

'*If* they prevail in an opposed landing, and *if* they can sustain themselves in such a barbarous country, and *if*...'

Chapter 5

The sun beat down on the soldiers forming up on the castle parade-ground. Baird had been insistent that, for the march of occupation into Cape Town, full regimentals would be worn and every opportunity taken for display. 'Find a pair of carriages,' he growled at his aide. 'I shall ride in the first, my commanders in the second.'

The Dutch governor's open carriage was brought out, still emblazoned with the arms of the Batavian Republic on its side. Another arrived and the parade formed up, led by the full panoply of a massed pipe band of the Scottish Highland regiments and followed by one thousand soldiers.

Kydd boarded the second carriage with the senior military, and they set off to the heady squeal and drone of the pipes, the skitter and thump of drums ahead, and the regular measured tread of the soldiers behind. It felt so unreal for him, Thomas Kydd of Guildford, to be in Africa, in such circumstances of pomp and occasion, to be admired – or hated – by the crowds as though he were a potentate.

With Baird in regal solitude, the parade moved away, finding its rhythm as it crossed the vast parade-ground. Then the drum major signalled a left turn into a broad avenue leading to Cape Town proper.

Kydd sat alert: would the conquering army be greeted with violence or resignation? As they passed characterful white-painted residences and imposing stone buildings on the long, straight roads, people began to gather: not sullen masses or threatening crowds but curious African labourers, a *huisvrouw* with a shopping basket, couples in a style of dress not at all out of place for the England of twenty years ago, multitudes clearly just about their daily business.

They marched on. More arrived, standing on street corners, spellbound at the show. Here and there Kydd saw a Dutchman on his stoop in an easy-chair enjoying a long pipe and pointedly ignoring the invaders.

An immensely long span of oxen crossed ahead, causing the drum major to step short, but nowhere was there any sign of disorder or insurrection: in its normality there was almost a sense of anticlimax.

With the whirling of an ornate baton and flourish of drum-sticks, the parade came to a halt in a square outside an imposing double-storeyed white building. Kydd supposed the dozen or more men standing there apprehensively were town worthies.

Baird descended from his carriage and approached them; words and extravagant bows were exchanged. As he returned to his carriage a detachment of redcoats marched forward purposefully and took an on-guard position at either side of the entrance.

The bands struck up and the parade moved on towards a long, spacious garden and stopped abreast a palatial mansion. Baird descended again. With numbers of interested onlookers gathering on the road to witness events, a party of servants headed by a nervous major-domo presented themselves. Baird nodded in acknowledgement, then turned and indicated that those in the second carriage should join him. 'Government House,' he grunted. 'I rather think I should show appreciation.'

Flanked by his commanders, the new governor of Cape Town went to claim his residence. The cool of its rooms was very welcome and the glasses of chilled champagne even more so. Baird relaxed a little. 'Well, gentlemen. It does seem we shall not be assailed by vengeful Dutchmen, which is a mercy. General Ferguson, I desire you shall give orders as will see your troops march off and be posted at the lesser places within the town until further orders.'

He drained his glass and beamed. 'So, here we are. I am now the colonial governor. What shall be first?'

'Sir, the defences against a landing by the French would—'

'I rather think not. No, sir, I mean to rule well and wisely, and for this I will need an administration of talent and probity that'll assist me in making decisions of such moment as you now raise. Yet even before that there are matters of confidence and discretion that I can only entrust to one on whom I must rely completely. In short, I'm in pressing need of a colonial secretary.'

'Why, surely your aide would serve, would he not, sir?'

'No military, sir. Recollect, these are folk who are joining the British Empire and may not be considered a species of conquered people. The complexion of our governance should be of a civil cast – as it is in England, the military subordinate to the body politic under the Crown.'

'Where, then, will you find such a one? Here surely all men are in a military way of things?'

'I'm in no doubt that, at hearing of the accession of this territory following our small feat of arms, Whitehall will quickly dispatch a parcel of government officials fit for colonial rule. It's the weeks and months before then that I'm more concerned with, first impressions being so much of the essence.'

'If I might make a suggestion . . .' Kydd found himself saying.

'Captain?'

'I know one of particular suitability. He's learned, worldly and desires no more than to study the ethnicals of his fellow creatures. And for this man I would pledge my honour that you may entirely trust him with your confidences.'

'Really? Who is this fellow?'

'Sir, my own confidential secretary, Nicholas Renzi.'

'Ah. He knows discretion?'

'His assistance to the Duc de Bouillon in a delicate matter has been much remarked by Mr Pitt himself.'

'Extraordinary. Is he, who should say, ambitious? The post is only of a temporary nature and I should not want him to get airs above his station, sir.'

'Renzi? Not at all, sir. I rather think he sets the world at a distance unless it suits him.'

'Very well. Your own services now being concluded, you will wish to return to your ship. Do ask your Mr Renzi to wait upon me at his earliest convenience, would you?'

Kydd doffed his hat politely to *L'Aurore*'s quarterdeck and then her recent acting captain. 'How goes she, Mr Gilbey?' he asked, noting the smartness of the side-party and the spotless appearance of his vessel.

'As an Irish thoroughbred, sir,' he replied, with a trace of smugness.

'*L'Aurore* made fine practice at her gunnery,' Kydd acknowledged, loud enough to be heard by others. 'As General Baird himself did allow.'

'It went well for us, did it, sir?' Gilbey asked, obviously consumed by curiosity as to what had gone on ashore.

'His Majesty's arms did prevail,' Kydd said, and, feeling his words a little pompous, added, 'You may say that Cape Town is now ours.'

Kydd was aware of the intent stillness of inquisitiveness around him, but all he wanted at that moment was the peace and familiarity of his cabin.

'Um, sir – the gunroom would like t' invite you to dinner b' way of a welcome back,' Gilbey ventured.

Kydd smothered a grin: the man's motives were transparent. 'Why, I'd be honoured, Mr Gilbey.' The watch on deck would just have to wait until evening, which would see not only the officers in the know, but the stewards and others, who would be sure to relay what they'd heard to their shipmates.

Below, in his cabin, Renzi was waiting to welcome him. 'Nicholas, old chap – so good to see you.'

'My dear fellow – and in the like wise.'

Kydd tossed his hat aside and sprawled in his easy chair, twisting around to take in the view of the glittering sea and distant beaches. While Renzi brought up his own chair, Tysoe entered with a cool cordial.

'Should you wish a rest before you tell me of your experiences . . .'

Kydd smiled. Renzi was only a little more subtle than Gilbey. He closed his eyes for a moment, the broad Atlantic swell inducing a pleasing regularity in the heave of the deck, the comfortable shipboard smells and occasional sea sounds balm to the soul.

'Ah, yes. A near-run thing...'

He sketched out the events quickly, grateful that he'd been spared the horrors of a protracted siege and now quite certain that he could never make a soldier.

'. . . and if you ask why did we triumph so easily, they bringing out the white flag so precipitate, I have no idea. Our good general is troubled, suspecting some kind o' treachery, and is taking all precautions.'

'Er, Africa. What's it, um, like at all?' Renzi said, as soon as he decently could. 'How vexing it's been for me, seeing this fabled continent and never yet setting foot in it.'

'Yes, well, it's devilish hot, there's a mort of dust abroad, no jungle did I see nor less your hippo and lion. I suppose they'd be frightened off by our moil and numbers. But I can tell you, it's a big country – no, immense.'

Renzi's eyes shone but he asked casually, 'So, I imagine we're to step ashore shortly?'

'I fancy not. We have the castle and the town, but there's quantities of fortresses and armies at large in the country, which will occupy us for long before we may claim rest. I'll wager our orders are this minute on their way to us, and what loobies we'd look if we have half our ship's company on liberty, kicking up a bobs-a-dying!'

'Of course. But I could be of assistance to you, perhaps, by dashing ashore and setting up arrangements with a vict-ualler, seeing what passes here for marine stores, charts—'

'No. Your services are too valuable for that trumpery.'

Renzi's face fell.

'Of course. And, in any case, going ashore'll hold no interest – did you not say you'd put aside your ethnicals since the publisher frowned on 'em?'

'That's as may be,' Renzi said, nettled. 'I've not yet decided on my course. It would be a mortal waste to abandon the study, for I'm persuaded it does have its merits. And if this is so, it would be a cardinal sin to ignore an opportunity such as this to augment data. Why, here the economic response attendant on this insinuation of the Dutch culture into the land of the Hottentots would surely suggest—'

'Just so, Nicholas, just so. Yet we're to sail at a moment's notice and I don't see how – unless . . .'

'Yes? Go on!'

'But then it might not be to your taste, you being a scholar as is not concerned with trifles.'

'What are you saying?' Renzi said impatiently.

'General Baird – who we must now account to be governor – has pressing need of a secretary. Not your usual pen-pushing kind but a learned cove who knows how to navigate a hard-going paper, easy with word-grinding as will be needed in conjuring colonial laws and a gentleman who can steer small about politicals. Who can—'

'A colonial secretary? This is a post of significance, of standing in government. You can be sure Whitehall will dispatch such a one at the earliest.'

'And what o' the weeks and months before? I confide to you, Nicholas, he's a mountain of work to fit out an admin-istration, which he'll be sore pressed to do without he finds a right hand. I would have thought it most agreeable for you, old trout, this forging of a new piece of empire when all about are different folk – white, black, Dutch and so forth . . .'

'He'll never take me. I'm but a poor—'

'Nicholas, he asked for you by name. Said he'd be obliged should you wait upon him at your convenience . . .'

* * *

L'Aurore weighed anchor within a day, her orders brief and urgent. She was to sail south about the Cape of Good Hope as far as Mossel Bay, touching at forts and settlements along the way to inform them politely of recent events and invite their early co-operation.

And in the expected event of a successful conclusion, Kydd was to extend his voyage around the south of the continent then up to the Portuguese settlement of Lourenço Marques. There he was to let their old allies know that Cape Town was taken – but only as a pretext for assessing its suitability as a small naval base for operations against French predators operating against the India trade.

The first business, however, was his report of the ship-of-the-line lying at Simon's Town. Was it nothing but a floating battery or could it still put to sea? Either way, it was a menace and had to be neutralised.

With a playful wind from the south-east, the frigate had put to sea without a confidential secretary for her captain. Kydd had wished his friend well of the position; he would miss his company but it was only a temporary loss of his services and he knew he would be a boon to Baird.

It took several boards to double the Cape and make False Bay, but after they had rounded an outlying shoal there, the old battleship was in the same mooring off the victualling and small repair establishment. Kydd could see no sign of sail bent on, no singling up to one cable – but a huge Batavian flag flew at the main and figures were moving purposefully about her deck.

L'Aurore shortened sail; they were deep into the bay with an onshore wind. If things did not turn out well there was no easy retreat.

She rounded to well out of range and let go a bower

anchor. They were immediately met with the sight of a large fin lazily cutting through the water towards them: a great shark, thirty feet or more of deadly menace, just below the surface.

Shouts of loathing came from seamen along the deck as the monster disappeared under their keel. The sight struck a chill of horror in Kydd: some years before, in the Caribbean, sharks had attacked his sinking boat.

He fought down the memory and took in the Hollander. Would a ship-of-the-line haul down his flag to a light frigate? He would either strike his colours or make a fight of it; there was no other possibility.

'Call away my barge, Mr Gilbey.' As it was put in the water he went below to change into full dress uniform.

The boat, with a white flag prominent, pulled strongly towards the distant ship, but Kydd was conscious that it would be easy to antagonise the proud Dutch, an unwitting remark or perceived slight leading to resentment, gunfire and bloodshed. These were the descendants of the Dutchmen who had laid waste to the Medway in the century before.

As Kydd drew nearer, the ship's old-fashioned build became clear but it was also evident that this was more like an 80-gun vessel, just as large as Villeneuve's flagship at Trafalgar. Along the deck-line men were watching their approach. Surely they would not be there if their intention was to repel visitors.

He was hot. The glare of the sun glittered up from the sea, and beat down from the sky, making him itch and sweat.

As they neared the side-steps of the grand old ship, Kydd noted the wonderfully carved work at the rails, the side-galleries and sternwork. It was a standard of ornamentation that would never be seen again in this modern day of utility in a warship. A senior captain in tasselled finery on her quarterdeck bellowed, '*Ahoj de boot!*'

Standing to let his uniform be recognised, he hailed back. 'Captain Kydd, His Britannic Majesty's Frigate *L'Aurore*. We wish to come aboard!'

'*Niet* – keep clear or we fire into you!'

'I wish to discuss—'

'There's nothing to discuss. We're at war, Captain. I open fire in one minute!'

'I have news!' Kydd shouted back importantly.

There was a pause. 'One only to come aboard.'

Punctiliously the boat rounded the great stern where '*Bato*' was etched in an arch of gold letters on the lower transom. Poulden glided to a stop one inch from the side-steps and Kydd stepped across, noting on the dark hull below the surface long streamers of weed swirling in the current. This ship was sailing nowhere.

Kydd broke into the stillness of the upper deck and, removing his hat as he appeared, bowed to *Bato*'s haughty commander. 'Sir, I'm commanded by the governor of Cape Town to enquire your readiness to quit this ship and turn her over to us—'

'This is your news? A rank impertinence, sir!'

'Here are my orders,' Kydd said, handing over a carefully worded document telling of the surrender and enjoining him peacefully to relieve outlying commanders, signed by Baird. A similar one in Dutch was signed by Baron Prophalow, lately commandant of the castle and town.

The man scanned them quickly, then snorted angrily. '*Zottenklap!* This talks of the castle commandant signing away a naval ship. He has no jurisdiction over the Batavian Navy and therefore this is worthless.'

'It does state, sir, "the defences of Cape Town and all appurtenances thereto"—'

'You mean to apply that *kletspraat* to the capitulation of a line-of-battle ship? When our army has suffered but a temporary reverse and its general places his trust in our loyalty? Do you take us for poltroons, sir?' the captain spat, his colour rising.

'Not at all, sir,' Kydd said hastily. 'It is rather that I deplore the violence and bloodshed that must result from a mis-understanding. Should I not make myself plain, then I have failed my commodore – who is in possession of a squadron of ships-of-the-line – and unfortunate consequences must surely follow.'

From the exchanged glances Kydd knew the implication was well taken. 'Should you concur,' he continued smoothly, 'then, naturally, the honours of war shall o' course be accorded you in respect to the long traditions of your gallant navy and—'

'You presume too much, sir!' the captain snarled. 'Get off this ship – now!'

'Sir, if you would—'

'Now!'

Kydd drew himself up and bowed. 'Then I am obliged to point out that it is my duty to convey your . . . views to my commodore and the matter will be taken out of my hands. Sir, I beg you will reconsider, if only for the sake of the brave men who must soon die.'

The expression was stony and he went on doggedly with the only card he had left to play. 'I'll take my leave, sir, but shall delay my return to the commodore for the space of one hour.'

He paused significantly, looking about the other officers

III

on the quarterdeck, then turned quickly and left. There was a chance that, even given their proud history, he would relent under pressure from the crew, hearing of a squadron of feared Royal Navy battleships nearby.

The passage back gave Kydd time to think. It was a hollow threat he had made: Popham would not take kindly to a request to deal with a situation that should have been resolved diplomatically, that risked his valuable fleet assets with damage that could never be repaired in this distant outpost. In fact, it was most unlikely that he would quit his station directly off Cape Town at this critical time.

Should he leave *Bato* isolated for dealing with later? There were already soldiers heading south to Simon's Town in a hazardous march to occupy the only pretence at naval facilities in the colony. If they were met by the murderous broadside of a ship-of-the-line . . .

Expectant faces met him in *L'Aurore*: was there a likelihood of prize money? They were the only ones present and rules on gun money and head money were very clear. Kydd, however, was in no mood to indulge them.

The dilemma was his alone. At the end of the hour, what should he do? Run back to Popham with his tail between his legs – or fight it out? Or wait until dark and perform a daring cutting-out operation? Against an alerted ship-of-the-line?

His thoughts raced, with no solution in sight. He couldn't talk it over with Gilbey. A captain made his own decisions and this would be seen as a worrying weakness by his first lieutenant.

The deadline approached. Should he give them more time? How much?

Gilbey broke into his thoughts. 'Some sort of signal, is that, sir?'

Kydd snatched the glass. 'That's their national Batavian flag,' he said peevishly. 'I'd desire you'll take the trouble to recognise it in future.'

Something made him linger on the image. Did this mean they were about to open fire? The flag mounted up the main-mast halyards – but at the truck it rested for a moment, then slowly descended to half-mast where it remained. 'Barge alongside this instant!' The hoist could have only one meaning: capitulation. His heart leaped.

Kydd took the surrender in the huge old-fashioned great cabin, fighting down exultation. To his knowledge, not even at Trafalgar had a ship-of-the-line struck to a mere frigate. The terms agreed were straightforward enough: colours to be hauled down immediately and unconditionally, in return for the officers and crew to be allowed ashore to await their fate in the Simon's Town establishment rather than endure confinement aboard. That was most convenient: only a token party from *L'Aurore* needed to take possession while the crew would be held in custody later by the approaching soldiers.

Kydd allowed the captain his sword in recognition of the fact that the capitulation was *force majeure* other than an act of war by *L'Aurore*. That it was the threat of an English battle-squadron in the offing remained unspoken.

Even as they returned to the upper deck, boats were being swung out and manned by Dutch seamen. The captain kept aloof, avoiding Kydd's eye.

The seamen, dark-tanned and lithe, tumbled into the boats with their sea-bags as if desperate to be quit of the scene, and it wasn't long before the captain went to the side, turned stiffly and, after a short bow to Kydd, looked up to where the Batavian flag still flew and removed his hat. After a few moments, and without a second glance, he swung over the ship's side and was gone, leaving Kydd gloriously alone on the quarterdeck.

He savoured the moment, taking in the forlorn disorder about the decks and the odd smell of a Dutch ship, then strode to the side and signalled for his barge. It came alongside and he motioned the rest of the crew aboard. 'Haul down the colours, Poulden,' he ordered. His coxswain had an English ensign under his waistcoat and proceeded to bend it on, sending it soaring up.

'A fine day's work,' Kydd pronounced, to the grinning men, 'as will give you a dog-watch yarn none may beat.' There were eight altogether. With none of the usual challenges of a new-captured ship – securing prisoners, frantic pumping to keep afloat and the rest – it would be enough.

L'Aurore was under orders to keep off until he returned, in case of a trick, but it didn't matter for he'd simply leave a couple of hands and, on return, send back more. He smothered a sigh and sent his men to carry out a quick inspection – it would not do to have to rouse out later any drunken and resentful crew who'd remained onboard.

The afternoon sun beamed down, and while he waited, Kydd considered what to do next. To keep men aboard *Bato* in idleness while *L'Aurore* sailed away was not the best use of a frigate's prime seamen. If he delayed for a day or so he could send to Cape Town for guard-duty soldiers, but his orders were for critical haste.

A muffled cry came up the main hatchway – and another. If it was a trap it made no sense: Kydd and his men had been outnumbered before – why wait until now to spring it? Kydd raced over to the hatchway as two of his men burst up from below, horror on their faces.

'S-Sir! Ship's afire, sir!'

Over the fore-hatch Kydd saw a shimmering that did not owe itself to noon-day heat. Somewhere below . . . 'Follow me!' he roared. The Dutch had fired the ship, but if they moved fast they had a chance. It was worth taking almost any risk – at stake was a ship-of-the-line. The guns alone were . . .

He raced down the fore-hatch. The air below was hot and acrid with resinous smoke from Stockholm tar, which was almost certainly what they had used to start the blaze. It was a sailor's worst nightmare, but Kydd knew his men were with him. He flew down the steps to the next deck. Now smoke was swirling around him but there were no visible flames.

Was it even further below? The orlop? He made out a flickering orange glow in the gloom forward. Coughing, he plunged into it, tripping on rubbish strewn about the decks, and soon saw a hasty pile of carpenter's stores – chippings, glue, resin – well alight.

'The fire engine! Find it 'n' rig it!' he shouted hoarsely. Poulden beckoned a seaman and hurried aft. 'The rest, grab a hammock to smother it – move y'rselves!'

He looked round wildly: there was a roll of old canvas to one side. 'Get the other corner,' he spluttered at a seaman, and they drew it clumsily at the fire. It died away for a moment but, choking, they had not managed to aim well and flames began licking out from under the material.

One seaman screamed, the whites of his eyes vivid in the gloom. He fell back, mesmerised. Kydd tried to reposition the canvas but now it was only fuelling the fire.

'Sir – we found an engine but it was in pieces, like,' Poulden shouted nervously from behind.

Flames eagerly took to the canvas flaring some old paint

encrusted on it and Kydd felt real heat now. The fire engine was wrecked: what else was to hand? He shielded his eyes from the glare, looking about wildly. The cunning Dutch had started the fire low in the ship – a bucket brigade was useless this far down and even a whole crew would be hard put to stop it now.

Some of the braver souls unfurled hammocks and dragged them over the fire but it was hopeless and the flames rose even quicker, licking at the deckhead, spreading evilly. There was a dull *whoomf* as some tar barrels caught and then a general retreat through the choking smoke.

Suddenly there was a scream from the hatchway. 'Save y'rselves, mates! There's another fire forrard!' On the upper-deck, flames had followed the lines of tar and leaped to the rigging.

There was an instant stampede; there came a point when a fire became a ravening beast let loose with death in its heart, and this no man could withstand.

It was time to leave the ship to her fiery doom. 'Muster aft, all the hands!' Kydd bellowed. A quick tally revealed two were missing. 'Poulden,' Kydd ordered.

The coxswain snatched at the sleeve of a sailor and they disappeared below. The others shuffled nervously, but Kydd was damned if he'd let them save themselves before the four returned.

The fire forward was spreading astonishingly quickly. The rigging was stiff with preservative tar and the flames shot up the foremast halyards voraciously, catching the varnish of spars and racing along tarry ropes between the masts to start fresh blazes.

One by one they gave way, swinging down in a shower of cinders. Yards robbed of their suspending gear jerked and swayed dangerously. Then sparks began dropping on Kydd and the others from the main-mast, whose rigging had caught.

'Into the boat, then!' he snapped. They needed no urging and, yanking it alongside, began scrambling in. Kydd stayed on deck, praying Poulden would soon appear as a rain of burning fragments drove them further aft.

Then Poulden's smoke-blackened figure burst out of the after-hatchway with his mate, dragging a body with them. 'Couldn't get t' Lofty,' he said, his voice breaking. The other man looked around piteously and Kydd shied from the thought of what must have passed below.

'We're leaving now,' he said brusquely, and they hurried to the side, Kydd pausing to snatch a line from a belaying pin and fashion a bowline on a bight to lower the corpse down. Anxious faces looked up, flinching at the burning fragments falling from aloft.

Without warning there was a loud, splintering crack above them. Before Kydd could look up, a weather-darkened spar swung down jerkily, trailing flaming ropes and brutally knocking them aside. It ended its careering rush through the centre of the boat, like a giant's spear.

A shriek of agony from an unfortunate who'd been skewered ended in choking bubbles of his own blood. The cries of the trapped turned to frantic gurgling as the smashed boat filled. Frightened seamen scrabbled back up the side and joined the shocked group on deck, staring at the wreckage containing their dead shipmates settling low in the water.

'What d' we do now, sir?' Poulden asked, ashen-faced. 'No boat.'

Kydd had no quick answer. *L'Aurore*'s orders were not to approach *Bato* on any account, to guard against trickery, and simply await their return. The firing of the ship would have been spotted and the assumption made that it was Kydd's action. But, worst of all, the boat was on the blind side and nothing would have been seen of their catastrophe. There would be no rescue.

The crackle of blazing timber from forward redoubled; in the light winds flames leaped vertically and now spread across the width of the ship, advancing aft in an unstoppable wall of fire. Kydd saw there was no longer any option – at any moment the fire would reach the ship's magazines and they would be blown to kingdom come. 'Into the water!' he shouted, throwing aside his coat. 'The magazines are ready to go!'

The seamen raced to the side but stopped dead as one shrieked, 'Jus' look at 'em!' He pointed down, terrified. Lazily flicking past was the huge pale bulk of a shark. Another pallid blur cruised further out, accustomed to the ditching of 'gash' overside from *Bato* – galley scraps and the like.

'Mr Kydd, *sir*?' Poulden beseeched.

The fire – or the sharks? He was the captain.

Kydd snatched another glance over the side. At least three of the monsters were now in view. And the magazine could blow in the next second.

'We go in!' he ordered. 'On m' order, we jump together next to the boat as will frighten the buggers off. Soon as you're in, pull yourselves into the wreck.'

It was a last and very desperate hope, but he didn't allow the men time to think about it. 'Ready, all? Then go!' He plummeted into the sea. The others joined him in a confused crash of bodies. Gasping for breath, Kydd saw what was left of the boat, awash and at a crazy angle with the spar projecting, and clumsily struck out for it.

Almost immediately there was a burbling scream and frantic

splashing. Twisting round, Kydd saw a giant shark fin cleaving the water towards them at shocking speed. Before his frozen mind could react, it was on them – but, incredibly, it passed them by. Kydd felt a glancing touch from the hard, muscular body.

With frantic desperation, he flailed for the boat, grasped the gunwale and was about to heave himself in when he realised why the sharks had left them alone. Attracted by the blood in the water, they were going for the trapped bodies in savage, battering charges.

More came to join in the frenzy of snapping and tearing: when that meat was gone they would turn on anything to sate their lust for flesh. They had seconds to live.

Against the brutish frenzy the distant hoarse cry was like a dream: '*Raak niet in paniek Engelsen, we komen!*' Kydd jerked around. A Dutch longboat was pulling strongly out for them – they had seen what had happened and humanity had overcome the imperatives of war. They were saved.

Chapter 6

'I suppose we must address you now as "Mr Colonial Secretary Renzi", should we not?' Baird harrumphed, but he was clearly taken with his first appointment as governor.

'As you wish, Sir David.' Renzi was secretly gratified at his elevation – the honours of the post had not turned his head but at Baird's right hand he was above the petty manoeuvring yet at the centre of events, well placed to gather his ethnical curiosities.

'There'll be a mort of hard work for us both, you may be sure – but satisfying for all that.'

'Sir.'

Baird paused, then looked at him keenly. 'Forgive me, Renzi, but you do present as something of a man o' mystery. What makes you tick, sort o' thing? Wine, women – any vice as will be revealed to me in due course?'

'To me, sir, the pleasures of the mind are the more perdurant and grateful to the senses. I've been these last years labouring over a study that seeks to relate ethnical character to economic response and . . . and it's showing promise,' he ended abruptly.

'Ethnicals! Then, sir, you should go to India. There you'll find every kind of God-forsaken creature and outlandish practice as would be meat for a thousand tomes!' He guffawed, then sobered in reflection. 'With cruelty and corruption in great palaces, side b' side with the deepest sort o' thinkers, who'd give pause to Pythagoras himself.'

'As opportunity permits, of course,' Renzi answered politely. 'The Dutch as incomers to a tribal Africa should be a diverting enough ethnical spectacle.'

Baird's eyes narrowed. 'You have objection to the civilising of savages?'

'Sir, the deed is done, as is the way of the world. My interest is in its outworking, the play of peoples and nature, threat and reply, never the sterile confrontations of politics.'

'Then I declare I've a colonial secretary of the first water! You'll find there's the conquered Dutch, the Hottentots o' various stripe, and who knows what we'll see up-country? All these to keep content and govern for His Majesty, and I've a notion you'll have a contribution to make.'

Baird sat back, contemplating. 'So, we begin. You have experience of conjuring a government *ex nihilo*, from a vacuity as it were? No? Then neither have I.'

It was going to be a task of monumental proportions: the creation of a system of rule, its codifying, and then its declaration and promulgating on a subject people. From the detail of ceremonials to the rule of law. Allegiance, tax revenues, land-holding, defence of the realm, municipal water supply.

'I conceive, as first step, a committee, a cabinet of advisers as will give their views when asked. Not too big, say . . . half a dozen? Hmm. Dasher Popham, of course, and a military type? Ferguson will do. We'll have a doctor – public health and so forth. Munro would like the job, I'm sure – he's our senior regimental surgeon.'

'Could I suggest a gentleman of an accounting persuasion?' Renzi offered quietly. 'We'll be facing problems of revenue and expense of quite another kind.'

'Just so. Then I think it's to be Tupley, our quartermaster general. Dry old stick, but knows his financials. There'll be others, but this will do for a start, I believe. Well, now, I must see about finding you an office and assistants, Mr Secretary. Oh, and in the matter of a salary, I fear at this stage we must be cautious. Would, say, four hundred per annum satisfy at all?'

Incredibly, his income was now greater than Kydd's. 'There's need of a residence of sorts,' Renzi replied, greatly daring.

'Why, most certainly. Grace 'n' favour of the Crown, of course. Can't have a secretary as won't be found when needed.'

'I'm most grateful, sir.'

'Right! Then let's whip in this kitchen cabinet and start our business.'

'Gentlemen. I'm grateful to see you all here at such short notice. Time is of the essence, as you'll understand.'

It was an informal gathering: Baird at one end of a table, pointedly in civilian dress, and Renzi at the other. The rest were in military uniforms.

'You'll be remarking this room.' By its location it was certainly discreet, but although smallish it had rich hangings of Dutch origin. 'I choose to make my headquarters and reside here in the castle rather than at Government House, from where all administration of a gubernatorial nature will be conducted.' A ghost of a smile passed. 'Apart from feeling a damn sight safer within these walls, I judge it to be a nod to Dutch sensibilities – recollect, their governor is still at large at the head of an army.'

He neatened the papers in front of him deliberately. 'We all know each other, o' course, no need for introductions. Except Mr Renzi here.' There were curious looks as he added, 'Who is to be acting colonial secretary.'

'Renzi?' Popham frowned. 'Is he not some sort of clerk in one of my vessels?'

'Confidential secretary to Captain Kydd, Dasher. You'll probably not be aware he's something in the philosophical line, corresponds with Count Rumford and others in London.'

'A philosopher clerk? We'll be tackling high problems as will be requiring more than a mort of discretion.'

'I've placed my trust in Mr Renzi, old chap. I desire him to be privy to our discussions. Now we've pressing business – shall we get on with it?

'The first.' Baird waited until he had their attention. 'I've just this morning discovered the true reason for their abrupt yielding of the town.'

He grinned mirthlessly. 'Simple. Cape Town is within three weeks of capitulation by starvation.'

There was a stunned silence. 'After a catastrophic failure of the harvest the total amount of grain in store does not exceed two days' consumption, and external supply by the Batavians has been very effectively discouraged by fright of our navy.'

He broke through the murmurs of concern and added, 'Which places us in a near impossible situation. Not only have we the entire population to feed but thousands of useless mouths – our prisoners-of-war, Dutch and French, who may not be suffered to go at liberty.'

He gave an expectant look across the room. 'General Ferguson?'

'Send out to the farms, seize the corn stocks,' the old soldier growled. 'It's their skins we're saving.'

'Except that the grain regions are dominated by Janssens's army, which has moved into the Stellenbosch. We can count on nothing from the country – is it expected we'll be starved into quitting?'

'God forbid. No, we must send out for supply.'

'The nearest friendly settlements are St Helena and Madras. I shall certainly dispatch ships there for flour and rice but, gentlemen, these are weeks distant, are they not?'

'Simon's Town. Isn't it some sort of victualling post?' Dr Munro offered.

'It is,' Popham said, 'but still lies in the hands of the enemy, guarded by a ship-of-the-line no less. I'm having a frigate call but am not sanguine about the outcome.'

There was a reflective quiet, then Baird said mildly, 'Therefore it's in my contemplation to release the fleet immediately to proceed to India, as was planned in the event of a successful outcome to our expedition.'

'What – now?' Popham was dismayed. 'David, this requires I detach escorts in the face of a French retaliation. I cannot guarantee—'

'Noted. It's imperative, you'll agree, either to increase our grain stocks or substantially reduce numbers of those on government corn. Failing the first, I'm obliged to accept the latter.'

Ferguson looked up bleakly. 'Losing troops when there's an army at large opposing us?'

'I'm keeping back elements of the Seventy-fourth and Eighty-third as will take the field against Janssens for an early accounting.'

'Ah.'

'And the India fleet sails now.'

Popham frowned, but refrained from comment.

'Very well. The next point is security. We have Cape Town. My best information suggests there are some twenty-eight forts and batteries in the outlying districts. My intent is to severally reduce these before moving on Janssens – and, General Ferguson, you will oblige me by presenting a plan for so doing.'

He glanced at Popham and smiled. 'The Navy is our ever-present bulwark and a comfort to all to see anchored there in the Roads. All matters marine accordingly I'm grateful to leave with the distinguished commodore.'

He sighed, fiddling with a pencil. 'We're beset with worriments, gentlemen, but we will prevail. The Dutch made this a green and pleasant land and I won't see it decline. The problem I would most ask you to reflect upon therefore is that of how best we are to reconcile its inhabitants to our rule. A sullen and rebellious population, ready to rise at little provocation, will be a sore trial.'

'Um, er . . .'

'Yes, Colonel Tupley?'

The quartermaster general, a precise individual, whose intensity of gaze was disconcerting, came back, 'I've not heard anything yet, sir, about what shall be done concerning our trading position.'

'Trading position?' said Baird, blankly.

'Indeed. We lost two-thirds of our specie when *Britannia* went down in the Brazils. I'm expected to pay the troops with just what cast of exchange? Implicit is that we must satisfy them and local suppliers by note of hand on the British Treasury, which in course will be discounted on the local market. And for which form of return? Goods in kind? Some barbarous foreign coin?'

'An early decision will be made, Colonel.' Before Tupley could reply, he announced briskly, 'The meeting reconvenes tomorrow at nine sharp. Thank you for your attendance and please do give our problems your deepest thought – I need your ideas. Good day to you all.'

Renzi remained, and when the others had left, Baird slumped in his chair. 'By heavens, just talking about what faces us brings on the blue devils,' he said moodily.

'I can't help but observe that if the people wished to rise against us, I believe they would have done so by now,' Renzi said. 'I'm supposing the nature of this entire settlement is as a Dutch merchant-ship victualling stop and, in a small way, a trading port. If this can be restored, then it would go well with the merchantry.'

'Umm. Now that's something that I *can* do.'

'Sir?'

'Make it a free port! Open to all nations – that'll please 'em. Where before they'd only what was left of the Batavian and French trade calling here, now they've all of the British Empire to welcome! I'll make a proclamation to that effect immediately.'

'It'll be many months before it takes effect, the word needing so long to get out.'

Baird beamed. 'Yes, but it's the effect on the merchants I have an eye to. Gives 'em something to thank us for.'

Renzi thought for a moment, then added, 'But then I observe there is a further course – one that links their self-interest with our desire to govern wisely.'

'Oh? Do go on, Renzi. I've a fancy this will be worth hearing.'

'It does cross my mind that the chief objective of our being here is to deny the French the strategic advantage of holding the Cape. That being so, we have no interest in its exploitation – the planting of colonies, the establishment of manufactories and the like. In fine, we have no real wish to disturb the present order.

'However, conceive of the consternation, the dismay, at recent events in the hearts of these folk. The merchant and honest citizens will long have accommodated to the subtleties of opportunity and advancement in society afforded by their traditional and familiar system of law and culture. Now this is taken away and they're confronted by a situation not of their choosing or control.

'Are the English to be a brutal conqueror, exacting tribute, imposing our language, alien forms of law, taxation? Are they to be dispossessed by arbitrary laws of their ancient lands, losing their ancestral homes, their investments against old age?

'Everything is set on its head and they will listen to any who promises to restore the old ways. Sir – I have a proposition. Should we do as the Romans did, then we will be at considerable advantage.'

'Pray continue . . . Mr Secretary.'

'We keep the structure of native rule in place, complete with laws and customs, without interference, merely ensuring the ruler is complaisant. Do you declare by proclamation that this be so, that none may fear loss or seizure, that we English do hold ourselves under the same laws and that—'

'A radical conceit, sir!'

'– providing always that such is not in conflict with any English common law. Sir, the Dutch system is derived from the Roman tradition, as ours is. I'll wager there are paltry differences only, and the customs are harmless. For a little given, much is gained.'

'I'll reserve opinion on the Romans as an exemplar, but your proposition is interesting. Damn, it, very interesting . . . It means they'll have little to complain of, they ruling themselves, and if they wax fat on the trade we put their way, most will frown on any who seek to trouble it.'

Renzi said nothing, giving space for Baird to explore the thought.

'Hmm. Laws 'n' customs – I suppose this includes their currency? Then here we have a solution to our lack of specie. Let 'em keep using their old money, whatever that is. Pay our soldiers in suchlike, and the market can't refuse our coin, it being theirs . . . Yes, it'll raise eyebrows among my colonels but we have possibilities.'

His forehead creased in concentration. 'Ha! Another fine thought – we treat with their old town council or whatever with a view to adopting it in its glorious entirety, lord mayor and all! This way we'll have no need to face the tedium of forming our own with all its devising of pettifogging ordinances and drain to the Treasury. Yes, by Jove!'

He reflected for a moment, then slapped his hand down. 'We'll do it! Nothing to say I, as governor, can't make it so! Um, first thing is to get it down in a form o' words. Then we trot it by the former Dutch nabob in charge, who'll see it in his interest to be restored to power, and we'll then get it cast into the local lingo.'

'Do we have any familiar with the law, sir?'

'Umm – no. And it has to be safely in the legal cant.' Baird was downcast for only a moment, then brightened. 'No – but the Dutch have. This nabob making common cause with us you can be certain will leave nothing to chance in this way. Splendid! I'll trouble you to draw up our draft form o' words while I send out for the chap and we'll have something to show for a good afternoon's work.'

Kydd was only too aware that for sailors a death at sea, when not in the presence of the enemy, must always be attended with the proper forms of respect – a muster at the ship's side, prayers and then a flag-draped body consigned to the deep.

For the three who did not return there could not be all of this. But regular service at sea saw many a fall from the yard at night, a rogue sea sweeping the fore-deck and other hazards taking life and leaving nothing, and there were long-hallowed traditions of the captain gathering the men, ensuring the right words were said. As was the way of the Service, *L'Aurore* put to sea immediately afterwards, duty bound.

They sailed away from the sunset, the seamen at their mess-decks muted over their evening grog. Later there would be the traditional ceremony about the foremast as the dead sailors' kit and treasured possessions were auctioned to their messmates, the proceeds always many times the actual value of the items, to go eventually to their loved ones – but it would be many months or even years before they would hear of their loss.

Kydd missed Renzi. Through the years they had contrived to stay together and now he was no longer there, so Kydd would dine alone. Most captains did, of course, unless invited by the gunroom, or at breakfast with the offgoing officer-of-the-watch and a brace of tongue-tied midshipmen, but Kydd had grown used to Renzi's company.

Would Renzi soon tire of acting the scribe for a precarious land-bound bureaucracy? Like himself, Kydd knew his friend relished the broad horizons and freedoms of the sea, and perhaps the fetters of unchanging routine would become irksome.

The long but slight southerly swell gave a pleasing rhythm to *L'Aurore*'s easy leg seaward; in the morning she would close with the land to resume her easterly course, the next fortress marked as Onrusberge. And in the meantime he would try to let sleep soften the images of the day.

A rose-tinted dawn saw the frigate raise the long rocky spit at Hangklip; their position secure, a couple of tacks into the south-south-easterly, and they were approaching an immense stretch of bright sand-hills as far as the eye could see, at its northern end a small settlement below rumpled umber heights that stretched away inland.

'To quarters, if you please,' Kydd ordered. Their chart was a dozen years old, and the modest battery on the hill above might well have been strengthened since then to give them an unpleasant surprise.

Located well into the hook at the end of the bay, Onrusberge was on a dead lee shore and *L'Aurore* prudently came to well clear, conveniently out of range of any guns. Taking the officer-of-the-watch's telescope while his barge was being prepared, Kydd carefully inspected the land. Set many miles to the south-east and separated by formidable country, there was the prospect that the news of Cape Town's surrender had not reached it, if the terse notations on the chart were to be believed.

Their appearance had created something of a stir, for there was noticeable activity ashore. He swept the heights, searching for the fort. There was none evident, only a low jumble of square grey structures. Could this mean that it was in some way concealed?

Under sail, his barge made for the distant cluster of houses, surfing before the swell with bellying sails, a large white flag high and prominent. He had a minimal boat's crew and was unarmed, and noted warily a gathering of figures along the shore.

Kydd directed the boat towards its centre. A small file of soldiers appeared and began to form up. When they were closer, he could see that they were at the head of a projecting flat tongue of rock, which had a rickety jetty perched along it.

The swell urged them inshore with dismaying rapidity. Kydd glanced at Poulden at the tiller; unusually, his calm features were set in a frown. It was a delicate judgement in seamanship: wind abaft, the swell translating to white-capped seas driven ever higher as they surged in, and the small jetty with barely a boat's length to come up to. In this craft it would be lunacy to make a direct approach, the seas only too ready to smash against its pretty but squared-off transom before Kydd could make it to dry land.

He said nothing, letting Poulden make his decision. A hundred yards off, both sails came down at the run and oars thumped into their thole pins. For a moment there was an awkward slewing as the boat lost way before they could find their rhythm, but then Poulden saw his chance and brought the boat round, head to seas.

It was masterly: now the barge was keeping position against the onrushing combers, edging across until it was within oar's length of the jetty.

'Sorry, sir,' Poulden said, trying to work out what was happening ashore.

Any but a lubberly crew would see the need for a rope thrown to bring them in the last few yards but the reception party just stood like statues. 'I'll go for'ard,' Kydd said, finding his way down to the bows, and when Poulden brought them in at an angle, he would be ready for that split-second moment when bow touched jetty.

He saw his chance: he would seize one of the vertical top timbers of the jetty and pull himself over. The bow approached, touched, and he sprang for the upright, heaving up with all his strength. The barge fell away immediately – but suddenly there was a rending crack of old timber and he dropped to his waist in the swash of the next wave.

Energised by anger, he performed a topman's trick, rotating to let his feet walk up as he hauled in on the sagging timber until he could twist up and on to the ramshackle decking, in the process losing his gold-laced cocked hat to the waves.

He straightened, trying to fix a smile as he faced the five rather quaint-looking soldiers and their elderly officer, who had wisely not ventured out on the old jetty. A moment of mutual incomprehension passed, and then a quavering but jaunty air arose from the fife-player.

Sloshing forward, Kydd approached the little group, the smile still fixed. The officer drew his sword and energetically saluted him, his gaze carefully averted. Without a hat to raise and feeling more than a little mutinous, Kydd bowed shortly.

Knowing that the Batavians and French were allies he declared importantly, *'Je transmets les salutations de sa majesté le roi George, et les frères néerlandais, félicitations—'*

'Do you come from the Grand Admiraal Nelson, sir?' the officer asked abruptly, in English.

Nettled, Kydd ignored the question. 'I am here to treat with your fort commandant on an important matter. Be so good as to take me to him.' His wet clothes clung annoyingly.

'I am he,' the officer admitted, the sword-point drooping a little. 'Ritmeester Francken. And these are my men.'

'Ah. Captain Thomas Kydd, my ship *L'Aurore* of thirty-two guns,' he said, indicating the frigate nobly at anchor out in the bay. 'May we go to your fort to discuss a delicate matter, sir?'

'We must surrender to you, *hein*?' Francken asked politely.

Kydd blinked, then collected himself. 'Er, shall we go to the fort?'

'*Het spijt* – and it's not fit for such as *you*, sir,' Francken said admiringly.

Kydd took his arm and propelled him away from the gaping onlookers. 'You've heard of Blaauwberg?'

'Sadly, yes. The fishermen. Sir, are you sure you're not sent by Admiraal Nelson at all?'

It was becoming clear. 'He has other business and asks me to treat with the gallant defenders directly. Sir, do you—'

'Certainly. But with the conditions.'

'Sir, you lie helpless under our guns! And you talk of *conditions*?'

Francken drew himself up. 'I must insist,' he said stiffly. 'Sir – we are a nation of honour! I cannot allow—'

'Very well. What are these conditions? Be aware that I cannot speak for my commander-in-chief should these terms be adverse to His Majesty's arms.'

Stubbornly, the officer tried to explain. Eventually Kydd understood. He excused himself and went once more to the jetty. 'One boatkeeper,' he bellowed to his barge laying off. 'The rest to step ashore.' A shame-faced urchin came up with his sodden hat, retrieved from the breakers, which he shook and clapped on, glowering.

The boat's crew scrambled up and assembled behind Kydd.

He bowed to the officer and turned to address his bewildered men. 'Stand up straight, y' scurvy villains!' he growled. 'We're about to take a surrender from the Dutch but he's insisting on a good show in front of the locals. We've no Jollies right now so you'll have to do.'

Stirk caught on quickest and wasted no time in hurrying out to take charge as 'sergeant'.

'Stan' to attention!' he roared hoarsely, glaring at them.

They obeyed with enthusiasm, if in highly individual poses. 'Belay that, Toby!' Poulden blurted in dismay. 'I'm cox'n an' it's me as—'

'Silence in th' ranks!' Stirk ordered gleefully, then twirled about and knuckled his forehead to Kydd. 'Surrender party ready f'r inspection, sir!'

So it was that grave military courtesies were exchanged that marked the reluctant yielding by one to the overbearing forces of the other, and while Kydd and Francken solemnly conferred, the barge was sent back with orders for the ship.

On the flagpole at the landing place, the Batavian flag descended as a gun salute thudded out importantly from the frigate. The English Union Flag was bent on, and as it slowly rose an identical salute banged out.

Honour satisfied, there was nothing more to do than shake hands and depart, with a promise to send later perhaps a more permanent form of soldiery for an official ceremony.

Mossel Bay, the last defensive work on Kydd's list, was some way further along the coast and was very much an unknown quantity. A port serving the frontier region of Boer settlement, it had tracks radiating out into the vast interior to exchange produce for trade goods.

How had the Boers taken their colony's sudden reversal

of fortune? Would they fight to the last for their lands? Or had they no inkling of what had befallen their largest town?

Stretching out along the scrubby red-brown coast they made the prominence of Cape St Blaize before noon of the second day. Mossel Bay lay around the point, and at this remoteness the sudden appearance of a frigate could have only one meaning.

The foot of the cape was seething white with, further out, a welter of conflicting seas betraying the presence of Blinder Rock, carefully marked on the chart. In tiny words along the edge the information was offered that, centuries before, the Portuguese navigator Dias had reached this far to prove that there was a route east to the riches of the Indies and Cathay. Kydd gave a wry smile: Renzi would have delighted in the knowledge.

Like so many of the havens in the south of Africa, this was open to the south-east and thus a lee shore, but as they rounded the cape well clear, the defending fort was quickly spotted. Squarely at the tip of the promontory, the national flag streaming out, this was a much more substantial structure. Low, squat and pierced for guns, it was well placed to command the scatter of buildings below and could reach out and destroy any who dared to threaten the score or so of various craft huddled within the curl of shore beyond.

Once more his barge put out, its large white flag prominent, *L'Aurore* at single anchor with her colours in plain view. As they neared the shore the landing place came into sight, a sturdy pier advancing into the sea, quite capable of taking alongside coastal brigs – or smaller troop transports.

Well before they reached it, a file of soldiers trotted out and formed line. An officer arrived, dismounted from a white horse, and stood watching their approach, his arms folded arrogantly.

Kydd mounted the boat stairs, conscious that, despite Tysoe's best efforts, his uniform sagged and was tarnished with seawater. The officer waited, obliging Kydd to come to him. Dressed distinctively in a blue coat with red facings and silver epaulettes, his black boots were immaculately polished and he wore a tricoloured sash about his waist.

His features were dark-tanned and hard, and he stood with ill-concealed animosity.

'Captain Thomas Kydd of *L'Aurore* frigate. I bring greetings from His Britannic Majesty,' Kydd opened. In his limited experience, most Dutch had English, unlike the French. 'Sir, I come with news of—'

'Major Hooft, Fifth Regiment of Pandours. You wish a parley, sir?' he snapped, slapping his side impatiently with a riding crop made of the tail of some African beast.

'Sir, I bear tidings from the governor concerning the present situation,' Kydd said carefully.

'Ver' well.' He spat an order at the African sergeant and stalked off towards the small town, leaving Kydd to follow in undignified haste. There was a factor's office near the wharf and Hooft went in with a crash of doors. '*Uit!*' he bellowed. '*Iedereen krijgt uit!*'

Frightened clerks spilled out into the sunlight, blinking and confused. 'We speak now!' Hooft threw at Kydd. He took the biggest chair and sat legs outstretched, looking up at Kydd. 'Well?'

Kydd handed a document to him. 'The governor prays you will understand the necessity of coming to an early arrangement for—'

'*Wat een zottenpraat?*' Hooft shouted, waving the paper. 'How dare you, sir?'

'Major Hooft, I don't understand—'

136

'Why, this is signed by an Englishman! Governor? *Apekop!*'

Kydd held his temper with difficulty. 'You may not be aware that after a recent battle there is a capitulation. Here is the proof – signed by Baron von Prophalow himself.'

'Ha! I have heard of Blaauwberg – a temporary reverse at arms only. Prophalow had no right to sign a capitulation while our forces regrouped. It's a treachery! The true governor of the colony is at Swellendam at the head of his army, and if you think I betray him while our colour still flies then you insult me, Captain,' he thundered.

'I beg you reconsider, sir. Our landings are complete, we—'

Hooft shot to his feet. 'Go, sir!' he said in fury. 'Go before I order my men to deal with you as you deserve.'

Kydd forced himself to remain calm. 'My ship—'

'Will be fired on if it's still there in one hour.'

'Sir. If you fail to come to terms with me, it must be reported to my commander and unfortunate consequences will in course ensue.'

Lifting his crop, Hooft slowly advanced on Kydd, smacking it into his palm. 'You threaten me? I'll remind you, Mynheer, that we are enemies and we are still at war.'

Kydd stood his ground, holding the man's gaze steadily.

'So!' The whip hovered an inch from his nose. 'I give you five more minutes on Batavian soil – then I come for you, *hein?*'

Kydd had no option but to return to his ship and did so. On the face of it the encounter had been absurd. For all the man knew, the frigate in the bay could well have held numbers of troops ready to storm ashore – but then again, he would be aware of how fraught a task that would be for Kydd under the guns of his fort.

There was no way Kydd's orders included starting a war

on his own. He must allow the arrogant prig his triumph, return and admit to General Baird that there was still one significant defensive work manned and active in his rear.

He looked back at the fort on the heights, glowering down, dominating the little harbour. It stood on three-hundred-foot near-vertical cliffs, and any attempt to bring *L'Aurore* inshore to threaten bombardment was risking too much.

The coast on either side away from the harbour was rock-girt and forbidding and, as far as he could tell, had nowhere suitable to land a boat of any kind. The only conceivable place was the pier.

Quite close by, and firmly under the guns of the fort, a convenient fresh-water rivulet lazily issued over the sand.

A road leading along the foreshore was fringed with houses, then disappeared up into the scrub.

Risking ship or lives in a gesture was not warranted. 'Get us under way, Mr Gilbey,' he snapped.

'Um, where to, sir?'

'West'd. We return,' Kydd said, with a look daring the lieutenant to comment.

'Aye aye, sir.'

They fell away before the brisk wind and soon Cape St Blaize turned to an anonymous dark grey and sank below the horizon as he slumped in his chair moodily. Tysoe came and set his table for dinner.

He accepted a glass of claret and as he sipped a thought came. One that swelled and blossomed until he laughed aloud. 'Ask the master to attend at convenience,' he ordered, and sat back in satisfaction.

'I see, sir,' Bowden said admiringly, putting down his breakfast coffee. 'During the night we stood out to sea and completed a triangle that sees us the *other* side of Mossel Bay, and when we appear, it's as if we're another ship!'

'Not quite.' Kydd helped himself to another roll and applied the plum jam liberally. 'It's not *L'Aurore* that will appear – but a local coaster as will need watering. It arrives near dusk and can't begin until sun-up.'

'With men concealed, sir?'

'Not only men – but a surprise for our biggety Dutchman.'

'Sir?'

'First things first, Mr Bowden. We've to catch our vessel or we have no plan. Is the coast in sight at all?'

'The master thinks we're some six leagues beyond Mossel Bay, sir.'

'Good. We'll keep well in with the land and I desire a sharp lookout for any small vessels. I'm to be called the instant one's in sight.'

As if catching word of their escapade, not a sail blemished the horizon, just simple native craft, a mussel-dredger, after which the bay was named, and a Moorish vessel with a soaring lateen, an exotic token of the utterly different world that lay around the tip of Africa. But no coaster.

Then a hesitant hail from the maintop. 'I see a – a barky, lying inshore!'

They had just passed a small but lofty headland and opened a very pretty inlet nestled in green bluffs, with a near perfect triangle of white sand at its head. Moored safely to seaward of the breakers was a high-sided two-master – a lugger or schooner: with her gear struck down, it was difficult to tell.

A few buildings perched on the side of one steep slope – was the owner there and willing to hire his vessel? 'Away the cutter,' Kydd ordered, after *L'Aurore* had hove to. Would the local settlers deal with the English enemy? If not, then they were in trouble – by their own admission they were now at peace, and seizing a coastal trader would be deemed piracy.

The boat surfed in on the backs of eager combers in an exhilarating ride through the shallows, and beached with a hiss. Kydd, in plain dress, moved to the bow. He sprang over the gunwale and up the beach before the next wave. Poulden and Stirk loped to his side.

There was a feeling of placidity in the hot sunshine as if the ancient continent were asleep. On the left were a few huts and shanties and Kydd trudged towards them, the pungency of drying fish reaching out to him.

As they neared, a dog started barking, then another. The animals rushed over, mangy and odd-coloured, disputing their progress. An astonished African woman with a basket of fish on her head came to berate them, but stood open-mouthed.

Stirk kicked at the dogs with an oath and they raced off. The little group trudged on. At the end of the beach one shack, larger than the others, had a wide terrace on stilts with wicker chairs and tables proclaiming its trade.

'We'll try the tap-house,' Kydd said. It looked deserted in the afternoon heat but as they mounted the steps an unshaven and tousle-headed white man emerged, wiping his hands on a rag. He stopped in astonishment. Then, on seeing *L'Aurore* offshore, his face cleared.

'Do you speak English?' Kydd pronounced loudly.

A chuckle emerged. 'I reckon,' he grunted, 'seein' as I was born in Stepney.'

'Then you're the very man to help us. Captain Kydd, two of my crew. Now, we'd like to discuss—'

'Hold hard, Cap'n! This here is the Red Ox mug-house,

what th' Dutch call a *wijnhuis* on account you'll get no beer. Now what'll you be havin'?'

'Tell me — is there a fort or soldiers close by? If we're seen . . .'

'Never. Closest is Mossel Bay an' he never stirs his arse unless there's a profit in it f'r him. No, rest easy, shipmates, ain't no one going to disturb ye here. I c'n recommend the blackstrap, out o' Stellenbosch, it is. So that's three, then?'

Kydd gave a tight smile — as long as they had a result by nightfall . . . and there was, of course, the necessity to obtain local information. Aware of the expectant looks from Stirk and Poulden he offered a shilling. 'Will you take this?'

'Lord love yer! O' course. Now m' tally is Jones, shall we say, an' I'd admire to know how th' old country is faring. I don't get t' see too many o' me countrymen out here — I tell a lie, I've never even seen hide of an Englishman since—'

'Later, Mr Jones. What we'd like to do is hire that two-master out there. Do you think it possible?'

'It's possible if I say so.' Three heavy china cups appeared and a rich scarlet liquid was splashed into them from a name-less bottle. 'Take a snorter o' that, then. Tell me what ye thinks.'

It was remarkably good: full-bodied and honest, quite distinct from a European claret. 'A fine drop, Mr Jones,' Kydd said sincerely, adding, 'And we'll need a muzzler each for my stout boat's crew.' There would be ribaldry on the mess-decks later as it was learned that the captain had stood a round for them in the line of duty.

He took another sip. 'You said Major Hooft is interested in profit?' he prodded.

'Ye've had dealin's with the bastard already? He's a militia major only, puts on these dandy-prat airs and he's aught but a jumped up revenooer, takes a tax on the grains comin' from up-country an' there's not a soul but hates the sight o' him.'

'So his fort's really nothing to speak of?'

Stirk jerked to his feet, swearing and lashing at his trousers until a large lizard scuttled away. He sat again slowly, trying to look casual.

'Fort? It's big enough, wi' great guns an' all. Tell me, Batavia bein' y'r enemy, have ye any thought o' making a strike agin the Cape? It's a right dimber place as would—'

'Less'n a week ago we defeated the Dutch at Blaauwberg. Cape Town is ours.'

'Glory be! So the Cape is British . . .'

'Well, er, the Dutch governor is still in the mountains with an army – but, never fear, our redcoats are on their way to dispute with him.'

This was met with a cynical smile. 'Oh? In back-country mountain kloofs he knows s' well? He's a-waiting f'r the Boers to come from the veld t' reinforce him. Then he'll be down on ye.'

Kydd grimaced and changed the subject. 'Mr Jones – how is it you, as an Englishman, are suffered to remain free under Batavian rule?'

'Another *beker van die wyn*, Cap'n?' Grinning, Stirk and Poulden pushed their cups forward. 'It's like this. There's every kind o' human on God's earth livin' here, an' as long as we don't kick up a moil, the country's big enough f'r us all, so it is.'

'But—'

'We're two thousan' leagues from Europe, an' we live different in Africa. Enough worryin' about bein' took by a rhino or lion without we start marchin' up 'n down. Xhosa war drums on th' frontier an' Khoikhoi going scared, we've plenty t' vex us without we take after your Napoleyong an' friends.'

Kydd slapped at an insect but was too late: its spiteful sting lanced his arm. 'That's as may be, Mr Jones,' he said irritably. 'I'm to ask you again. Are you willing to hire your vessel to the Crown?'

'Well, as t' that . . .' He flicked a rag expertly. 'It's not rightly m' own. Belongs t' Joseph M'Bembe. Ye'll need to speak wi' him.'

Swallowing his annoyance, Kydd asked, 'Where can we find him, then?'

'Oh, I c'n send a younker when we're ready. Stayin' f'r vittles? There's a right fine mutton bredie as is waitin' f'r attention . . .'

Kydd found another coin and slid it across. 'Do you ask Mr Bemby to call and I'd be much obliged,' he said heavily.

'No hurry, Cap'n. We've time – you'll tell me o' London this time o' year. How's y'r—'

'I'd take it kindly should you send for Mr Bemby NOW!'

With a hurt look Jones put fingers into his mouth and whistled. A barefoot child rushed in, his hand held out meaningfully. He looked askance at Kydd's coin but after a scolding in some native dialect he scampered off.

'Well, now, we was speakin' of London an' what sport's t' be found this time o' year . . .'

The dark bulk of a massively built man appeared at the steps up to the terrace, then stopped, looking suspiciously at the three white men. '*Se vir my wie jy is?*' he said softly, in a voice that was rich and deep.

'They's English, Joe, like me.'

'What you want?'

'To hire your vessel, Mr Bemby,' Kydd rapped. If he didn't

get satisfaction in the next five minutes he would think again about the whole venture.

'That your ship?'

'It is.'

'Why you want mine?' The eyes were small but shrewd.

'I'm offering to hire your whole vessel for three days, its crew not needed. The purpose is our business.'

'English. You's going agin the Dutch an' you need my ship.'

'I didn't say—'

'It's Mossel Bay – you're takin' on Hooft.' His face creased with mirth and he became animated. 'That *rakker* Hooft! Not easy, not a-tall. He's three hund'erd Pandours in that fort – Ndebele, no good. How many men you got in that ship?'

Kydd hesitated to take a stranger into his confidence, especially a country trader like this. But if he didn't, there could be no move against Hooft.

'I'm not starting a war with Major Hooft, Mr Bemby. Just a-persuading him is all. My plan is to bring ashore a howitzer – an army gun that throws a shell that explodes where it lands.'

There was a pair in *L'Aurore*'s hold from the Blaauwberg battle not yet returned to stores and one would make an excellent frightener for troops not expecting it. Stirk and Poulden exchanged knowing glances.

'Where you take it on land?' M'Bembe demanded.

'I thought to come in just before nightfall as if we were watering. There's that stream by the pier?'

'Ever'one uses it, this is true.'

'We sling the gun under a raft of four barrels, wait for dark and, um, get it up on the heights behind the fort ready for daybreak. I take it there's no guns pointing inland?' It would be strange if there were.

'No. A good plan – and will never work.'

'Oh?'

'The soldiers will be curious why you water at night. The road to the top, ver' steep, ver' long. You never do this in time. An' peoples will see.'

'Then we'll have to—'

'No, man, we can fix.' M'Bembe reflected for a moment then said, 'I like your plan. This what we do.'

The timing was perfect. As the sun went down over Hartenbos peak in Mossel Bay a well-known livestock coaster doused her sails and found a place among the scatter of fishing boats off the beach.

The boat-boys sang cheerfully as they rafted the water-barrels together alongside, then seemed to think better of working into the night and instead set up an awning and lantern on the after-deck for an evening's conviviality.

As the warm violet dusk faded into night, anyone looking closely might have made out a few figures busy with block and tackle on the opposite side who had not yet joined the party. But before it could get under way there was an irritated bellow from the beach. It seemed that there would be no slacking until the water-casks had been brought ashore ready.

The little double-ended boat was manned, Lieutenant Bowden himself taking an oar and suppressing a giggle at the sight of other *L'Aurore* seamen disguised in low conical hats, faces and limbs well daubed with galley soot, and muttering under their breath at the indignity.

The raft was ponderous and slow with the weight of the concealed gun but, of course, these were resentful sailors not about to exert themselves unduly and it was pitch dark before the gun grounded and was dragged ashore.

A low curse and a frighteningly loud wooden squealing and jingle of harness came out of the night as the promised ox-wagon came over the sand, animal snorts with the rank smell of the barnyard heavy on the air.

The squat bronze gun was small but heavy; hidden in a square box, it was satisfactorily anonymous. Ropes were brought and it was heaved around to the tail of the cart. More men jumped down to help, their white teeth showing as they grinned in delight at being part of the adventure.

Suddenly two soldiers materialised out of the blackness and asked suspiciously, '*Wat doen jy*?' All movement ceased.

An easy chuckle came from the drover. '*Het hulle jou nie vertel nie*?' He sauntered up and held out a packet. The soldiers muttered between themselves, then took it, waving them on before they left.

'Quick!' the drover hissed. The gun was heaved into the wagon with nervous energy, the cart settling with a thunderous creak. The boat arrived with the carriage and five heavy bags – shells and charges.

Bowden hauled himself up to the seat next to the drover. 'How did you—'

'Gave him bung for Hooft,' the drover said, lightly cracking his whip over the leading oxen, which stolidly started the wagon in motion.

Curiously he asked, 'Er, how much did you give him?'

'A lot – of ol' paper!' he chortled. The ox-wagon dipped and swayed as it ground up a steeply sloping road into the night.

Some miles past Mossel Bay *L'Aurore* came to and anchored in ten fathoms. Kydd was taking a grave risk by stripping the frigate of every last man save a token five; all had a crucial role in a very few hours and to hold back could be fatal.

One by one the ship's boats pulled ashore, landing the *L'Aurore*'s at the end of a wide beach, which marked the beginning of the heights above Mossel Bay. Kydd had the men mustered and they set out up a steep track into the African dusk, led by guides, the Royal Marines following and insisting on marching in proper form.

Sweating in the hot night, Kydd was thankful when they reached the top. Following the guides, they swung right and moved out on a turtle-back of high ground. Beneath, the lights of the settlement twinkled, but the massive dark bulk of the fort lay closer.

Now all depended on Bowden's arrival. It was not until a bare hour before dawn that the unmistakable sound of the ox-wagon intruded into the stillness from the other direction. The men positioned themselves in accordance with orders, hunkered down and out of sight of the fort.

The howitzer was assembled, the gun crew hand-picked by the gunner's mate. Kydd waited patiently. As soon as it was light, the howitzer was carefully sited and loaded, and when the faint sound of the reveille sounded on the still air, he gave the first order. The ugly little gun banged angrily into the morning peace and, seconds later, a shell exploded short of the rear wall of the fort.

The distant trumpet's sound was cut off, as if with a knife. Moments later it was urgently baying the call to arms.

Another shell detonated close to one side. 'Easy, Mr Stirk – this only to wake 'em up.'

After the third, men were at the embrasures to repel the mysterious attackers from inland, then began issuing out and massing for a counter-attack.

Time for the final order. Kydd stood and gave the signal. As one, *L'Aurore*'s entire complement, seamen, marines, every man and boy in her crew, dressed in anything that was red, slowly stood up – and all along the skyline, hundreds of English redcoats could be seen forming line for a merciless attack from the unprotected direction.

The effect was instant: in moments there was not a man left outside the walls of the fort.

Another shell burst close, its smoke wreathing the air and wafting back over the defenders.

'Last round, sir.' It duly banged out, but its effect was decisive. As Kydd watched, the colours were jerked down in ignominious defeat.

Chapter 7

'Ah, Renzi – I'd like you to meet Mijnheer Willem van Ryneveld,' Baird said jovially, although his eyes remained cool and appraising. 'In the last government under Janssens he was head man, as, who's to say, their fiscal. Sir, this is Mr Nicholas Renzi, our colonial secretary.'

Civil bows were exchanged and, murmuring a greeting, Renzi took in the neat and intelligent features, the sharp beard and restrained but stylish dress.

'Shall you entertain Mr Ryneveld, old fellow?' Baird went on. 'I'm to consult on military matters this morning, I believe.'

It was prearranged, but Renzi pretended to be taken by surprise and suggested a walk outside in the early-morning air. 'I do suppose there's much to consider,' he said, affecting a leisurely stroll.

'Yes, Mr Renzi,' Ryneveld said, in a quiet and precise tone, falling into step beside him.

Renzi hesitated. This was a crucial time: if the previous ruling class took against them, their position would be untenable. If, on the other hand, concessions were offered, would it be taken as a sign of weakness?

His task was to sound out the chief figure in the previous administration, get a view on the distribution of allegiances and delicately allude to the advantages of co-operation.

He stopped to admire the rearing bulk of Table Mountain, so close. 'Such a magnificent prospect, Mr Ryneveld,' he said. 'A sight to transport the Romantics to ecstasy!'

The man stood attentive, but silent.

'And how curious it is that the mountains in Africa rear out of the earth so very abruptly,' Renzi continued. There was still the same polite attention as he added, 'Is this perhaps why we can so easily distinguish ranges at a distance, with none other to obtrude?'

He let the question hang and eventually Ryneveld answered: 'Singular, perhaps. I've heard that the Great Winterhoek is still visible at eighty miles.'

They reached the end of the parade-ground and turned together. Then Renzi saw a tiny ghost of a smile. He couldn't help but grin back and they chuckled. The ice had been broken.

'Shall we talk?' Ryneveld said.

'By all means.'

'Then I'd hazard that if I should be so impertinent as to make query as to the intentions of the new order, you would be exercised as to how these might be implemented.'

Renzi allowed a measure of concern to enter his voice. 'The colony faces hunger and danger – common humanity demands we come to an understanding.'

'Then might I know how your governance is to be achieved?' Ryneveld asked cautiously.

'I cannot speak for General Baird—'

'Of course.'

'– yet I do sense that he appreciates the care and tolerance of the Dutch in their past administration and is minded to emulate it.'

'A pity if that were so.'

'I beg your pardon?' Renzi said in surprise.

'The previous establishment – the Batavians – were in thrall to Bonaparte, who controls their nation. Decisions here were not necessarily taken in our best interests. Shall you?'

'Sir, our purpose here is not in the character of conqueror. We are, as it were, obliged to make landing and occupation in order to prevent the French from seizing a strategic position that would enable them to sever our trade routes to India, nothing more.'

'That much is apparent, sir.'

'Therefore it is not in prospect to exploit the colony for its manufactories or resources.' Renzi paused, then said significantly, 'Which supposes our best course is to allow the continuance of the system of government that prevails.'

He saw an unmistakable gleam of interest. 'This to include the code of law, currency, rights of property – what say you, sir, to a restoration of all the traditional customs and trade practices as have been in place in Cape Town for these centuries past?'

'All?'

'Just so.'

'Then I'd be compelled to describe it as a mistake, sir.'

Renzi was taken aback. This, from the previous first man of government? 'May I know why?' he asked, after a space.

'The Batavian government is recent, a *parvenu*. Our origins are far in the past as we were founded by the Dutch East Indies Company to be naught but a victualling stop on the way to the Spice Islands. They ruled until a handful of years ago and their motives were selfish, their loyalty only to their shareholders. A polity such as this has no right to rule, still less to be imitated.'

'Are you then a radical, sir? Do you despise the former ways?' Renzi asked. If he were, it would instantly disqualify him for any position in the administration they were trying to bring together. A revolution would be a distinct liability in their precarious situation – and where would be their ready-made civil service?

'Not at all. The Dutch ways are direct, practical and well suited to this land.'

'Then?'

'I was fiscal in the previous government. There are regulations I would strike down and there are laws I would strengthen. It's a small, inward-looking society of many races and beliefs and requires careful nurturing. Do you know that in Cape Town today the slave population exceeds the free by thousands? That the Malay Muslims demand their own burying ground? That the Xhosa people speak by the clicking of tongues?'

It was becoming clearer: Ryneveld was making a bid for power in the new administration on the grounds of indispensability. But would he commit publicly to collaborating with the conquerors?

'For myself, I'm a newcomer of days only,' Renzi said neutrally. 'These curiosities deserve attention, and insights from one of undoubted understanding would be well taken. However, it's in contemplation to go much further – to entrust the well-running of the settlement to the people of Cape Colony themselves. Do you think it wise to allow the upper reaches of such a governance to be in Dutch hands or would it be prudent to staff it with English appointees?'

'If you are sincere in your desire to bring forward the natural aspirations and feelings of the inhabitants of the Cape, then only the totality of what exists, the continuation of the known order, will bring the confidence and contentment in its administration that you stand in need of.'

Renzi nodded gravely. 'If there will be one who stands for the people of Cape Colony, would it not be seen that such would be in the pay of the English and therefore betrayed his countrymen?'

'No,' came the firm reply.

'Come, sir. This land was settled by the Dutch, now another has usurped their ancient rights. Do you not believe this to be injurious to their feelings?'

Ryneveld gave a tiny smile. 'In turn, I'm astonished you English have not railed against the usurping Dutch – after all, it is you who have the prior claim. Was it not in 1620, a generation before our Jan van Riebeeck, that your Captain Shillinge took formal possession of the Cape in the name of King James?'

'It had slipped my mind,' Renzi said smoothly.

'Then, sir, I think it true to say that should affairs be conducted in the old ways, congenial to the sensitivities of the honest citizens of Cape Town and conducive to the swelling of trade, you shall have a contented colony.'

'Upon the advice of one of discernment and discretion, intimate with the delicacies of public affairs at the Cape . . .?'

'Naturally.'

*   *   *

153

'Capital!' Baird said. 'If he's willing to serve it means he's others of like mind behind him. I do believe we have a way forward. Tricky that Janssens is still in the field – two governors, divided loyalties and such.'

'Never mentioned, sir.'

'Then he shall be appointed fiscal again.' Baird laid down his pen and smiled expansively. 'Excellent! No offence intended to my soldier brothers but a civil complexion to our rule is essential and now we have it. A rather good wheeze I came up with, hey? We may now move forward, I believe.'

'Shall you wish your cabinet to meet?' Renzi asked.

'I'm not intending in the future to conduct my affairs by committee, my dear Mr Colonial Secretary. It shall be informed of the resumption of a civil administration and then dissolved. Any advice I might require I'll ask for at the time. Now – I do think it about time we made a few proclamations. Let's see . . . one about allegiance to His Majesty, o' course, but at the same time a grand one as sets 'em a-twittering, opening the port to trade and such.'

'Allegiance? Could not this be seen as somewhat presumptive, the Batavians being as yet undefeated?'

'Then what do you see as standing in its place?' The tone, however, was pleasant and encouraging.

'Um, I'd say a stern admonition of sorts from your own good self, urging citizens to abandon General Janssens's cause as hopeless in the face of garrison reinforcements from England expected daily.'

'And pointing out the undoubted advantages of settling down to an enlightened domestic rule – yes, that will do. Now, while I summon Ryneveld, see what a fist you can make of the wording, there's a good chap!'

As Renzi reached his office, a terrified woman escaped

with her mops and buckets and a distinguished-looking elderly gentleman presented himself. 'Sir – Oudtshoorn, chief clerk. I do hope your office will be satisfactory. If there's anything . . . ?'

'Thank you, er, Oudtshoorn.' They entered and a younger man at a small desk to one side rose awkwardly.

'Stoll, your private clerk. You may rely on his discretion.' Renzi was astonished that so many Dutch had such an excellent command of English.

Oudtshoorn turned to Stoll. 'Do you soon acquaint Mijnheer Renzi with the present workings of the secretariat. He may wish to make changes.'

'Sir,' the young man said, touching his forelock in an old-fashioned way.

After the chief clerk had left, Renzi was obliged to cut short Stoll's earnest conversation and sat behind his vast desk to compose his thoughts.

How utterly unreal it was! After a near-mortal fever, years ago, had led to his quitting the Navy he had not, since then, held any post of consequence he could boast of, and his attempt at establishing a new life in New South Wales had failed miserably.

Since then his closest friend, Thomas Kydd, had provided him with board and lodging in the form of a position aboard his ship while he pursued his studies. It had worked most agreeably, well suited to his character, his horizons always new, never the limited ones of the scholar in his fusty rooms, yet in his own eyes he'd never *really* been gainfully employed.

Now here he was, sitting in state as a colonial secretary, with all the trappings and influence that came from being so close to the summit of power.

He had no illusions about why he had been chosen. For

Baird he was perfect: educated, intelligent, of an appearance and, above all, with no loyalty to a faction. He was not ambitious and, in his *tendre* for scholarship, no threat – and immediately available. His evident connections at the highest with London might prove useful in the future but would at least ensure that he was not trifled with by others.

Out of the corner of his eye he could see Stoll watching him covertly as he busied himself. Renzi bent to his task of finding a form of words for nothing less than the coercion of a people to accept foreign rule. It was a challenge that would test his literary powers to the limits.

He stared ahead, his quill at the ready. Fragments of Pausanias on helotry in conquered peoples drifted into his mind. The Athenians had robust views on rulers and the ruled, pithy aphorisms that went to the core of what it was to extend conquest into dominion.

Pulling himself together, he gave a wry smile. His studies into the vanished worlds of long ago had not prepared him for producing actual decrees and proclamations, of turning political intent into workable public instruments. This was going to be an interesting occupation.

'Whereas . . .' Everything official began that way. Then what? He glanced about for inspiration and found himself catching Stoll's wary eyes. He looked away: it was this man's lands and heritage he was dealing with.

'Whereas a party of Batavian troops, under the Orders of Lieutenant General Janssens is attempting to oppose the authority of the British when further resistance is—' Is useless? The usual denunciation of the oppressor? No – something like, 'injurious to the settlement and its trade' would better serve.

Stoll darted anxious looks towards him. It was no good.

Renzi could not concentrate. He rose slowly and Stoll shot to his feet. 'Oh, er, whose is that office?' Renzi asked, indicating a small side room.

'That is where Mijnheer Höhne, your sworn translator, goes when you call for him, sir.'

'Very well. I shall work there for the moment.'

Stoll blinked in consternation, but said nothing.

Alone at a small desk in the modest room, with a rather charming painting of a Dutch family scene on the wall, Renzi set to with renewed purpose and soon had a draft. He reviewed its phraseology, aware that it would be pinned up in public places.

> *... to inform the Inhabitants of this Colony that being in possession of the Town and principal Places the whole be subject to His Majesty's Authority ... most strictly enjoin them to have no communication with the aforesaid Corps ... will draw upon themselves consequences of the most serious nature ...*

He concluded with a solemn reference to the inevitable miseries of a protracted state of warfare set against a future of prosperity and growth under a settled population, and took it to Baird.

'Exactly so! Fine work, Renzi. You've a translator? Then we'll get it cast in Dutch and set out beneath. We'll have, say, two hundred struck off immediately and posted up. Then we'll need to get our heads together on how we deal with this damned grain shortage.'

Renzi made to leave but Baird called after him, 'Ryneveld took the position. I rather think it a good idea should you make an early official acquaintance.'

'I will, sir.'

'Oh, and – How shall I say it? I'm sure there's a half-decent tailor in town – you'll soon be looking to dress for the part, hey?'

'Point taken, sir.'

If anything the office of the fiscal was grander still than his own and was a hive of activity as the engine of state was in the process of being set in motion.

'Ah, Mr Secretary Renzi!' Ryneveld greeted him with outstretched hands, clearly relieved that order was emerging from chaos. 'Are you content in your accommodation?'

'Why, yes, indeed.' He graciously enquired after the fiscal's own situation, as the playful thought crossed his mind that, if he himself was not happy, he had the power to eject Ryneveld from his office in favour of himself.

'The problems will pass,' Ryneveld said, in happy exasperation. 'My closest post-holders wish to serve, which is gratifying. A working administration is not impossible, I believe.'

He hesitated then added, 'You will not have had the time to set up an establishment of your own – if it is more convenient, my wife Barbetjie and I would be honoured should you dine with us tonight.'

Of course, Renzi realised, as he was now at some eminence in society, he must cut a figure, graciously entertain. He would see to it. But now what better public demonstration of his aligning to the British cause could there be for Ryneveld? 'That is most civil in you, Mijnheer. I should be delighted.'

The afternoon passed pleasantly, the two drawing up a table of positions obtaining in the previous government for reference in forming the new. The wisdom of adopting completely the existing body of governance quickly became apparent – everything from the Court of Justice to the

Chamber for Regulating Insolvent Estates, the Lombard Bank and Orphan Chamber, Tide Waiters and Matrimonial Court, Lands and Woods, all with their subtle interweaving of loyalties time-honoured, understood and ready to serve.

It remained only to win them over, or end with them sullen and obstructive – or worse.

'A good day's work, Mr Secretary. I think we have earned our dinner,' Ryneveld said, first carefully locking his papers in his desk.

'I would rather it were Nicholas.'

'We Dutch are jealous of our honorifics, you'll find. I am Schildknaap Ryneveld to others and would resent its overlooking. Please forgive if "Mr Secretary Renzi" offends, sir.'

Outside, Renzi stood squinting in the late-afternoon sun, admiring the square ramparts of Table Mountain so dominating the landscape.

'My carriage.' Ryneveld beckoned.

The open-topped vehicle was compact and expensively appointed with a youth holding a wide green umbrella over them. The driver clucked at the stocky horse and they lurched forward.

Renzi took in the sights with interest. It was a settlement like no other, at the end of Africa, a vast and mysterious continent that separated it from the old European civilisations of the north. Here, men had settled, their destiny shaped not just by the land but also by surging events happening far, far away.

The town was well laid out – neat, with wide streets and the sun-baked glare of whitewashed houses set off with green shutters and doors. An amazing variety of peoples were abroad: Malay slaves with bundles of faggots, grizzled Bushmen carrying bundles, hard-looking countrymen in broad-brimmed hats, hurriedly followed by a score of men with baskets on their heads – and well-dressed women primly stepping out, each followed by a maid with a silk umbrella, as could be seen in any avenue of Europe.

Ryneveld lived in the lower town, in a relatively modest mansion that was set about with a shady and colourful garden, which Renzi politely admired as they passed through.

'My wife Barbetjie.' A plump, practical-looking lady with an elaborate hair-dressing came to the door and curtsied gracefully to Renzi's formal bow. 'Do enter, good sir,' she said, in quaint English. 'A welcome awaits.'

He was ushered in and offered chilled wine as they sat in the drawing room. With its dark panelling and tiled floor, it was remarkably effective in preserving a cool against the heat outside.

'A singular place, Cape Town,' Renzi ventured.

'As no other,' Ryneveld said firmly. 'Even the flowers, the *fynbos* – and for its beauty and richness of species it stands alone in the world. And where else in this tropical continent might you encounter penguins and fur seals both?'

'Er, are you perhaps inconvenienced at all by the more . . . forward species? The lion and elephant do spring to mind when thinking of Africa.'

'The Cape lion was much feared around Table Mountain in Riebeeck's time but has not been seen this age. The leopard and lynx are still to be encountered, but never the elephant. Nevertheless, if you mean to travel it would be wise to give heed to your guide.'

'Even in town?'

'Here at night you may meet hyenas on their way to devour offal on the foreshore, in the day troops of baboons. More to be respected is the spitting scorpion or perhaps your Cape cobra, its poison every bit as venomous as that of the black mamba,' Ryneveld added.

'Oh. Then the hippopotamus—'

'Our dinner is served, gentlemen.'

They sat down at what was clearly a family meal; Ryneveld at the head, Renzi at the other. Opposite Mevrouw Ryneveld was a shy girl who darted glances at him and next to Renzi a young man with a look of patriotic defiance on his face.

Ryneveld pronounced a Dutch blessing on the meal and raised his eyes. 'Our humble repast – a *bobotie* only,' he said quietly. 'Haasje, do help Mr Secretary Renzi to a portion.'

Renzi enjoyed the spicy dish, meat studded with dried fruit and nuts and topped with a savoury custard. It was clearly a family favourite.

After dinner, the men retired to the library, a discreet and well-appointed room. Renzi stood admiring the volumes while Ryneveld found a bottle with a wax-sealed cork and opened it carefully. 'A Cape liqueur, made with the skin of the naartjie fruit and orange blossom.' Two glasses were produced and filled. 'And named after Admiral van der Hum of the Dutch East India Company who did so admire it.'

The thick golden liquid had a tantalising tangerine flavour but was very sweet. 'A little too sticky? Then we'll add some brandy.'

Ryneveld was the perfect host and Renzi relaxed in his company. Here was a man of the world, an acute observer, whose interest in his guest was not contrived and who took an intelligent pleasure in the discussion of philosophies and the arts.

But the talk petered out when Ryneveld's manner turned grave and introspective.

'The grain famine?' Renzi asked, with concern.

At first the man did not answer, then said woodenly, 'For your nation, if this affair turns out against you then you'll sail away. For me, I shall be left to answer for my conduct.' He set down his glass very carefully. 'Until now we've been able to console ourselves that we have our independence, but for all that, we must understand that we are merely holding the colony for Bonaparte.'

'He's still "protecting" the Netherlands, I gather.'

'The French Army occupies the Low Countries,' Ryneveld agreed, 'but the Batavian Republic forced on us in imitation of the glorious French Revolution is still headed by our own Grand Pensionary Schimmelpenninck, who stands staunch.'

'You're concerned for the mother country,' Renzi said sympathetically.

'I am – but this is not what disturbs me. I was recently given some very unpleasant news concerning it that directly affects us here.'

'Oh?' Renzi felt the warmth of the wine fall away.

'What I have heard confidentially is nothing less than that Napoleon will shortly end the Dutch Republic and place his own brother, Louis, on the throne of Holland in contempt of all the principles of the revolution.'

It was a bombshell. Presumably there was now nothing that could prevent the French taking formal possession of the Dutch colony for themselves.

With a cynical smile Ryneveld continued, 'It's always been said that the Cape is a feather in the hands of the Dutch and a sword in the hands of the French. You can be sure that, now the way is clear, they'll stop at nothing to recover it!'

Renzi's mind raced. Baird must know of this, of course,

but it left him in a frightful situation. Within days of taking possession he faced two major problems: an army still in the field opposing him and the pressing need to reduce numbers by sending away a large proportion of his troops. Would his fragile defences hold against a determined assault?

'I'm no soldier,' Ryneveld said, 'but I'd think that the advantage must still lie with you as defender.'

'Possibly,' Renzi said, with a wry smile. 'Yet Cape Town fell to us, you'll agree.'

'Of course. Your commanders will probably know by now that we were much outnumbered. Goewerneur Janssens did what he could, but who is able to stand against those devilish Highlanders? No, with a professional general of the army at its head, the defenders will make good account of themselves. I suspect that General Baird will want to fall back on the defences of the castle and town – with your ruling of the seas he will not be in want of supply.'

So much depended on Popham – and here such a tiny force to set against a determined foe. 'The Navy will do its duty,' Renzi found himself saying.

'I'm sure it will, if only to honour its great Admiral Nelson. Yet the gravest threat is not to be met on the ocean waves – it is here.'

'The people?'

'Quite. There are those who would be rid of the English, who would think it a duty to take cause with any who could overthrow you.'

'May I know . . . ?'

'I will tell you.' Ryneveld sipped his liqueur. 'The feeling among the general populace is that the French will soon return and overthrow you. These people will fear retaliation for having collaborated and will be reluctant to fall in with you. But the good people of Cape Town, those of property and standing – those we call the Cape Dutch – will see a settled and prosperous future under the free-trade rule of the British as much to be preferred, especially should you stand by your promise to abide by the old laws and customs. They're tired of being cut off from the world, threatened with wars and upheaval not of their making. You'll have no trouble from them.

'They are in small numbers, though. Even counting the lesser sort, the population is only some six thousand, and outnumbered therefore by the slaves who, if you take the rural as well, are some twenty, possibly thirty thousand. These are the Cape Malays from Java, others from Madagascar and the east of Africa, but never from the south. Now, if some hothead or *provocateur* stirs them up I'll leave you to consider the consequences.

'But it's the folk of the country, the *boeren*, whom you must never trust. They are poor, hard, uncouth and restless – and therefore well suited to existence up-country, at the edge of civilisation. You must understand that, since the early days of the VOC – the Vereenigde Oost-Indische Compagnie – which is our Dutch East India Company who founded the colony at the Cape, they've always been rebellious and hostile to rule.

'When the last Stadholder of the Netherlands fled before the French Revolution to England, it was the Boers who supported the Batavian Republic against the VOC here. They'll have no love for a country that shelters the old enemy. And know that they're the core of Janssens's army, some of the best irregular mounted troops anywhere, and loyal only to him.'

Ryneveld picked up his glass again and looked shrewdly at

Renzi. 'So what we must say, Mr Secretary, is that you have made conquest, but how long will you be able to hold it?'

'And so I give you a toast. Gentlemen – t' *Billy Roarer* as is Neptune's right royal favourite!' Gilbey spluttered, red-faced and happy.

'Which is to say includes her noble crew of souls,' Curzon said languidly, knowing it would niggle the first lieutenant, whose efforts to deny his own humble origins led him to keep Jack Tar at a snarling distance.

'And never overlooking the Royals,' Kydd came in, with a gracious nod to Clinton, the young lieutenant of marines, who blushed and raised his glass in return to his captain.

L'Aurore had now rounded southern Africa and was standing out into the Indian Ocean in flying-fish weather, bound for Lourenço Marques and utterly in her element.

Bowden, as Mr Vice and having acquitted himself of the duty of the royal toast, now joined in the merriment. 'Damme, but Mossel Bay was well done, sir!' He chuckled. Their blood-less success there would never make it to the history books but it was the tonic the ship's company needed to put behind them the grim scenes with *Bato*.

He posed, theatrically hanging his head and intoned:

> *When first on board this ship I went,*
> *My belly full, my mind content –*
> *No sorrow touched my heart:*
> *I view'd my coat, so flash and new,*
> *My gay cockade, my hanger too,*
> *And thought them wondrous smart;*
> *But now, alas! My coat is rent,*
> *My hanger's pawned, my money spent;*

Shiv'ring walk the quarterdeck,
Dreading first lieutenant's check
Who struts the weather side!

Amid the appreciative applause Curzon came in with another, delivered in a charming boyish falsetto:

I'm here or there a jolly dog,
At land or sea I'm all agog,
To fight, or kiss, or touch the grog –
O! I'm but a jovial mid-ship-man!

About to launch into the second verse, he stopped awkwardly and ribald cries went up. 'Go on, sir! Can y' not remember the words?'

But in the august presence of their captain it would never do to continue the rest of the racy ballad. Bowden came to the rescue, the only one in the gunroom who knew their commander had a voice. 'Sir, can you feel it in your heart to favour us with . . . ?'

Kydd quickly reviewed his repertoire, which now included pieces from salon and drawing room, but they were not what was wanted. Instead he held up his hand and in the respectful hush began in a soft but manly baritone:

Tom Truelove woo'd the sweetest fair
That e'er to tar was kind;
Her face was of a beauty rare,
More beautiful her mind;
This tale, his mess-mates sorrowing tell,
How sad and solemn three times rang;
Tom Truelove's knell . . .

When he finished there was an incredulous silence then a storm of acclamation. It had brought a rush of sailorly feeling, the age-old warmth of mariners alone together in a far-off sea, tender remembrances of a native land stealing into their thoughts to soften their existence.

Another wistful song was offered by Bowden, one more from Curzon and, after obliging remarks on the efforts of the officers' cook that evening, the gunroom lapsed into an introspective quiet.

'I'm thinking we should be raising a glass t' our little piece o' empire,' Gilbey reflected moodily, 'as they've got so much going against 'em.'

Clinton snorted, his face flushed. 'Blaauwberg showed Johnny Dutchman what we can do, damn their eyes!'

'An undefeated army in the field, nothing in the granary and a country half the size of Europe to hold down – I'll wager we'll be packing our bags for England in the space of a three-month,' Peyton said cynically, helping himself to the bottle.

'Never so, Doctor!' the master, Kendall, rumbled. It was the first he had spoken that night and heads turned to listen. 'We've a navy second t' none other, c'n keep ourselves well supplied an' them Hollanders starving. An' never forget, any wants t' take the Cape back has to get past us.'

'Get past us?' Peyton drawled sarcastically. 'Then you haven't heard of the heavy squadrons Bonaparte sent to sea after Trafalgar? Three, or was it four, sir?' he challenged Kydd.

'Five, I believe,' Kydd said mildly. 'Let me see . . . We've L'Hermite in the Gulf o' Guinea with frigates, Leissègues with four o'-the-line – but he's for the Caribbean, I fancy. La Meillerie with four frigates off West Africa, but Willaumez with six battleships in the South Atlantic at this moment and Maréchal still in the Indian Ocean.'

'And we with a couple of paltry sixty-fours and a single pair of frigates – even if one be none other than His Majesty's Ship *L'Aurore*,' Peyton returned, his words heavy with irony.

There was an edge to Kydd's voice as he replied, 'I should leave the strategicals to us, Doctor. The gentlemen here are not concerned, neither should you be.'

'Has anyone stepped ashore in this Lourenço Marques?' Bowden asked lightly. 'I've never heard of it before now.'

It seemed there were none who had in fact done so. 'As it needs our Mr Renzi t' tip us the griff,' Gilbey said, solemnly regarding his port. There was a general murmur of agreement: Renzi was a valued member of the gunroom and his presence missed.

'The pilot hasn't much t' say,' Kendall said thoughtfully. 'Around twenty-five south latitude, one o' the last half-good harbours sailin' south.'

'Portuguese,' Kydd said. 'Been there since the fifteen hundreds, the south part of their old empire they share with the Moors – Zanzibar and other places. Should be a fine place to stretch the legs.'

The mood brightened at the prospect of an exotic foreign port with novel sights and smells.

'Then here's to Lorency Marks!' Peyton said gleefully, raising his glass.

L'Aurore stretched out willingly, slashing through the glittering seas away from Africa to reach her destination in two boards, not only to make her northing in the face of the north-easterly monsoon but as well to avoid the fast south-going Agulhas current close to the coast.

It was a time to gladden the heart of any sailor. Close-hauled with gear set for long watches at a time, the frigate was rock-steady and predictable, her motion easy and sweet, an occasional burst of salt spray over the bows carrying aft.

Forward, the old sailmaker Greer smiled with satisfaction as the boatswain and his party sent up a patched staysail while the watch on deck sat cross-legged around the main-hatchway teasing oakum, an unassailable excuse to tell yarns and gossip.

At the conn, Lieutenant Bowden gave a shy smile at Kydd, clearly relishing the conditions. Kendall, beside him, was taking in the vast blue bowl of sky with a tranquil gaze, and the quartermaster, having little to do, contentedly chewed his tobacco, gazing with a faraway look out over the headsails.

On impulse Kydd removed his hat and began a leisurely pace forward, enjoying the sights of a frigate in her prime on a bowline, the comfortable creak and thrum of her passage, the gratifying symmetry of masts and lines, sheer and camber, the—

'*Saaail, ho! Saaail three points t' the weather bow!*'

The urgent hail from the foremast lookout cut into his thoughts. At deck level it would be some time before they became visible and it could be anything – there were active trade routes in this part of the world that made it likely to be a merchant ship. But this far out?

'*Deck, hooo! I see three sail – an' big 'uns!*'

Three men-o'-war? Only too aware of the French heavy squadrons at sea, Kydd turned and hurried back to the quarterdeck. 'Close as she'll lie!' he snapped, now fully alert.

L'Aurore was in no real danger: she could wheel and make off downwind at any time she chose, and if these were indeed Willaumez or Maréchal, then his duty was clear. He would shadow them until he could establish their course, then clap on every stitch of canvas to get the news to Cape Town. At this distance he could be sure of reaching there days ahead of lumbering battleships.

Another hail. *'I see eight of 'em – no frigates!'*

Kydd breathed a sigh of relief: scouting frigates ahead of the squadron could make it very hard for any shadower.

Away to weather, tiny pale shapes interrupted the horizon as they hove into view, three, four and more until all eight were visible. Gilbey had his sextant up, held flat as he measured the angle between the strangers and *L'Aurore*'s course. Another sighting, minutes later, confirmed that the distant ships would pass ahead by some margin.

'Stand down the men,' Kydd ordered.

'Sir?' said Bowden, puzzled.

'Do you not think it significant that they're holding course?'

'That they think us not worthy of attention?'

'Not at all . . .'

'Ah! They've other business – they're a John Company convoy!'

'Well done, Mr Bowden. However, I do think we'll make our number – for a certainty they've not heard of our taking Cape Town.'

For any mariner, after weeks in the oceanic vastness, another ship was always of the deepest interest and the calling to of an important East India Company convoy must seize the attention of every soul in the fleet.

'Then what is your news, sir, that I'm obliged to stop my progress?' the commodore said loftily, but with barely concealed anticipation. 'Consols above five per cent? The nabobs combining against the tax?'

'I'm to inform you that His Majesty's arms have met with success on the field of Blaauwberg before Cape Town and as a result the colony is ours.'

'And?'

Kydd blinked. 'This is a development of some significance, sir.'

'Really? I can't see why. It's never been our practice to rely on touching at the Cape, and the Dutch have never seen fit to interfere with our trade. What, then, is it to us?'

'To take on fresh victuals, allow your passengers ashore – er, to fettle your ships?'

'Hmmph. Your notions on what is of significance to us is singular, sir. I'll have you know the concerns of a convoy commodore are many. At the moment I've no notion where two of my most valuable sail are – they scattered in a blow during the night.'

Kydd bristled – then realised that the stately convoy must have been outward bound for over a month and would not have had word of the greatest news of all. 'Of course, this is not the reason why I've seen fit to speak to you, sir.'

'Oh?'

'It's my duty to acquaint you of a great battle, the grandest this age in which the combined fleets of France and Spain were finally met by the British fleet under Admiral Lord Horatio Nelson off Cape Trafalgar.'

'Yes? And?' the commodore said incredulously, jerking upright.

'Sadly, Lord Nelson died of his wounds at the height of the battle and is now lost to us.'

'Good God!' The commodore fell back, stupefied.

'As it happens, I was present at the engagement,' Kydd added.

'But – how was . . . Did we prevail? How many – Sir, can I offer you sherry? You're in no hurry at all?'

'That is very kind in you, sir, but the progress of your convoy . . .'

The change of attitude was gratifying, and Kydd gave a powerful account of events, then added sombrely, 'Now Bonaparte has changed the French conduct of the war at sea. Not able to face our fleet, he's sent numbers of his battle squadrons to harry our trade.' He went on to detail the forces unleashed.

The man's face lengthened: the big privateers based on the French-held Indian Ocean islands were bad enough and the pairs of frigates sent roaming the sea-lanes were worse, but to have to cope with a naval battle squadron was unthinkable. 'This is grave news, sir. This ship alone bears some six chests of specie and silks to a very great value. Its loss would be catastrophic. And the others – why, in sum it could bankrupt entire trading companies, even cause panic and a run on 'Change! So what does the Navy propose to do, Captain?' he challenged.

If sail-of-the-line were taken from their blockade to chase the enemy squadrons it would achieve what Villeneuve had failed to – a lifting of the clamping hold on the French ports and thus the ability of their navy to combine and fall on England. The Admiralty would never countenance it.

'I'm not privy to the dispositions of my commander-in-chief, sir, but you may be sure that there are fast squadrons of our own in close pursuit.' Whatever could be scraped together from a badly overstretched navy, and set to find their quarry anywhere in the immensity of oceans across the globe, he reflected cynically.

Kydd concluded with a promise to send newspapers of

Trafalgar – the gunroom would still have them – and took his leave. In the boat returning to *L'Aurore* he looked back thoughtfully at the convoy: grand ships of the illustrious British East India Company, run on a discipline little different from the Navy's and in their bellies the treasure that was allowing Britain to defy the whole of Europe. They must win through.

L'Aurore took up again eagerly, a picture of grace and warlike beauty as she leaned to the wind. In a short while the last of the Indiamen were hull down and then their sails disappeared below the horizon, and the seascape was as if they had never been.

Alone once more, the frigate sped on. 'I'll tack about now, I believe, Mr Kendall,' Kydd said. The manoeuvre was performed at a leisurely pace – there was no point in straining gear – and then they were on the final leg, their course set direct for Lourenço Marques.

Almost unbelievably there was another cry from the masthead. '*Saaail! All t' weather, three – no, five saaail!*'

It couldn't be another John Company convoy. Then came another hail. '*Deck, hooo! They're all alterin' course towards!*'

This was the confident act of warships but it was vanishingly unlikely that this was a British squadron for he hadn't been told to expect any. It was the enemy.

Kydd hailed back: '*Whaaat shiiips?*'

There was a hesitation as the lookout strained to see, clinging to a line, his body unconsciously leaning forward while he shaded his eyes. '*I see two sail-o'-the-line, three frigates!*' he finally called down.

Kydd's orders were straightforward: he was to shadow and report. Yet here was a puzzle: why was the entire squadron going after his single frigate?

Then the icy thought blasted in that this powerful force was in the wake of the East India Company convoy, bare hours astern of them.

Upwind of them, the French were in a dominating position but only one thing stood between them and the convoy: *L'Aurore*. Against two line-of-battle ships his brave vessel would not survive the first broadside. Yet to step aside and let a catastrophe happen was intolerable. He must try to buy them time.

'Mr Kendall—' Even as he was about to give his orders the answer came as to why they were crowding after *L'Aurore*: they assumed she was an outlying escort and would lead them directly to the convoy.

'Lay us on the other tack,' he called to the sailing master, 'with all haste, and I do expect you to miss stays.'

While *L'Aurore* floundered in her fright and confusion at sighting the French, Kydd ordered the master's mate, 'Make a signal, Mr Saxton!'

Bewildered, the young man fumbled for his notebook then took down, 'To commander-in-chief: my fore-topsail yard is sprung. I request leave to both watches and – numeral five – men overboard.'

Saxton opened his mouth, then thought better of it and hurried away. Soon three hoists were urgently fluttering aloft as the frigate plunged off to warn her convoy – in precisely the opposite direction.

Would it work?

The topgallants of the enemy were just in sight from the deck; if they took the bait, the tiny white sunlit sails should foreshorten as they hauled their wind in chase. If not, *L'Aurore* would pass them by and they would disappear.

His mouth dry with tension, Kydd stared out at the distant

cluster, willing them to change. Slowly their aspect altered, the glare of white from the sun fading. And it was . . . all of them. Every one of the French squadron was now in pursuit of *L'Aurore*, being drawn away from the convoy.

But for how long? Any false move on his part and *L'Aurore*'s bluff would be called. For a certainty the French commander would then fall back on his original track, straight towards the convoy.

The leading ships were hull-up now, their angling course allowing them closer. At that moment, therefore, *L'Aurore* was under tight scrutiny from telescopes. Kydd kept his own glass on them for there was one move that would turn the tables – if the French detached the faster frigates to deal with him and then, ranging further, found nothing.

But the frigates were kept back: the cautious French were playing safe in case *L'Aurore* was a scout for a distant British squadron, tasked to lure them on to bigger ships. They were left unmolested to play out their gambit and Kydd's anxiety began to subside. If he could keep them on this course after him until dark they would be drawn sufficiently clear of the convoy.

One piece of irony was that *L'Aurore* was easily outpacing the French when she should be keeping well in sight, leading them on. If this squadron was Maréchal's then it must have been at sea for months, if not years, and was slowed by marine growth. He ordered a discreet drag-sail over the bows that would keep them in sight.

Kydd was gratified: a classic manoeuvre of evasion and deception had saved the priceless argosy at the cost of not a single shot. And probably not too severe a delay in reaching Lourenço Marques. All in all it was— He was interrupted by the sudden cry of a lookout. '*Deck, hoooo! A sail – no two, right*

175

ahead!' It was absurd – three sightings so close, here in the vast reaches of the ocean.

Was this the other jaw of a trap? It made no sense – why was the whole squadron involved? And, in any event, how could these two know which course *L'Aurore* would take? If it was all by chance, was this the rest of Maréchal's scouting force? Or an English naval detachment? Or innocent strangers caught up in a larger war? Whatever the reality, a decision had to be made. If—

'*They's Indiamen!*' came the disbelieving cry from the lookout. Then Kydd remembered the commodore had mentioned that two of his charges had been separated in the night. And, by the cruellest misfortune, *L'Aurore*'s ploy had led the French straight to them. In one stroke it had altered the situation decisively and he must take the consequences.

'Cast off the drag-sail!' he roared forward, and snapped the orders to make straight for the pair. Forcing his mind to an icy coolness, he weighed up the alternatives. Abandoning the two merchantmen to their fate in the face of such odds was unthinkable – it would make his name a byword for dishonour. This left only the heroic and ultimately useless sacrifice of *L'Aurore* in their forlorn defence – the logic of war demanded it and that was what had to be done.

He would not make it easy: it would be played out to the last throw. There was the tiniest chance that if he could get the Indiamen to wear about and flee for their lives then, with the enemy slowed by their bottoms being foul, the two Company ships could disappear into the enfolding night – but that was hours away.

In the Indiamen someone quick-witted enough to work out what was afoot had them wheeling about without being told, seeing Kydd's colours if not his nonsense signal.

All too soon, however, it was apparent why they had separated from the convoy. One of the two that flew the bright red stripes of the Company was favouring her foremast. She had unseasonable reefs in her topsail and course – probably the mast had sprung in some squall, unbalancing other sails and making for poor sailing. The other was low in the water, no doubt having sprung a leak in the same blow from wrung timbers. They had almost certainly come together for mutual protection against privateers but, thanks to *L'Aurore*, they now faced a battle group.

It was the damnedest, most evil luck, and before long the last act must be played out. The mercy was that it would be very quick: once battle was joined they had not the slightest chance. The only question was whether the French commander would send in the frigates to finish it, preserving his 74 from damage.

Kydd would use *L'Aurore*'s speed and superior wind-holding to best advantage, but the act of protecting would sadly limit his manoeuvring options to just a small space of sea. In terms of tactical planning, there was nothing he could do.

When they had overhauled the Indiamen, Kydd hailed the closest with a speaking trumpet as they bucketed along close together. Few words were spoken, the unknown captain opposite acknowledging with a heartfelt 'Good luck!' and sweeping his hat down in an elaborate bow.

Kydd's instructions to them had been brief: course would be altered to more full and bye, and when the point came for play with the guns *L'Aurore* would fight for time, while they fled in opposite directions to what safety they could find.

L'Aurore then took position on the enemy side and the

three made their best speed for the far horizon. Ironically the conditions were perfect for sailing, the north-easterly steady and urging and no more than a slight swell from the east. Overhead the sky was an immensity of glorious blue with little cloud, and in any other circumstances would have the watch below spending their leisure on deck, admiring their racing motion.

After an hour it became clear that they were losing the race. The French were now in sight from the deck and beginning to spread out as manoeuvring positions were being taken. There would be gunfire before dusk.

Then Kydd heard an indistinct shouting from the men on the fore-deck and saw some pointing away to the east. One broke away and ran to the quarterdeck. Kydd cursed under his breath – settling a quarrel was the last thing on his mind.

It was the seaman Pinto, obviously distracted. 'Sir – sir, look! T' the east'd!'

Taken aback he looked to where Pinto was pointing at a cloud not as big as man's fist but somewhat darker than the others and with a distinctive reddish centre some thirty or so degrees above the horizon.

'Sir! This I been told b' my shipmates as have traded wi' Africa is the Ox-eye!'

'Get back for'ard, y' Portugee fool!' Gilbey flared. 'We'll have none o' y'r Papist notions aboard this ship!'

'Hold!' Kydd said. Before he'd been elevated to the quarterdeck he had been mess-mates with Pinto and knew the man not to be given to superstition. 'What's then your Ox-eye?'

'Is called "*Olho de boi*" – the eye of bull – an' we see it before a terrible kind o' storm.'

'Have you heard of this, Mr Kendall?'

'I never have, sir. That's not to say the Portuguese don't have a right steer on things, they being in these waters a mort longer'n we.'

'Tell us more about your Ox-eye.'

Pinto looked scornfully at the first lieutenant, then explained that it was portent to a tempest of unusual severity, one coming with no warning other than the Ox-eye, which would grow in size until it dominated the heavens.

Kydd regarded the seas, as easy as they had ever been, a low swell from the east, no omen of a tempest in the offing, all in hand. He looked again at the cloud: small, ovoid and with a red centre; harmless in itself. Then back at the pursuing French. If Pinto was right, they should batten down for the storm soon – but if he was wrong it would be madness to shorten sail at this point: they would then be most surely delivering themselves up to the enemy. On the other hand, if he was right and it was ignored, the ship was in grave danger. How the devil could he confirm the truth of it?

'Mr Gilbey,' he said formally, 'I desire every officer and midshipman to muster in the gunroom.' What he had in mind was nothing less than the violation of a gentleman's privacy.

When the mystified group had assembled he told them, 'I've been advised that the odd-looking cloud to starboard means there's a right clinker of a blow coming.'

The officers looked at each other uneasily. 'Sir, you're surely not giving ear t' the Portuguee?' Gilbey growled. 'Such cat-blash as—'

'We've a chance – a small one – to find out. If he's right, we need to know about it. If he's wrong, no harm done. There's one whose intellects I've reason to trust, but he's not aboard this day.'

The purser arrived, looking confused. 'Ah, Mr Owen. Be

so good as to open Mr Renzi's cabin. Gentlemen, you are to make use of the library you'll see there to discover references to this "Ox-eye" or in the Portuguese, "*Olho de boi*".'

He smiled at their astonishment – he was sure Renzi would appreciate the drollery of the situation. 'And I've no need to mention that time is pressing,' he added, stepping aside to let them in.

They set to, each selected a volume from the neat racks occupying two sides of the cabin up to the deckhead, and brought it to the gunroom table where brows furrowed in concentration.

Even Kydd was amazed at the abstruse variety of Renzi's reading. Thick works on the philosophies of the Ottomans, others on the agricultural practices of native peoples, still more on jurisprudence considered culturally – and, blessedly, a shelf and a half on travels and histories.

Curzon was the first to spot it. In a frayed book a century old, *Mechanism Macrocosm* by one Purshall, there was reference to 'those Dreadful Storms on the coast of Africa, which the seamen call the "Ox-eye" from their Beginning'.

It was tantalising but more was needed. Bowden came upon a slim and very old piece, *Discoveries and Voyages to the East and West Indies*, a translated Dutch work with a passing reference, but then he struck gold in a dictionary. '*Olho de boi*' – from *Vocabulario Portuguez e Latino* of the Lisbon of eighty years before. But it was all in Portuguese.

'Get Pinto!'

Awed to be in the presence of so many expectant officers, he took the book gingerly, and frowned. 'Ah, the Portuguese navigators o' the Orient Sea, is what we call t' the east of Africa. Where we is now,' he said, in dawning wonder.

'Get on with it!' Gilbey said peevishly.

'Be silent, sir!' Kydd snapped. 'Carry on, Pinto – anything as can show us what we face.'

'Says, Ox-eye start from little, grow wi' colour o' the funeral, until the face of heaven he turn scareful an' then the wind come. Captains mus' lower yards an' topmasts for is sudden an' dreadful. It say our Bartolomeu Dias when he sail in this sea in 1488 he—'

'Thank you, Pinto,' Kydd said, and summoned the sailing master. 'Mr Kendall, your opinion, please.'

He listened to the description, then rubbed his chin. 'Aye, well, it sounds main like a weather gall, the most common being a rainbow. If that's what it be, an' so quick, then I've a notion it's talking of a tropical storm in the character of a local blow, but it has to be very . . . intense, if y' gets my meaning.'

'We batten down.'

'If 'n the signs are there, sir.'

The Ox-eye had grown, spreading laterally across the horizon, darkening and adding livid yellow to the red in its centre in a menacing show of aggression. Oddly, there was no indication of an approaching tempest, no high winds, heaving swell – nothing but the broadening ugliness.

'Frenchies don't mind,' muttered Gilbey. There was no sign of a slackening in the pace of the pursuit.

'I'm thinking it'll be all of a sudden, like, when it comes,' Kendall said, troubled. 'All that talk o' striking topmasts an' such.'

Kydd hesitated – there was still a wild chance they could make the safety of night, and if he was wrong he would be for ever damned as a looby in the Navy. Then, there was a flurry in the steady north-easterly, a flaw that set the sails to a momentary bellying and slatting before settling. And it had come from out of the east – right in line with the baneful Ox-eye, which was now distorted and barely distinguishable in the crepuscular wall of melancholy occupying near half the horizon.

'We do it!' he muttered. He turned to the master and ordered, 'Lay us alongside each of the Indiamen – they'll have to know we haven't lost our wits.'

The first was disbelieving and tried to object but Kydd was adamant. The second had heard vaguely of the phenomenon and was more prepared to comply. Both were sent to strike tophamper and distance themselves from each other.

'Mr Kendall, bosun – we're to douse all sail and send down topmasts. And we bring down the lower yards a-portlast!' This action of laying the heavy spars down across the gunwales would lower the centre of gravity.

The pursuing French were visibly put out: as sail vanished from their prey they themselves took in canvas, unsure, wary of a trap. But it was becoming very apparent that something dire was brewing.

By the time *L'Aurore*'s yards were down the sky overhead was darkening, the sunlight cut off and the entire eastern aspect hung in livid, hideous greens and ochre upon the mass of dark grey. It had been only an hour or so from the first sighting of the Ox-eye when the winds began to break loose, slamming in from the north-east off the bow to past the beam, directly from the east. If sail had not been brought in they would certainly have been caught aback.

More spiteful blasts rattled the rigging, and combers could be seen here and there, startling white against the grey, the wind now driving almost always from the east. There was little talk along the decks, as men stared out at the gathering phenomenon.

Then they witnessed a strange sheeting across the surface of the sea: unnatural, flat, fan-like shapes of torn white instantly spreading and being replaced randomly by others, so when the wind hit, it was with a shocking force that sent men teetering and set *L'Aurore* to an uneasy rolling.

This was like nothing Kydd had experienced before. He grabbed a line and tried to peer into the lunatic hammering from the east. The entire sea was now flattened into a tortured expanse of white, yet waves had not appeared – was it that the 'fetch' of the winds was too short to build up a sea?

Again strangely, there was no rain – the darkness overhead threatened a deluge but the slam of wind remained dry, then grew damply warm in a ferocious onslaught, droning and howling dismally among *L'Aurore*'s stark rigging. The frigate for some reason started a nervous wallow and Kydd saw that it was because her head had fallen off the wind, which bullied and blustered mercilessly at her side, slewing her broadside to it.

It could only be that the sea-anchor, prudently led over the bows, had parted. Broadside to the blast *L'Aurore* rolled like a log, viciously and frighteningly, but Kydd knew the experienced fo'c'slemen would be doing all they could to get another out quickly.

Then the rain came: in storm-driven downpours, bruising torrents that had Kydd bent double to breathe, his sodden, flogging garments a trial as he held on grimly. There was a perceptible quiver and lurch, and *L'Aurore* was sullenly jibbing to the second sea-anchor, bringing round to face the wind once more.

The merchantmen had long since disappeared into the

chaos of spume and darkness and the immediate need was to endure. God knew where they'd have been if they had not struck the topmasts and laid the yards down. No doubt in times past ships must have encountered this terrifying phenomenon and never lived to tell the tale, just vanished into the deep.

In an hour or so the rain had diminished and the frenzied battering lessened to a steady hard driving from the east. There was no navigating in this but there was sense in trying to reduce the awful strains aloft. Kydd raised salt-sore eyes to meet Kendall's. 'We'll scud,' he croaked, 'reefed fore-topsail, fore-topmast staysail.' The topsail would impel *L'Aurore* before the blast, lifting the bow, and the staysail would act to damp any deadly yaw.

The rain cleared and a desolate grey seascape was revealed – an empty expanse with not a sign of any of the ships that had occupied his attention. When their sails tentatively took the fearful wind, *L'Aurore* immediately began to roll. It was not the characterful motion they were used to, running before the wind, but a vicious, screwing heave that had each man reaching for a solid hold.

At the same time there was a near unstoppable yaw from one side to the other that left the four helmsmen struggling. 'A cable, let out over each quarter,' he shouted hoarsely at the boatswain, clinging to the mizzen shrouds.

Oakley nodded and, working hand to hand, made his way below. Kydd watched him go – his was a near impossible job: in the insane rolling, he had to rouse out a substantial hawser and heave it overboard to trail in their wake as a damper on the yawing.

It was finally done. The yawing eased and *L'Aurore* plunged on before the wind into the gathering darkness. Mercifully, with the night, the winds eased, and with little in the way of swell, the waves subsided. Only a few hours had passed, from the first appearance of the Ox-eye to its dissipation. Kendall had had it right: it was a species of local tempest that was short but shockingly intense, a product of the tropic regions.

The morning brought an innocent sky, the wind a kindly north-easter once more, the sea a picture of blue tranquillity. It was time to take stock.

Thanks to their precautions, there was no serious hurt to the frigate, and hands were set to clearing away between decks the broken articles, mess slopping about, all expected consequences of foul weather.

But where were they? They had been some hundreds of miles from the coast of Africa and south of Madagascar when the Ox-eye had hit. Then they had scudded before the wind – an easterly, so ironically they had been urged on towards their final destination, Lourenço Marques. They must now find their latitude, which would be possible with precision at noon.

The French were nowhere to be seen, but neither were the Indiamen. Who knew what had happened to them in those wild hours of the previous day? One mystery was solved later that afternoon: two ships close together were sighted ahead and away to the north. They turned out to be the Indiamen, one under tow by the other and relieved to be still afloat. The big ships' much higher freeboard had enabled them to survive the rolling at the cost of offering a larger area for the wind to press against and they had wisely chosen to scud before it.

Their latitude placed them comfortably south of the Limpopo River further up the coast from Lourenço Marques and it was with some relief that Kydd shaped course towards it, closing with the coast. That left just one concern: where were the French?

The immediate task was to get the Indiamen to safe harbour. As the three storm-lashed ships made their way slowly south, Kydd and the master conferred.

The only chart Kendall had been able to locate was a private Dutch one of ancient provenance. It seemed to warn of a breaking bar across the entrance to the port, one Baixo Paiva Manso. Past that, it opened into a dismaying twenty-mile expanse of shoals at the estuary of the Rio Espiritu Santo. And in several places at the point where the river discharged into the sea there was the ominous-sounding *zand-golven,* which had been underlined by an unknown hand. It didn't need much guessing to realise it meant sub-sea sand waves, shifting, unchartable hazards.

Without a pilot, it was going to be a difficult passage, and when they arrived off the sprawling whitish sand-hills and sliding overfalls of the river mouth, the bar was breaking and visible, but not the treacherous sand waves.

With a seaman at the fore-chains chanting the depths and another aft, they slipped past the scrubby margin of Africa in the rising heat until they were within the twin low arms of Ponta da Macenta and opposite, the Ponta dos Elefantes, the wind fair for their goal.

Lourenço Marques lay ten miles further, and Kydd had kept quiet about his fear that, if this was the only port worth the name on the coast to find safe haven, would not the French head for it as well?

It was too late now: they were within the bay and the wind that made it fair for entry would at the same time make a hasty exit impossible. They went on, the coast to starboard rising in dark-green cliffs. Here and there palm-tree clumps rose above the vegetation, and as they closed with the land, the fetid fragrance of Africa reached out to them.

Then at the sharp turn into the river there it was: a decaying fortress set about with palm trees and scrub, a scatter of humble dwellings and fishing boats. Lourenço Marques, the most southerly outpost of the ancient Portuguese Empire.

And not a Frenchman to be seen.

Chapter 8

It was a masterly stroke, Renzi conceded, and one that could never have been contemplated in any modern state. The grain shortage was the biggest single problem facing them and Baird, in a direct, soldierly manner, had found a way to solve it.

Recognising that it was a matter of survival until the ships he had sent out returned, he had set about looking for an interim local supply and reasoned that there had to be those who would hide supplies with a view to cashing in at famine rates and farmers who were withholding their grain in the hope of higher returns.

By a simple device he had trumped both. A regulation was introduced that repealed duties but specified that sales of cereal crops would henceforth be at a fixed price, which would be rigorously enforced. In fairness, the government would also be bound by this and in fact was opening its grain stores for immediate purchases.

Before long creaking lines of ox-wagons materialised as

hoarded stocks were brought in and government stores swelled. The crisis had been averted.

The question of currency had not been so easy. As most English specie had been lost in the Brazilian wreck what was to be the common coinage? There had been only two options: print banknotes against the Treasury in faraway London or continue to use the current system.

Baird had chosen to avoid the risks of runaway inflation in printing their own, which left no option but to persevere with what existed. The trouble was that ships touching at the Cape for centuries had left the colony awash with the most exotic forms of coinage, each one of which had to have its English equivalent.

The official medium of exchange was the *rijksdaalder* or, as it was more commonly known, the rixdollar, and it was Renzi's task to draw up a table of equivalence: the rixdollar of forty-eight *stuivers* against each coin of foreign origin and that against English sterling.

It was a far from trivial undertaking, for there were those who stood to make a tidy sum if the conversion was struck in their favour. It was no longer to be the sentiment of the market that decided rates, and opinions were sharply and loudly divided.

With Ryneveld's canny assistance Renzi completed the wording of the grand proclamation. It allowed that, for the better regulation of trade and the prevention of disputes, the values of money in circulation in Cape Town should be fixed in accordance with the table shown.

Only the more common were listed: the doubloon, Spanish dollar, rupee and ducat, the pagoda, johanna and Venetian sequin, and each with its value in *stuivers* and sterling. It had been a long task but diverting, complexity to be discovered in even the seemingly simplest economic activity of man.

Baird read it carefully then frowned. 'And you'd let us be ruined, Renzi, old chap?'

Puzzled, Renzi took it back. 'Er, you're in dispute at the rates, sir?'

'No, not at all.'

'The wording?'

'Splendid, as far as it goes.'

'But?'

'My dear fellow, you're too honest for this world. What if our fixed rate for the gold mohur is less than what some rupee wallah offers in Bombay? Why, next thing every merchant worth the name will be sending 'em over by the sackful for the premium, leaving us bare.'

'Um, quite,' Renzi said uncomfortably.

'Don't worry about it, old chap – I'll add a bit about export o' specie in use in the settlement being forbidden under pain of confiscation. Do get that in and posted up quickly. Oh, and one more thing. I'm supposing it's your first public appearance, so to speak?'

'Er?'

Baird chuckled. 'On the proclamation, under where it says all that about "Given under my hand and seal this day," and so forth, surely we'll see "By Order of His Excellency, N. Renzi, Colonial Secretary," shall we not?

'But now – some disturbing news. This was found in a waterfront *taphuis* by one of our redcoats.'

He handed across a handbill roughly printed in Dutch.

'It's Janssens's work, urging all patriot Boers to rally to his colours in the mountains. I have to deal with it – there's too many of these fellows up-country he can call upon. I'm without delay sending General Beresford with a column to invest his redoubt.'

'These are military operations, sir.'

'They do concern you, Renzi. The only effective move is to send an overwhelming force to smoke him out and persuade him of the hopelessness of his position.'

'You're going to strip Cape Town of its garrison?'

'I am. While this is in train the settlement will be as near as damnit defenceless. I want you and your fiscal friend to give ear to every rumour, keep an eye on those who stand to gain by an uprising, and let me know the minute there's a hint of unrest. We'll deal with it together in some way.'

'Sir, there's no question of a spying against the citizens?' Renzi asked.

'Good heavens, no. I'll not stand for it. Just do your best, get close to the locals and don't delay in alerting me. Do always be aware – I've sent my dispatches to London after Blaauwberg, but it'll be months before we get a reply, let alone supply and reinforcements. We're on our own out here, Renzi. The only ones we may rely on are ourselves. We're free to make decisions but then we take the consequences – as I'd want it, wouldn't you?'

Baird's bullish confidence was infectious. 'Exactly so, sir,' Renzi agreed.

'Then here's some more decisions. You're going to say I'm leaving us defenceless. However, I've an idea that Janssens's Hottentots, who did so nobly at Blaauwberg and, o' course, are still prisoners under guard in barracks, these fellows would find it not impossible to contemplate continuing service, this time for the King. I'll raise some sort of Cape Regiment with officers seconded from our forces.'

Renzi nodded in admiration of the move: the civil security

of the town assured and so many fewer useless mouths to feed.

But there was a question. 'Would you not be concerned for their loyalty?'

'Ah – that's where you come in, Renzi.'

'Sir?'

'Draw me up a form of oath. A pledge of allegiance to the Crown as all citizens must swear, good and simple so even the dunderheads may understand.'

'Very well.'

'Quick as you can, there's a good fellow.'

Renzi left for his office, thoughts whirling. So this was what it was to create a brave colonial outpost that would develop in later years into a city and state of consequence. At school, children would be taught about the beginnings of their society and receive a smooth account of it but never know the reality – men of initiative and quick thinking taking the lead, chance events shaping the direction matters must take, individual acts that in sum made hopes possible . . . or not. In essence, here was the crucible forming history – and he, Mr Colonial Secretary Renzi, was centrally involved, forging the very instruments of state.

He felt a surge of excitement and pride as he lifted his pen and got to work. It did not take long: the ancient preamble was in use in so many other documents and the intent was clear. He looked at the draft and fleetingly wished his prose had more of the romantic and grave majesty that lay behind the great utterances of England but consoled himself that this was for an immediate purpose, not the handing down over generations.

His Majesty George the Third, by the grace of God King of the United Kingdom of Great Britain and Ireland, being now in possession of the Settlement, I do promise and bind myself by my oath to be faithful and bear true allegiance to His said Majesty so long as He shall retain possession of the same.

It would do. He wrote out a fair copy and returned to find Baird at his desk, his head in his hands at the burdens he was facing. 'Do you wish me to return later, Sir David?' he asked gently.

Baird smiled tiredly. 'If you do your duty, Renzi, then so must I. Let me see what you have.' He scrutinised it carefully, then laid it down. 'Yes, a very competent production. We shall have every burgher and Boer in the land take oath on it.'

'And if they demur?'

'They shall be regarded as prisoners-of-war and shipped out with lands and chattels forfeit. Fair enough?'

Renzi gave a half-smile. 'Then, sir, I shall have these printed and start a register of those complying.' A little ceremony in the castle courtyard, some form of witnessed signing by hand? He'd leave the details to Ryneveld. 'Is that all, sir?'

'Not quite. It does cross my mind that perhaps at this time we should extend the hand of friendship, offer reconciliation, fraternal regard and so forth. After all, if we're all going to be Afrikaners together . . .'

'An assembly – a reception of sorts?'

'I was thinking more along the lines of a ball. Here at the Castle of Good Hope, at which we might see the good Dutch matrons with their daughters and our handsome young subalterns consort. Nothing like a bit of manoeuvring together to get the fraternal blood up.'

'In company with the great and good of Cape Town?'

'Naturally.'

Renzi chose his words carefully: 'I do see the possibility that it may not achieve the object we desire.'

'Go on.'

'If the mood – which is to say the temper of the Dutch people – is such that they feel out of sympathy with our rule, what better way to show it than to make their excuses, leaving their governor and lord to throw an extravagant ball to which no one comes?'

'I'll take that risk,' Baird said firmly.

'The ball will need to be advertised widely, and well in advance of time, sir. All the greater the scandal if it fails.'

Baird sighed. 'But we need to woo the people. You're right – yet we must show willing. I'm going to try.'

'Er, who will be the one . . . ?'

'As there's no Lady Baird, my trust must be in you, Renzi, old fellow.'

'Oh.'

'No expense to be spared – it has to be an occasion that's talked about for years to come. The historic coming together of two peoples to create one. Make it a good'un, old chap.'

'Very well, sir.'

'Oh – I may have omitted to tell you that in my last dispatch I made particular request that Whitehall do confirm you in post. I hope you'll entertain the thought of a permanent position. As such, you'll not want for honour and style – and shall we say we need not be mean in the article of your recompense?'

Renzi was thunderstruck. It was the last thing he had expected.

Before he could say anything, Baird added, 'It'll be long before I get an official reply so let us say that for all intents and purposes you are now the reigning colonial secretary of

Cape Colony and in consequence will be shown due respect and obeyed accordingly.'

'I – er, thank you, Sir David, and will endeavour to—'

'I'm sure you will. Now, about this ball . . .'

Renzi's quarters in the castle were nothing short of palatial – large, well furnished and quaint in an old-fashioned way. His bedchamber looked out over a spacious ornamental pond, decorated with the head and tail of a spouting dolphin. With four rooms, each with attendant maids and servants, he felt heady with achievement.

There would be time later to attend to the domestic niceties, and he dismissed the servants after allowing wine to be brought and left. He poured a glass and sipped appreciatively. Bright golden in colour, it had a delicate green tinge and an enfolding fragrance of orange and peach with a long, nutty finish, quite unlike the sombre whites of northern climes.

He savoured it, then sat back with a smothered sigh. The appointment of colonial secretary was his for as long as he wanted it.

But was his relationship with Kydd now to end? Their adventures together had been many and no doubt could continue – if he turned down a permanent position. Kydd was holding a berth open for his friend and they could resume their voyaging – but not if he took this post.

And was it morally right to abandon Kydd at this point? Could he fill the appointment at this remove from England? He also knew his value to Kydd as confidant and close friend.

Being the man he was, Kydd would let him go with every wish for his success, of course, and in a surge of feeling Renzi teetered on a decision to refuse the post.

And what of Cecilia? His moral principles had prevented

him making suit for her hand while in reduced circumstances before – but now! Here he was a full colonial secretary of a new-born piece of empire with every prospect open for the future. He could lay before her the life of a lady of conse-quence in society, while with his salary, a country estate and a Cape Town villa would be her demesne.

Yes! He would send for her, allow her to see for herself this extraordinary country. A society wedding here in Cape Town, then together they'd make journey into the interior – lions and jackals, elephants and . . . and . . . But only if Baird's gamble paid off that Janssens would tamely surrender at a show of force, if the French did not return in a vengeful invasion, if there were no bloody uprising . . .

And if she was not already married, as he himself had urged her to do.

There was no time to be lost. He sprang from the chair and went to the desk to find pen and ink, but hesitated. What if any of these dire events swept away the fragile colony? Given all the uncertainties, was it fair to promise so much?

Distracted, he nibbled the end of the quill and then decided. He would do it! He would pour out his passion for her, confessing his love and admiration – holding back nothing, allowing her to see the depths of his feeling and then laying out his proposal for wedded bliss.

It was an intoxicating thought: there were threats hanging over them but these would be resolved in a few months, if not weeks, and it was unthinkable that Whitehall could refuse the governor's direct request. He would write the letter, crying up the beauty and splendour of life under Table Mountain – but delay sending it until things were settled.

That was what to do. He began scribbling in a fury of passion.

*   *   *

Renzi entered the Burgher Senate with suitably grave features and in the severe attire that he would wear from now on at every official occasion. Behind him in the little procession were Ryneveld and Höhne, his sworn translator.

The assembly slowly rose to their feet, their gaze disdainful. The president, his expression stony, at the last possible moment yielded his high chair. Renzi gave a civil inclination of his head and sat, the Senate conforming in an unnerving hush.

This was the powerhouse of Cape Town, the merchantry, professionals and captains of trade meeting together to run their community as they had done since the Dutch first arrived. They had built this characterful 'Town House' in the middle of the last century when it had become clear that the colony had a future. Its three-arched portico and elaborate mouldings were finished with the white and yellow plasterwork and green shutters so distinctive of Cape Town.

Renzi braced himself. It was vital that he put across messages of reassurance, respect and hope to a people whose land had been taken in conquest by his own country.

He stood and looked about the room. 'Mr President – Mijnheer de Voorzitter van Nuldt Onkruydt,' he said, with a wash of relief when it seemed he had pronounced it acceptably, 'I do thank you for your invitation to speak and for your kind welcome.' He turned and, with a smile, bowed to the granite-faced man while Höhne droned out the translation.

The rows of faces gazed back at him, hard men of money and power whose very dress seemed alien and foreign.

'We bring you opportunity and prosperity by freeing your colony from the oppression of the Corsican Bonaparte. Now you may trade freely with the world, succouring the fleets of the Indies and finding full commercial advantages in the status of free port that His Excellency has bestowed . . .'

It was unnecessary to explain that free trade would never extend to the King's enemies or their friends, and that the fleets of the Indies were those of England, not the Dutch, whose trading empire in the Spice Islands would now wither without supplies and support from the Cape.

'Your customs and traditions in the practice of commerce will be respected by this government . . .'

In so far as they did not conflict with English mercantile law and the revenue raised was adequate for the purposes of government.

'. . . as will be the ancient rights and privileges of this House here assembled.'

He had not detected a single movement in the impassive rows of men facing him; their faces — individual, broad, tanned and seamed — betrayed no trace of feeling.

'Therefore I commend to you the Acts of His Excellency the Governor . . .'

Höhne finished the translation and Renzi smiled. 'If there's any question that I'm able to answer for you, gentlemen?'

In the front row a thick-built man with a brooding expression stood slowly.

'Yes?' Renzi said pleasantly.

A stream of guttural Dutch and the man waited, arms folded.

Höhne leaned forward. 'Herr Maasdorp asks, *which* governor?'

Ignoring the jibe, Renzi came back with what he hoped was a robust summary of the situation.

Afterwards, in the carriage, Ryneveld tried to make light of it. 'The first time they have met you. Hollanders do not readily put hearts on their sleeves, as you say. However . . .'

'Your point?'

'It's troubling they do not see their interests coinciding with yours – ours. That they did not see fit to applaud your appearance does not speak of contentment and reconciliation – rather resentment. Maasdorp can be a troublemaker and all it needs is for some fool to spark a spurning, a turning of the back, and Cape Town will be ungovernable.'

The ball was now assuming increasing importance as it was becoming clear that this would be a breakthrough event, throwing the two cultures together – or turn into a ruination. According to Ryneveld, it was fast becoming public knowledge but attracting contempt from some; Renzi felt the beginnings of despair. He so wanted it to be a success, not least because this would be his place of settling with Cecilia.

'You'll pardon my straight talking, Sir David, but I find it a rum thing that we're to discuss defence in depth and we've emptied the barracks of troops to send 'em out to Hottentots Kloof. A singular thing, sir!' Lieutenant Colonel MacDonald had strongly opposed General Beresford's all-or-nothing march against Janssens and wasn't going to let it rest.

'Mine the responsibility, yours the duty,' Baird said mildly, smoothing the campaign map. 'At this moment my chief task is to provide as hot a reception as may be conceived to any enemy who dares threaten us in our new possession. Which is to say, until the form of the French response is known, like good soldiers we must cover all lines of approach.'

He looked around the room. 'Now, gentlemen, we face a near insufferable problem in defending our new possession. I detail our vulnerabilities for your earnest reflection.

'The castle and all the batteries may be relied on to secure the Table Bay anchorage but a determined enemy might land at any point up the coast unseen by us, and when numbers are sufficient march upon us in strength.

'That's not my main anxiety – the Navy is there to discourage them – but what disturbs my sleep is what the Dutch before don't seem to have considered well: the three points of approach that'll see an army poised high above us, ready with guns to pound us into surrender, our batteries all seaward facing.

'The first and second are on the western flanks of Table Mountain. Should any enemy land there' – he held up his hand to silence Popham's protest – 'then in less than a mile they are at the Kloofnek to the south, or more probably between the Lion's Head and Rump. Either will see their guns dominate a helpless town.'

He gave Popham a wry smile. 'The commodore does assure me that a sailor might find a hundred reasons why this is impractical but it does not ease my mind. If the French have seamen half as daring as our doughty tars then they'll find ways. Need I remind you of that Caribbean rock you captured, fortified and called a ship? Brought Martinique completely to a stand with just a few guns perched up high.'

Knowing glances flashed around the table; all were aware of Commodore Hood's feat just two years previously. Against overwhelming odds he had established a gun-post on a barren pinnacle off the island to become a thorn in the side of the French.

'As to the third, this is the eastern flank of Table Mountain, past the Devil's Peak. Any landing in the north of False Bay will see 'em without delay above the town, this time to the east. And if there are simultaneous landings . . .'

Another tight smile. 'Therefore our options are few. Fortifications at these points will take too long to build, so I conceive that a body of troops must be posted at each to perform what I can only describe as a "Thermopylae" against the foe.'

MacDonald stirred restlessly. 'And while these soldiers are out of reach, in siege of General Janssens?'

'Then, of course, even this is denied us,' Baird answered testily. 'Do you question the Navy's resolve to exert the utmost vigilance in denying the French the opportunity to land in the first place?'

He sighed, then continued firmly, 'Given this outline of what faces us, we must get to the details. Colonel Pack, tell us the state of the batteries.'

Pack snorted fiercely. 'Damn it, they're useless! We've four hundred guns and on some the carriages have crumbled to powder. Others wi' bird's nests in the muzzles. Honeycombed iron guns, rotting bronze 'uns. We open fire, the French will fall about wi' laughter is best we can hope for, sir.'

'I'd have thought there's more 'n a few serviceable. Did not your frigate – what's her name?'

'*L'Aurore*,' glowered Popham.

'Did she not smell powder when making her sally through the anchorage?'

'Captain Kydd's report speaks of fire from four batteries but their practice poor. Why, *L'Aurore*'s easy escape is best evidence of—'

'We can't rely on the harbour batteries, then. Perhaps we—'

He broke off at a tentative knock on the door. 'Come!'

His aide, Gordon, entered with an opened dispatch case.

'Er, urgent from General Beresford from before Hottentot Kloof,' he said crisply, drawing out a packet. 'The galloper asks for its immediate attention, sir.'

Around the table officers rose to make their excuses but Baird waved them down. 'This will be a deciding engagement – or a crushing disaster. Either way you'll have need to know it.'

In expectant stillness he slit the seal and smoothed out the sheets. He read quickly and looked up with a strange expression. 'It is neither. A development of unexpected and crucial significance – gentlemen, without meeting us in the field, General Janssens is by this letter offering to treat for the outright capitulation of all Dutch forces.'

The stunned silence broke into an excited babble as Baird read on, then fell quiet as he continued, 'It seems that his Boer farmers are deserting the colours in large numbers, more interested in harvests than honour. And with military supplies denied him by the Navy, he's concerned to spare the colony needless bloodshed in a lost cause.'

He laid the letter down slowly. 'An honourable and courageous man – I salute him.'

The meeting broke up, the news without doubt now fast spreading through Cape Town. Baird wasted no time, and Renzi set to on a proclamation of thanksgiving for the peace, his heart full at the knowledge that with the threat removed, and with its strategic value, the British would never abandon the colony. Soon he could make the plans that would have Cecilia by his side.

The last menace, of course, was the French, but with re-inforcements from Britain their hopes of seizing Cape Colony must fade. It was only the short period before they arrived that was the danger – and they still had to win the loyalty of town and country before the colony could settle down and prosper.

The ball: this *must* succeed! So much to worry about, to plan and prepare – who to invite and who would be offended if omitted. And a formal ball would imply refreshments and supper as well as a master of ceremonies who could be trusted with both the Dutch and English forms; music at a suitably august level, and if this were in the English mode, a discreet separate area for cards and dalliances.

Then there were equally challenging details ranging from the protocol of the receiving line to locating decorations and flowers fit for vice-regal patronage. If only Cecilia were here, she would revel in the task . . . but she was not. He picked up a pencil and glumly continued with his endless to-do list. A muffled thud interrupted him. It would be the gun from Signal Hill on the Lion's Rump – with its view to both sides of the Cape, it reported ships' arrivals. Renzi hastened outside to see what vessel it could be.

There was no three-flag red hoist, so no enemy. Curious, he remained for the ship to show, either to the north or around the point from the south.

And there it was – from the south, bursting into view close in with Mouille Point in a fine display of seamanship, a frigate under a full press of sail undertaking a showy flying moor on the inshore side of the naval anchorage.

It was *L'Aurore*.

Kydd left *Diadem*'s great cabin not greatly put out by the surly manner of Commodore Popham for he knew *L'Aurore* had done well. Lourenço Marques had turned out to be little more than a forlorn outpost, perpetually in conflict with the savages, that was hanging on to the last sad vestiges of

Portuguese rule and could offer nothing in the way of dockyard facilities or similar of interest to the British.

The two Indiamen were still there, undergoing repair with materials *L'Aurore* had sent over and had every hope of a successful resumption of their voyage. He'd brought reliable news of the size and capability of the French squadron, even though Popham had dismissed the threat, assuming after the blow that they would fall back on their Indian Ocean bases.

In light-hearted mood he boarded his barge and directed it ashore to pay his respects to the governor. The boat came smartly alongside the jetty and Kydd mounted the rickety side-steps, surprised to find his confidential secretary there to meet him.

'My word, but this sea life is suiting you, dear fellow,' Renzi said genially.

Kydd laughed, and they walked companionably towards the castle. It was good to see his friend after so much had happened. 'Shall we sup together after I've seen Sir David, or must his secretary keep close station on him always?' he asked.

'Er, I'm not, as who should say, his secretary, old chap. He has his own,' Renzi said, a little uncomfortably.

'Then you didn't get the position? The dog! I'll wager even so he's working you half to death, Nicholas.' Renzi did look more than a little harassed.

At Kydd's full dress uniform, the castle sentries presented arms with an enthusiastic crash of musket and gaitered boot, and they passed into the inner courtyard and across to the governor's suite. Seeing Renzi, the aide-de-camp rose respectfully. 'Sir David is with General Ferguson, sir. I'll let him know you're here.'

'Never mind, Lieutenant,' Kydd said crisply. 'We'll return later.'

The aide ignored Kydd with a pained expression and knocked gently on the connecting door. 'Mr Renzi and a naval gentleman, Sir David.'

Moments later a disgruntled general emerged, looking sharply at Renzi before being ushered away. Baird appeared beaming. 'You've brought me Captain Kydd, then, Renzi, old chap.'

'As he's bringing report of the French, sir,' Renzi said smoothly, standing aside for Kydd. 'Do go in, Captain, I shall wait outside.'

Later, a much-chastened Kydd was settled into a chair in Renzi's inner sanctum by a protective Stoll. '*Your* secretary?' he asked wryly, when the man had left.

'Well, one of them,' Renzi admitted.

Kydd looked around the well-appointed office. 'And I had my concerns that he'd been working you like a slavey. Shall I be told what you do with your day at all?'

Lightly covering the detail, Renzi explained what it was to be a colonial secretary while Kydd listened first in astonishment and then in good-natured envy. 'In the first rank of Cape Town society no less – I must take off my hat to you in the street, I find!'

'It has its compensations, the position,' Renzi agreed.

'As will make it a sad trial for you to return to *L'Aurore*.' Kydd chuckled.

Renzi's face shadowed. 'Er, there's every reason to suppose that will now not happen, Tom.'

'What do you mean?'

'Sir David has done me the honour of asking me to consider this a permanent situation,' he said gently, 'and is communicating with Whitehall to have me confirmed in post, my friend.'

'Nicholas – is this what you desire, or is some villain—'

'It is my wish. You see . . . I shall now have a situation in life that is both honourable and secure, that yields a competence that is quite sufficient, you see, to . . . marry.'

Kydd was dumbfounded.

'A *sufficient competence*?' he managed.

'An acceptable term, I'd think, for an emolument some seven or eight times your own.'

Kydd smiled awkwardly. Renzi's high moral principles had prevented his seeking Cecilia's hand in marriage while unable to provide for her, and through sheer chance he had been given the means to do so and obviously had seized it with both hands – or . . .

'Oh, er, Nicholas, by your talk of marriage, do you mean to say, um, to Cecilia, not some Dutch lady of your recent acquaintance?'

'To your sister,' Renzi said frostily. 'In the event she is free and accepts my proposal, I mean to send for her to approve Cape Colony as an appropriate place of our *domicile de mariage*.'

'Ah.'

'To be wed in the Groote Kerk, I shouldn't wonder.'

Cecilia – out here? Kydd had doubts, but if she still had the feelings for Renzi that he'd been witness to before, then all was possible. 'I see. Then . . . then you'll not be wanting your cabin aboard,' he ventured, still dazed by the announcement.

'It would seem not, Tom.' Renzi's voice was awkward. 'I would take it kindly if you'll—'

'Your books 'n' effects will be landed as soon as they may.'

'Thank you.'

There was a long pause while Kydd tried to find something to say. 'Er, you're still looking a mort mumchance – can this be some delicate question of state that's taxing the intellects?'

Renzi smiled ruefully. 'No, dear fellow. It's naught but the throwing of a grand ball for which I bear both the honour and responsibility. You'd never conceive the worry of spirits this is causing me – such quantities of vexing detail that would drive a saint to drink and ruin.'

'Ha! That's easily solved, I'm persuaded,' Kydd said immediately.

'Oh? How so?'

'You may claim the services of Tysoe, who, as you know, has served a noble family – but, mind you, I shall have him back!'

Renzi's face cleared. 'A capital idea! My mind is quite eased, believe me. Er – shall we adjourn to another place? My apartments are commodious and overlook such a quaint and sublime fountain . . .'

The evening stole in, a thankful cool with a violet tinge to the light adding to the nervous elation in the group standing about the doors of Government House. Baird had fallen in with the idea of holding the reception there, in the palatial surroundings of the Dutch governor's residence, then moving to the larger castle for the ball, involving as it would a jingling panoply of sumptuous carriages through the streets for all Cape Town to see.

'I don't spy any of 'em yet!' Baird rumbled, twitching his military stock and peering past the goggling crowd pressed up to the railings. 'If we dance alone they'll hear about it for years to come in every club in London!'

'Sir, the evening's yet young,' Renzi soothed, trying not to let the feathers of his ridiculous ceremonial helmet tickle his nose. 'And I'd believe every matron will be concerned not to let a single hair go unfrizzed.'

The governor did not appear mollified and Renzi fell back briefly into the entrance to confront an immaculate Tysoe. 'Is everything ready?' he hissed. 'Should this night be a disaster then . . . then—'

'All is to satisfaction, sir,' Tysoe replied serenely, 'Being under my direct instructions.' At any other time the distinct elevation of his tone would have brought amusement.

The impeccably dressed regimental band stoically continued playing their light airs and the members of the receiving line – himself after Baird, Ryneveld, two generals, Popham and three members of the Senate – hovered in readiness.

It wasn't until an interminable forty minutes had passed that the first carriage arrived and one Overbeek, vice-president of the Orphans Chamber, wife and wide-eyed daughter arrived. A genial Baird granted a full five minutes to the bemused worthy, his wife and daughter the breathless centre of attention of the rest of the line.

Soon after, to Renzi's surprise, the grim-faced Slotsboo, treasurer of the Burgher Senate and implacable enemy to the currency-exchange proclamation, stepped out of his carriage, himself handing down his extravagantly dressed wife and approaching the governor with an ingratiating smile.

Behind him carriages joggled for a place as more and more arrived, to the intense gratification of the onlookers. Both the collector and comptroller of Customs claimed noisy priority over the dignified Truter, secretary to the Court of Justice, and when the crowd caught sight of the young wife of the deputy fiscal in her beribboned gown, there was a long collective sigh.

The evening was made! Renzi looked around at the glittering splendour of the animated throng, the jealously hoarded finery of the ladies and the naked jostling for social position – there was no doubt that Baird had been right and that society was beginning to cohere as one around the person of the governor.

Renzi did his duty happily, passing among the great and good, graciously bestowing kind words upon those brought to be introduced by Ryneveld and allowing himself, the influential colonial secretary of Cape Colony, to be both seen and admired.

Then it was time to make the short journey to the castle and the ball. The governor rode alone first in an ornate carriage; Renzi with Ryneveld was next, the military behind.

Following Baird's example, Renzi affably acknowledged with a wave the shouts of the crowd as they passed by and then on to the parade-ground where, by torchlight, a massed band and marching troops crashed into motion.

With a sense of unreality Renzi sat rigid as they drove through the ancient gate to the inner courtyard. Opposite, lined up outside the governor's residence, were the lesser invitees – colonels, post-captains, heads of departments, ward masters, church ministers, others.

Baird descended from his carriage and began passing along the waiting guests, Renzi close behind, finding polite words for each. Then it was Kydd who was next in the line and they played their parts, the only concession to the situation being a solemn wink from Renzi and a wondering shake of Kydd's head.

The long ballroom was splendidly lit with candelabra stands

by the dozen and infinite tawny gold points reflected in the many mirrors. At one end a regimental band in evening dress played softly as the room filled and champagne flowed.

Kydd was sure that he was going to enjoy the heady evening, not unaware that in his full-dress post-captain's uniform he cut a striking figure.

'Mevrouw – the first dance?' Baird led out a proud Mrs Ryneveld, and Kydd claimed a shy, light-featured Dutch maiden, whose English, he discovered, was not the equal of her charms. They stepped out prettily together, though, and after two dances he graciously allowed her to be taken by a red-faced young subaltern.

Then, in the next dance, dutifully bowing and rising to a dimpled matron, he caught sight across the room of a beautiful dark-haired woman, whose grace was drawing admiring glances from all parts. When the dance finished he determined to go in search of her.

She was surrounded by fawning men, fluttering her fan but giving her entire attention to Renzi, who was holding forth. Her ivory gown was cut low, revealing an alabaster bosom, and her lustrous black hair framed striking Gallic features. Kydd thrust through and gave a sweeping bow. 'Shall this round be mine, Mam'selle?'

He had noticed what the others had not – that Dutch maidens did not mark cards for dancing partners and he was therefore free to ask. He was met with a cool gaze from her and a startled look from Renzi, but she consented, lifting a sequinned gloved hand, which he took with a wicked glance back at the group of envious men.

The first words of his small-talk in English were met with a cold expression in French of her inability to converse easily, but Kydd was equal to this – his painful lessons from Renzi during the blockade of Toulon had matured into a passable competence in the language.

She seemed not impressed, however, and he had to wait impatiently for the dance round to come back to him before he could continue. As he spoke, her eyes darted to where Renzi was the centre of a circle of admirers.

Did he know Colonial Secretary Renzi at all? Such a handsome and charming man! And so elegant a turn of phrase for an Englishman. Was he married? A lady friend?

Kydd admitted that indeed he knew the gentleman and with relish went on to point out that the colonial secretary's intended was to be sent for shortly to join him at the Cape.

This got her attention and the coolness went as she observed respectfully that he himself must be a gentleman of importance to know the colonial secretary so well. Kydd explained that Mr Secretary's bride was to be none other than his sister and that he was certainly well acquainted with the gentleman.

After the dance he led her back to the side of the room and was rewarded with a charming smile. He lingered, blasting with a glare the subaltern who had the effrontery to cut in. The young soldier retired, wounded.

Was the next dance promised, or should they stand up together once more? He whirled her into the cotillion, blood singing.

All too soon he had to surrender her and wandered back to the refreshments table, where Renzi was in earnest conversation with a grave Dutchman whose wife stood shyly back. Kydd helped himself to a plate, waited until Renzi was free, then said casually, 'Rattling fine ball, Nicholas.'

'Oh? I'm gratified to hear it, old fellow.'

'Um, just curious, that French-rigged lady you were speaking to earlier?'

Renzi gave a slow smile. 'Why, brother, the mysterious damsel that's set all the men to talking?'

'She says I'm to call her Thérèse,' Kydd said.

'That is much easier on the tongue than Marie Thérèse Adèle de Poitou.'

'Er, who was that again?'

'Who the Dutch call the French princess, although she is but the youngest daughter of the Baron de Caradeuc. Apparently royalists fled from France and settled here, keeping to themselves, with a modest vineyard past the Stellenbosch.'

'You seem to know enough about her, Nicholas.'

'As a moderately successful vintner, the baron is entitled to an invitation, I find. He expressed his regrets and trusts that his daughter's presence might suffice.

'Quite a coup,' Renzi added, with satisfaction. 'The baron lost his wife to the guillotine and lives alone on the estate with his daughter. They were seldom seen in town before now.'

The ball continued joyously – but Kydd had eyes for only one.

Chapter 9

This had been an edgy voyage. Kydd had been tasked to search out any lurking French squadrons so *L'Aurore* had ranged along the track of the Indiamen as being the most likely hunting ground, meeting each dawn with the utmost vigilance, as the starry night faded to first light, extending out until the wave-tossed horizon could be meticulously searched.

Nothing had been seen of the enemy, but there had been some moments of heart-pumping tension: as one night lifted, it had shown a fleet of ships bearing down on them. These, however, had proved to be an outward-bound John Company convoy, who were glad to hear of the capture of Cape Town but had no news of the French.

For Kydd it was always something akin to magic, the diligent application of tables and the wielding of sextant and chronometer, then land conjured from the immensity of ocean. He stood on the quarterdeck, gazing at the jagged blue-grey that was St Helena; unspeakably remote, a speck in the watery vastness of the South Atlantic but a valued rendezvous point for the rich India convoys.

Kendall knew St Helena well and, as they drew near, directed *L'Aurore* to pass to the west. Close to, the island was a spectacular sight: massive crags pounded by waves driven ceaselessly a thousand miles or more by the constant open-ocean trade-winds that ended their run in a thundering assault on the south-east of the island.

The interior was riven by rocky valleys; strangely, on this island it was the summits of the mountains that were clothed in verdure, the lower slopes bare and precipitous, some shrouded in cloud and mist.

'We'll enter t' leeward, o' course, sir – Jamestown on the north is where we lands,' Kendall said confidently. 'An' that there's Lot an' His Wife,' he added, pointing to two contorted columns of dark basalt rearing high above the broken scarp.

Rounding the sharp western extremity they passed into relative peace to leeward of the island, *L'Aurore*'s barrelling roll before the wind finally easing after so many days at sea. Jamestown was marked by several ships at anchor offshore and *L'Aurore* did likewise, her sailors agog at the new-found land. There was no need for salutes or ceremony because this entire island, complete with its governor, was a fiefdom of the East India Company.

'Open the hold, Mr Oakley – we'll take aboard fresh greenstuffs and water while we've the chance. And let the passengers know our boat will be going ashore in one hour,' Kydd ordered. They were carrying three gentlemen with business on the island.

He went below to prepare. There was no real necessity for him to visit: his orders were to return by way of a voyage east to Africa, then down the coast back to Cape Town, keeping a weather eye open for the tell-tale signs of a French landing. But St Helena was a strange and haunting island, set at such unimaginable remoteness – who knew if he'd be this way again? Besides, Renzi would never forgive him if he did not bring back an account.

They landed at the foot of a long, narrow valley, the town not much more than a single street. A gateway through the sea wall led them in and Kydd stood for a space, admiring the bluffs that soared five hundred feet on both sides. 'You're for Plantation House?' Moore, one of the passengers, asked pleasantly.

'The governor?'

'Yes, Robert Patton. I'll advise a *calesa*, Captain. The house is at some miles' distance.'

At the Mule Yard they secured their conveyance. 'The castle on the left is near crumbling with ants,' Moore chuckled, as they ground up an incline, 'and there is our snug Grand Parade and our steeple-less St James's Church.'

'Er, how old is it at all?' Kydd asked, out of courtesy.

'As it was building when Captain Cook chanced by. Your first visit?'

Plantation House was in the pleasantly cooler uplands, fronted by a lawn set about with myrtles and mimosa thirty feet high, an exotic mingling of bamboo and eucalyptus, laurel and cabbage tree.

Kydd walked past a giant tortoise contentedly munching grass and was politely conducted to Governor Patton, who greeted him with a warm handshake and invited him to sit in one of a pair of fine antique chairs.

'I bring news,' Kydd opened. 'Cape Town is ours, and—'

'This I know, Captain. Is it possible *I* have news for *you*?'

'Oh?'

'There's been a hard-run battle off San Domingo that's

ended the career of your Admiral Leissègues. Quite destroyed by Admiral Duckworth in as fine an action as any I've heard.'

This was welcome indeed. One fewer battle squadron to worry about at the very least.

'And Admiral Willaumez has been sighted to the suth'ard . . .'

Kydd started. What the devil was such a threat doing in the south – a strike at the Cape? He stood immediately. 'I – I must get this news to Commodore Popham.' What could be achieved with a pair of old 64s and lesser craft would soon be put to the test.

Patton gave a reassuring smile. 'A company schooner is already on its way, sir.'

Kydd left as soon as he decently could and made his way back aboard. *L'Aurore* was part of the Cape squadron and his thoughts were very much on the little outpost at the tip of the great continent in its time of lonely defiance.

And then, of course, there was Thérèse. At the ball he'd been much taken with her cool poise and striking attract-iveness, which had made it irksome to sail the next day. When he returned, if she had not retreated back to her wine estate, he would most certainly pay her a call . . .

He waited impatiently until Oakley had reported stores and water aboard, then, although it was well into the first dog-watch, he ordered the ship secured for sea and they sailed into the evening to return to Cape Town.

Close-hauled on the starboard tack in the fine south-easterly trades, *L'Aurore* made a good crossing, raising land soon after dawn. Notorious to every sailor, the African coast at these latitudes was treacherous, desolate and unutterably remote,

216

a burning wilderness, what the old Portuguese called *a costa dos esqueletos* – the coast of skeletons.

There was vanishingly little reason for the French to be here – but, then, what better place to conceal a secret refuge, a location where a fleet of ships could be assembled out of sight before making their strike south? Kydd dutifully went about and headed south, closing with the stark shore as near as he dared, keeping with the inshore south-westerly.

Through the telescope he peered out at an endless march of tawny sand dunes, shimmering in the heat behind the white line of breaking surf. Occasionally a twist of rock, a low hillock or dry wash-way caught the eye, but the unrelieved boredom of the prospect soon reduced its novelty and the seamen got on with their work with no more glances shoreward.

Shortly after the men settled to their noon meal there was a low cry from the lookout at floating wreckage across their path. It was not unknown to come across derelicts – sad, waterlogged remnants of ships abandoned in storms – and Curzon told the conn to leave it safely to leeward, but as they drew nearer sharp eyes detected movement.

The watch were set to back the fore-topsails to lose way, and as the frigate slowed, it appeared they had stumbled upon a stove-in ship's boat with a ragged sail stretched over what looked like two bodies. As they approached, a hand threw aside a corner of the canvas and a face burned scarlet by the sun stared up, unbelieving. With an inhuman screech, the figure tried to rise but flopped sideways. Then came husky, tearing cries, piteous in their pleading.

Aroused by the noise, Kydd was soon on deck. 'Heave to, if y' please. Away the gig.' At sea, his orders were to keep the small boat always at the ready in the stern davits, the watch-on-deck to man it.

With a squeal of sheaves, the gig descended and quickly pulled towards the pitiful sight, one of the figures now in a paroxysm of waving and crying. The bowman went over the side into the perilously swaying wreckage, tender hands easing the transfer, and the boat returned with its cargo of suffering humanity.

'Sorry, sir, an' he won't leave the dead 'un behind,' the coxswain apologised, while a bloated corpse was awkwardly slithered over the bulwarks. The survivor fell on the deck, alternately blubbering and giving vent to hoarse howls.

The surgeon arrived. 'Extreme desiccation,' he said, after no more than a cursory look. 'I'd be surprised if he sees another dawn.' He stood back and folded his arms.

'Well, what's to do, Doctor? You'll not let him suffer?'

'I suppose a measure of opium, water, of course, but sparing . . .'

Kydd was about to have the man taken below but paused; obviously in the last extremity of thirst, he continued with his urgent cries. And his eyes, though pits of suffering, were still rational, constantly flicking from Kydd to the others. 'He's trying to tell us something . . . His shipmates – he's been sent to find help!'

But the harsh gobbles were impossible to make out. Then the babbling stopped. The man gathered his strength with desperate intensity and mouthed a single word: '*Danske!*'

'He's saying as he's a Dane, sir,' Kendall said positively.

To Kydd's knowledge, there were none of his kind aboard – the English were at war with Denmark. 'Get him below and comfortable,' he said, 'then pass the word for any who think they can understand the poor wretch.'

Later, Kydd was sent for. Olafsen, a half-Swedish

sailmaker's mate, was standing by the hammock in which the man lay, exhausted, eyes still restless, haunted.

'Says he's a foremast hand off the *Grethe*, a trader from Christianborg, sir,' Olafsen said.

'Where's that?'

There was a short exchange. 'A Danish fort up the Guinea Coast.'

Then the man went into a muscle spasm, his eyes bulging with the effort of trying to get something out – but eventually Kydd had the story.

His ship had taken the ground and been driven ashore over the bank. Most of the crew and passengers had saved themselves, only to face a fearful arid desolation. In a desperate attempt to get help the one surviving ship's boat, with three seamen, was launched through the surf, commanded by the mate.

During the night the mate and one seaman had been swept over-side, their water lost and the boat swamped. The man's remaining companion had died in heat convulsions the next day.

'Ask him where the wreck is,' Kydd told Olafsen. If they moved quickly, the rest had a chance.

'He can't say. He doesn't know navigation. They knew to head south for Cape Town, so he thinks maybe north of here a few leagues.'

Kydd shook his head. This simple seaman could not know of the cold, surging Benguela current thrusting up. Once swamped and helpless, the boat would have been carried inexorably north. The likelihood was that it wasn't too far ahead on their original course – to the south.

'How many aboard?'

It turned out to be forty-seven, including passengers, but

of these the captain and nine seamen had been lost in the wrecking.

'Tell him we're starting to search for 'em now.'

With no shortage of lookouts, *L'Aurore* sailed south and almost immediately sighted a wreck. Stark against the glare of pale sand, it was thrust up near a sand-spit. Lieutenant Bowden was sent to make contact, but returned quickly.

'Not ship-rigged and looks to be old, sir.'

In the early afternoon another wreck was sighted. This one was at an angle to heavy breakers and still showed mast stumps – it had to be recent or would have been reduced to a grey-ribbed carcass. Careful searching with a telescope, however, showed no sign of life.

'Give 'em a gun.' A six-pounder forward banged out. There was no response.

'Another.' Nothing.

'See if our survivor can be carried up on deck to identify it,' Kydd ordered, eyeing the way in.

There was no mistaking the Dane's pitiful response and Bowden was sent in once more, this time in the whaler. On his own initiative, Kydd had acquired for *L'Aurore* a whaling boat: double-ended and sea-kindly, it could be landed through heavy surf, unlike a flat-transomed boat.

He watched its progress. Sped ashore through the final lines of breakers, it grounded and was rapidly hauled clear. The men quickly went to the wreck, disappearing out of view, but after some time they reappeared, and went over the dunes, searching.

After a perilous launch into the surf, with the boat in a demented rearing and bucking, a soaked Bowden reported, 'It's the *Grethe* well enough, sir. And not a soul alive, I'm sorry to say.'

'None?'

'There were eight or so bodies in the 'tween decks aft, but I couldn't make good search as she was breaking up.' He shuddered. 'Some African beast had got to them, sir, I – I didn't look closely.'

'Your men found nothing?'

'Not a sign.'

It didn't make sense. If they'd abandoned the wreck, surely there'd be a camp somewhere close. And lookouts to watch for a rescue vessel. Or had they already been picked up? No – they would have buried their shipmates first. If he now sailed away, he could be dooming thirty-three people to a terrible end.

'I'm going to see for myself.' In all conscience, Kydd couldn't rob them of their only chance of rescue without one more look.

'It's fearfully hot, sir,' Bowden said, 'and if this swell rises, getting off again in the surf could be hard.'

'I'll bear it in mind. Poulden – pick a good crew.'

Kydd stripped off his coat and, with a quick apology, borrowed a seaman's flat sennit hat before boarding the whaler, taking the steering oar himself. It was a dizzying ride in, and the final rush to the sand was as exhilarating as it was hazardous.

'Haul in.'

While the boat was dragged clear Kydd looked about him. High sand-hills, a very few small ragged bushes and strangely coloured dunes that stretched away into a limitless distance. A sense of utter desolation beat at him as he trudged towards the dark-timbered bulk of the wreck.

From shoreward it was not difficult to get aboard by the ropes that trailed in the water over the stern. What Bowden had not mentioned was the squeal and barking of tortured timber and the crazy working of the planking as the decks sagged on to each other. Or the stench of putrefaction mingled with bilge and sea smells.

Bent double, Kydd worked his way forward and saw the first body, its parts scattered. In the gloom he caught the flash of eyes – some sort of hyena circling. There were other bodies – now just butcher's carcasses – that he dimly perceived rolled together in the lower part of the canted deck.

There was nothing to be gained by staying and Kydd made for fresh air, relieved to be away from the cloying fetor of death. He had once been wrecked in the Azores and knew how rapidly a doomed ship turned from having been a neat and trim home for sailors into a crazed death-trap.

The *Grethe* was not long for this world – in a short while it would be a gaunt, grey-timbered skeleton. But where were her people? There were simply nowhere near enough bodies. It could only be that they had left the wreck and got ashore.

Back on the vast beach he gathered his thoughts. Had they headed inland, hoping to reach some sort of civilisation? The constant wind with its sibilance of rubbing sand-grains had obliterated all tracks – even Bowden's were now rounded and filled.

Kydd toiled up the face of the highest dune. At the top he looked out on the most parched and bleak desert landscape he had ever seen: endless vari-coloured sand-mountains, some with dark ridges protruding, rising from a flat desert floor and stretching away into a shimmering distance, where several rounded copper mountains lay, all in the torpid stillness of a terrible desert silence – vast, brooding, impenetrable. And not the faintest human trace.

Away from the sea, there was no cooling wind and the heated sand beat mercilessly up at him.

Had there been a fierce attack by a native tribe? Surely nothing could live here in this landscape. The survivors had vanished – and it must remain a mystery for ever.

He turned to go, but stopped. What if they had not accepted their fate and in desperation had struck out to find their own deliverance? It would have been a dreadful decision: to leave the relative comfort and shelter of the wreck for the unknown. Perhaps the bodies were of those who had argued for staying until rescued, while the others had taken their fate in their own hands and started out.

Only a madman would enter the hellish aridity inland when by the sea there was some degree of coolness and hard-packed sand for travelling. The more he thought about it, the more certain he became that this was what had happened.

They would have gone to the south. The impossible dream of Cape Town would be always before them, but Kydd knew that this was an unreachable eight hundred miles away – a comfortable week's sail for *L'Aurore* but an impossible march for survivors in this sun-blasted hell.

He decided to go after them. In these conditions he could not hazard the frigate inshore close enough to pick out individual figures. It would have to be done on foot along the beach, but this should not be too difficult for fit men. He would necessarily be delaying his return to the Cape, but if there was no sign in a single day's march, he would abandon the search.

'Stand by to launch the whaler, Poulden.'

His coxswain hesitated. 'We're t' leave 'em, sir?'

'No – we're following them. You're to take the whaler to *L'Aurore* and bring back these things – make a note, if y' please.'

Kydd had already decided that he should be with the searching party in case decisions had to be taken, but it needed only a few others – a couple of marines used to marching, the doctor and possibly someone with sharp eyes. And each to carry three military canteens of water at the least. Everyone to wear but a covering shirt, seamen's trousers and sennit hat. Perhaps a scrap of canvas to lie under, some ship's biscuits, anything easily portable to eat.

He also scribbled an order to Gilbey to take the ship, his instructions to keep with their progress until signalled to send in a boat. And there would be three signal flags, he'd decide the meanings while the boat was away, and in the event of strange sail, he'd leave this to the discretion of the acting captain.

The whaler launched in a mighty rearing and exhilarating explosion of rainbow spray and fought its way over each successive line of breakers until it had won the open sea and could erect its mast and sail.

Kydd was left on the beach, feeling curiously lonely away from the company of men, just the sound of wind-driven sand and the relentless bass pounding and seethe of surf. He stripped himself down to shirt and trousers and stared over to the wreck, pondering on its gradual ruin at the hands of the ceaseless breakers.

He took out his notebook and jotted down some elementary signals: 'boat to come in', 'survivors sighted', 'send more water', and others. Satisfied, he snapped it shut and waited.

The boat returned in a wild rush through the surf and a wide-eyed Calloway, Sergeant Dodd and his corporal, Cullis, scrambled out. The boat's crew threw out their gear after them and helped the surgeon over the gunwale, cursing as he came.

'I just hope you know what you're doing, Mr Kydd!' spluttered Peyton, thoroughly soaked, nursing a bag of medicines.

'I do. And you'll not be wanting that coat, Doctor – do take it, Poulden.'

The whaler was being bullied sideways by the onrushing waves and Kydd didn't want to detain it, but Poulden asked, in some concern, 'An' shall we stay wi' ye, sir? Could be cannibals an' all behind them dunes.'

'We'll be fine, thank you. Goodbye.'

The little group formed up, the two marines trying not to be awed by the daunting spectacle of the limitless wilderness. Canteens were slung, small bags swung over shoulders and they set out.

The sun was ferocious, the heat almost like a weight bearing down as they paced along, grateful for the hard sand underfoot. Sergeant Dodd carried a light pole, at its tip signal flag numeral one fluttering out to signify to watching telescopes, 'Am proceeding normally'.

Conversation was an effort, and they swung on in silence until, after an hour, Kydd called a halt.

Peyton sat in the soft sand, his head in his hands, but Kydd was not inclined to be sympathetic. 'I'm looking for signs – clues that tells me they've been this way. Anything at all – cast-off pieces of baggage, empty water canteens, things thrown aside.' Glancing scornfully at Peyton, he added, 'But if there's no evidence by sundown, we return aboard.'

They each took a careful swallow of water and moved on. Ahead there was nothing but a featureless glaring haze, a glittering white mist hanging over the crashing breakers, as far as the eye could see. By midday it was clear they needed to shelter from the blazing heat.

An outcrop of rock ahead had a shadow underneath and

they thankfully plodded up to it but the sun-heated slabs were like a stove-top, burning to the touch. They rounded the ridge and found a deeper ledge, which offered a haven of cool in its shade.

Seeing Peyton's red face, Kydd suggested, 'Cullis – take the doctor's kerchief and soak it in the sea, will you?' The marine collected one from all of them and returned with blessed coldness for each man. Kydd fretted at the delay but in these inhuman conditions there was little choice and they stayed in their crevice.

At about three he ventured out. They had to get going and with a light onshore breeze it was just bearable. 'On your feet, gentlemen – remember what we're about.'

The shape and colour of the dunes was changing, a dramatic deep yellow-brown shading into iron red but always the pallid under-colour of bleached desert sand. Twisting valleys leading into the interior appeared in the dunes, and once they crossed what surely was the broad emerging of a dried-up river. Here and there were splashes of faded green, vegetation hanging on to some kind of existence in this infernal region.

A little further on a small salt marsh opened up. Calloway froze, then slowly pointed across to the base of a rearing sand-hill.

'Wha' . . . ?'

Slowly and methodically, as if in a dream, five elephants plodded past in the sand, ears flapping and occasional snorts proving their reality. Winding around the sand-hill, they disappeared from sight as if they'd never been.

The little party went on, one foot in front of the other in mechanical rhythm. At one place they stumbled through a field of sea-rounded pebbles, a startling profusion of varicoloured granite, lava and agate, and every so often a gaunt, sand-scoured ghost tree leaning out of wind-sculpted pastel dunes, some of which were near a thousand feet to their sharp summits.

A point of rock protruded out in the beach, obscuring the view ahead. When they rounded it there was another surprise: the bizarre sight at the tide-line of the carcass of a beached Antarctic whale. As they passed it what they saw brought them to a standstill – an animal had been recently feeding on it, the claw and toothmarks savage and massive.

'Lions!' It could be nothing else.

Fearfully they looked around. It was past imagining – a lion feeding on a whale! This desolate coast was proving to be anything but that.

'Stay together!' Kydd could think of nothing else to say – going after shipwreck survivors armed with heavy muskets would have been nonsensical. They resumed their monotonous tramping, tired muscles burning.

More mighty whale-bones were passed; was this why the first Portuguese had called it the coast of skeletons? Then the beach ahead began to curve, a long sweep that allowed them to see ahead for miles into an empty distance. And still there was no sign whatsoever.

'We carry on to an hour before sunset!' Kydd snapped, at a comment from the doctor. Then they would make the signal and quit this God-forsaken place, reluctantly leaving the survivors to their fate.

They trudged on, each wrapped in a private world of heat, weariness and fiery muscles until, the sun descending to the sea, it was time. Looking out at the horizon Kydd tried to make out *L'Aurore* but she was far offshore, out of sight at their height of eye.

Uneasily, he saw there was now a difficulty: mesmerised by their plodding progress he had not noticed that the seas had imperceptibly increased, their regular booming roar and hiss being no more than a constant background he had filtered out. Now they were foaming in at a height that would cause the whaler to swamp over the gunwale, or be uncontrollable and end tumbling broadside. Against the odds, the boat might make it in but would certainly not get off again.

They were trapped ashore.

Dully, he tried to focus. He cursed his stupidity in overlooking the elementary check. They'd simply have to spend the night ashore and try again in the morning.

'Take down that flag and hoist numeral two and three,' he told Calloway. The message would tell *L'Aurore* that the seas were too high for boat operations, and Gilbey would realise that this meant they would necessarily be staying ashore overnight.

'Let's find somewhere to get our heads down,' he said apologetically, after explaining their predicament.

With loud groans from Peyton they went up the beach to a stony bluff and, in the fading daylight, found they had a choice between lying on hard rock still warm from the sun or the open beach, which was noticeably cooler now. To a man they lay on the soft sand; with painful limbs, and trying not to think of roaming wild beasts, they sought the solace of sleep.

Did lions sleep at night? Where were the elephants now? What other beasts were out there beyond the dunes? Aching and weary, tossing and turning in the gritty sand, Kydd finally drifted off.

After a few hours he woke to pitch darkness, damp and cold. A heavy dew had descended and they were all sodden to the skin; in the night breeze they began to shiver un-controllably. Peyton cursed endlessly in a monotone, hugging his knees, while the marines stoically endured.

There was no question of sleep now, but as a full moon rose none could find words to appreciate the haunting beauty of the stark and mysterious scene that unfolded.

The moon rose higher, the light almost enough to read a book by. One of the marines got to his feet and paced up and down, flapping his arms for warmth. He was joined by the other and then Calloway stood and asked, teeth chattering, 'Sir, the survivors – it sits bad with me, we're leaving 'em now. While we're stranded, just to get warm can't we . . . go on a-ways?'

'Sit down, you fool boy!' Peyton snarled, but Kydd was touched.

'I'm putting it to the vote, Doctor. All those agreeable to pushing on for a bit longer . . . ?'

The two marines instantly nodded, and with Kydd and the midshipman also in favour, there was nothing Peyton could do. 'So we go on for a while. Of course, Doctor, you're free to remain here, if you so wish.'

Grumbling under his breath, Peyton got up, brushing the sand away while their gear was collected and distributed.

The trudging pain resumed, but this time in a surreal land-scape of silvered contrasts. Then, within minutes, the whole situation changed.

Dodd spotted it first. Above the tide-line and close up to the shifting base of the dunes a little mound stretched length-ways. When they went over they saw a crudely fashioned cross at its head.

And there were footprints, not yet entirely filled by the rest-less sand, proof that this had occurred recently. The survivors, therefore, were somewhere ahead.

Kydd guessed they were moving by the cool of the night so he and his party must also. Forgetting the pain, they pressed on, and in another hour Calloway's sharp eyes picked up a cast-away leather bottle and, further on, some pieces of clothing.

Into the night they continued, hoping against hope for a sight of faraway moonlit figures and the end of the quest. At one point there was an ominous sound to their left – a reverberation so low-pitched it was more sensed than heard. They tried to make it out: a long, muffled, dull roaring somewhere out in the sand-hills. Numbly they waited for the nameless beast to emerge – then the noise slowed and stopped: some inscrutable force of nature at work in the towering dunes.

It was another hour before they came upon the corpses, dark shapes on the edge of the dunes. Closer, the moonlight pitilessly revealed an elderly man, burned to disfiguring by the sun, laid out in dignified repose, his hands crossed over his breast, eyes closed. And a woman by his side, one arm over his body, her sightless eyes staring up, horror and suffering still on her face.

The doctor examined them, then stood up slowly. 'No more than hours ago,' he said, his voice falsely brisk. 'I conceive that the man could not go on and . . . and his wife stayed by him.'

Sergeant Dodd dropped to his knees and began scooping out the sand. Cullis joined him and a little later the two bodies were laid to rest for ever.

In the cold hours before dawn they found faint footprints, but this time meandering, scuffed, meaningless. Then the moon faded and darkness returned for a time. The swell had quietened during the night, now only a lazy boom and hiss.

Daybreak finally came, and with it, the cruellest stroke. It brought a dank mist that developed into a full-scale rolling sea-fog – there was now no way of signalling to *L'Aurore*.

A dense fog to rival any on the Thames here on this scorching desert coast! They were trapped ashore.

Their hard tack had long since gone and their precious water was unlikely to last for much longer – should they go on?

Visibility dropped to yards and it became difficult to make out even themselves, but nobody seemed to want to slacken the pace. Hunger biting, limbs afire, they slogged on – but then Kydd held up his hand for silence. He'd heard a commotion ahead: faint cries, a general hubbub.

Pushing through the swirling fog-bank, they hurried forward, tripping painfully on dark, jagged rock shards protruding from the sands at what must be a point of land – and beyond they found themselves in the middle of a colony of seals, which, in their quarrelling, completely ignored them.

They stumbled through the bedlam. It was bitterly disappointing. At the end of his stamina, Kydd knew it would be asking too much of his men to carry on blindly in the hope of reaching the survivors, who might be a mile – five miles – ahead and still moving. They had to give up – it was not humanly possible to—

And then the fog lifted.

Chapter 10

'And then?' Renzi prompted, caught up in the drama of the story Kydd was telling. He made much of topping up his friend's lemon punch and waited impatiently for him to continue.

Kydd eased his legs on the foot-cushion. 'Nicholas, well, the fog lifted and there they were – when we got to them they fell on their knees and blessed God, because they'd taken us for savages about to finish 'em.'

'Why ever did they think to walk to Cape Town?'

'A falling-out. After the wrecking, with the captain dead, it was the first mate who took charge and set out in a boat with three men, leaving the second mate to command. He lost authority and was murdered by those who thought they were done for anyway and had taken to drinking.

'It was a brave passenger who led the party out, not even knowing how far but thinking it better to do something than nothing. They were twenty-nine to begin and lost several on the way, but we ended taking off twenty-six, including a plucky mother and child.'

'As are all singing paeans of your action in coming after them,' Renzi said warmly. 'It's the talk of the town, brother!'

'Er, Nicholas – they being Danes, shall they be . . .'

'The governor has graciously deemed that as shipwrecked mariners they be given the liberty of Cape Town and may freely return to their homes when convenient.'

Kydd heaved himself up in the chair and changed the subject. 'So, since I was away, the Dutch have given in.'

'They have indeed, so quickly that General Beresford complains he's robbed of a famous battle. In fine, the Articles of Capitulation were signed, which makes over the whole of Cape Colony to His Majesty, after General Janssens was satisfied that the honours of war would be accorded, which Baird did right nobly by him.'

'I hear he's been granted residence at the Governor's House.'

'Until he is to return to Holland, with all his troops and arms under cartel.'

'To go back freely?' Kydd said, in amazement. 'This is an astonishing thing in an unconditional surrender.'

'But a masterly stroke. Here Baird's concluded a rapid peace. He's won the sympathy of the Cape Dutch, with his extravagant expressions of respect for the previous governor and, above all, he need not feed and guard thousands. The French in Dutch command, of course, are prisoners-of-war and will not taste freedom.'

'I can't see why Janssens surrendered when he was in such a strong position among his people in the country.'

'No mystery. His numbers were always fewer than we supposed, and Baird let it be known that we're daily re-inforced, allowing him to send as many of our troops as he chose. It was a brave gamble but it had its effect – there was no stomach to face those devils the Highlanders again in a lost cause, and in any case, the majority of his soldiers were Boer militia who deserted the colours, placing their desire to return to their farms above their duty.'

'Then it might be said we've completed the conquest of the Cape.'

'Indeed. Governor Baird is now undisputed ruler of Cape Colony, the soldiers are stood down before the civil authorities and, as we talk, are creating a bob's-a-dying in every s*hageerijen* in the town. Our ball has done its work for there's much expression of amiability in the people, the merchants seeing undoubted advantage in falling in with the new order.'

'So now we've nothing to worry of, you'll be spending your days setting taxes and hearing grievances, m' friend. Hardly a life of adventure.'

'Well, until we get our reinforcements from England, we're in a fragile state. In confidence, I have to tell you that a determined assault will place us in a perilous situation indeed. And Baird is troubled that we have no idea of what form the French retaliation will take, as surely it must.'

'Never fear, old fellow! You may rest easy while the Navy's here to look after you.'

Renzi gave his friend a conspiratorial look. 'On quite another note, when you're of a mind to taste the delights of the Cape, a certain lady seems to have delayed her return to her wine estate, a most uncommon thing, wagging tongues are saying. I've a notion that should you pay your addresses there will be an eager listener to the hero of the hour recounting his ordeal . . .'

Kydd smiled lazily. 'Thérèse? Perhaps I shall find time to call upon the lady. And your plans?'

'Ah. As colonial secretary my responsibilities do include

the country folk. I've a yen to take a visit – see the lie of the land, so to speak,' he said casually.

'To see your curiosities of Africa is your meaning, you villain,' Kydd chided.

Renzi chuckled. 'All in the way of duty, of course . . . I'm minded to go to Stellenbosch, not so distant and highly regarded for its wine-growing. I may tell you of it on my return,' he added.

Vastly content after his meal, Renzi sipped his prime Constantia, delighting in its freshness and zest, quite different from the fashionable but sombre European offerings that must make the long passage from the Cape across the equator.

The developing African sunset was at its most compelling: the quality of the spreading blaze of orange and smoky reds exceeded anything he had seen before and he absorbed it in a reverent silence.

'Another *koeksister*, Jonkheer Renzi?' Van der Riet, the *land-drost* of Stellenbosch and his host, asked politely. Renzi declined, surfeited by the sticky confection, but the large man helped himself to another two. They sat together in comfortable cane chairs on the stoep of the residence.

'A good day, Mr Secretary.'

'It was indeed,' Renzi agreed. A steady stream of the hard-working people of this second oldest Dutch settlement had come to take the oath of allegiance, and the returns of the government muster were in scrupulous order, as were the revenue books.

'And a splendid repast to conclude the day!' Renzi added, in praise of the roast hindquarter of bontebok. 'The bounty of this fine land continues to amaze.'

His heart was full. The Cape was all that could be wished for in a new life, healthy and with limitless prospects for growth. Here, Cecilia and he would put down roots and begin their life together.

'Do you mind, sir?' Van der Riet drew out a long clay pipe and stoked it with dagga, the sweet Cape-grown tobacco. 'I find it eases the mind after a day's concentration.'

After a few satisfied puffs, he went on quietly, 'You wonder why we accept your rule so readily. I will tell you. It is because we hanker after the *lekker lewe* – the good life that comes from the taming of a hard land. Any that can provide us with the security and freedom to do this, we will submit to.'

Unspoken was the other side of the bargain: if security was not provided, neither would be the loyalty. 'I understand you, Mijnheer,' Renzi replied. If the French established themselves ashore, this tenuous fealty would evaporate and they would be left to their own slender resources. But, of course, all they had to do now was to hang on until the consolidating troops and support arrived from England and they would be impregnable. But in the meantime . . .

The *landdrost* took another puff. 'Did you find your expedition to the mountains agreeable?'

'Why, yes, Mijnheer.' It had been only a few days, travelling into the Hottentots-Hollands, but he had encountered a country of fierce grandeur that was boundless and challenging – and one that Cecilia would certainly adore. It had been a dream-like progress: the jog and jingle of the long narrow ox-wagon, the *voorloper* with an immense whip driving his sixteen wide-horned oxen along crude tracks over the mountains; the slow climb into the dark, contorted ranges rearing steeply from the flats; impossible hairpin turns with jagged crags to one side and a precipice to the other; then a perilous scramble into the Drup Kelder, a cave of ghostly petrified columns and icy streams.

Before sunset each day a halt was called and a fire started while the wagons were outspanned. Then, a delicious supper of ostrich eggs cooked in the embers under a blaze of stars and, after a companionable Cape brandy, a comfortable bed had been waiting in the wagon.

As they had wended their way back, Renzi made acquaintance of the mountain *fynbos* and the carrion flower, and quantities of springbok antelopes performing their curious pronking. No giraffes or lions, but once he caught sight of a tufted-eared lynx peering resentfully over a rock ledge.

Renzi took another sip of his wine. 'Mijnheer, Franschoek is a singular place, set so in the mountains. Here, you're rightly content with your vines, but what about your farmers there?'

The *landdrost* courteously explained: it was the Boer farmers who were the pioneers in this, pushing the boundaries of settlement into the trackless interior; they laid down their isolated farms and by their own hands carved a living out of the hard ground. They were a stern, independent breed.

Of another sort were the Trekboers who, like desert nomads, moved about the country with their herds, living out of their wagons, while some went even further and scorned any contact with conventional civilisation to the point at which they turned their backs on even their Dutch kin.

And the original inhabitants? The Khoikhoi were peaceable cattle-herders who had come to terms with the white man, but the rising power were the Xhosa, whose warriors were displacing the Khoikhoi and pressing the settlements back from beyond the mountains to the east. An uneasy truce was keeping them at bay along the Great Fish River but anything could set them off on the blood trail again.

Renzi was building a picture of a country that was not yet a nation but had its future before it – could it be said that the accident of external forces that had brought them to take the Cape would be to its eventual advantage? The prime motivator for the British Empire had always been less about glory and more about trade, the establishing of markets and sources of raw materials, and thus great efforts were always made to bring peace and the security to allow this to flourish.

What would not be possible here, given a long period of peace and the world's markets thrown open? If he and Cecilia could—

A polite clearing of the throat interrupted his thoughts. 'Er, shall we go in, Mr Secretary? My daughter Josina has been persuaded to play the fortepiano for us and is anxious for your opinion of her Clementi . . .'

As he rose Renzi had a fleeting image of his friend, the picture of a thoroughbred seaman. Now their paths would diverge into two very different life courses. At this very moment where was he? What new adventure was *L'Aurore*'s captain sailing into without him?

From where he lay, Kydd could make out the vast black bulk of Table Mountain blotting out the stars – the Southern Cross constellation was just about to be swallowed up in its turn. The house seemed to be in a charged silence, broken only by the mournful baa of a distant goat and the muffled sound of revelry down by the water's edge.

He smothered a sigh. There was sleepy movement next to him and a pair of legs slowly entwined in his as a female voice demanded huskily, 'Kiss me again.' Her resulting passion released his own in an erotic flood, and then they lay together in a long, silent embrace.

With a final caress she rolled over, but for some reason sleep eluded Kydd. Was it the strong Dutch coffee they had shared on arriving here – or the heady shock of the evening when the distant and haughty Thérèse had melted into the passionate and imperious woman who now shared her bed with him?

It had happened so quickly: he had paid his call at her town address, a large and well-appointed house where she was apparently the only lodger, and been received graciously. He had stayed to take tea and was able to tell her something of his recent ordeal. She had listened politely but when he had asked about her own tribulations as a French royalist noble she had declined to talk about them, saying they were too painful to her.

Instead she had asked about his naval career, anxious to be reassured that everything was being done to prevent a French onslaught. He had answered soothingly but she had pressed the issue, asking if he was privy to the highest levels, that they might be concealing the truth from the people. Only when he told her that he regularly spoke with both the governor and the colonial secretary personally were her fears allayed and the first real warmth entered her smile.

She talked a little of the wine estate her father cultivated up-country, as close to the climate of their ancestral estate in France as it was possible to achieve and ended with a vague suggestion that he might visit her there some day.

Before leaving he had found himself inviting her to the theatre the following day, being surprised and pleased when she had accepted. Accompanied for the sake of propriety by the unsmiling Widow Coetzee, the keeper of the lodging house, they had attended the fine theatre in Riebeeck Square.

Kydd had been gratified at the astonishment and envy he saw on all sides, for he was aware that this daughter of a baron was not known for appearances in public, let alone accompanied by a friend of the opposite sex.

Afterwards he had returned her to the residence and accepted the offer of refreshment. When Vrouw Coetzee retired, they were left alone. He had been taken aback by her ardour – but had responded in like kind, hers a possessive, hungry need, his a startled but willing response.

With a glance at the now sleeping Thérèse, he could only wonder where it would all lead.

Kydd waited impatiently at the old jetty for the dawn when he would be seen from *L'Aurore* and a boat sent. He watched as the light spread, taken with the delicate tints falling on the seascape. It would be hours before the sun appeared over Table Mountain, and until then the entire town and anchorage would be spared its heat.

The boat came; he acknowledged Calloway's greeting genially and took the opportunity of viewing his ship from the outside. With no dockyard worth the name, they were on their own resources and were thus spending their time at anchor performing all the tasks of fitting and fettling that were so necessary in keeping a ship seaworthy.

Topmasts had been sent down for inspection after their encounter with the Ox-eye, giving a stumpy look to the vessel; the larboard shrouds were in the process of being rattled down – the retying of each of the ratlines to parallel the waterline – and the old sailmaker Greer would have much of the upper deck spread with sails a-mending.

A dull thud ashore told him that the castle had deemed that day had broken; it was answered by the flagship *Diadem* and aboard *L'Aurore* on the quarterdeck the Royal Marines were performing the solemn ceremonies attendant on a new day. He ordered the boat to lay off until these were completed, then came aboard.

As his breakfast was prepared, he asked Tysoe to shave him while Gilbey recited events since he had gone ashore and clumsily asked when Kydd might be returning there. It was of some interest to him, it seemed, as there was to be racing at the Turf Club at Green Point and, of course, the captain and first lieutenant could not be ashore at the same.

Kydd waved Gilbey away while Tysoe finished his ministrations. The man had a moral right to the liberty but he was eager to see Thérèse again.

The deeper *crump* of another gun sounded distinctly. Guns were not fired in a naval anchorage without good cause and he snapped to full alert. There was a sudden clatter and the sound of running feet. A breathless messenger burst in. 'Mr Curzon's compliments, an' a gun from Signal Hill wi' the hoist "enemy in sight", sir!'

Kydd pushed him aside and made for the upper deck, heart pounding. He snatched Curzon's glass. Three red flags vertically. As he took it in, there was a silent puff of smoke as the flags were snatched down to be replaced with another, the numeral one, followed by the thud of the discharge arriving seconds later.

This was not making sense: a single ship could conceivably be sighted ahead of the main body but this would be at a distance that made firm identification as an enemy very unlikely.

There was no time for puzzles. Kydd roared the order for

quarters, the marine drum in a frantic volleying at the hatchway, and men scrambled to obey in what might be a fight for their lives.

It had come at the worst possible time. *Leda* and *Encounter* gun-brig were still returning after a false alarm to their usual scouting station and the only other, *L'Espoir* brig-sloop, was under repair and therefore there had been no warning.

Caught at anchor: no worse fate could have befallen them. In a reverse of Nelson's famous battle of the Nile, was it now the French who would sweep in and, one by one, destroy their unmoving victims?

'Flagship, Blue Peter, sir!'

Kydd nodded. Popham was ordering them to get under way to meet the enemy on the open sea and fight whatever the odds. It would take some time to weigh anchor and get sail on, but with the advantage of height the signal station would have sighted it at a far distance – they probably had time.

Furiously Kydd tried to think. *L'Aurore* had her topmasts down, not only cluttering the decks but seriously affecting her speed and manoeuvrability. Should he obey and put to sea or stay at moorings until they had been swayed aloft?

Her twelve-pounders would be of little deciding value against ships-of-the-line, and any other frigate-like service would be impossible with topmasts struck down – there was no alternative: he had to stay until they were a-taunt. But failing to sail in the presence of the enemy was a serious court-martial offence, and if the worst happened, an ignorant press would crucify him.

'Sir! Sir! Look!' The upper sails of a ship were close in on the other side of the point, the vessel about to put into Table Bay. And flying brazenly out was the tricolour of France.

It was a disaster. Not only had they been caught at anchor but the enemy had come from an unexpected direction, throwing them utterly into confusion. It was masterly timing, and if this was the first of the battle squadron, they had less than an hour to live.

Unexpectedly, a gun from *Diadem* drew attention to the next signal. The Blue Peter jerked down: Popham wanted the squadron to stay at anchor. Then the Dutch colours rose on the ensign staff and at the same time, along the ship's side, the rows of bristling guns vanished as they were hauled in and the gun-ports shut.

Kydd quickly caught on: the commodore had reasoned that the ship that had been identified as an enemy had familiarly sailed close to the Cape peninsula because it was expecting Cape Town still to be in the hands of the Dutch. She was probably a stray from one of the battle-groups come to re-victual or repair. They would find out soon enough: if the ship shied away in alarm it would be proof, but then it would be free to draw down the rest of the French squadron. Unless . . . ?

The other British ships followed the flagship's lead, but there was another gun – the Dutch colours on *Diadem* dipped, then rose again, a stern reminder to the castle ashore, which was slow in sending up a Dutch standard.

The French ship came into full view, a heavy frigate that made a show of hauling her wind as she swept around and, with a signal hoist flying, headed directly into the anchorage. Assured by the tranquil early-morning scene, with everything in place as it had expected – men-o'-war peacefully at anchor and with the colours of an ally floating lazily out from every vessel – the unsuspecting frigate made for the flagship.

Kydd held his breath: at any moment there could be the panic of recognition, a sheering away – but still it came on.

Sailing by the first, a sloop, it pressed on, passing *L'Aurore* so close that individual sailors and the three officers on the quarterdeck could be seen plainly.

As far as Kydd knew no 64-gun ship was found in the French Navy and therefore *Diadem* would seem very Dutch to them – and, of course, *L'Aurore*, recently captured herself, had unimpeachable French lines.

The ship brought to opposite *Diadem* in a fine show. There was unbearable tension: any false move now and they would take fright. All now depended on Popham's timing.

Every eye was on the stranger's fo'c'sle – her bower anchor let go to plunge into the sea at the same time as her sail was taken smartly in. Unbelievably, it had happened.

And in an instant the Dutch colours were struck in *Diadem*. Watching for the signal, in every ship rows of gun-ports flew open and, with a deadly rumble, guns were run out in an unanswerable challenge.

It was check and mate.

Aboard the hapless ship, after a moment's hesitation, the tricolour dropped down in short, angry jerks.

As nearest, and with a boat already in the water, *L'Aurore* was ordered to take possession. Out of consideration for the feelings of the other frigate captain, Kydd himself went, with Saxton and a file of marines.

As they approached he noted the weather-worn appearance of the vessel; this ship had kept the seas for months and therefore was almost certainly part of the feared battle squadrons. The loss of a frigate would be felt keenly.

He was first up the side, punctiliously doffing his hat to the quarterdeck and then to the group of officers standing rigidly awaiting him. '*Je suis le capitaine de vaisseau Thomas Kydd du navire de sa majesté* L'Aurore . . .'

It transpired that the tight-faced captain was named Brettel and had the honour to command the French National Ship *La Voluntaire* on a peaceful voyage to Cape Town and wondered at the temerity of the English to act so in Dutch waters.

Kydd bowed extravagantly. '*Capitaine Brettel, je suis désolé de vous informer que . . .*' It took only a few moments to tell the luckless man of the capture of Cape Town and therefore the necessity of relieving him of the command of *La Voluntaire*. He paused significantly. The man reluctantly unfastened his sword in its scabbard from his belt and presented it with a stiff bow. It was done.

Passing it smoothly to Saxton, Kydd nodded to Poulden, who went to the mizzen peak halyards and toggled on English colours above the French, hauling them up with a practised hand over hand. 'And I'll trouble you for the keys to the powder magazine,' he added politely.

Sergeant Dodd took them and, with his corporal and two men, went below to mount guard. Then it was just the closing act. 'Ah, it would oblige me, sir, should you accompany me to the flagship to meet our commander.'

Popham would get the sword but, much more importantly, he could speak with the man who knew where the battle squadron was. Saxton would have the sense to get below with the rest of the marines and confiscate any charts and papers he could find, and the French seamen would be landed to an inglorious captivity, all in an hour or so of arriving at what they thought would be a welcome run ashore.

Dodd returned hurriedly up the hatchway. 'Sir! Mr Kydd, sir! There's men below – English soldiers, an' main glad they be t' see us!'

The French captain gave a tired smile. 'Taken in a transport.

It was my intention to land them here – the reason we touched at the Cape.'

They started to come up from below, blinking in the sunlight, stretching and rubbing their limbs, in their dozens, scores – too many to count. Their rising joy was infectious as they laughed and shouted incredulously, and tried to shake hands with every Englishman they could reach, some weeping openly and a few staring gape-mouthed at the overwhelming sight of so many ships and the grand bulking of Table Mountain.

'Er, Sar'nt Dodd – get those men into lines or something!' Kydd chided, in mock indignation. This was an altogether unexpected bonus and at the very least a welcome addition to Baird's forces.

'And you're welcome to that heathen beast we have below,' the captain said sourly. 'It took seven good men to put him in irons, no less.'

Kydd toyed with leaving the troublemaker for later but, in the general joy, decided to give him the benefit of the doubt. 'Go below and see if he'll come quietly,' he told Dodd. 'Any trouble and he stays.'

When the sergeant returned it was with a barrel of a Chinaman with fiery eyes and a scowl. Kydd recognised him instantly. 'Ah Wong!' He laughed delightedly. It had been many years but at one time he had been messmates with the circus strongman and seen his skill at scrimshaw.

Wong's face showed suspicion and surprise, then creased into happiness. Hurrying across, he gave a respectful Oriental bow and touched his forehead. 'Ah, Tom Kydd, sir! You now officer. Plissed to see!'

Aboard *L'Aurore*, Wong was overwhelmed when he found another old shipmate, Toby Stirk, there to greet him. Kydd soon found out what had happened: discharged from a broken-down man-o'-war in Sheerness, he had signed aboard a transport on the India run, which had had the misfortune to encounter the Willaumez battle squadron, and he had done his best to make known his displeasure at captivity.

What he would do when he found Doud and Pinto below as well could only be imagined, but of one thing Kydd was sure: they had just won a valuable addition to *L'Aurore*'s company.

Kydd's invitation to the cool promenades of the Company Gardens was accepted with a coquettish pout. 'Why, of course I should, *M'sieur le capitaine grand*!'

It was the place to see and be seen and Kydd strolled with Thérèse on his arm, flaunting her beauty before the gentility of Cape Town. With Vrouw Coetzee at a discreet distance behind, he nodded graciously to those who doffed their hats in admiration, bowing civilly to others, all the time his heart swelling with pride.

She did not deign to glance at anyone, her head lifted in patrician disdain, but Kydd didn't care. She was openly admitting that a liaison existed between them and from now on the world would not be the same.

From the gardens they made their way to the first race meeting at Green Point Common and, in the senior officers' enclosure, absorbed the excitement and atmosphere of the racing. The fine spectacle and fierce thud of hoof-beats brought a flush to her cheeks and an animation that was directed to him alone.

Enjoying the many looks of curiosity and envy, Kydd bowed extravagantly to the governor and the fiscal, flashing a barely concealed look of triumph at Renzi, who was standing with them. Beside him, Thérèse curtsied in dignified court fashion and was rewarded by an exaggerated bow from Baird.

More social interchanges would come later, at a governor's levee, perhaps, but for now Kydd was supremely content. The acknowledged beauty and reclusive French princess had made her choice and all the world knew it.

'A small matter, *ma chère*,' he apologised, when the racing was over. He had chosen the recently formed Africa Club on the Heerengracht to make his social *pied-à-terre* and, besides a subscription of forty rixdollars, rules dictated he deposit twenty-five bottles of wine in the club's cellar. Who better to select them than Thérèse?

Duty done by the delighted club secretary, he stepped out with his lady into the fine evening, a French dinner *à deux* promised for later. He fought off a feeling of unreality as his mind allowed a fleeting but alluring image: returning to Guildford, a post-captain with a royalist French beauty of noble birth. It would be a breathtaking sensation in the little town, to be talked about for years . . .

'I'm sorry, Mr Secretary, but he's insisting he's to see the governor and no other,' Stoll said apologetically, explaining that the man outside was one of the recent survivors so much talked about.

'I'll receive him here.' Renzi sighed.

He was called Knudsen and was of an age, bowed and with his silver hair still dull with the privations he had suffered, face cruelly burned by the sun.

'I am the colonial secretary,' Renzi said courteously, 'and I'm to say that unhappily the governor is not to be disturbed at this time.'

'I understand, sir,' Knudsen said, in a voice barely above

a whisper, and in curiously accented English. 'My business, however, is of the greatest importance and must not be delayed.'

He leaned forward confidentially. 'A serious matter for His Excellency, concerning as it does the safety of this settlement.'

There was something in the man's calm but earnest manner that triggered unease in Renzi. 'I'll see what I can do,' he said, and went to find Baird.

The general was in a genial mood. 'Send him in, Renzi – and, mark you, he'll not get a moment over ten minutes.'

Knudsen was shown to a chair. He looked up at Baird, clearly having difficulty in finding the words. 'Sir. You must believe me to be a true citizen of Denmark. Our countries are at war and this has placed me in a most odious moral position.'

'Please go on, sir,' Renzi said, in an encouraging tone.

'I have fought with my conscience since we were in all humanity granted our liberty here in Cape Town and now have come to a personal decision.'

'Yes, Mr Knudsen?'

'It was a noble act that your frigate captain did, to land and search for us in hazard of his own life, and another that we were given our freedom as shipwrecked souls in this place.'

'And . . . ?'

'Therefore I'm come to a determination, even if it might be said to be a betrayal of my country, to tell you of a deadly threat to this settlement, one of which unhappily I cannot provide the details but which none the less appears to be of a fatal nature.'

'Please be plain, sir.'

'Our ship was on its way from Christianborg to the French

249

islands in the Indian Ocean. On board were passengers, and two of these were French officers of the Army. They caroused much and what I overheard I will tell you now.

'There is an enterprise afoot, which is intended to restore Cape Town to Bonaparte's empire. It involves supplies, timing and that their navy plays its part. I cannot tell you more, except to say that one boasted to me that Cape Town would be theirs to plunder within the month.'

In the shocked silence, Renzi was the first to recover. 'Sir, it is of the first importance that we know whence the assault will come. From the sea? A privy landing on the coast far from here? Or a direct descent on the town, perhaps.'

Knudsen shook his head sorrowfully. 'I sincerely wish that was in my power. As you might expect, talking between themselves, there was no general plan laid out, and as a merchant factor, my interest was never in any military adventure.

'Sir, I tell you this in violation of my feelings as a Danish citizen, but in respect of my obligation to you for your kindness. I know no more.'

After he was shown out, Baird sat down slowly, his face grey. 'I knew the French would retaliate – but this! We know nothing of it, how or where they will come, except that it must be very soon. What can I do to defend against what we've just heard?'

Renzi had no answer.

'Very well. Not a word of this must get out to the common people. We can only hope that the French show their hand early so we can move to delay them until the reinforcements get here. All I can say is, God help us, Renzi.'

Back in his office, Renzi tried to think it through. That there was a threat was not in question – the source was unimpeachable. That it was well advanced could be deduced from the facts as told – an attack before the month was out.

But that could not be, for the news of Blaauwberg would only very recently have been received in Europe and any expedition mounted as a consequence could never have been planned and put into operation within the time-frame.

Therefore it was a local response.

This raised as many questions as it answered. To overwhelm a prepared defence even of the order of what could be mustered at Cape Town implied a massive landing by a major force, together with a powerful naval squadron to sweep aside the sea defences. Where was that coming from on a local level? And the transport shipping required: this must be of a similar scale. It simply did not add up. Or did it?

He went back to Baird and explained his reasoning. 'If it's local it's unreasonable to think they can deploy enough military resources to succeed in a landing. Therefore we must consider how else it can be achieved – and I believe I know.'

'Yes?'

'They're already here.'

Baird blinked. 'Do tell me, Mr Secretary.'

'Sir, it's my belief that somewhere beyond the mountains among the Boers the French are building up a secret army. Instead of a direct landing, they're sending troops overland from the east to add to this force until it's ready to challenge us. Then they'll descend from the mountains to crush us, our navy powerless to stop them.'

'Umm. Not impossible. You mean, they're being infiltrated somewhere along the coast past the settlements and marched inland? There's many a reason a military man might find to say how this might fail, but for now I'll allow it.'

He considered for a moment and added, 'I'd think to have

heard something of any build-up of soldiery but, as you say, if it's placed among our Boer friends they've everything to gain by keeping quiet. No matter, I'll send out patrols and—'

'Sir. You've an immense country to cover and there's simply not the time – and, besides, you'll set the colony to speculation and panic. No, sir – there is another way.'

'Which is?'

'I make a surprise tour of the interior, the purpose of which is let out to be of ensuring that our administration is fairly and truly conducted, namely, that the books of register and account are well kept and in their proper form.'

'You have a reason.'

'Certainly. An army has to be supplied. From these accounts I can easily see if the receipts of foodstuffs in Cape Town no longer match production in the country – that they are being diverted for other purposes.'

'Quite so – well done!' He grunted ruefully and added, 'Although it offends my military sensibilities that the French might be thwarted by mere books of account.'

'Then I'll set out immediately, if I may, Sir David. There's not a moment to lose.'

'Of course. And I'll ask the commodore that a ship be sent to look into the coast to the east as well. We must move on this as quickly as we can.'

Chapter 11

I t was true that, with impunity, Janssens had held out in the mountains until his army of unreliable militia had melted away, but if now there was a core of Napoleon's professionals, gathered up from the garrisons in Mauritius and other Indian Ocean islands . . .

Popham had thus been obliged to send his lightest frigate to the east to join *Leda*, already on station.

Kydd's orders were brief and open: he was to cruise off the long south coast of Africa to intercept anything that looked like a supply train or to acquire any intelligence that would reveal something of a clandestine force.

With the desolate coastline now under his lee he summoned Gilbey and Kendall to discuss a plan of action.

'This is a puzzler, gentlemen. Here we have a secret army being landed but no port available to them.'

'Mossel Bay?' hazarded Gilbey.

'The only place possible, I'll agree, but we've since sent in the lobsterbacks to keep order. No – that leaves no docking worth the name on this whole stretch of coast. They'll have thousands of troops, stores and guns to get ashore, and you've seen the beach surf in this part o' the world.'

'A river, then?'

Kendall harrumphed. 'Not as who's t' say. Never seen such a continent without it has its river navigations,' he offered, adding that the south part of Africa had not one river capable of taking sea-going vessels.

'Up the coast, somewhere uncharted b' us?'

'We can say no to that, Mr Gilbey – the French are good at marching but in your case they'd have to sweat along for many hundreds of miles across to reach us. And by our intelligence they're but a month away from a descent on Cape Town, so must be nearer. And, as well, if they land in unexplored country they'll be in the middle of savage tribes who'll resent 'em crossing there.

'My suspicion is they're closer, the Boers hiding 'em somewhere among themselves. And if we smoke out how they victual, we'll find it.' It was an easy thing to say but the reality was quite another matter. It was a long coast, and if they discovered nothing, did this mean there was no secret army?

'Sir, may we know how far out the Boers have settled away from Cape Town? This'll limit the search a mite, I'm thinking.'

'I have this map from the colonial secretary's office. They're saying they've spread east as far as this' – Kydd indicated a point two-thirds along the blunt heel of Africa – 'as they call it, the frontier. That's the Sundays River and after this there's nothing but tribes o' savages pressing in.'

'Which a mariner might know as Algoa Bay,' Kendall murmured.

'Which Mr Renzi would tell us is as far as Dias got before his men informed him they'd cut his throat if he took 'em further, the land so unfriendly.'

'Aye, sir — but where's to go, these nor'-easterlies an' all?'

Kydd nodded. It made more sense to make a fast board out to sea past the end point, then search the coast on return with a favourable wind all the way.

There was little else that could be profitably discussed and *L'Aurore* was set to making her offing, an exhilarating swoop in the swell with the steady winds, a regular crash and burst of spray at the bows, the weather shrouds bar-taut.

On the return board, however, the day had lost its shine and the cloud became sulky and low, the deep-sea combers showing a vivid white against the greying waters. It persisted, and when the coast was raised once more, the bearings that placed them in position for their run down the coast were taken through a misty layer of spindrift.

A sea kicked up that had *L'Aurore* corkscrewing along, now with curtains of driving rain passing that made observations close inshore both uncomfortable and chancy.

'Let's find some shelter an' ride it out, sir,' Kendall offered. 'No use in trying to search in this'n.'

Kydd agreed, but it was not until some distance further that an offshore island providentially appeared, not a large one but sufficient. 'We'll go to single anchor in its lee.' This would have the added bonus of facing the shore to keep it under observation.

A cold rain squall blustered while they shaped course to round the end of the island. When it passed by, a simultaneous yell came from the two lookouts. There, as large as life and doing much the same as them, was another frigate, and it was not *Leda*.

'Hard a-larboard!' Kydd snapped. 'Take us out again, Mr Kendall.'

L'Aurore came round hard up to the wind and started

255

thrashing seaward as Kydd took in the scene. An unknown heavy frigate, no colours but not Dutch, sails still in their gear and men on the fore-deck – almost certainly coming up to the moor – and, curiously, just beyond, there was a large brig of undoubted merchant origin. Ship and escort? Unlikely – a single brig with a frigate escort was not how it was done.

L'Aurore was completely outclassed by the 38-gun stranger who would no doubt be mounting a battery of long eighteen-pounders and therefore it was both prudent and honourable to withdraw. But what the devil was a big frigate doing so close inshore here? Was it something to do with the secret army, or a chance encounter with one of the French frigates set to range the sea-lanes for prey? Kydd could find no answer.

Should he stay and shadow, or tiptoe past and continue his mission? But the choice was taken out of his hands – sail was cast loose on the big ship and it took the wind, curving about the far side of the island to re-emerge on a course directly towards them.

This was insane! The first duty of a commerce-raider was to avoid battle – even if it became the victor, any damage incurred far from a friendly dockyard could end the cruise at that point. Kydd didn't like so many unanswered questions, and not only that: until he had the measure of his opponent's sailing qualities there was no certainty that in this blow they could even get away.

He glanced up: after her long voyage from England, *L'Aurore*'s rigging was no longer new and her sails were stretched and sea-darkened. If there was to be a chase, it would be prudent not to put too much strain on the gear aloft. They had a heavier suit in the sail locker but it would be suicide to stop now and bend them on.

'Ease her, if you please. We'll wait and see what that one's made of.' The frigate was a mile or more astern and there was no need for heroic measures yet but Kydd watched it keenly.

Its sails visibly hardened as they were sheeted in, a top-gallant briefly appearing and then disappearing as it was trialled, and a bone in the teeth grew larger as the frigate leaned into it. *L'Aurore* was under topsails and courses – Kydd dismissed the idea to spread reefed topgallants because any risky venture aloft that did not come off could end in dismasting and ruin.

Patience and safe seamanship were what was necessary at this point, holding on until the hunter tired of the chase. Cold spray dashed him in the face; they were having a hard time of it in the strengthening wind, which was at cross-purposes to the swell, resulting in abruptly mounting triangular wave-forms that *L'Aurore* struck heavily as she fled.

Within the hour it became clear that there would be no early abandoning of the chase and, worse, the gap was closing. It was now getting serious – as the weather deteriorated it would favour the larger vessel, and any advantage *L'Aurore* had in manoeuvrability would be nullified.

They'd go about now. Kydd had the utmost confidence in his ship's company: they'd been well tried and had settled into a fine body of seamen. 'Hands t' station for staying!'

In this fresh weather it would require the utmost concentration. 'Ease down the helm,' Kendall ordered, allowing *L'Aurore* to quarter the wind to her best speed.

'Lay aloft.' Men scrambled up the shrouds to clear away the rigging, while along the deck, braces were thrown off their pins and laid out for running.

There would be no second chance: if they missed stays it could be disastrous.

'Helm's a-lee!'

They were committed. With the stakes all too apparent, the men threw themselves at the tacks and braces as the orders cracked out, one after another.

'Rise tacks 'n' sheets!'

'Mainsail haul!'

'*Haaaul* of all!'

Responding nobly, *L'Aurore* swept about, sail taking up on the other tack with a thunderous slatting and banging, the seas now meeting her weather bow with explosions of white.

Kydd watched the other frigate intently. The unknown captain was not to be hurried – given that *L'Aurore* had the initiative, he nevertheless held on until he was ready, then made a faultless stay about, falling in astern with little ground lost, an indication of a competent and well-tested crew.

The seas were resulting in an uncomfortable bucking and stiff roll, and still the Frenchman came on – and still no reason as to why he would risk taking on even a smaller ship, especially in these increasingly brisk conditions.

Kydd had to think of a way out. Standard tricks in a chase, such as lightening ship, would be of little use in these seas and smacked of desperation, but any attempt to set more sail would be risky – better to leave it as a last resort.

To wait it out in the hope that the other would abandon the chase was the only option, that and attend scrupulously to sail trim to wring the last knot from the ship. But it was as though there was a malignity in the other captain, a hostility that was hateful and personal, driving him to extremes in wishing Kydd and his ship destroyed.

They raced together over the southern ocean as if tied with an invisible rope. What looked like a goosewinged topgallant appeared briefly on the fore of the other vessel, but almost immediately blew out into ribbons streaming away. Now the deadly intensity of their adversary was palpable.

Kydd took stock. *L'Aurore* was fitted with chase-ports in her stern but these were intended only for the carronades used in defending against gunboat attack. Forward there were two nine-pounders and proper ports used as classic frigate chase guns against quarry – could these be brought aft to bear on their tormentor?

It would mean traversing the entire rearing and jerking length of the ship with near a ton of cold iron on the loose. But anything was better than a meek surrendering to Fate.

It took more than an hour of fighting the beast aft with handspikes, tackles and wearisome tying off by stages but then it was on the quarterdeck and aft to the taffrail. The port, designed by a long-ago Frenchman who had known nothing of carronades, was more than adequate and the gun was wrestled into place. Now they had teeth – even if they were only half the calibre of the other's.

Another hour saw their big pursuer gradually close until they came into range. Kydd didn't expect miracles, particularly with a single gun, but it might give the enemy pause in its relentless pursuit and there was always the remote possibility of a disabling strike.

Stirk chose his own gun-crew and set to work, but it quickly became plain that his task was impossible. The motion at the stern was a dizzying rise and plunge much faster than the gun could be laid. It bravely crashed out, the powder-smoke carried instantly away, but there was no sign of the flight of the ball.

L'Aurore suffered her first casualty, a gun-tackle number carried below, whose nimble avoidance of the weapon's leaping recoil had ended in his near-braining on the driver boom above.

Doggedly Stirk continued until a shame-faced gunner found that there was no more of the seldom-used nine-pounder chase-shot in the locker and their pathetic defiance ceased. He wearily shook his fist at the looming nemesis seething along in their wake.

The French had contemptuously ignored the firing; they had forward chase guns of their own but no doubt thought it a waste of ammunition in the circumstances. *Why* were they so bloody-minded in their chase?

Then – incredibly – the wind started to veer and, with it, its violence. The quirky and unpredictable southern weather had changed the entire equation. With less force *L'Aurore* could regain her greyhound speed. First, reefed topgallants were cautiously shown, and later the reefs were shaken out just as the sun reclaimed command of the heavens.

Now it was a more even contest. Free to choose her best point of sailing, *L'Aurore* lay into it and flew. As the wind eased there were the royals to set – and later perhaps stuns'ls.

Kydd had no doubts now, for he knew his ship was a thoroughbred. Slowly they were hauling ahead. Now was the time for the thwarted pursuer to break off the chase for the end was plain to see. Yet it did not! Instead more sail was crowded on as the two frigates sped across the sea.

In the sparkling weather *L'Aurore* pulled ahead triumphantly but powder-flash and smoke stabbed out of the enemy fore-deck. Chase guns! The seas were still lively, a complex cross-swell making predictions of deck motion problematic and the ball-strike was nowhere to be seen, but it was an unwelcome development. More than one engagement had been settled by a chance hit on a mast or spar.

A hail came from the masthead. '*Saaail* – I see sail ayont th' Frenchy!'

It could be friend or foe appearing beyond their pursuer. As far as he knew, the next India convoy was not due for some time. Another French frigate? They often hunted in pairs. Kydd was not about to investigate and they plunged on.

Within a short time it was clear that the sail was not accompanied by another. It had sighted them and was falling into the line of chase. And while the French frigate must know of it, there was no sign it was taking any notice. The chase continued, as did the harrying gunfire.

And then a sharp eye recognised a peculiarly discoloured topsail on the distant ship. By chance the gunfire had attracted an English frigate at the end of its patrol line – it was *Leda* and she wanted to join the encounter.

Exulting, Kydd saw the tables had been turned. Now the hunter was the quarry – between the two of them the French frigate would be at their mercy. It only needed considered teamwork and they would have it. Of course, Honyman in *Leda* was the senior but Kydd must deliver the Frenchman to him.

If the dogged pursuit continued it would be easy; otherwise Kydd's duty was to turn and engage to achieve a delay until *Leda* could come up.

'Helm down, alter four points to starb'd,' he ordered. *L'Aurore* fell off the wind and, with furious work at the braces, they were quickly making off downwind. Unbelievably, the other followed suit almost immediately, the foremost guns on her broadside firing a ragged salvo at an angle, one shot punching a neat hole in *L'Aurore*'s mizzen topsail.

Leda was now on the beam and on this course the tracks would eventually converge – yet still the Frenchman hung on. It could be that this was a determined attempt to crush them before *Leda* came up, but Kydd's course was clear: he must stay ahead until they were two, then turn at last on his pursuer.

The seas were now moderating, the winds steady, the land far off: it was a clear field of battle for an all-frigate action with the odds for once on their side – but would the enemy stay to fight?

As *Leda* approached there was no sign of a breaking off. Still *L'Aurore* stretched out ahead, the French frigate stubbornly in her wake and *Leda* angling in from to leeward.

And then the Frenchman put over his helm and wheeled to starboard. As his broadside bore momentarily he opened up on *L'Aurore*'s unprotected quarter in a storm of fire. Kydd staggered and fell to his knees with the wind of one ball, which went on to take the quartermaster squarely and send him into a bloody, squirming heap before severing a shroud with a bass *twang*. Another, blasting and splintering into Kydd's cabin, brought shrieks of pain from further forward and yet one more ended in a brutal crunch somewhere in the hull.

The sudden eruption of violence was shocking: the malevolence of the nameless French captain had reached out and savaged *L'Aurore*; it was now a punishing downwind fight against a cunning and tenacious enemy.

Even before he could struggle to his feet there was the sound of a further thunderous broadside – but this was from the frigate's opposite side and it hammered into *Leda*'s bows. Kydd gave a grim acknowledgement: to achieve a broadside on two opponents within such a short space of time was the work of a fighting seaman worthy of notice.

Kydd hauled *L'Aurore* around and now they were following. On an impulse he took out his pocket glass and trained it on the carved stern: *Africaine*. It now had a name.

They passed *Leda* beginning her turn, but then the Frenchman swung to larboard, and once again *L'Aurore* faced that deadly broadside, now to her bows. Time froze: but not a single gun fired. Kydd gave a cynical smile: this great captain had neglected gun drill in favour of manoeuvres, and despite the masterly tactics, he'd been let down by the gun crews and left with no guns ready.

And he would pay for it. Savagely, Kydd gave the orders that brought *L'Aurore* around parallel. Now the Frenchman must stay on course and endure what was coming – if he turned away he would take a full broadside to his high, scrolled stern. Kydd savoured the moment then roared, *'Fire!'*

Instantly *L'Aurore's* starboard broadside of twelve-pounders crashed out triumphantly, gunsmoke towering up between the two ships to be snatched away by the wind. To his intense satisfaction, Kydd saw the shot strike *Africaine* in gouts of splinters, the sudden appearance of black holes in the hull and the parting of ropes to trail in the wind. Their twelves would never be the battle-winners that the opposing eighteens, half as big again, could be, but they had hit back.

Something made him suddenly wheel around. He saw that the Frenchman had timed his turn precisely and had manoeuvred to be between *L'Aurore* and *Leda* leaving an impotent Honyman to curse Kydd for a fool in masking his guns. Face burning, Kydd was about to give the orders to sheer away when he realised with horror that to do so would be to fall in with the expectation that he would present his stern once again.

In a fury of self-accusation, thoughts flashed through his brain – then he bellowed, 'Hard a st'b'd!' It was crazy but it would not be expected that he would throw his ship entirely in the other direction – towards, instead of away. Understanding, the boatswain tore men from the guns in a frenzy to man the lines as *L'Aurore* swung about, taking up close-hauled hard to the wind to place herself directly in the path of the French frigate. There would now be a fearful and crippling collision if one of them did not give way – and it would not be Kydd.

At first the other frigate stood on, as though in contempt of the move, but Kydd knew his man now – at this moment he would be coolly reasoning that if *L'Aurore*'s reckless tactic ended only in tangled rigging it would nevertheless give *Leda* all the chance she needed to close in and that was a risk he simply could not take.

Grimly holding to his course, Kydd saw the other's bowsprit, like a spear, swinging round to aim at their vitals – then it wavered, slowed and began falling away. Within less than fifty feet it shot by the awkwardly turning frigate, Kydd regretting that with men away from the guns he could not slam in a broadside as it passed.

There had been a sputtering of musket shot but otherwise they were unscathed, and once past, Kydd lost no time in wheeling about for battle again. The frigate was taking punishment from a vengeful *Leda*; Kydd's larboard broadside being ready, he would ease in and resume his pounding when the range was clear. This was how it must be – teamwork.

Leda's cannonade ceased and she fell back while *L'Aurore* came up to take the other side. This would be the final act – a brutal battering between two fires until colours were struck. It could take hours – the frigate was still full of fight and, in the hands of its bloody-minded, devious captain, was capable of anything.

Kydd sent *L'Aurore* forward, her men at the guns keyed up for combat – but before she was in position the big frigate yawed widely to starboard and its broadside hammered out ahead of their own. Again the shock and violence of the enemy's malice, debris falling from above, the insane flapping of a ragged sail and a hoarse, morbid bubbling from a doubled-over member of a gun crew. Then their own broadside opened up into the gunsmoke, sounding so puny against the eighteens.

So it was to be a smashing match! *L'Aurore*'s topsails were shivered to spill wind and she eased back to allow *Leda* to come up for the next bout. Both ships fired simultaneously in a fury of gun-flash and smoke, *Leda* every bit a match in size and guns for the Frenchman, who nevertheless fought back furiously.

Guns reloaded, *L'Aurore* began her run in, Kydd alert for any ploy, but this time there were no broadsides. As they began their overlap *L'Aurore*'s forward guns fired one by one, as soon as they bore in a deliberately aimed cannonade, but were answered gun for gun by the French in a display of cold courage that demanded respect.

But before half her guns had fired, there was the shock of a shot-strike on *L'Aurore*'s lower fore-yard, and with a rending crack it broke in two, instantly ripping the fore-topsail from top to bottom and descending to the fore-deck in a tangle of ropes and torn canvas.

The sails thus unbalanced had an immediate effect – *L'Aurore* reeled like a drunken man from side to side as the helmsmen fought to keep her from surging into the side of *Africaine*. Quick work on the quarterdeck had the driver boom sheet thrown off and the big fore-and-aft sail in brails to correct for it. However, to all intents and purposes, *L'Aurore* was out of the fight, falling away while the other topsails were doused until she was dead in the water.

Kydd waited for the boatswain's report, knowing Oakley would not be rushed. 'Could be worse, Mr Kydd. A clean break t' larb'd. I've a notion t' fish the spar with stuns'l booms an' capstan bars. We've a chance!'

Kydd trusted him. It would be hard work, laying along the strong bars and tight-lashing them to the wounded yard, while above, the jeer and other large blocks must be overhauled and much of the rigging re-rove. It would take time, and even as he watched, the two duelling frigates moved away, still firing. Honyman in *Leda* would know that they would rejoin as soon as they could – perhaps two or three hours?

While the work went on, Kydd paced up and down. The strange events leading up to the battle didn't make sense, and neither did the peculiar action of the frigate in falling on them as if utterly to destroy *L'Aurore*, to remove her from the world of man. The ships had never met before; whoever the astute and skilful French captain was, he could not have known Kydd was *L'Aurore*'s captain and therefore any element of personal vengeance was highly unlikely.

And close to the coast, frigates simply did not hazard themselves like that unless they had duties of watching the shore, which had no meaning in these regions. Was it something to do with the secret army? Was there a connection with the brig? What if the brig contained something of such value to this secret army that it needed an escort of force – so important, in fact, that its very presence in that location had to be a closely guarded secret in itself? The more he thought about it, the more it added up. That was why the Frenchman had tried to crush them – to stop the secret getting out.

Was it guns, gold, a famous general? Whatever it was, it could prove the key to solving the whole riddle of the boastful threat to take Cape Colony.

A growing conviction rose that he should be where the brig lay, unmasking its secrets, and not here, contributing in a minor way to a battle. Impatiently he strode up to where the boatswain had his crew splicing, heaving, stropping and seizing in a frenzy of activity. The *L'Aurore*'s were clearly in good heart, laying in with a will and, judging from their banter, relishing a re-match.

'As quick as you know how, Mr Oakley,' Kydd urged.

'Aye aye, sir,' the boatswain responded, aggrieved.

A mysterious brig? Supposition? In the cold light of reason it didn't seem much to set against the action he was now contemplating. The easier thing would be to forget about it and rejoin the fray, but he could not.

'Let's be having sail on her, then!' The fore-yard was now in place at the slings and the running rigging led along. Bending on the new topsail would test the repair and he was eager to be under way.

On the footrope of the fished yard as it took the wind, a gleeful Oakley raised his arm in acknowledgement as it eased to the strain, and Kydd gave the orders that saw sail drop from the yards and brought *L'Aurore* back to life.

'Cast to larb'd,' he ordered crisply.

'Larb'd, sir?' said Gilbey, puzzled. At best this would have *L'Aurore* at right angles to the course of the battle. The two ships were far off, hull-down with only their upper rigging barely visible, an occasional mutter of thunder and slowly rising smoke a token of the continuing combat.

'That's what I said.'

'But that'll take us clear of the fight!'

'We're going back to investigate the brig. Are you questioning my orders, sir?' The deck stilled as men stopped to listen.

Gilbey stepped back as if he'd been struck. 'You're – you're leaving *Leda* to fight on alone?'

'She's perfectly capable of standing up to the Frenchy – we've got more important business. To find out what that brig's about.' There was now no one who was not agog to hear what was being said.

'Sir, this is hard to take.' His face grew pale and set. 'Am I t' understand you're not resuming the engagement?' he said thickly.

'We're not, and that's an end to it, sir!'

Men took position behind Gilbey as he stubbornly continued, 'Mr Kydd, there's those who'd say you're in a fair way of having to explain y'self before a court-martial should you take such an action.'

If Kydd was wrong, there was, of course, nothing more certain: the Articles of War were as strict and unbending on captains and commanders as they were on the common seaman. After court-martial, Admiral Byng of the Royal Navy had been shot on his own quarterdeck for irresolute conduct in the prosecution of an engagement, and what Kydd was intending was nothing less than the abandonment of the field of battle in the face of the enemy.

'I said, are you questioning my orders, sir? If you are, you'll face a court-martial yourself for direct disobedience, Mr Gilbey.'

He stared down his first lieutenant, who looked away, then drew himself up with wounded dignity. 'Then, sir, I would be very much obliged should you log my objections to this course of action.'

'Are you sure you wish to go on record?' If Kydd was right about the brig it would go against Gilbey at the Admiralty, but if he was wrong . . .

'Sir.'

Kydd nodded at Kendall, who looked uncomfortable but made a note in his notebook, then told him, 'Clap on all sail, if you please – we're going back to the brig.'

Curzon moved across beside him. 'Mr Gilbey has a point, you know, sir,' he muttered. 'To quit the scene of action and—'

'It's not your decision, Mr Curzon. Obey my orders and *your* yardarm is clear,' Kydd said cuttingly. He was conscious that Bowden stood apart, avoiding his eye. Was this because he shared the general opposition to his action, or that he did not want to be seen siding with his captain, trusting that there was a good explanation for his order?

It was essential they make the coast without delay. The brig would wait for the return of its escort to continue on its way, of that there was little doubt, but for how long? And if *Africaine* got away from *Leda* would it come back for its charge?

'Rouse yourselves, y' lubbardly crew!' Kydd roared, at the men slowly moving in the tops.

It was the wrong thing to say: these men were keyed up for a fight and were resentful and sullen at the abandoning of their step-ashore mates in *Leda*. But Kydd could not shrink from what he believed was the right moral course.

He grimaced, his face hardening. That mystery brig had better reveal a world-shaking secret . . .

Chapter 12

'Over the ridge only, Secretary,' Stoll said encouragingly. Renzi grunted testily. That was at least another mile ahead in this heated, iron-hued and barren landscape, and he was tired and saddle-sore after days on the trail.

Quickly moving inland from Stellenbosch, he'd crossed the mountains to descend on remote settlements without warning, then reached Swellendam, a pretty town set among forbidding mountains of the Langeberg range and the last that might be thought civilised. In other circumstances the grand scenery would have been diverting: colossal rock formations, black ramparts of mountains stretching away endlessly, but Renzi was not of a mind to take it in. There were still no tell-tale indications of undeclared movement of provisions hinting at the rapid gathering of a secret army.

After Swellendam, he'd insisted they press on into the fringes of settlement, shifting to horses and a small country wagon to make best time, in a fever of anxiety that he would be too late.

Stoll, not informed of the real purpose of the mission, no

doubt thought him some form of administrative maniac. Arriving in small hamlets unannounced, he'd demand of the honoured but mystified *landdrost* or field cornet that he inspect their books that very minute – and then, refusing all hospitality, leave for the next.

It was now getting to the end of what was possible for he had travelled through the entire settled area of the colony without detecting anything suggestive of a concealed army. But nothing else fitted: if it was not to be a mass landing from seaward and the onslaught was to be within a month, there simply had to be an army building up in the interior.

Over the ridge there was no *landdrost* and comfortable *drostdy*, only an out-country farmhouse of the kind that took in weary travellers. It was the furthest he could think to go: beyond was the Great Karoo, a vast, sun-blasted and treeless upland wilderness inhabited only by nomadic Bushmen. The very edge of the frontier. If nothing turned up here, it had to be accepted that he had been wrong in his logic, for although there were Boers right out to Graaf Reinet, even Napoleon's famed soldiers could never cover such distances over this kind of terrain. In that case he would simply drop down to the coast and take ship from Mossel Bay back to Cape Town and ignominy.

But for now, ahead on the winding stony track, the kraal and scatter of outhouses at least promised surcease from the jolting, monotonous driving. They could be sure of something – there were only Stoll and himself; their two servants would be found other accommodation. As they approached, the house-slaves came out in curiosity, each with a shapeless animal skin over the shoulder and wearing a traditional conical straw hat. Behind them was the Boer, in broad-brimmed hat and blue shirt.

'*Ons wil graag'n kamer vir die nag he, Mijnheer,*' Stoll said politely.

The Boer looked at them shrewdly, taking in Renzi's travel-stained but finely cut clothing and demanded, '*En wie is jy?*'

Renzi nodded wearily at Stoll, who explained that he was the colonial secretary.

The Boer stiffened and glared at Renzi. '*Vir jou is daar geen ruimte hier!*' he spat, folding his arms.

There was no need to translate. 'Tell him we're tired, it's late, and I'm not to be trifled with. If there's no lodging his *gastehuis* licence will be revoked – here and now.'

The farmhouse was large but of homespun simplicity, no tiled floor, just hard-packed smoothed mud. In the main room, hams and strings of vegetables hung from the solid beams overhead; a long table and benches occupied the centre. At this altitude a fire was welcome, but with the scarcity of wood it was stoked with dried dung. A giant pot simmered over the hearth.

'Secretary Renzi, this farmer is named Reinke,' Stoll said patiently. 'Do you have questions for him?'

Renzi regretted his first words with the man. He should have put aside bodily weariness for the greater cause. 'I should be happy were he to join us for some brandy,' he said encouragingly.

Reinke sat on the other side of the table, his expression closed and suspicious. Renzi managed to sip the rough aniseed spirit. 'How is his farm – does it prosper?'

It was tough going. If the Boer had any curiosity as to why the colonial secretary was visiting he showed no sign and answered readily enough, but after an hour's questioning, Renzi had found only that the farm was in a small way of sheep, corn and the usual up-country side occupations. It was a way of life that was hard and, judging from the scrappy accounts, almost devoid of profit. He tried more questions but there was no undue change in the pattern of ox-wagon deliveries or sheep drives to the nearest market to the south, no variation in the hard daily round. Renzi had little reason to doubt the Boer, who in any case would not know what he was looking for. In essence this was the finality of his search.

A cheerful woman bustled in to attend to the pot, smiling at Renzi.

Reinke grunted something. 'The Vrouw Reinke,' offered Stoll.

Renzi nodded politely.

'Ah – plissed to meet!' she said shyly.

'You have fine English, Mevrouw.'

She dimpled and fingered her pleated cotton garment. 'I at Meester Dogwood school when a girl,' she said. 'Come – we fin' you a sleep room, but not s' great as castle.'

Ignoring her husband's sullen glare, she picked up a lamp and led Renzi into the gathering gloom to an outhouse. 'Here!'

It was small but adequate. The stretched bull-hide bed would probably have fewer fleas if spread with his bedding from the wagon, Renzi thought wryly. A capacious clothes chest at one end and two amateurish paintings of the dramatic ranges around them completed the décor.

'Excellent, my dear. This will do.' Knowing that his striving must now cease, Renzi gave in to his fatigue. 'If it does not inconvenience, I should like to rest before the evening meal. Pray be good enough to tell my assistant.'

'Yiss.' She smiled and, leaving the lamp, departed quietly.

Renzi flopped on to the bed, which creaked loudly, and stared up at the shadowy recesses. He refused to let his brain dwell on his failure and surrendered his aching bones to rest. Soon he dozed off into a light sleep. At one point he awoke to the sound of voices and a distant jingling of harness. A returning work party? More travellers? It didn't matter any more and he drifted off again.

Some time later a house-boy arrived with a bowl of water and towel. 'Din-nah,' he said, patting his stomach gleefully. Still feeling muzzy, Renzi went with him to the main house, his own stomach growling. The long table was set simply with several dishes, and Reinke sat, frowning, at one end. Renzi was placed apart from him with Stoll opposite, and a lithe young lad, scolded by Mevrouw Reinke – obviously a son.

'*Pens en pootjies*, Meester,' she said encouragingly.

Stoll raised an eyebrow. 'Tripe and trotters, Mr Secretary,' he said drily.

Renzi gave a polite smile.

There was one place not yet taken at the opposite end of the table. Then voices came from outside and a woman stepped into the room. Astonished, Renzi recognised her immediately. It was Thérèse.

But she was not the elegant lady he remembered from the castle reception. This woman was dressed in smart but practical bush clothes – a mannish tunic, leather gaiters, boots, her hair tightly gathered.

She stood for a moment in shock. 'Why, Mr Secretary!' she said in French. 'I – I hadn't thought to see you here.'

Renzi stood and bowed politely. 'Nor I you, Mam'selle.'

There was a sudden tension in the room and conversation stilled. She tossed her head, avoiding his eye, and took her place at table.

'Wine?' Mevrouw Reinke said, holding out a jug. There

were no takers, except her husband, who sat glowering, unable to understand what was going on.

Renzi turned to Thérèse. 'A most interesting country, I'm persuaded. Have you had time to see much of it?' He was intrigued by her transformation – and seeing her so far into the border lands.

Her expression tightened. 'No. And yourself, Mr Secretary?' Her voice was hard, commanding.

Renzi gave a saintly smile and pointedly looked around the gathering, sitting with varying degrees of bafflement. All had Dutch, none had French, and only one spoke English. She picked up on it and rattled off some Dutch, which eased the atmosphere and muttered exchanges began among them. Stoll did not translate but looked troubled.

'Cabbage *bredie*, sir?' Mevrouw Reinke said brightly, looking at Renzi.

'Thank you,' he said, and faced Thérèse again, adopting a tone of light conversation. 'If I might remark it, do you not miss the life in *la belle France* – the fashions, the salons?'

'Some things must be borne,' she answered flatly.

The meal went forward awkwardly. Then Reinke pushed away his plate and growled something, daring comment.

'He hopes that all present enjoyed their meal,' murmured Stoll.

Mevrouw Reinke began clearing the table, saying apologetically, 'He not himself, Meester. He's worry the Xhosa will cross the Zuurveld.'

Renzi stiffened. An incursion? 'Please tell me more, Mevrouw.'

She smiled. 'Reinke don' want me talking, but we hearing a crazy man live wi' them, givin' out muskets. They has guns – there's to be no stopping of 'em.'

The Boer snapped at her harshly and she fled.

Could this be the real secret army, an unstoppable flood of savages? No – it was weeks of travel across the mountains before they were a danger to Cape Town and the tribe would soon tire of it. None the less it should be attended to as soon as possible. Renzi lifted his head thoughtfully and saw Thérèse staring at him with a set face.

'Your pardon, Mam'selle, but I do find your presence here somewhat curious.' There was more than a little about her that was unsettling – known to be aloof and seldom to be seen in Cape Town, keeping to herself and now to be found familiarly in the furthest reaches of the colony, presumably far from her family estate. And what lay behind the brittle defensiveness?

She stood suddenly. 'I find the question impertinent. It's no business of yours, M'sieur, and I shall bid you goodnight.' She turned and left quickly.

'A strange lady,' Stoll murmured.

Renzi nodded.

At breakfast Thérèse was composed and icily calm. 'Did you sleep well, M'sieur Renzi?' she asked, over the corn and bean porridge.

'I did – but the dismal howling in the night was not to my liking.'

'The hyenas? You will be used to them.' One of her servants entered and whispered something. She nodded, replying briefly, and he left, a remarkably huge man, Renzi noted, with fingers like bananas.

'We will be leaving directly and I must now say *adieu*.' She stood up and held out her hand. '*Bon voyage*, M'sieur.'

Renzi felt the fingers move slightly and became aware that a small piece of paper was being transferred into his hand. He bowed elegantly. 'A safe journey, Mam'selle.'

He wandered over to the mantelpiece and discreetly read the note. It was brief and to the point: *I have information concerning the Xhosa. I do not want to be seen by others talking with you. I shall stop my horses beyond the first bend and wait.*

Renzi lingered a short time, then told his secretary, 'I do think I'll take a walk in the morning air for an hour, Mr Stoll. When you've finished, please prepare our wagon – we're returning.'

The freshness of the new day was bracing and he stepped out along the gritty track, careful to look right and left as though admiring the grand scene. Near the bend around the mountain flank, he stopped to inspect a pretty montane flower, taking the opportunity to look back whence he'd come. No one was watching.

The track wound sharply around. Thérèse was standing beside a string of horses with three hard-looking men.

'Did anyone see you?' she asked quickly.

'No. I'm expected back in an hour.'

Her tense manner eased fractionally. 'That's good. Now – why *are* you here?'

Renzi was taken aback by her question and its tone of blunt grimness. 'I beg your pardon?'

'So high in government, trekking this far up-country – there's more to you than it seems, Mr Secretary.'

He drew himself up. 'Mam'selle, if you have some information for me concerning—'

'I'll ask you again. What are you doing out here?'

'Which in course is confidential government business and not of your concern. Now, if you have something to tell me, do so, or I shall—'

'You're frightened, searching out something. Now, what would it be that it brings the colonial secretary himself out here?'

'If it's of that much interest to you, then I can say it's simple administrative matters concerning the form of mandatory returns for—'

Her eyes narrowed. 'That might fool your flunkeys but not me. And now you've heard of the Xhosa.'

'This discussion is to no account,' Renzi said stiffly. 'Therefore I shall bid you—'

She snapped something at her men. Two swiftly took position behind him, so close he could smell them.

'Now. Tell me what you're going to do about the Xhosa. Quickly!'

Renzi stood mute. He had no idea what he had come upon but it was rapidly getting out of hand.

'You're going south to raise an alarm, aren't you? And you're the only one in these parts with the authority to do so.' She bit her lip. 'And now I've to think what to do.'

'Mam'selle, I can only suggest you do nothing reckless to jeopardise your standing in this colony.'

She ignored it, looking at him for a long moment, then made up her mind. 'I can't take the risk. It would ruin everything. I think this means you must disappear, Mr Secretary.'

He couldn't believe what he was hearing, but she showed every sign of going through with it.

'You're aware I'm expected.'

'It has to be done.' There was no cruelty in her expression, neither was there compassion – simply the finality of a concluded decision.

He tried bluster. 'The *colonial secretary*? This is absurd! It will result in such a searching of the country as you must be found out!' With the two guards just behind him, any thought of making a break for it was out of the question.

'Then it must be an accident. I believe it will answer should you be taken by a leopard.'

Renzi gaped.

'Why, yes. They have the useful habit of dragging away their kill to devour in hiding. This will occupy your men for many days in hunting for your corpse – they wouldn't dare return to Cape Town without proof.' She shook her head sadly. 'So foolish of Mr Colonial Secretary to wander abroad at this hour in wild country such as here . . .'

The man next to her flexed his hands, his dark eyes unreadable. There was only the breathy silence of the hot slopes, broken occasionally by the distant harsh call of a wheeling buzzard and the clink of harness as the horses fidgeted.

In a detached way, Renzi was in admiration of her quick thinking to come up with such a workable plan. His neck would be broken here and the body rapidly conveyed to the nearest precipice and thrown down, to be torn apart by roaming wild beasts. And it would achieve the delay that would ensure she was not suspected.

'I see. Out of curiosity, might I be granted knowledge of what you're . . . involved with, at all?'

She looked at him suspiciously. 'You want to drag things out, *hein*? Better for you it was quick.'

'Nevertheless, it would gratify me to find out before . . .'

'You deserve to know, I suppose. It's simple enough – the Xhosa are being given muskets. With these in their hands the balance of power on the frontier is changed. They will push the Khoikhoi and Boers aside to flood in to take the land for themselves.'

'Is this by chance connected with any threat to Cape Town?'

'I knew it! You've heard something and have come to seek it out. Well, it's too late. As soon as this happens, your governor must send every soldier he has to stop them – and while Cape Town lies unprotected, a signal will be sent to our fleet to begin their assault.'

So no secret army – but a far better plan, one that needed only a few shipments of muskets and traditional African tribal enmity to bring about what otherwise would have taken a large army in the field to achieve.

'Then you have some kind of harbour, perhaps a hidden base to receive your shipments?'

'Of course, but this cannot concern you.' She was growing impatient – at any moment someone might appear. He had moments to think of something – but he had to know—

'How far advanced are your plans, may I ask?'

'Within five days it will begin,' she snapped. 'And no one can stop us!'

'But how will you—'

'Enough of this!' she flared, then stepped back and gestured angrily to the men. 'Kill him.'

Quartered by the winds, *L'Aurore* gathered speed, the distant sails and grumble of guns gradually fading astern as she closed with the land once more. It would be easy enough to pick up the island by progressing down the coast but what if the brig turned out to be simply an innocent that had happened to take shelter at the same time as *Africaine*? Kydd realised that not only would he have to answer for it before a court-martial but – which would hurt infinitely more – he would earn the contempt of the ship's company of *L'Aurore*.

His thoughts turned to Renzi, no doubt lording it as a high panjandrum in the Castle of Good Hope. This was a much more elevated situation than confidential secretary to a junior frigate captain and now his friend had a bright future. Who knew? At this very moment he might well be entertaining Thérèse at some high event or other.

He went below to avoid the accusing glances on deck and took refuge in carefully drafting the first part of the report to go in to the commodore, outlining his case for breaking off the action. Thank the Lord he had not been signalled to close action or received a direct order from Honyman, disobeying either of which would be very difficult to explain.

There was a knock and Bowden entered holding out some papers. 'The midshipman's workings, sir.' There was no need for this: Kydd's orders were that their instructor would be the junior lieutenant and he himself would inspect them only if asked to do so. But he knew why Bowden had come.

'Thank you, Mr Bowden. Do take a dish of tea with me.'

'Sir.' The third lieutenant sat awkwardly in one of the chairs at the stern-lights. 'Sir – er, the present action—'

'The gunroom talking wry, are they?'

'Well, some do say—'

'As so they may.'

'Sir?'

'They haven't the facts to weigh my decision and are making their judgements on what they see. They should know an active and diligent naval officer has his duty and that is to engage the enemy, which is all that counts.'

'So you have privy intelligence, sir?' Bowden asked daringly.

'Not as who might say,' Kydd said. 'Our secret army is not so easily flushed out. It is we, the eyes of the fleet, who have the duty to find it and report, and the present danger must take precedence over anything.'

'To abandoning an engagement?'

'Even so.'

'I see, sir.'

Kydd sighed. 'There are good and proper reasons that the brig so takes my attention, young Bowden, but shall we leave it that I do feel it in my bones? A sense much prized by captains, believe me.'

'And if *Africaine* returns while we're rummaging?'

'We have the legs of the Frenchy in anything of a breeze, and *Leda* will be taking her attention for some hours to come. As long as we don't delay our investigating then we'll have time.'

Bowden broke into a broad smile. 'Then we go forward in faith and cry shame on he who doubts! Thank you, sir.'

Kydd knew he had told him nothing of substance – in fact he'd virtually admitted that gut instinct was driving him on – but to the young man it had been enough.

In a state of high expectation, *L'Aurore* sighted the island and came up on its windward side, careful to round it close to.

And there was the brig, lying at anchor in the same position they had left her, nothing changed.

'Seems innocent enough, sir,' murmured Kendall.

'Then why's she still here?' Kydd said. 'We'll heave to abreast, give 'em a look at us.'

He took in the plain but serviceable merchant-service lines. Of medium tonnage, she was not deeply laden, judging from her marks. One or two sailors on deck were idly watching them and there was no flag, which was common enough as owners discouraged the wearing out of perfectly good bunting in vain display. For the moment he had to agree with the master's assessment.

Ignoring the muttered cynical comments of watching seamen, he ordered, 'I'll have the larb'd guns run out as we come up, on my command. And two boats in the water – four armed marines in each, Mr Clinton. I'll take the barge, Mr Curzon the cutter.' If he was going to be made to look a fool, he'd give them something to talk about.

In the light airs *L'Aurore* glided to a stop opposite the brig. Her gun-ports opened and, with a sudden rumble, the length of the gun-deck became filled with the deadly muzzles of her guns. There would be no mistaking her intentions now.

Kydd dropped into the barge and, taking position aft, growled to his coxswain to shove off. Poulden did so, then asked politely, 'Um, what're we lookin' for, then, sir?'

Just what would it be that could turn an innocent ship into a vital part of a great plot to seize back the Cape for Bonaparte? What evidence was there to find that could prove his instinct true? 'We'll know that when we find it,' Kydd replied firmly. As a lieutenant, he had conducted boardings all over the world; the arcane wording of ship's papers, bills of lading, manifests, equipage – all these he knew and the tricks as well, but this was another matter entirely. If the brig was a neutral he would have to tread very carefully to avoid an international incident, but at the same time ensure he did all it took to unmask any villainy. There would be no second chance.

As they neared, he looked keenly to see if there was the slightest thing untoward. The totality of offensive weapons were two pairs of what looked like ancient six-pounders and an empty port, nothing more. 'Mr Curzon, stand off until I hail,' he called across to the cutter, which obediently gave way to the barge, the men laying on their oars.

Poulden headed for the deeper waist of the vessel, where seamen were gathering, and brought the barge alongside. Conscious of being under eye, Kydd swung over the bulwark and rose to meet the resentful look of the brig's master. 'Do you have English?' he asked briskly.

The man shook his head but did, it seemed, understand French, so Kydd went on, in that language, 'My apologies for the manner of this boarding but we are on the lookout for a notorious pirate known to be in these parts. Your name and ship's port of registry, if you please.'

'Enrique, San Salvador.'

A Brazilian? Therefore Portuguese and an ally.

'Lourenço Marques in palm oil, bound for Rio de Janeiro.'

The seamen about him were tense and watchful, an officer avoiding his eye – in Kydd's experience, a sign of a bad conscience. He sniffed delicately. In the heat there were many odours but none that could be described as palm oil – all cargo in quantity stank richly, no matter how closely stowed, and he would lay money on there being none in this vessel.

'Ah, if that is so, Captain Enrique, then perhaps you'll show me your papers. Shall we go . . . ?'

The older man hesitated, his eyes sliding to the fore-hatchway.

'Come along, sir! It shouldn't take long – where is your cabin? Aft, is it?'

'Er, I . . .'

'Yes?'

'It would be better if . . .'

'If?' Kydd said, making a show of impatience.

Enrique turned to one of his men and muttered an order. The man gave a lopsided smile, padded off forward, knocked sharply at the fore-companionway and stood aside.

There was movement and the door swung open. One by one, blinking in the bright sunshine and dripping with sweat from their confinement, a stream of soldiers came up from below – a dozen or more, officers and sergeants, each in the unmistakable colour of French infantry of the line.

They glanced bitterly at the graceful frigate and its naked guns lying off and stood stiffly before Kydd. 'Poncelot, Chef de Bataillon de Chasseurs de la Réunion,' the oldest said haughtily. His face had cruel lines and held a barely contained rage.

The man had no choice in the manner of his surrender, no gallant stand against great odds, no hot-blooded declarations, simply a bald recognition of impotence, a species of checkmate, but Kydd was unmoved. He needed to know just what a senior infantry officer was doing aboard a lowly brig. And the others: each soldier as he emerged looked hard and experienced, some of Napoleon's finest, not the raw colonial troops to be expected in the French Indian Ocean islands – another piece of the puzzle.

Kydd bowed, as custom dictated. 'Captain Kydd of His Majesty's Frigate *L'Aurore*. I'm obliged to inform you that by the fortune of war this ship stands taken and its company are now prisoners-of-war. As you may notice, our force is overwhelming and resistance is therefore not possible.'

Poncelot smouldered. 'What are your conditions?'

'How many are you?' Kydd countered.

'Fifty in all.'

'Then, in the circumstances, as a gesture of honour, the officers may keep their swords but the men must drop their weapons over the side.'

'Very well. In the face of impossible odds we do capitulate.'

Kydd bowed again.

The merchant ship carried no colours to be hauled down

285

and these soldiers' standards or whatever were, no doubt, in their baggage; there would be no ceremonials to please the Royal Marines. Kydd signalled to Curzon to come aboard. 'Post guards where you see fit, and after these soldiers have thrown their weapons in the sea, keep them on deck while you do a thorough search below in case any have been, um, overlooked.'

'Aye aye, sir. Er, might one ask how you knew that—'

'Not every challenge in war is met with powder-smoke, Mr Curzon.' Nevertheless Kydd was gratified at his lieutenant's look of amazement and respect.

He turned to the French officer. 'My condolences on your misfortune, sir. Do let us take a little wine together. The captain's quarters?'

The cynical smile on the Frenchman showed that he knew full well Kydd's intention, and he sat in rigid silence in the homely little cabin.

'Sir, it does cross my mind it's a singular thing that an experienced and honourable officer such as yourself is only afforded passage in such a humble vessel. For a long voyage surely this is too much to be borne,' Kydd began.

Poncelot stared at him mutely, his lips curled in contempt. Kydd held back his irritation. It was going to be difficult, if not impossible, to pry any information from this man. How could he secure evidence of the secret army, the uncovering of a grand plot, an admission of intent against Cape Town?

'The armies of France are victorious throughout Europe, but it is in the colonies that they fail,' he continued, in a sympathetic tone. 'Is it because there's no glory to be won in these parts?'

There was no response. Muffled splashes and plunges announced that the arms were now being dropped overside.

Kydd was frustrated: *L'Aurore* would now have to accompany the brig as prize back to Cape Town. There was enough evidence to reveal French chicanery, but on such a small scale. Would it be enough to mollify his superiors?

He tried again, but was met with the same mocking silence.

Something was afoot but there was nothing to suggest it had anything to do with a secret army. So few troops: it made no sense, any more than that these were all battle-hardened veterans.

'We sail for Cape Town immediately,' he snapped. 'I'll remind you that you'll be constantly under the guns of my frigate, but in so far as there is no interfering with the navigation of this ship, your men will not be confined. Any attempt at a rising will result in their instant restraint in fetters below decks. Is that clear, sir?'

He got to his feet, angry at not having thought of some cunning ruse to weasel the man's secrets from him. Poncelot rose too, with a slight bow and clicking of heels in the continental way, still with his maddening smirk. What *was* he missing?

It was a straightforward enough task to ready the brig for sea. Bowden was appointed prizemaster and old Teazers, sailors from Kydd's first command, a similarly rigged vessel, were sent over to replace its crew, who were hauled aboard *L'Aurore*. Night hails and countersigns were issued, sea-bags swung into boats and the little convoy put to sea.

Kydd went to his cabin to write his dispatch. Dissatisfied with the wording, he went up for air, frowning at the anonymous low coastline slowly passing. Stirk was supervising his mate's crew at work on a carronade and looked up at Kydd's arrival, touching his forehead with a pleased grin.

Then Gilbey came up hesitantly beside him and doffed his hat. 'Sir, I'm t' say I stand well chided for m' lack o' faith.'

'As so you should.'

'A brig an' fifty Frog lobsterbacks – a good day's work, I believe.'

'No,' Kydd replied curtly. 'Not so. There's villainy afoot and I got nothing about it out of the Frenchman. Something wicked – we're having to leave it astern and it damn well sticks in my throat.'

He turned on his heel and went below to resume the dispatch. As he finished his work, there was a soft knock at the door.

It was Curzon, with a sailor standing a little way behind him. 'Gunner's Mate Stirk, sir. Wishes a word.'

'Very well.'

Tobias Stirk padded in, remaining standing but with a wolfish smile. His bare feet and big splayed toes on the chequered floor-cloth brought a smothered grin from Kydd in remembrance of times past.

'What can I do for you, Mr Stirk?'

'Ah. It's just t' say I overheard what ye said t' Mr Gilbey about the mongseer not bein' straight wi' ye an' all. Thought it not right, he a Frenchy. So me an' Wong just had an interestin' yatter wi' one o' the brig's quartermasters. A bit shy at first, but we got there in th' end.'

'He's not, as who's to say, damaged at all?'

'He'll recover, Mr Kydd.' Stirk grunted dismissively. 'Now here's what he let on about. Seems this is their third an' final voyage out o' Mauritius wi' cargo f'r some sort o' rat-hole along the coast. First they lands muskets, then powder an' now a parcel o' soldiers t' finish with.'

A secret base! This was more like it. 'Where is this, er, port?'

'Ain't a port as ye'd know it, sir, more like up a river out o' sight, jury-rigged like.'

'Go on.'

'They's to land their gaff, hand it over t' some cove who he's heard is goin' t' rouse up the blacks b' givin' 'em muskets against us. Right scareful, he says, they bein' such a fierce bunch o' cannibals an' all.'

Kydd felt a rising excitement – but there must be more to it. Then he realised that if there was a big enough insurgence, there would be no alternative but to send a strong force to quell it, leaving Cape Town open to a direct assault.

So devilish! So well planned – and it had turned out that the delivery of these soldiers to direct the native army was the final move before the frontier was set aflame. With so much at stake, no wonder *Africaine* had been sent as escort, and so desperate to see the brig to its final destination and do all it could to prevent word of their presence getting out.

None the less, the brig's capture would soon become known and replacements sent. The only sure way to prevent the inevitable was to destroy the base and its weapons.

'This is deadly important,' Kydd said, with intensity. 'We must find this port and wipe it out before everything takes fire. Did your friend say where it was?'

'No good askin' him,' Stirk said sorrowfully. 'He ain't got the navigation. Says as it's up a river, is all.'

To search every inlet, every river, in the south of Africa was out of the question. Should he put pressure on the officers? Renzi's logic would say that for the good of the greater number an individual might suffer, but this was not in Kydd's nature – besides, these hard-bitten characters would never talk.

But there was another way.

On deck Kydd hailed the startled officer-of-the-watch. 'Heave to the brig – we're boarding.'

Calloway was sent across with strict instructions to Lieutenant Bowden, and in short order was back with a bagful of material recovered from the captain's quarters and cuddy. It was emptied and spread out on Kydd's cabin table, pieces of screwed-up paper, the ship's log, nameless scribbles, receipts.

He called Gilbey in and they got to work. The ship's charts had not been found, probably destroyed, which was a setback. The log was disappointing as well: although it disclosed the name of the port and even the river it was useless information – they had been hopefully called Port Bonaparte and the Josephine River.

That left the hard way. Both officers knew intimately what they were looking for: the scratch workings of navigation for calculating a position; meridional parts, sun's total correction and the rest. The papers were smoothed out and examined one by one, and any that had revealing figures were carefully put aside. They were in two separate hands, presumably the captain's and the mate's, both slapdash and difficult to follow.

Then Gilbey had the thought that, as the vessel was approaching from the east, the workings with the longitude furthest west should be looked at first. And with that, wrested from the mass of numbers, a track emerged – which must lead to the mouth of the river. There, and repeated, was the precious information they sought: the latitude and longitude of the secret base.

Quickly they moved to the position on the chart – but this was a scaled copy of a Dutch one and showed little detail. No doubt the little river did not warrant notice but now it certainly would.

There could be no delay. The base had to be destroyed –
now.

Kydd and Gilbey set to on a plan of action. In this instance
a sizeable frigate was not an asset but she carried boats, and
these could be made to go up rivers. How to equip them?
Fitting for a standard cutting-out expedition or the boarding
of an enemy was well practised, but attacking some sort of
defensive position up an African river?

They needed more local knowledge and one source was
readily to hand. It was put to the brig's crew that if they were
helpful, their status as prisoners-of-war might well be
favourably reviewed. They most readily fell in with it. But
their information was limited: a sand-bar was across the
mouth of the river, which required boats to be kept inside;
cargo was landed on the beach and hauled over the bar to
the waiting boats, then taken up-river to the base, which was
a mile or so upstream. That, and – unwelcome news – an
army of ten thousand Xhosa warriors camped nearby massing
for the uprising.

There was little else they could add besides the fact that
a mysterious Frenchman living with the Xhosa was directing
the whole operation; he was keeping the muskets and powder
under guard until the French veterans arrived to issue them.

On the face of it, the odds were ludicrous, the only possible
thing in their favour being surprise.

How to get heavy boats across the sand-bar? How to cow
an army of ten thousand? How to achieve total destruction?
There were just too many questions, which could only be
answered with stealthy reconnaissance.

Returning to the deck to give his orders, Kydd suddenly
stopped at the problem he saw. The brig lying secure under
their guns couldn't come with them: the sight of it would

arouse the base and bring unwelcome attention. However, if it was left to return to Cape Town on its own, it would have to be heavily guarded and would be an intolerable drain on the frigate's manpower, just at the time when it was most needed.

Sink it? Let it go? Maroon the soldiers? Wreck it ashore? The answer was laughably simple. 'Mr Calloway. My instructions to Lieutenant Bowden are that he anchors offshore and his sailing crew does return with you in the brig's boats. Clear?'

It caused much merriment among the boat's crew, and renewed respect for their captain when they realised what he'd done. Aboard the brig, the soldiers were to be left quite at liberty to do as they pleased, with not a single guard to trouble them. They could eat, drink and make merry as they wished, only one thing denied them: as hopeless landlubbers they could not move the vessel an inch and without boats had every incentive to keep their prison safely afloat until L'Aurore returned to claim them.

'Let's be about our business. Mr Kendall, I desire we should be in this position at dawn, if you please.' This would give Kydd the night hours to review his options.

By the time the grey of dawn was stealing over the sea he still had no plan. An assault from the river by boats shipping a carronade? The Royal Marines holding up the army while the seamen set fire to the buildings, whatever they were?

Keyed up, Kydd waited impatiently for the distant coastline to firm. When close enough they would pass slowly by, positively identifying the river mouth before anchoring well out of sight, ready for the final act. He had done as much as he could. Now for the reconnaissance that would provide the vital detail to enable an assault plan to be put in place.

'Coming up to position, sir,' Kendall said quietly.

'Thank you,' Kydd replied, and brought up his telescope. With local information gained from the brig's crew, they had hand-drawn a chart of the river mouth and approaches and he knew what to look for – a low swirl in the sand-hills with, on the left, a characteristic rise topped with two trees and a crumbling hut to the right, and in the distance a serrated mountain range.

He scanned the shore carefully, but the flat coast, with its undulating, scrubby hillocks, went on and on without a break. Frowning, Kydd ordered the ship in nearer the land and continued. Without result. No discontinuity in the feature-less shoreline, not even a mountain range in the distance. One mile – five, ten. Nothing. He and Gilbey had checked their reasoning, were confident of their results, and with two independent workings to go with . . .

'Put about – we'll try on the other side.' If the brig was out in its reckoning it would only be minutes of longitude, no more than a few miles. It had to be close. *L'Aurore* came around and took up in the opposite direction, holding her course until she passed the expected position. Then she stood on for a mile, two, more – but it was obvious to everyone aboard that the secret of the base was going to stay that way.

There was no other conclusion than that they had been utterly and comprehensively fooled.

Chapter 13

'What are you waiting for? Kill him now!'
Renzi steeled himself but stood outwardly calm as the men made to seize him, hesitating for a moment in bafflement at his confidence. He smiled cynically. 'A rising of the tribes? I rather think not. You've overlooked the one thing that makes it quite impossible.'

Thérèse held up her hand. The men clamped his arms with an iron grip and waited with a growl. 'What do you mean?' she bit.

'Shall I remind you that I'm colonial secretary and few things are hidden from me? And what I know tells me your plan's worthless. You've utterly ignored one vital matter.'

'What's that?' she demanded.

'You can't see it? Then all I may conclude is that as a band of plotters you're both incompetent and amateur.'

'What are you talking about?' she flared. 'You're bluffing, aren't you?'

Renzi said nothing, his smile still in place.

'Tell me!'

He remained mute.

'Tell me, I said! Or I'll have you crushed!'

'I could say anything, which you must believe, and in the circumstances your threats are meaningless, Mam'selle.'

She bit her lip in frustration. 'Don't think you can be allowed to live!'

'Oh? You're going now to your leader to confess you destroyed the only one who can point out the fatal flaw in time to halt this misguided rising? I do pity you, dear lady.'

She stepped close and slapped his face twice, hard. 'I'll make you pay for this, Renzi. But not now. You've won yourself some time. You're coming with us and then we'll see what you've got to say before the *patron*.

'Bind him.'

Renzi's hands were tied behind him with rawhide thongs. Thérèse went to the string of horses and familiarly mounted one of them. 'He goes first,' she commanded, and Renzi was thrust ahead roughly to walk on the end of a rope lead, while Thérèse and the three men followed on horseback, the pack train strung out behind.

'Move!' she snapped. Renzi trudged forward, but after rounding another bend she ordered the party to stop and nodded to one of the men. 'Here!'

He dismounted and took a trussed chicken from a wicker cage, crudely cut its throat and splattered the side of the road with blood.

'Where you were taken by a leopard,' she said acidly.

Renzi glanced at her for a moment, before returning his gaze to the dark, rust-coloured mountain scene. The little convoy got under way again, Renzi's plodding progress setting the pace. After an hour she called a halt again. 'You're worse than useless, Renzi,' she said harshly. 'We'll never make it at this rate. You two – get the mule for this fool.'

The animal was relieved of half its load and Renzi was hoisted on its back, a rope at the bridle leading to one of the men's horses. It was bony and uncomfortable without a saddle and his arms restrained behind him made it near impossible to stay upright. After two tumbles Thérèse ordered his thumbs to be cut free and he was able to ride by holding on to the pack-straps.

They moved off at a brisker pace and, despite his discomfort, Renzi could not help but take in the grand panorama – the narrow trail rimming the spectacle of a great mountain range on one side and the trackless aridity of the legendary Great Karoo to the other. They had left the last farms and now were trekking into the unknown.

All Renzi could deduce was that by keeping the mountains to the south they were curving around to enter the wild Zuurveld well away from the habitations of white men. Thérèse kept up a punishing pace; with little idea where they were, there could be no estimate of how far they'd come, but it must be a considerable distance through the lonely, near silent landscape. There was no sign of Africa's fabled wild beasts other than an occasional wheeling eagle – or was it a vulture? – and unknown scuttling as they passed along.

At one point there was the click and tapping of dislodged stones above them. Thérèse stopped the party, dismounted soundlessly and drew out a long Austrian rifle, swiftly circling the base of the scree slope to disappear ahead. The men sat quietly, expressionless, until there was the sound of a distant shot when one dropped to the ground and loped off in that direction.

They returned, a baby antelope over the man's shoulders

and Thérèse in the lead, cradling her rifle professionally. Then without pause the little group set off once more.

A small valley stippled with the green of some spiky plant provided welcome relief from the gunmetal greys, the ancient reds and orange, and a rivulet tinkled down its slopes. A halt was called to water the horses.

'You,' Thérèse threw at Renzi, who looked up wearily. 'Since we've allowed no rations for useless mouths, you'll find your own supper.

'Show him some *veldkos*,' she told one of her men, who got to his feet and beckoned Renzi.

Aching in every muscle, Renzi followed the man into the stony expanse. He searched about, kicking at a patch of vine with leaves like a bay-tree. '*Camaru*,' he grunted, and pointed at the base.

Renzi scrabbled with his fingers and found a large tuber. He hacked at it with a jagged pebble until it was free, surprised by its weight, at least ten pounds. He found another, even bigger.

'Very good,' Thérèse said sarcastically, when they got back to her. 'Then perhaps you *will* eat tonight, Mr Secretary.'

They remounted and pressed on relentlessly. Clearly she knew where she was going, moving from one water-source to another until, as evening drew in, they ended at a small fold in the ground overhung by several trees of outlandish size and shape.

The men began setting up a pair of tents while Renzi was put to gathering firewood. As the evening came, the surrounding mountains grew darker and more daunting, and all attention focused on the fire over which a well-used cooking pot hung from a tripod. The darkness quickly became complete and by the light of the fire Thérèse doled out portions of stew.

Aching and sore, Renzi tried to make himself comfortable on the stony ground as he hungrily fingered hot gobbets of meat and the tasteless *camaru* tuber into his mouth, a knife denied him. They ate quietly, finishing with *rooibos* tea. Stars were coming out in a profusion he had only seen before at sea, hanging close above in a spell-binding silence.

Thérèse's face took on a demoniac cast as she stared moodily at the fire.

'Mam'selle, should your rising be successful, even to the recapture of Cape Town, it will be to no account so long as we rule the seas,' Renzi said, breaking the silence.

'What should you care? You'll be dead in three days.' Was this how much of the journey remained?

She tossed her head. 'Anyway, that's a matter for the *patron*.'

'Ah, yes. Is he a great man at all, learned in the military arts and—'

'He's my father,' she said flatly.

'The baron! Surely he—'

'He will know how to deal with vermin like you, Renzi.'

An expatriate royalist, plotting with the regicides? Incredible, but it had to be true – unless it was a double-bluff of some extraordinary complexity that he couldn't fathom.

'I look forward to the meeting,' he replied.

He sipped his *rooibos* and then ventured, 'Thomas Kydd – may I ask what he is to you?'

'Kydd? That's no business of yours.'

'I was simply curious.'

'Well, since you ask it – not as useful as I'd thought. A simple *matelot* who kept his mouth tight shut on anything to do with his precious navy.' Her face softened for a moment. 'But as a man he was . . . diverting.'

'Just that?'

'Who are you to quiz me?' she blazed, and stood up. 'Enough of this talking – don't think it will save you, Mr Secretary.'

She stalked off to her tent, the others following to theirs, leaving Renzi on his own at the fire.

It was quite impossible to think of flight. Prowling lions and other beasts would make short work of him, and even if he was still alive in the morning, on foot he would not last long in this oppressive wasteland.

Feeling chilled as the night took hold, he made his way to the horses and the pile of offloaded gear. They whinnied in surprise as he rummaged through, found some canvas covers and carried them back to the fire, spreading out a bed as best he could, a roped bag of clothing for a pillow.

At least now he had peace to think. How quickly his horizons had narrowed from the survival of Cape Colony to his own mortal existence. He turned his mind to the coming confrontation with the baron. It was a bluff that had saved his life; in reality, he had no idea what he could say that would turn the tables, for what kind of man would he be talking to? A royalist or a revolutionary? In any event, when he was seen to have nothing to reveal, he would be dealt with summarily.

His only chance would be to make a move before they arrived at the base. Unarmed, he wouldn't stand a chance against the three men, and there was then the question of what to do with Thérèse. There was nothing for it but a course of action that, in his very being, he despised: he would find a heavy rock and silently crush her skull where she lay, trusting that, the deed done, her men would see it in their best interests to lead him to safety.

299

He waited for an hour or so, then stealthily eased back his covers, raised his head and looked around. It was a dark night but brilliant with stars, the light just sufficient to make out the primeval terrain, the inky shadows of the tents and trees. The firelight was a problem so he got up, stretched and went out into the darkness with the obvious intent of relieving himself.

Careful to keep the glow between him and the tents, he felt around until he found a weighty piece of rock, then began painstakingly to circle towards her tent. A sound startled him. Ready for some terrible beast preparing to spring, he then realised it was just a snore from the men's tent.

He was coming close, but all it needed was for him to trip over a root or step on some nocturnal creature and he would be finished. The tent was hidden in blackness – he remembered there were ropes on all sides except the entrance, which would be laced up. That left the other end. He must work at raising the edge carefully and then, in the shadows, strike without seeing. To achieve a killing, silencing hammer blow on a woman.

Judging he'd nearly reached the end of the tent, he closed in, heart pounding. It loomed huge and he could hear no sound from within. All he had to do now was to get close, ease up the edge and do the deed quickly before the cold night air woke her. Crouching low, he moved forward – and froze, for the star-field had just been blotted out. For long minutes he kept motionless. Then he saw it was one of the men on guard and cursed himself; of course, they'd be taking it in spells through the night to watch for wild animals.

In a wash of disappointment he skulked back to his bed-place.

Days of soreness and tedium followed, as they progressed

over endless miles of scrubby bare red plains between the ranges until at last they began to descend into the green-clad downlands. They reached a river and Renzi sensed tension after they had splashed the horses across and made the low scrub the other side. This must be the actual frontier and they were now within the Zuurveld before Xhosa territory – and therefore near the end of their journey. Picking up another, smaller, river, they followed its banks as it wound through ever-flattening terrain.

Where the scrub thickened to light woods, they stopped. 'Tie him,' Thérèse snapped. He was made to dismount and the thongs tightly reapplied. A rope led from them to one of the men on horseback and they set off, Renzi plodding on in the lead.

They wound down a track into a shallow valley, dark green shrubbery thick on each side. His eyes cast down as he trudged on, Renzi saw that underfoot the trail was turning from the usual red and ochre to a paler hue, with the addition of white sand. Somewhere ahead they were nearing the sea. The blessed, limitless, friendly sea. It caught him unawares, bringing a sudden lump to his throat. Out there – somewhere – was Kydd, still in the first flush of glory of his frigate command, going about his duty with no idea that his friend could have been brought to such a pass. It was as if—

In a shocking flash, dozens of dark shapes shot up into view each side. They resolved into tall warriors, each with an assegai and a shield, clad in nothing but a loin-cloth with decorative tufts around their ankles and a tall headdress. Their fierce eyes glittered as they brandished their weapons.

Thérèse and her men immediately threw their arms wide, palms open and upwards in a gesture of peace, and one of her men spoke in a short, strangely guttural clicking language. The assegais were withdrawn but the warriors did not fall back; this was now an escort and they took position on each side as the trek resumed.

Renzi felt their eyes as they loped along next to him, their arrogance of manhood and ferocity of purpose fearsome. These were quite different from the harmless Khoikhoi of Cape Town, and if they were enabled to sweep in on the settlements, they would stir up an appalling tide of war. Baird could then do no other than send every soldier he possessed to stem the flood.

The river was now a broad, barely moving calm expanse, curving among the flat scrub and an occasional tree. They passed a rise, along its top many more warriors watching their progress. From somewhere in the interior rose an immense ululation, a swelling sound of tribal song that could only have come from countless thousands of throats. It beat in on Renzi.

Then, abruptly, they rounded a bend and ahead Renzi saw a sizeable native-style kraal stockade fronting the river, the roofs of huts inside visible and around it patrols of Xhosa warriors. Thérèse spurred on eagerly past Renzi and gave a shout, which was answered from inside. Several men came out swiftly from a far entrance. She threw herself at one whose reaction could only have been that of a fond father.

Renzi straightened, trying to ignore his aching limbs as he went forward.

'Good God, Thérèse! Who's this?' The man was tall, with a neatly clipped beard, and carried himself with effortless dignity. The eyes were intelligent but concerned.

'I'll tell you about it later, Father. First there's—'

'No. You'll tell me about it now, my child.'

She sighed. 'He saw me at the Reinke farmstead. I found out he knew too much and thought to bring him to you. He says he knows why the rising will fail.'

'Cut him loose,' he said firmly. 'Here we may fear no one man.'

He turned to Renzi. 'Why, sir, my daughter failing in her duty of politeness, therefore I must ask you to introduce yourself, if you will.'

Renzi returned his gaze with composure. 'Do I have the honour of addressing the Baron de Caradeuc? Then, sir, be introduced to Nicholas Renzi, colonial secretary of Cape Colony.' His elegant bow would not have been out of place in the court of the late king and was returned instinctively.

'An . . . unexpected honour, M'sieur.' Clearly taken aback, he flashed a troubled glance at Thérèse. 'However, it does leave me in some degree of perplexity as being how to . . . entertain such a notable personage.'

'He can't be set free now, Father.'

'And as we have not the means to ensure his, er, security while in the process of setting our plan in train, it does rather set us a problem.' His apologetic smile might have been seen on a parson regretting upset picnic plans.

Renzi knew he had to get through to the baron if he had any hope of getting out alive. But the man was a mystery – he was known to be a royalist, a refugee from the chaos of revolution, and here he was, patently of noble birth, with the delicacy of manners and graces of the *ancien régime*, in Africa fomenting a native rebellion.

'Sir, it would gratify me much to understand how a gentleman of courtliness and discernment is to be found in such distant parts as this. Do you not pine after the salons and civilities of *la belle* France? The home of Voltaire and

Montesquieu both – the mists on the Seine from the Pont Marie, the bookshops on the rue St Honoré even?'

'Why, I do believe you are acquainted with Paris, sir!'

'Not so long since I had the felicity of attending the Institut as guest of M'sieur La Place.'

'Then you are a scholar indeed!' the baron exclaimed, in wonderment.

'In the meanest way, sir. I have pretensions at a theory of the human condition that require extensive travel of which—'

'He lies!' Thérèse spat. 'I know him for a certainty as a humble clerk of sorts from off one of the navy boats. He must have bribed his way to the attention of their ruling general to get his grand post.'

'Possibly. A gentleman of learning certainly,' the baron mused, stroking his chin.

'And one who is in some mystification as to the meaning of your present actions, sir,' Renzi said civilly.

'I believe, Mr Secretary, you are referring to this current enterprise. There is no mystery, sir. I'm engaged in the raising of the Xhosa tribe to fall upon the eastern frontier, thereby attracting the military forces of the English occupier while Cape Town is retaken. As you may imagine, I have some considerable interest in what you have to say concerning why it must fail.'

Renzi swallowed. 'None the less it exercises me considerably why a distinguished member of the *noblesse* does so support the Emperor Bonaparte in such a forward manner.'

The baron winced. 'I abhor the upstart Corsican. Probably more than you do! He has the manners of the *banditti* and the instincts of a wolf and while he tears down the old order he replaces it with his own aristocracy. A vainglorious and contemptible creature.'

'Then why—'

'There are principles of honour and destiny that must rise above all else. At the present time the country is ruled by that scoundrel but will not be always. There will come a time when we emerge from this state of eternal war into a bounteous peace. Then, sir, the age of empires will begin and undoubtedly whosoever has possession of the fulcrums of trade will inevitably accrue the most glorious and enduring dominion.

'France shall no longer be denied her place as queen of nations, her right by virtue of culture and civilisation! No more in the shadow of other more thrusting realms, she shall step forward to take her role as leader and exemplar, ruling over the greatest empire the world has yet seen.'

'And for this you—'

'For this I abjure my title and honours, for what are they compared to the glory of one's country? For this, too, I have invested my entire fortune in the equipping of the expedition, for nothing but celerity and swiftness of purpose will secure the prize.'

'I honour you for it, sir,' Renzi said sincerely. The baron was a patriot of the highest order and had dedicated himself and his wealth to the service of his motherland. And he was impeccably correct in his logic: whoever ended the war with the most possessions would dominate trade and world empires – and he must be aware that the British were at that moment, thanks to their navy, beginning to detach French possessions and adding more of their own. A strike back now, before military reinforcements and the apparatus of permanent rule could arrive from England, was their only chance. He was privately funding the uprising to overcome delay and bureaucracy, yet had been able to arrange in time the necessary deadly counter-stroke – a direct assault by some powerful squadron already at sea.

The baron gave Renzi a curious look. 'And now you will infinitely oblige me with your views on why we must inevitably fail.'

'I vow I shall tell you everything I know, but find it necessary to learn further of your preparations, sir, it bearing so on the elements of success.' What was he reading of the man? The stakes were higher now by far than his personal survival.

The baron beckoned graciously. 'Then I shall be your guide and show you our little enterprise.'

Walking side by side they began their tour within the kraal. 'A contemptible little fortification, you'll agree, but then it's for a temporary purpose and, besides, what have we to fear, no one knowing of our existence?'

It enclosed a wide area: to one side were numerous thatched huts in the native style and, set apart, others with a small stoep that resembled a Dutch country dwelling. 'Our living quarters. And over there those of our closest warriors.' There were many such men nearby, some standing on one leg with the other crooked against the knee while balancing with the assegai. 'The main band numbers some ten thousand, four paramount chiefs and their Nguni followers. A formidable force to unleash, I'm persuaded.'

'And there?' Renzi indicated directly across to the other side. It was a long, low thatched structure away from other huts covered by canvas and well guarded.

'Ah. That is where our muskets and powder are stored. Dear me, you have no conception of the pother and vexation it has been to mount this uprising. The Xhosa are not to be trusted in the article of muskets – if they got hold of them before time they'd turn them on their brothers to seek some petty vengeance or other. No, the only way for me has been to send first for the weapons, useless, of course, without powder. This was to attract the avaricious attention of the warriors to flock to me and, as you can see, has succeeded handsomely.

'Then the recent shipment of powder. To prevent its looting and ransacking, I have made my selection of those who will bear my arms and they have every interest in guarding the store. Tomorrow is the final move, which will set match to fuse.'

'What is that, pray?'

'I had hoped to have the services of fifty soldiers of France to aid us but their vessel seems to have been delayed. I can wait no longer – the warriors are hot with blood-lust to begin and I risk my standing with them should I attempt to hold them back. Therefore I've given orders that the arms will be issued. Tomorrow.'

Renzi felt numb at the sheer impossibility of stopping the tidal wave of savagery about to engulf the frontier. And shortly he would be asked to reveal the fatal flaw.

'Out of the gates here, we have but a short walk to the landing jetty.'

A rickety but strong pier jutted out from the riverbank. Two cargo-loading boats lay alongside and Renzi estimated that there was at least four feet of water available. Was the river tidal, he wondered.

'It is made from what the local people so quaintly term stinkwood. Now, is there anything else you wish to assess before you share with me your objections?'

Renzi looked about him. There were above a hundred warriors in sight and Thérèse and her men were paces away:

he would be chopped down before he had gone yards if he tried to run.

He drew himself up and said quietly, 'Sir, I promised to tell you everything I know. And I have to say to you now, that I know . . . nothing. Nothing at all. There is no reason I can think of that might halt your scheme.'

'I don't understand you, sir.'

'The claim was a subterfuge only, practised on your daughter to enable me to gain the satisfaction of learning who it was that is about to set the frontier ablaze. That has now been achieved.'

The baron stared at him, then laughed. 'Upon my word, sir, that is rich! You're a man of courage and spirit such as few I know.' He chuckled again.

'Father!' Thérèse snarled.

'Ah, yes.' A shadow passed across his features. 'It grieves me more than I can say that such a noble soul shall pay for his knowledge with his life, but with what you know, sir, you will see that it is beyond my power to preserve it. Let me assure you, however, that when the time comes it shall be done swiftly and with mercy shown.'

Renzi went cold.

'Yet the very least we can do is offer you the pleasures of our table this night. It does pain me to observe, however, that on the morrow I expect the ship to arrive with the soldiers – no doubt it has been lately delayed by the poor weather we have been having. Or in its absence we must shift for ourselves. We shall then be very busy, as you will understand, and therefore, most regrettably, I beg you will think of this night as your last.'

True to his word, the evening passed in a blaze of colour and feasting, lines of Xhosa women dancing in the firelight, the glitter of their bangles vying with flashing eyes amid the hypnotic thunder of drums. Gourds of drink followed the devouring of roasted ox and *umngqusho*, a maize and bean delicacy. Tribal choirs sang full-throated melodies, lithe solo dancers writhed and gyrated, but the honours of the night went to the warrior dance – countless numbers arrayed in the full panoply of war, by their hoarse shouts and brandished weapons leaving no doubt about what was to come.

Renzi saw it only through a haze of distraction. There was no conceivable escape: two of Thérèse's men stayed constantly within a few feet of him and the Xhosa knew full well his status – should he make a break for it, they would instantly skewer him with assegais for the kudos of bringing him down. At least the baron had promised a merciful end.

In the early hours the festivities waned and the participants streamed back to their encampment. Visibly embarrassed, the baron bade him goodnight. Renzi was escorted to a hut and guards posted. He was left alone on a rush bed with his thoughts for the time that remained to him.

In the last hour of the night a small line of grave-featured witnesses called for him: the baron, Thérèse, and the inevitable heavy-set brutes, each carrying a flaming torch that illuminated the scene pitilessly.

'It is time, sir. Are you ready?' The baron carried a small, ornately chased box, which Renzi recognised. So it was to be a pistol.

He looked up at the vast profusion of stars. In such a short while they would fade as the day stole in – one that he would never see. 'As ready as any mortal can be,' he said, without emotion.

'Er, most would wish that it be carried out privily, away

from prurient eyes. Do you have any preference, Mr Secretary?'

'Yes, Baron. I have a yen that my last sight shall be of the sea. Is this at all possible?'

'I'm desolated to have to refuse you – that's over a mile or so away. Perhaps a fine view of the river – it does join with the sea, after all.'

'Then that must suffice.'

The little party started out down a path by the barbarous light of the torches and then the baron paused, turned, and said firmly, 'Not for your eyes, my dear. I shall be back presently.'

'A pity,' she said callously. 'I'd hoped to hear him beg for his life.'

Chapter 14

'We were gulled,' Kydd said in a low voice. To use the captured vessel's own reckoning to find the base had seemed foolproof. 'Take us back to the brig, Mr Kendall.'

The master hesitated, shuffling awkwardly. 'Sir, it's not f'r me to criticise, but in setting up y'r workings, did ye get a sight o' the charts they had?'

'No, the rascals destroyed 'em.'

'Well, here's a possibility as ye might think on . . .'

'Yes, Mr Kendall.'

'If the brig's really out o' Mauritius or some such, then they'll be using Frenchy charts.'

'And?'

'All their reckoning will be with those charts – which, in course, uses the Paris meridian.'

It hit Kydd like a thunderbolt. 'O' course! Damn it to blazes!'

It was so obvious, once brought to mind. All British charts had the line dividing the eastern and western hemisphere – 0° of longitude – passing through the Greenwich Observatory in London. The French had theirs running through Paris. Therefore any given figure of longitude would be off by the difference, probably some hundreds of miles.

Kydd retrieved the situation in seconds. With the longitude of Paris being precisely 2° 21′ 3″ to the east of London, this correction was applied to the figures and they had a position near a day's sail away to the west. 'Well done, Mr Kendall! We'll flush 'em yet.'

Next morning they raised a serrated mountain and later the other sea-marks came gloriously together at the new position, hardly needing the brig crew's confirmation. As *L'Aurore* sailed serenely past, half a dozen telescopes were up on the quarterdeck, eagerly sweeping over the shore to take in every detail possible, for it was vital the frigate continued on her way without showing any sign of interest.

It was a perfect hiding place; in the unremarkable and characterless coast the entrance to the river and its sand-bar were barely visible, any secret base well concealed.

L'Aurore sailed on until two headlands separated her from the river mouth, then went to a buoyed single anchor as though snugging down for the night.

Kydd turned to his first lieutenant. 'Mr Gilbey, I desire you shall find me a poacher.'

'Er?'

'Come, come, sir! As premier you are best placed to know our ship's company. Find me a young lad who knows well his pheasants and hares.'

'I, um – aye aye, sir.'

It took the additional good offices of Kydd's coxswain, however, to discover the talents of the shy Leicestershire lad the lower deck called Buttons, down on the ship's books as Ordinary Seaman Harmer.

Kydd then summoned Sergeant Dodd. The perplexed marine was hailed aft and told to find more suitable clothing than his fine red coat for an important mission ashore.

'Now, call away the whaler for sailing, Mr Gilbey – I shall be undertaking a reconnaissance with Dodd and Harmer. You shall remain aboard in command.'

'Sir, you can't—'

'I can and I will. You'll have my written orders.' If he was going to make decisions that sent his men into peril he wanted to see for himself.

In the face of Tysoe's vigorous protests, his captain was clothed in old seamen's togs. The stout-hearted sergeant donned the cooper's work clothes. With young Buttons red-faced at the honour, the whaler was manned and rigged. Poulden took charge and the little boat shoved off.

Leaving the reassuring familiarity and size of the frigate brought a cold wash of reality. They were proposing to trespass on a territory held by an army of ten thousand no less! Only the thought that the enemy would believe it preposterous that any would seek to challenge such a horde made this mission possible.

They laid course for the first headland, staying just outside the line of breakers until they were in its lee, then raced through the surf until they grounded with a spectacular rush.

'Out!' Kydd ordered. The three members of the shore party raced up the beach and into the scrub, where they hunkered down, aware of the strange but pleasant fragrance of the sparse vegetation above the odour of hot sand.

'Now, Buttons, do you go over the headland towards the river as carefully as you may, and see if you can sight a sentry. Off you go, lad!' He needed no urging, disappearing expertly into the low scrub.

It was some time before he returned but Kydd had anticipated this. A poacher would be concerned to ensure that no gamekeeper was in front of him and equally that none was out to the side who could cut off his retreat. 'A lookout, sir. Sittin' on the beach by the river,' the boy panted. 'None else as I could see.'

'We'll get closer.'

Kydd and Dodd bent down and moved on through the scrub behind Buttons until the young lad held up his hand, signalling they were near. He crouched and beckoned them on, bellying forward until they topped the sand-hill and looked down into the river.

The rise of ground was too slight to see much beyond a glitter of darker water inside the paleness of the sand-bar – but there was the lookout, not a hundred yards away, sitting by the twist in the river mouth that hid the interior so well and staring out to sea, his figure stark against the near-white sand.

Kydd cursed silently. It was critical to the operation to get depth of water over the bar but that was in full view of the lookout. 'I have to get to the sand-bar,' he whispered.

'Shall I take 'im, sir?' Dodd asked.

'No, he'll be missed and they'll be warned something's afoot.'

'Don't fret, sir, I know how,' hissed Buttons, mischievously, and faded into the undergrowth.

Minutes later, for the first time in Africa's long history, the distinctive harsh call of a mating wood grouse was heard, rising from a regular *chuck-chuck* to its irresistible strident climax.

The lookout's head jerked up and he looked around in astonishment. Kydd took up the cue and began circling to the edge of the river behind the man. The bird's call stopped, the lookout stood up and gazed about. Then it started again, further away, alluring. With a quick glance out to sea the man padded inquisitively into the scrub.

Kydd had his chance: he stepped into the river and waded out, not daring to look behind, heading for the centre of the sand-bar. The white sand was firm, the river placidly sliding over it to meet the sea, but to his dismay he saw that in places it was barely inches deep. A sinuous deeper channel of sorts was at the far side, but with a foot or so of water there was going to be no rousing swift assault by boats.

He returned to the bank quickly, glancing upstream to note the river disappearing into a sharp bend. That produced one more complication: to get a sight of the base itself there was no alternative but to follow the riverbank up.

He waited until he was joined by the other two. The base would be guarded, of that there was no question. But would there be outlying pickets or sentries? The probability was that the French were feeling secure in their hidden outpost with such a huge army in the offing – but all it needed was for one only to spot them . . .

'Go ahead, lad – if you see anyone, play the bird.'

With evening drawing in, after nearly a mile of nerve-racking progress they turned a bend and saw the base, palisaded and of a considerable size with distant figures entering and leaving by a gateway leading to a jetty. Faintly on the air came the sound of drums and massed chanting from a vast throng.

Kydd took out his pocket telescope. Close up, the scene was even more intimidating. The base looked impregnable, the palisaded fort, or whatever it was, large and sprawling with countless warriors passing to and fro. The only thing in their favour was that Kydd could see no embrasures for cannon.

'What do you think, Sar'nt?' Kydd said, in a low voice, passing across the telescope and trying not to let his worry show. He had deliberately selected the experienced NCO to assess their chances rather than the young lieutenant of marines.

Dodd took his time, studying terrain and cover, fields of fire, exposure. When he lowered the glass his face was grave. 'Not good, sir.'

With night coming on, there was nothing to be gained by further reconnaissance and it was time to leave. Kydd took one last look before moving away.

'Sounds like they's workin' up to a right gleesome night!' Buttons whispered to Dodd, as they followed.

'We must give 'em best, is my thinking, sail back with our prize – it's no shame to recognise when the odds are over-bearing,' Curzon said sorrowfully. Next to him Gilbey pursed his lips but did not contradict him.

Kydd turned to look at Bowden, who started at being consulted and could only mumble something about the difficulties they faced.

Kydd's gaze moved to Clinton. 'What do the Jollies think?'

The lieutenant turned pink and stammered, 'From what Sar'nt Dodd informs me, I – I'm inclined to agree. Without field artillery and cavalry, we stand no chance against such numbers. A frontal assault on a fortified position . . . er, well, I can't see—'

'Then we have to think again,' Kydd said heavily. 'If this base is not destroyed before it sets off the rising, we fail in our duty. Time is not on our side and any and every plan must be considered. Gentlemen . . . ?'

The discussion grew animated, but when there were no fresh ideas forthcoming, Kydd said, 'Let me rehearse the situation. An attack of the usual sort will, of course, fail against such numbers. A surprise landing will not fare much better, for native warriors need only snatch up a spear and they're immediately effective.

'Very well. I feel Mr Gilbey's suggestion of arming every boat with carronades and bombarding the fortification before a party of marines lands to set fire to the palisades is not practicable. I can tell you, armed boats cannot get over the sand-bar and, besides, if the material of the defences is wet by rain there can be no fire.

'I like Mr Curzon's proposal – that we blow up their powder store, thereby destroying the muskets stored with them as well. This will stop the rising directly. But I need hardly point out the gravest obstacle of all: how to approach without being overwhelmed.'

Bowden brightened. 'Sir, as to that, my uncle served in the American wars and tells that the Indian savages never venture to fight at night for fear of the spirits that are abroad. Might we think these are no different? This would allow us to get close enough to lay a charge without being challenged.'

Kydd shook his head. 'A good notion, Mr Bowden, but I can't allow it.'

'Why not, sir? There's every—'

'Because, Mr Fire-eater, we'd lose the whole party when the powder-store blows and ten thousand angry savages swarm about looking for whoever destroyed their new weapons.'

'We could take 'em off by boats. That'd thwart the . . .' Remembering too late, he tailed off shamefacedly.

Their plans all fell down at the same hurdle. No boats.

317

Kydd had gone to the tide tables to see if they could wring just a little more depth of water over the bar but even at the highest state of tide they would still ground on the hard sand by a considerable margin. With enough men – say, a hundred or more – they could manhandle the boats over the bar, but bringing them ashore would leave *L'Aurore* helpless if *Africaine* showed up.

No, they had to give up. It was not humanly possible to—

Or was it? The *Naval Chronicle* of a year or two ago, in an article on Venice – that was it – had related how even ships-of-the-line could be built at the famous Arsenal, which was set in the midst of a shallow lagoon. On each side of the vessel was lashed a series of half-sunken lighters. These were pumped out and rose in the water, lifting the ship, which was floated out of the lagoon.

There was some peculiar name for them – yes, camels. They'd devise their own camels and float the boats over the bar.

Kydd took in the uncomfortable expressions around the table and couldn't resist a delighted smile. 'So this is what I've decided. We do both – lay the charges *and* send in carronade-armed boats, which'll serve to take off the party too.'

'Sir – boats?' Gilbey stuttered.

'Why, yes. With camels!'

It was the breakthrough, and after Kydd had explained the operation, the plan quickly came alive.

A sapper party would approach overland unseen while the launch and pinnace were brought over the bar. When these appeared off the base they would open fire, drawing the attention of the defenders, while the charge was laid. In the confusion after the explosion, the sappers would race down to the jetty to be taken off and all would retire.

It was a neat solution. The number needed for the operation was minimal, the sapper party could be retrieved and,
above all, in one stroke it would stop the rising before it
began, giving Baird enough time to find a more permanent
answer.

There was just one problem: at night it would be impossible to reload. While cannon fire would cause an adequate
diversion, the guns would then be useless if called upon to
deter swarms of warriors turning on the fleeing sappers.
Some other distraction would be needed.

'Who will lead the boats, sir?' Gilbey wanted to know.

'I will,' Kydd said firmly.

'Sir! I must protest. Surely the honour is mine as first
lieutenant.'

'No, sir. Did you ever see Lord Nelson hold back when
hot work's to be done? That wasn't his style and neither is
it mine.' He softened at Gilbey's expression. 'There'll be many
more such in this commission, I'm in no doubt. If a plan is
your conceiving then most certainly you will lead. And in
this action, why, you'll in course be to the fore – in command
of the other boat.'

Then to the other details. The camels: casks lashed upright
together in a row with lines connecting them under the boat,
fashioned so the cradle could be floated under and then the
casks emptied to raise the boat bodily. The charge: this would
be two powder barrels brought together and a length of
quickmatch leading into one. The timing: this very night, in
the darkness before dawn when the tide was at its highest.
And finally the volunteers: Gunner's Mate Stirk would think
it an insult to his profession and honour if he were not asked
to lead the sappers, and Kydd would allow him to decide his
own party.

They set to. The boatswain laid out the lines to form the cradle, the cooper and his mate trundling the barrels into place where they were seized together in a string. It needed some thought to arrive at a means, when the time came, of emptying them quickly, but one was eventually found.

In the magazine the gunner and his mate prepared the quickmatch fuse. This was in the form of three cotton strands, much like candle wicks tightly twisted around each other, which had been steeped with spirits of wine in a mixture of saltpetre and mealed powder. Forty-foot lengths of the deadly cord were connected together and threaded into a linen powder-hose, then coiled into a cartridge box for safety.

From their stowage below were swayed up the eighteen-pounder carronades. These were fitted to slide beds in the bows of the two boats, complete with gun-locks and lanyards, Kydd finally settling on one round shot and two canister each. Although it was not feasible to consider reloading at night this was a precaution in case of delay until after daybreak.

Even the cook was roped in, for the galley funnel needed to be tapped to provide soot to conceal the faces of the sapper party. Stirk knew who he wanted – he and the strongman Wong would lay the charge while Doud and his tie-mate Pinto would see to the diversion. It was a good team, and when the time came to board the boats there were high spirits and confidence.

Once on their way it was another matter. Barely visible out in the blackness, the pinnace was a slight dark shape on their beam with the occasional white swash of wake. Kydd felt it a monstrous tempting of Fate to challenge such odds with just a pair of boats against an army of ten thousand. So much could go wrong – an alarm given as they were halfway across the sand-bar, an overlooked strongpoint – but these were the familiar anxieties of any clandestine operation and he crushed the thoughts.

Their timing was good: they arrived at the ghostly silence of the river mouth some hours before daybreak. There was no lookout posted, but all whispered as they worked.

Kydd's launch nosed in first, the men leaping out and steadying it as the clumsy cradle was passed under the boat, the big casks, heavy with seawater, thumping shins and balking every inch of the way. Sweating and cursing silently, they succeeded – and then a most remarkable sight followed. Two dozen brawny sailors, each armed with a galley pot, began furiously bailing out the casks.

Even before they had finished it was clear the boat was going to make it over the bar so Kydd ordered it forward, men guiding it around the twisting channel to the deeper water beyond. The other was brought through but it was taking longer than planned – time was ticking by and to be caught in daylight would be utterly disastrous.

Stirk retrieved his gear: gunner's pouch, a cartridge box with the precious quickmatch sealed inside and a satchel of 'come-in-handies' that no self-respecting gunner's mate would be without. Wong and Pinto were each burdened with a barrel of powder sewn in canvas and strapped to their backs, while Doud carried a carpenter's bag with a mysterious glint of brass inside.

The two boats were manned again and Kydd looked across at the four burdened figures standing in the shallows. So much depended on their courage and cool-headed devotion to duty. He tried to think of something encouraging to say but words failed him at the enormity of what he was asking them to do and he could only fall back on a hissed 'Good luck!' as they hastened away.

From the first, Stirk took the lead. The directions given were easy enough, and the almost luminous white of the sand beneath his feet made choosing a path easy. 'Shift y'r arse, Pinto!' he growled, as the Iberian fell back with the weight of his barrel. Concerned, Doud closed with him and, after a while, insisted on changing burdens. Pinto gasped his thanks and the party pressed on.

It was only a matter of twenty minutes or so before they came to the last bend and made out the secret base and the stark height of its palisades, with here and there the red glow of dying fires. Now oriented, Stirk took the little band in a wide circle to where they must lie-up. He dropped his gear and, on hands and knees, went silently forward. Almost immediately he saw the black shape of a warrior with a spear against the sky. Another was standing idly by.

He froze, fixing the position in his mind. Part of him rebelled in horror – he remembered the cannibalism he'd witnessed on a Pacific island – but this was no time to take fright. He backed away slowly to rejoin his friends. 'There's African bastards all about, mates. Doud – go out 'n' give it y'r best, cuffin.'

Hefting his carpenter's bag, Doud grunted, 'Let's go, y' Portugee shicer.'

Leaning across, Wong whispered hoarsely to them, '*Baak nin ho hop, pang yau!*'

'Thanks, shipmate,' Doud threw back, with a grin, and they disappeared into the night.

There was one thing that was sure. Either their diversion worked or the entire expedition would fail – and their death would be certain.

It was the end for Renzi and it were better he accepted it. Prisoner and executioner followed the path as it wound around the bend and emerged facing the dark expanse of the wide lower reaches of the river, the starlight laying a pearly opacity on the still waters, so beautiful and infinitely poignant.

As graciously as at a garden party, the baron indicated a thicket of greenery at the water's edge.

Renzi took position there, then turned to face the river, remembering to stand still so as not to upset the aim. It was odd but in his last moments he had no particular thought, no last-minute hot rush of memories – simply a wistful regret that for him there was to be no more future, in fact ... nothing.

Behind him he heard the box open, the steely click of preparation and he waited for the extinction of life. Taking his last look at the innocent sky, he emptied his mind of thoughts. Behind him the pistol was cocked with a lethal finality, and then—

A deep, ghastly moan swelled away in the bush to the right, rising to a tortured howl that overwhelmed the senses with a primitive horror, baying at the night before finishing in a groan of despair.

In the split-second that the torch was dropped by a man paralysed with fright, Renzi ducked and the pistol fired blindly above. He swung round savagely and cannoned into the baron who was knocked sprawling. The sputtering light of the dropped torch revealed an assegai thrown away by the panicking men as they fled. He snatched it up with a snarl and held it to the baron's throat.

'Get up, sir! We have company!' Nothing else could explain the existence in the African bush of a standard stirrup North Atlantic fog-horn dutifully groaning its message into an unheeding world.

As the cries of fleeing warriors faded, Stirk stood up. 'Right, mate. We've work t' do.' He hefted his gear and made for the palisade. Wong joined him with the powder barrels.

Up against the heights of the palisade, the dense inter-weaving of laths and vines over hardwood uprights looked impregnable. They had nothing with them that had a chance against it. It was too high to vault over and, anyway, the top was ridged with sharpened stakes. Distant rallying shouts sounded in the night – they had minutes only before the warriors returned.

'*Gau ch'oh!*' Wong growled in exasperation. He pushed Stirk aside, placing himself squarely against the palisade and reaching with his big hands up and out. Carefully adjusting and testing his grip, he paused for a heartbeat. Then, with a roar of grunting, he heaved back mightily. The fabric shiver-ed and bowed. Wong held his grip and, leaning outward, climbed up and jolted backwards. Once – twice – and, with a thunderous crack, first one, then another of the uprights gave at the base.

Cries of alarm and savage shouts from the darkness could only mean they had been discovered. Stirk fumbled under his shirt and yanked out a silver chain. Into the night, for those who could know, came the pealing stridency of a boatswain's call piping, 'Repeat the last order!'

An instant later the terrifying howl was heard again – much closer, erupting in a hideous swell of agony that could only have come from the undead of the nether regions.

The shouts turned to frantic wails and rapidly faded into the distance.

'I'll bear ye a fist, Wong,' Stirk said, and added his weight, heaving down heartily as if at the jeer-tackle of the main-yard. There was another splintering crack and the whole section lurched and drooped. Stamping it clear, he looked into the compound. As described, there was a low structure nearby and he darted across to it. 'Over here, mate,' he called.

To prepare took seconds only: a hasty slash at the canvas cover of the first barrel to expose a makeshift fuse from its interior. The end of the quickmatch was joined to it; he shoved the second barrel next to it and retreated, letting out the reel of quickmatch as he went. Through the palisades and out into the bush as far as the cord would go – there was no knowing just how much powder was in store.

In a pierced tin box a length of slowmatch was alight, of the kind kept in a match-tub next to guns in case of misfires. He tenderly took it out, blew on it and was rewarded with a healthy glow. 'It'll do, me old cock. Ready?' Quickmatch burned at nearly the same pace as an open powder-train – as fast as a man could run. When it started, they had seconds to flee for their lives.

He jabbed the glowing stub at the quickmatch. It caught in a bright fizzle and disappeared as a red glow into the tube, racing unerringly towards its destiny. 'Go!' Stirk blurted, and careless of noise, they hurled themselves out into the bush.

When it came the detonation was cataclysmic, the livid flash picking out every detail of the scene, the fiery column of destruction reaching high into the night sky before it was hidden in roiling smoke, the gigantic blast lifting both men off their feet and sending them sprawling. Then round and about there came the patter and thud of falling fragments.

Disoriented by the numbing roar, Stirk staggered to his feet and, urgently gesturing to Wong, lumbered off towards the river and the vital jetty. Still half blinded, he nearly knocked over a silent figure, a white man, standing over another. 'Sorry, mate,' he said automatically – then started, as though he'd seen a ghost. 'Er, Mr Renzi? Ye'd better have it away on y'r toes wi' us, sir. We've t' be at the jetty before—'

'Thank you, but first I'd be obliged if you'd relieve me of this gentleman and present him to Mr Kydd with my compliments. Tell him this is their ringleader. I've, er, other business to attend to – I'll be at the jetty presently.'

Gaping, they watched him hurry off.

Kydd was warned by the fog-horn and, knowing attention was away from the river, positioned his boats in the outer darkness. The thunderous explosion shattered the stillness like the end of the world.

'Give way, y' swabs!' he roared. The launch shot forward, towards the shore – and the general pandemonium. Warriors running aimlessly, shrieking their fear, small fires breaking out on all sides where burning fragments had landed. The jetty could just be made out but no anxious figures waiting.

'Hold water!' he ordered. They lay to fifty yards offshore, fearful that once they were seen, the panic could easily turn into a killing vengeance. In a frenzy they searched the river-banks for their shipmates. Nothing.

Gilbey's orders were to stay out and cover their approach with his carronade. Ashore, the disorder seemed to be subsiding – at any moment the horde could turn on them. Kydd left the sternsheets and scrambled forward to stand in the bows at the gun, peering to see.

'Sir!' one of the oarsmen said urgently. 'Over t' larb'd!'

It was clearly Stirk, and the others with him, struggling along towards the jetty and dragging another – but from the opposite side came a roar of anger. They'd been seen – and it was clear they were not going to make it to the jetty before they were overwhelmed. After all their immense bravery, to be slaughtered in sight of their salvation.

'Ready the carronade,' Kydd said steadily. In the dark, without the possibility of a reload, there were two shots and two only available between both boats.

'*Fire!*'

The crash of the eighteen-pounder from out in the night with its heightened gun-flash was shocking as a heavy round-shot was sent skipping and slamming over the water to end smashing and rampaging through the undergrowth – a very visible blast of terror that renewed the panic.

'Go for your lives!' The oarsmen needed no urging and the big launch flew in towards the jetty.

'Move!' bellowed Kydd, frantically beckoning to the waiting figures.

Stirk roughly pushed in the stranger, who fell protesting into Kydd's outstretched hands. 'Who the devil—?'

'Y'r ringleader, if y' please, sir,' Stirk said laconically, urging in his men before clambering in himself.

'Be damned!' Kydd spluttered, and hastily turning to the bowman roared, 'Bear off, there – let's away!'

Stirk grasped his arm. 'I'd be waitin' a mort longer, sir, as beggin' y'r pardon,' he said firmly.

Something about his old mess-mate's manner made him pause but the warriors could now see what was happening and started to storm forward once more – then out of the blackness came another thunderclap: Gilbey had seen what was happening and fired his own carronade.

They were now defenceless – but Stirk had seen something and muttered, 'They's coming now, sir.'

To Kydd's utter stupefaction, the unmistakable figure of Renzi loomed. Then, to his even greater astonishment, his friend theatrically produced Thérèse, sullen and tattered.

'Might I present to you the Baron de Caradeuc, whose daughter I believe you're already acquainted with?'

Kydd could only stare.

'Er, we gets under way, y' said, sir?' the anxious bowman pleaded.

'Aye – let's be back aboard, by all means.'

Tired but elated, Kydd and his victorious men stepped aboard *L'Aurore* to a roar of welcome. 'Get these two below under guard,' he told Bowden, briskly, indicating the prisoners. 'I don't want to see 'em again before Cape Town.'

When he'd finally disengaged Renzi from the throng they went to the sanctuary of Kydd's cabin. 'Tysoe! Mr Renzi is near gut-foundered and craves a restorative.'

'I understand, sir.'

The officers' cook came personally and busied himself with supervising several tempting dishes, and Tysoe murmured, 'We have still one of the 'ninety-two Margaux, which I recollect Mr Renzi particularly favours.'

'Make it so, you rogue, and be damned to the hour!' Kydd said happily, and fussed about a protesting Renzi in his old chair.

Soon glasses were raised and limbs eased. 'Now, Nicholas, you'll tell me what the Hades you were doing in such a place – or should I not ask?'

Between wolfed mouthfuls of mutton cutlets, Renzi told his tale, ending with 'So when that fearful fog-horn let go, how could I not remember those times off the Grand Banks in *Tenacious* when the damned thing was going morn to night? And here's to that old barky, dear fellow!'

'And here's to Toby Stirk, the cunning dog, who thought of it!'

'Which I'll second – I understand we owe our rapid withdrawal afterwards to the disinclination of our Xhosa friends to venture after us in the darkness where such dreadful spirits must lurk.'

After finishing his food Renzi laid down his knife and fork with a shuddering sigh, and closed his eyes. 'There were times, my friend . . .'

'Quite,' Kydd murmured, in sympathy. He knew better than to go further – Renzi would talk more in his own good time. He toyed with his glass for a moment, then said, with a trace of defiance, 'You must think me a sad looby to be gulled by Thérèse. I'm to say I never suspected for a moment, even while she dunned me with all those questions.'

'Of course not, old trout. There's others who've been deceived by her beauty and mystery, the chief of which must be my own self. And I'm here to tell you that her scheming to prise intelligence from you she considered a waste of effort, but as a man you proved to be . . . diverting.'

'She said that?'

'Indeed. Er, might it be hoped that this unholy experience has not soured you on the female race?'

'Not at all,' Kydd reassured him, with a wicked grin, 'although perhaps I shall take a little more care where I set my cap in future . . .'

Two days later, *L'Aurore*, her prize astern of her, rounded the point into Table Bay. Surprisingly, it was considerably crowded, with more than two score weather-beaten ships moored all along the wide anchorage.

'A convoy from England, Nicholas!' Kydd beamed. 'Our reinforcements have arrived at last, thank God.' Baird's dispatches must have done their work, for now not only had Whitehall received tidings of the action at Blaauwberg but had responded with all that was needed to make their presence permanent.

There were transports for garrison soldiers, store-ships with military supplies, merchantmen, no doubt laden with necessaries and luxuries, and stately Indiamen with notables on their way to India, who were now freely touching at their new port-of-call – Cape Town.

'Well, m' friend, I think we can say that Cape Colony now exists on the books in London. You'll no doubt have such a scurrying about, quantities of forms to return, new regulations and laws – not to mention the accounting of it all. I almost feel sorry for you!'

'Yes, it will be a challenge,' Renzi said gravely, his eyes on the massive grandeur of the African country before him.

After hearing Kydd's report Popham not only ordered him to inform the governor directly but insisted on accompanying him, along with the colonial secretary. 'Good God, Renzi!' Baird spluttered, aghast as the three were brought into his presence. 'You're – you're alive! We thought you were taken by a leopard!'

Renzi set out the plot and its foiling briefly and succinctly, taking pains to give due recognition to Kydd and his intelligent reasoning, followed by his decision to go forward with the attack in the face of such odds.

When he finished, Baird shook his head. 'The greatest

stroke I've come across this age,' he managed at last. 'Have you ever heard the like, Dasher?'

'Never,' said Popham, warmly. 'In the best traditions of the Service, Sir David. In particular I'd like to commend Captain Kydd on the moral courage he showed in breaking off the action with *Leda* to pursue the higher purpose. Captain Honyman was much annoyed as the Frenchy frigate slipped him by, but I shall speak with him on the matter and I'm certain he'll hear no more of it.'

'So,' said Baird, with feeling, 'here's a what-a-to-do before me, I must declare. We can't let it become public property in the colony that we were ever affrighted by the French or a rising by the Xhosa, so how can we decently hail it as a triumph? At the very least, gentlemen, in my dispatches I promise you I shall make it my business that it is not forgotten.'

He held out his hand in sincere admiration.

'Well,' Renzi said, with a sigh, 'after the excitement it's back to work for me, I fear. My desk under a monstrous pile, I shouldn't wonder.'

'Ah, as to that, er . . .' Baird looked uncomfortable '. . . um, there's someone I'd like you to meet, Renzi.'

He went to the door and called, 'Ask Mr Barnard to attend me, if you please.'

A studious gentleman, with a careful but intelligent manner, entered.

'Renzi, there's no way I can think to break this to you without disappointment, therefore without further scruple, I have to introduce Mr Andrew Barnard, who is to be the permanent colonial secretary for Cape Colony.'

Turning white with shock, Renzi stood for a moment before awkwardly returning his bow.

'Whitehall has seen fit to ignore my earnest recommendation on your behalf and is insisting on a professional civil servant in post. I'm – I'm truly sorry that this has been denied you, especially after your recent, er, experiences, of course.'

Seeing Renzi's stricken features, he hastened on, 'I'm sure Mr Barnard will be kind enough to desire that you remain in your quarters in the castle until your affairs are, um, more settled.'

'That – that won't be necessary,' Renzi said faintly.

'Ahem. I'd wish it were possible to offer you a lesser post in keeping with your undoubted talents but these have all been taken and I fear that the financials would frown on my creating a sinecure.'

'I understand, sir.'

With the utmost dignity, he turned and left.

The bottle of Cape brandy was half gone, and Renzi stared bleakly out of the mullioned stern windows at the grand sight of the majestic mountain and the pretty town beneath it.

His eyes brimmed as he murmured brokenly, 'Cecilia would have loved it here. Such a spirited creature! It must have been for her that Pliny wrote, "*Ex Africa semper aliquid novi*."'

He sobbed just once, then looked up. Seeing Kydd hadn't understood the Latin, he said distantly, '"There's always something new out of Africa."'

'And now this great land denied me.'

He buried his face in his hands.

'There's some who would rejoice it,' Kydd said.

'How so?' Renzi said, raising his head.

'Those who've missed having their friend to share adventures and triumphs.'

Renzi gave a wan smile. 'But I'm destitute – no future, no—'

Kydd bit his lip, then spoke in rising irritation. 'Nicholas, I find I'm to talk to you as I must to a foremast jack who's clewed up before me at the captain's table for the seventh time and needs a steer in life. I speak plainly, for you are my closest friend. You're a man of colossal intellect and logic, who's also the bravest person I know. How then can I put this? With all your talents, m' friend, there's one thing you lack that's sorely needed.'

'Oh? And what's that?' Renzi said defensively.

'Damn it – a firm hand on the tiller o' life!' Kydd exploded. 'A pox on it! Now, mark well what I have to say, Nicholas, for believe that I mean it! As God is my witness, do I mean what I say!'

Renzi was ashen-faced at his outburst.

'You shall have your position back in *L'Aurore* but on one stipulation – which is the strictest possible condition for the post, which you refusing will see you put ashore directly, to languish in this destitution you seem to crave.'

At Renzi's mute stupefaction, he continued more calmly: 'We're near to finishing our business at the Cape and must return to England soon. The condition is that the very *instant* we touch at Portsmouth you do post to Guildford and that very hour – not a minute longer, do you hear? – you do go down on your knees and beg Cecilia to marry you.'

'What?' Renzi gasped. 'I can't – she—'

'*She*'ll be the one to say whether you'll be wed or not – and never your poxy logical backing and filling until we're all dizzy!'

'But – but I haven't the means,' he said piteously.

'Then find some! Take your courage in both hands and *ask the woman!*'

'I – I . . .'

Kydd sighed heavily. 'Good God! Do I have to make my meaning plainer? You shall never set foot in *L'Aurore* again without you swear this thing – that is my last word, damnit!'

In great emotion, Renzi finally nodded agreement.

'What do you swear? Say it!'

'That when our ship touches English soil . . . I . . . I will beg Cecilia's hand. I'll ask her . . . to marry me.'

Kydd helped himself to a stiff brandy. 'She may turn you down as not worth the wait, o' course.'

At the look on Renzi's face, he hurried on, 'As to means – I know you'd forswear charity from me but, Nicholas, there must be a way, damnit!'

He began pacing the cabin, then stopped.

'Have you considered, well, that your publisher friend might be on the right tack? Should you not give the public what they crave, then later indulge yourself in your noble work? If it's a novel they want, give 'em one. I'm persuaded you've one or two adventures to draw on as will set hearts to beating, keep feminine eyes to the page and even rouse out a hill o' coin from the booksellers.'

Renzi was taken aback. 'A novel?'

'Yes!'

There was a long pause before he responded. 'Well, um, I suppose I can see that there's been one or two, er, instances in my life that may be of interest to others.'

The idea seemed to take hold and he brightened visibly. 'But, in course, Cecilia must not hear of it – I will write under a pseudonym and you will vow never to tell anyone.'

'I so promise.'

Renzi poured another brandy each and pondered for a

space. 'Hmm, how does – *Portrait of an Adventurer* by Il Giramondo sound to you?'

Kydd beamed – and the two friends roared with laughter and raised their glasses.

Author's Note

The triumph of Trafalgar may be seen in two ways: it lifted the fear of invasion for England on the one hand, and on the other it gave command of the seas to the Royal Navy, which they immediately put to good use. One by one Britannia relieved the French of their possessions and added to her own, so by the end of the war in 1815, there was an empire that was truly global, and which, even in my own lifetime, accounted for a quarter of the world's population. Kydd's adventures in *Conquest* therefore mark the start of an exciting new episode in his naval life: the race to empire.

Kathy and I had the great pleasure of visiting Cape Town on location research for this book in November 2009. Much of what Kydd knew there remains to this day. The Castle of Good Hope is in immaculate order, astonishing in a fortification nearly four centuries old. Government House still stands regally in the very pleasant Company Gardens where Kydd promenaded with Thérèse. And the Chavonne Battery, which fired on *L'Aurore* during her daring reconnaissance, has been preserved for posterity.

But, of course, there have been changes, most notably around the seafront of Table Bay. In the early nineteenth century it boasted just a single rickety jetty; today it has been extensively reclaimed to produce a world-class harbour. The battlefield at Blaauwberg is now near a pleasant beach town with a stunning view of Table Mountain. Simon's Town was much developed for the Navy and later became famous during the Second World War convoy battles.

As always in my books, I follow the historical record and take pains neither to distort nor exaggerate history. For instance, some readers may be sceptical about the French frigate I have sailing in unsuspectingly into Cape Town harbour to be taken by the British without a single gun fired, but this did actually happen, as did the bizarre scenes at the sinking of *Britannia* when the madman vowed he would die rich at last.

South Africa today is a vibrant multi-cultural society. Soon after the period in which I set this book, the Xhosa increased their warlike activity on the Eastern Frontier and later fought several wars before they in turn were pressed from the east, this time by the Zulus. The Xhosa eventually displaced the Khoikhoi to become the most prominent population group in Cape Colony, Nelson Mandela and Desmond Tutu among them. At the entrance to the Cape Town public library I was delighted to come across a poster in isiXhosa: *Ngabafundi abafundayo abaziikokeli* – 'Leaders are always readers'!

This book is dedicated to the Lady Anne Barnard, whose warm and delightful letters, journals and drawings informed much of my research on colonial Cape Town. I feel some degree of guilt in not being able to acknowledge everyone I consulted in the process of writing this book but they all have my deep thanks. Special mention, however, must be made of the assistance provided by the staff of the National Library of South Africa, the Cape Town Archives, the Simon's Town Museum and the South African Maritime Museum. And, of course, I would be remiss in not expressing heart-felt appreciation to my wife and literary partner, Kathy, my agent Carole Blake, and my editor Anne Clarke.

Glossary

ahoo	awry
assegai	light spear designed for throwing
ayont	beyond
belfry	protective canopy over a ship's bell
bicorne	two-cornered officer's hat; originally worn across until Napoleon adopted the style, then worn fore 'n' aft
Billy Roarer	sailors' nickname for *L'Aurore*
bobotie	baked spicy minced-meat dish, topped with a savoury custard
bredie	spicy slow-cooked stew, usually containing mutton
British East India Company	English chartered company formed for trade with East and South East Asia and India; 'John Company'
broadsides	opening fire with the battery of guns on each deck the entire length of one side of the ship
calesa	small horse-driven carriage
carronade	short-barrelled, large-calibre gun for use at close range
castellan	administrator/keeper of a castle
'Change	the Royal Exchange in the City of London
cobbs	sailor's term for Spanish coins
coxswain	in charge of a boat; captain's coxswain – in charge of the captain's barge
cuddy	small cabin or compartment
Dutch East India Company	English for the VOC, Vereenigde Oost-Indische Compagnie
field cornet	subordinate to the *landdrost*
fo'c'sle	the foremost part of the main deck

gimcrack	cheap, showy object
goose-winged	running with one corner of the sail clewed up to give half the area drawing
Great Karoo	vast semi-desert area in southern Africa beyond the Swartberg range, north of Mossel Bay
gunroom	wardroom of a frigate
howitzer	a gun that lobs an explosive shot in a parabola
Jonkheer	honorific for a person of note or high birth
Khoikhoi	original peoples met by the Dutch in the Western Cape
koeksister	spiced syrup-coated small cake
landdrost	local magistrate, responsible for order and collection of revenues
lee	side opposite to that from which wind is blowing
lobsterbacks	nickname for soldiers, from their red uniforms
loon	slang for lunatic
louring	dark, threatening
Mevrouw	Mrs
Ox-eye	large-scale wind-squall associated with north-east monsoon
pens en pootjies	casserole of beans and trotters
pickets	soldiers detached from the main body to act as lookouts
pinnace	one of the smaller of the ship's boats
plain sail	when the ship sails with all sail set except extras, such as stuns'ls
quarterdeck brace	authority position adopted by officer-of-the-watch; legs apart, arms thrust down behind
Quarters	after the ship is cleared for battle, the hands go to quarters for action
rijksdaalder	'royal dollar', rixdollar, main Cape currency
rooibos	native red bush, leaves of which are used to make a herbal tea
rutter	old term for pilot book in navigational use
Seringapatam, battle of	4 May 1799; final confrontation of the fourth Anglo-Mysore war
shageerijen	pot house frequented largely by sailors
swallowtail	distinctive v-shaped cut in a flag
tarpaulin	officer who has risen from before the mast and doesn't care who knows it
tie-mate	special friend, helped plait each other's pig-tail
umngqusho	savoury porridge, a traditional Xhosa dish
vrouw	housewife, woman
Zuurveld	buffer area between the Great Fish river and Sundays river to separate Boers and Xhosa